M000106024

THE BOOK OF HOURS

Maria Elena Alonso-Sierra

THE BOOK OF HOURS

Copyright © 2015 Maria Elena Alonso-Sierra

ISBN-13: 978-09862095-0-5
ISBN-10: 0-986-20950-3

Cover design by Scott Carpenter

To all Gabriela's and Richard's fans…the wait is finally over.

Prologue

Monterey Bay, California 1997

The past, figuratively, had been stooping over Gabriela Martinez's shoulder all morning long. Now it rode copilot on the drive home, laughing like a psychotic macaw at her feeble attempts to staunch the memories.

Hell. It was not as if this battle was new. For four years, Gabriela had been sparring with her past and its mockery, its unexpected hounding, its inconvenient ambushes, and its vicious pouncing with a relentless force of will. It was harassment, plain and simple, implacable, the transformative memories slithering unbidden into her consciousness: a soft caress that made her tremble, gray eyes that bored into her soul, arms that held softly or protected, and, oh God, lips that made her feel things she had never felt in all her married life.

That's because it wasn't your husband who made you feel them, her past snickered.

Well, hell. Score.

Past: one. Gabriela: zero.

She rammed the clutch. She really needed to snap out of this self-pity buffet she was dishing out today. With a practiced move, Gabriela downshifted to second and the BMW sedan slowed on cue. She veered southbound onto the last leg of her journey home, grateful she was only a few miles away. Focus, she ordered. Time to snap out of my-life-is-just-a-smorgasbord-of-misery crap. Today, she didn't have time for self-pity or memory lane flashbacks. Now that her meeting with her manager, Jean-Louis, about the upcoming auction was over, she had a nightmare of scheduling to organize. There was no time for the past and her thoughts. The better and more efficient undertaking was to keep the gear in second, give her brakes some respite, and focus on this downward gradient of road, which had more twists than a pretzel.

Brave words, her past intruded, then proceeded to remind her exactly who was in charge. Because when she looked about at the trees bordering the road, at the granite peeking out from behind curtains of pines, bushes, and dark earth, she was reminded of another similar road, another similar drive four years ago.

With Richard.

Damn.

Another score.

Past: two. Gabriela: zilch.

Renewed pain pierced her at the fleeting thought of Richard, launching once more a gamut of emotions—pleasure, longing, and heartbreak—some worse than others, and all linked to her memories of him. The worst were the constant yearnings entangled with a sense of abandonment, which wasn't fair, either. Hadn't Richard asked her to eliminate all doubts before reaching out to him, free and clear, with no regrets? She'd been working on exactly that for the past four years, and God only knew she had tried to keep her marriage afloat. But something in her relationship with her husband had splintered even before Richard had appeared in her life back in 1993. Had been irrevocably fractured in France, where her life had been threatened and almost snuffed out. And now in California shattered beyond redemption. There would be no turning back. And through it all, this piercing silence from Richard had been crushing. Year after year, she increasingly suspected his proclamation of undying love and the, *I love you with a terrible need,* had been crap written on paper. She feared Richard had moved on with his life, had married, and had a family of his own. *Forgotten her,* came the awful whisper. Unlike her. And during those moments, supposedly brave Gabriela turned into a veritable wimp.

He could be dead because of his job.

The car swerved.

Damn.

Score another hit for her past.

Three versus zero.

Gabriela straightened the Beemer and made a concerted effort to pay attention to her driving. That last thought had shaken her, badly. She tapped the brakes before the next curve. The response was slower than usual. Hell. What now? Her mechanic had finished servicing the car not two days ago and had boasted it drove like a dream machine. If he had overlooked some stupid thing, it would place the final cherry on top of her life's bitter sundae.

She took her foot off the accelerator and let the gearshift slow the car's momentum.

For a minute or two, she hummed along with the Vivaldi concerto on the radio's classical channel, a lame attempt to distract herself for a bit. But her thoughts refused to follow this new path, wandering back, once more, into familiar territory. Why on earth did she keep fighting herself, her memories? Why on earth didn't she *do* something, finally? She had her answer for Richard, but she now needed his. Jean-Louis had been after her for over a week on that subject. But she wasn't sure reaching out was a good idea. Not yet. Frankly, she was afraid to hope, and downright afraid, period. And ever since that desolate day at the *Marbriére*, she wouldn't be able to deal with a final rejection or abandonment from Richard as well. Besides, she wasn't free to make any kind of decision at the moment, either. Which brought her full circle. Why the hell did she continue this farce? Why on earth did she keep going back, day after day, to visit Roberto?

Gabriela's breath hitched as she tried to suppress her tears. Did she really believe things would end well and she could finally be free?

Guilt brings no freedom, a ghostly whisper teased her brain.

Round four, hands down, to the past, the nasty bastard.

Double damn.

Gabriela sighed. The ache in her soul felt like a sprain in need of Bengay. Guilt—the other taskmaster from hell. It hovered like a miniature avenging angel, lacerating her conscience every single day. Slash. You fell in love with another man. Slash. You gave birth to that man's child. Slash. You kept the child's identity a secret. But the biggest whiplash was asking Roberto for a divorce the same day he wound up in a coma.

Gabriela's thoughts screeched to a halt. *Whoa. Just one damn minute,* she told herself. *Let's be honest here.* She did not feel guilt at asking for the divorce, just guilt at her timing. Gabriela actually owed Roberto a grateful 'thanks' for plopping the overflow drop into the bucket of her restraint. Nothing attached her to him anymore, except Robertico and Gustavito, their two teenage sons, and Luisito, her energetic three-year-old. Gabriela hadn't even been upset by the fact Roberto had taken a mistress—had been sleeping with the woman for over four months, to be exact. On that day of confrontation, Gabriela had finally realized her marriage was indeed dead, with nothing worthwhile to rescue except the children. She had felt no jealousy at Roberto's admission, just a boatload of sadness at the waste of it all. And, if she were equally, brutally honest with herself, she had remained with Roberto this long simply because life had taken over, with routine and comfort replacing love and passion.

And you wanted to make sure there was nothing left in the marriage, as Richard had wanted, before you made an irrevocable decision, her past snickered.

Oh, shut up, she fired back, thinking that Fate was ever fickle. Right now, she had no choice but to keep forging on. For the sake of her children and, now, for her husband's legacy, she needed to keep the farce going for just a bit longer.

Chuck it up to penance, her past chided.

Gabriela flipped her past the figurative finger.

Score: One, for her.

Tires squealed on asphalt from taking the curve too tightly. Startled, she slammed the brakes. The car responded slower than before.

"Mannie, I'm going to kill you if this car needs to go back to your garage."

The venting out loud, however, made her feel better. Definitely. She would call her mechanic and let him have an earful, something similar to the earful she'd received last night from, what was this idiot of a person's name? Wickeham. God. Did she really need this now? The man was obsessed with snatching her rendition of an illustrated medieval manuscript before it went up for auction. At all costs. He kept calling her, insisting she sell her work for a fraction of what she knew it would be worth. Sounded like a professional nagger, raised finger and all. Suggestive, rather than threatening, which irritated the hell out of her. She better sell, or she'd be sorry. Yadda yadda. Arrogant gall.

But therein, possibly, lay the reason for the extended boxing match with her past today. The parallels to some events four years ago were just too damn close. Too damn déjà vuish.

No wonder her past had a smirk on its face. The odds were stacked in its favor.

The gradient on the southbound road turned steep and the car swerved heavily to the right. That snapped her completely out of her self-commiseration.

Taking a steadying breath, she pushed down on the brakes and prepared to downshift to first. The car didn't even hiccup. She pumped the brakes, thinking she had misjudged. Nothing. Her foot went all the way down to the floorboard and stayed there.

Gabriela froze. For an instant, her brain refused to capture the enormity of her current problem. Her muscles didn't twitch and she didn't breathe. *No, this is simply not happening to me. There's a mistake.* She released and pushed once more. The brake pedal slid down in slow motion.

All the way down. No resistance.

It stayed there.

She was *not* wrong.

Oh. My. God.

The sudden influx of adrenaline surged through her body like a savage beast set loose on a hunt after a famine. Her heart hammered her rib cage. Her eyes, hoping something, anything, would help her, darted frantically around. What was she going to do? She had a fifty-foot drop on one side of this two-lane road and a granite wall on the other. Traffic would get heavier as she went lower. Sweat pooled on her inner elbows and nape. She was in serious trouble.

The car sped up.

She started hyperventilating.

Take a deep breath…stay with me, Gabriela. I need you to guide me. Richard.

The thought of him fighting another car, on another road, somehow steadied her. She rammed the clutch and shifted to first. The car bucked. Almost stalled. Her seat belt bit into her shoulder and torso, and the whine from the motor became a distressing grating of metal. Did the car just slow down a bit? Concentrate, damn it. Concentrate. The next obstacle, the road ahead, was a hair-raiser. It veered away from the drop at a tight angle and twisted back immediately toward the western horizon, the ocean, and the road below.

Prioritize. Slow down the beast. One sucky situation at a time.

Gabriela eased the car into the median, giving herself more driving room. "Please, please," she begged no one in particular. "Don't let anyone come my way."

Tires screeched as she started the turn. Her hands slipped as she maneuvered the steering wheel with the small up-and-down jerks she remembered Richard using. But the car felt heavy, like a lumbering beast wading through thick mud, resisting her directions and weaving farther to the edge of the road. She increased her movements on the steering wheel. The car's rear dragged heavily to the right. Her first instinct was to compensate. She tamped down on that gut move quickly. Defensive driving taught overcompensating would trigger a dangerous spin.

She needed to break the car's momentum before she reached the next turn, the one facing the ocean. She grabbed the emergency brake lever and eased it up a fraction at a time as she kept turning. An acrid smell filtered into the car, but she ignored it. Her eyes scanned the road ahead. No oncoming northbound traffic, yet. Gabriela swallowed and steered diagonally to the opposite side of the road. Horns blared behind her, drivers frantic to get her attention.

She ignored them and concentrated on the approaching section of mountain.

She didn't quite ram the car against the granite, but rather scraped the entire driver side into the rock. Steel and granite pushed against each other. The car bumped once, refusing to stay parallel to the stone. Her side mirror snapped and slammed into her window. Glass cracked. She cringed and gave a frightened squeal. But she forced the car back to the granite. Metal ground against stone, filing the car's exterior like a fingernail. The steering wheel vibrated, hard, and with it her forearms. Keep the car steady became her mantra, despite sweaty hands, despite them slipping on the steering wheel. She increased the pressure on the leather there. *Oh, God. Oh, God.* The car would be pulp before she finished.

More cars blared horns, accelerated, and zipped past her. She caught a brief glimpse of a man gesticulating frantically while on his cell phone. Must think she was crazy, drunk, or high. Hysterical laughter bubbled up but came out as a keening wail.

Oh, God. Oh, God. She needed to stop the car or she was going to die.

Chapter One

London, England 1997

Richard stared at the *St. George and the Dragon*, his thoughts reverting to the woman whose beautiful hands had created such powerful drawing.

Gabriela.

His only love. His Achilles heel.

His redemption.

His friend Maurice was right. It was time. Time to save her and to get her back.

He strode out of his office and stopped next to his assistant.

"Please call a Father Ramirez at this number," he said, his voice frayed to the edge of emotion. He handed over the scrap of paper Maurice had given him moments before.

Vivian scanned the telephone number.

"Now?" she asked, startled. It would be four in the morning in California.

"Yes. He's expecting my call."

"I'll buzz you when I get through."

Richard returned to his office and approached the bank of windows that displayed the hectic London streets below. A cursory inspection of the weather outside confirmed it was still as cold, miserable, and gray as the color of his eyes. He rested his sleek six-foot-four frame against the wall of solid transparency and watched as traffic, human included, wove around each other like swarming ants.

Incredible that Maurice, in a visit so fleeting, had ignited a conflagration of hope, altering his prior restlessness to a fulfilling purpose, a goal.

Action. Finally. What remained now was for the first bell of the boxing match to ring. This go around, though, he would fight hard and dirty for the only woman he loved, still craved for, and thought lost.

If she wanted him back. If...

He rarely pondered on the past, avoiding it at all costs, but right now, it flooded his mind like a tsunami. After the debacle in France four years ago, that first year without Gabriela had been brutal. His heart, like his voice, had held a visible emptiness; and if anyone had bothered to look at him throughout that year, they would have seen eyes as equally lackluster, corroborating the vacuum in his life. During that year from hell, he'd been a man with no hopes, no illusions, a man who had lost his soul and his way. Sprinkled in between were the black moments of jealous fury as he thought about Roberto touching Gabriela, sleeping with her. She was his, damn it, he recalled railing at the walls, overcome by a murderous rage that consumed him. Gabriela belonged to him in a way she had never belonged to her husband. Never would.

Richard fisted his hands. Those had been his bleakest hours. Added to those had also been the moments of bitter, crushing longing, not to mention the myriad sensual dreams that had plagued him almost daily—warm skin caressing his own, the soft scent of jasmine filling his nostrils, lips trembling beneath his in reaction to his touch. By the end of that year, he'd been a mess, feeling only defeat and seeing only blackness for a horizon. Her absence had almost killed him. His need had made him careless on his last mission. It had almost ended his stay on this earth.

Fortuitously Maurice, his counterpart in French intelligence at the time, had arrived at the hospital where Richard was convalescing from a bullet wound too close to the heart. Functioning similar to a smirking Archangel Gabriel, he had announced the great news of hope, literally—potential salvation in a glossy, eight-by-fourteen photograph of Gabriela but, especially, in a small DNA report.

Maurice's visit had changed him. Richard shook his head. No, Maurice's words had branded him, had transformed him, his comments forever etched in his brain.

"She's an exceptional woman," Maurice had scolded him, and with reason, despite Richard's features reflecting his annoyance and the heart monitor his growing despair.

"Against all odds," Maurice had continued with the excoriation, "and the nightmares she must have had after the incident, she's been trying to rebuild her life from the ashes and the pain, like you asked her to do, even with paparazzi, journalists, and the debriefings from my unit and yours—which, by the way, were brutal. Getting over the trauma from her wounds must have been a nightmare as well, I'm sure. But she plows along stubbornly from what I hear. She's trying to keep her life together, unlike you."

Maurice's *pièce de résistance*, however, had been tossed over his shoulder at his departure.

"Gabriela is giving herself a chance, trusting you will be there in the wings if she ever needs you. Don't fail her by not being there as you promised." Maurice, who usually had a grin to rival the Joker's, had not been smiling. "Don't fail the precious new life you might very well have created with her."

At those words, and for the second time in his life, Richard had stepped beyond himself, beyond his emotions, walking in her shoes and realizing she was stronger than him, better than him, less selfish than him. Realized he'd acted like a self-serving bastard, more worried about his wounds than taking into consideration her own. He was still not worthy of her, not the man she believed him to be, nor the person he could be with her.

He had changed that, he hoped.

His moment of reversal.

He had stopped acting the wounded animal, stopped feeling guilty at leaving her. Removing himself from her life had been the only option for them at that moment, the only option if there was ever to be a chance for a healthy future together. He'd asked Maurice to keep tabs on her and had immersed his soul in work.

Her continued silence, however, had tortured him, but he had coped.

His working fury these past three years had also proved cathartic. Emulating Gabriela, he'd developed a lucrative business from the ground up, something of which he was extremely proud. There remained, however, a kernel of dissatisfaction digging at him, despite his success. Now he understood his triumphs were incomplete if not shared with Gabriela, the only woman who evoked in him yearnings that still subsumed every atom of his soul.

As he smirked, his sudden chuckle echoed around the office. Never knew he could spew such melodrama. However, Fate was a fickle bitch, wasn't she? Before, nasty Lachesis had manipulated things in such a manner there had been no choice but to let Gabriela go. Now, Fate was back for round two, neatly gift-wrapping Gabriela once more, this time leaving her across his path to unwrap, to take back, to cherish, and to possess—a gift to never relinquish. Would she want him back? Would the preposterous idea, which had popped to mind seconds ago, work? Hell, he'd make it work. But, first, he needed to assess Gabriela's danger and the magnitude of the threat. The next step would be to actually manipulate the priest into accepting a fait accompli. Once he had Gabriela on his turf, well, the rest would be up to him.

This time, he was not going to remain empty-handed. Not unless she chose otherwise.

Chapter Two

"Do you have the pictures?"

The bulky man standing in front of Wickeham's sofa handed over the articles in question.

Bogdan Ljubic was communist born and bred by way of Yugoslavia and had become a proud irregular in Britain since all hell had broken loose in his area of the Balkans in '95. His occasional liaison with the Yugoslav DB, the communist state security service, had proven profitable, both during his years in the Yugoslav army and, now, in his adopted country. By upbringing, he was ruthless, a natural bully who relished the power of his fists, who now used them to his employer's advantage, and who occasionally kept his wife in check by using her as his primary practice, punching bag. Because of those skills, certain jobs had kept him financially afloat during his journey across Europe and during his first few months in England.

It had created his share of enemies as well. But, he didn't care.

His apelike physique—with excessively wide shoulders, elongated arms falling lower than the knees, and a profusion of reddish-brown body hair— had also served him well. A sagging chest belied the fact that he, like the primate he resembled, was stronger than most men, his well-honed biceps and deltoids religiously worked for tone and strength. To complete the simian image, his oval eyes, pinched down at the corners, graced an ovoid face, sagging jowls, and a jutting chin with lips that cut across it in a straight line. It was the expression in those eyes that made most people avoid him. For some, it was the last thing they saw.

"Any news from your contact, Mr. Ljubic?"

Arnold Wickeham accepted the photographs from the man he fondly called his enforcer with a fastidiousness born from years of study and concentrated practice.

He was his own creation and he took pride in perpetuating the myth. Every article in his house, office, or on his person was for effect and perception. The interior of his house resembled a coveted Condé Nast architectural magazine model home. He dressed impeccably, with top-of-the-line designer clothing and underwear. His speech was moderate, his cadence slow, and his intonation flawless; the air of sophistication with which he'd surrounded his life had been achieved through years of observation and rehearsal. What he knew of survival, front businesses, intimidation, and coercion, he had learned while running errands for Ronnie Kray as a child in the late sixties. Now, very few people doubted his crafted persona of breeding and affluence, and many would be truly surprised to realize Wickeham had actually clawed his way out of a brutal East End neighborhood. To those very few perceptive people who usually watched the world with a jaundiced eye, there was always a sort of fakeness about Wickeham, something decidedly not quite genuine, as if he were an expensive imitation—something cheap that had tried to vanquish its own vulgarity by throwing some expensive window dressings over itself.

His signature token, a David Yurman, hand-engraved, fourteen-carat signet ring, glinted off his left pinkie as he perused the photographs of a Mission-style home, its grounds, retaining wall, and staircase. As he flipped photo after photo, he scratched his wide, bulbous nose, ever a source of embarrassment on his sadly disappointing face. It was the first thing he noticed on waking and the first thing everyone noticed when face-to-face. It was deeply etched by severe acne and chicken pox marks, with nostrils splayed out across his cheeks to the width of his lips. During harsh winters, it swelled and resembled an appendage stung multiple times by wasps. His longish brown hair, stylishly and meticulously cut, covered ears that were too long, framing a flattish face, as if someone had tried to press down on it to create a two-dimensional model rather than a normal three-dimensional one. Maybe his former psychiatrist was right in saying his need to surround his life with everything that was materially beautiful was a direct correlation to his perceived unattractiveness.

Perceived, my ass, Wickeham chuckled at his own witticism. The moment that quack had offered his ridiculous euphemism for a reality with which he was too familiar was the last time he'd visited the asshole. Shame he couldn't use his influence to retire him permanently. But there was always hope.

Wickeham paused, closing his eyes, his posture almost prayerful. Focus. He needed focus in order to formulate a new strategy, to find additional motivation to convince Mrs. Martinez to budge on her position because, damn her, she was not budging at all, not even after his latest phone reminder had hinted he'd arranged her car mishap. His lips thinned. She had scoffed at his warning, had outright laughed over the phone. She would not be laughing the next time he took action. She would capitulate. She would cringe in fear of him.

His thoughts shifted. Time was of the essence. Ever since setting eyes on her exquisite creation, he knew he could not allow it to go to auction. That manuscript could not go to anyone else. And, bugger it, he wanted…

Wanted…

Now that was a rather tame description of the emotions evoked within his psyche. The moment his contact at Christie's had shown him two of her folio pages, his need for Mrs. Martinez's work had ratcheted up beyond wanting. He rummaged through the glossary in his brain. Ah, yes. He *coveted*. He *craved*. And that *Book of Hours* would be his.

He wet his lips. To possess uniqueness was a dangerous compulsion, he knew. According to his ex-shrink akin to an aberration. Wickeham didn't experience this compulsion frequently, but, upon rare occasions, artifacts would surface which called to him, drew him to such extent his need to possess hurt. And rarity…now, rarity was something for which he would go to extremes. Her manuscript was such. No. Worse. It was one of a kind. He simply could not allow anyone else to have it. Could not allow her to create a facsimile.

He almost crushed the next photograph in his fist. He'd been beyond insulted at her apology. Furious, actually. Mrs. Martinez had informed him she would never recreate another *Book of Hours*, but she had suggested duplicating several folios, of lesser quality, for him. A lesser copy. Even now, thinking about her suggestion, his mind churned with acid. Her proposal had been akin to his accepting a cheap lithographic print as a replacement. What cheek. If she'd been facing him, she would have been the recipient of his displeasure. He'd had Bogdan intimidate his targets for less.

His lungs expanded in an effort to regain his center. He would triumph in the end. He always did in these cases. But timing was of the utmost importance. The piece must never go to auction. If it did, this priceless work of art would be handed over to multimillionaire bidders in Saudi Arabia or Hong Kong with whom he could not compete financially—unappreciative people who would place her magnificent work in a vault to gather dust.

Not him. He already knew where he would exhibit it, what antique furniture to obtain to display its exquisite pages and craftsmanship. He would ascertain its pages were turned, the tome pampered, admired, and shown. He had to act before it was too late, to ratchet up the pressure and gain her capitulation quickly. His lawyers were already working on an unbreakable contract of sale with a stipulation she never duplicate this work. Nothing would stand in his way, especially not her.

"The incompetent was dealt with," Bogdan interrupted his thoughts. "No more mistakes from that end."

Wickeham smiled. He so enjoyed tidiness, and those who were, should he say, inept, needed to conveniently disappear, to not grace this planet on a permanent basis. Messes were intolerable when paying premium prices for services rendered.

"Evidence?"

"Disappear tomorrow or next," Bogdan replied.

"How about current availability?"

"When you wish."

"Perfect."

Wickeham flipped to another photograph of the area and thought this Gabriela Martinez was a woman after his own heart. Her house was expensive and expansive, the grounds even more so, perched over Pacific granite and facing the rolling sea. Very little frontage to the house on the street side, with an iron gate framed by thick, impenetrable eight-foot hedges of perfectly clipped ficus. Limited access from the road. Smart of her. Problematic for him. He spotted two security cameras facing the area. The remaining property would be peppered with them as well, he was certain. Another challenge, but he ever so loved circumventing them.

The next photograph caught his attention. The terrace to the home was L-shaped, with the longest arm on its right. That section was kidney-shaped and stretched the length of the living areas of the house. The short arm veered left to abut a large rectangular pool with some sort of building corking it. He scanned the single-level structure, architecturally matching the main home. It was too big to be a simple changing room. A guest house to accommodate visitors? Possibly. But what interested him was the area to the left of the pool. Framed by a thick hedge of what looked like oleander bushes, a winding path of about forty feet joined that area of property to a hedge bordering the neighbor's driveway and the street beyond. Private, yet accessible.

His fingers, with perfectly manicured and buffed nails, flipped to the next picture. It displayed the terrace's elbow, with a wooden staircase leading downward, in stages, to the rocks below and beyond. Uneven, flat areas of granite, dotted haphazardly with what looked like twisted dwarf pine trees, stretched several yards seaward until huge boulders, smoothed and shaped by the relentless sea, now stood as suffering sentinels before the endless expanse of the Pacific. He studied several other photographs taken from different angles to afford the best vantage point of the area. No beach that, Wickeham thought, just an area to enjoy the view when the surf was not riled up and pounding that rock wall, the only natural barrier between land, sea, and home. The sunsets there would be truly spectacular.

Taking a few more moments to consider the photos, Wickeham finally decided on two and culled those out of the stack. He discarded the rest by handing them over to his silent employee. He sedately covered the short distance from his seat to his work area, a nineteenth-century mahogany partner's desk that stood in the middle of his home office. He reached across the desk, opened the middle drawer, and took out his magnifying glass. He clicked on the desk lamp and began a meticulous sweep of every inch of ground imprinted in those photos.

First, he studied the path leading from the pool area to the neighbor's property. At the very edge, there seemed to be a small opening there, like a service gate. If that was an easement, possibilities could ensue. He then reverted his attention to the other photograph, specifically to the area below her terrace. A wooden staircase hugged the brick wall for the first eight feet, leveled off into an ample, semicircular viewing area containing several lounge chairs and tables, which then angled down the next stair four feet to end on the rocks below. Access might be tricky there, but not impossible. He carefully re-examined the area. No security cameras posted anywhere. Interesting. Another set of possibilities came to mind.

The next maneuvers in his strategic plan began to coalesce more clearly in his mind. He turned to Bogdan.

"I believe it is time to send Mrs. Martinez a more personal message." He looked at his man. "When can services be rendered, you said?"

Chapter Three

The telephone line buzzed softly. Richard walked to his desk, reached for the telephone, and heard Vivian tell the overseas party to go ahead. A high-pitched voice then asked, "Mr. Harrison?"

"You wanted to talk to me."

The voice at the other end whispered a relieved "At last."

"Father," Richard said. "I'd appreciate it if you got to the point." Especially when Gabriela was the point.

Father Ramirez sighed. "Maurice Nôret, your colleague…"

"Ex-colleague. We don't work together anymore."

The priest cleared his throat. "Well, he did say you'd be impatient, especially since I've taken the liberty—"

A hell of a lot of liberty, Richard thought, but said instead, "If Gabriela needed my help there was no need for intermediaries."

Father Ramirez, a veteran priest of twenty years, didn't miss the tone of reproach. His voice turned conciliatory. "She doesn't know I've contacted you. She'd be furious."

Furious. That single word, savoring heavily of rejection, struck Richard like a blow to the solar plexus. His reaction to that, however, was immediate and visceral. Fierce. No. Rejection was not an option. He refused to swallow that bitter pill, even after all this time, not unless her lips uttered them.

"Besides," the priest continued. "Gaby doesn't take the man seriously, you see, even after the accident."

Richard's muscles tensed. "What accident?"

"Her car almost dived off Canyon Road two days ago, that's what. That's nearly a fifty-foot drop straight down onto the road below. Only by God's grace and His blessed Mother's protection is Gaby alive and able to tell about it. Frankly, I'm still in shock. I honestly don't know how she managed to downshift like a maniac, or what made her ram the car into the mountainside until that finally stopped it. Of course," the priest continued, ignorant of how his words were affecting Richard. "The gearbox was wrecked, and the car looks like it went through a demolition derby. By God's grace, she only suffered a few minor cuts, a bloody nose, some bumps and bruises."

Richard shifted the receiver and wiped the sweat off his hand on his pants. Four years ago, when Richard's ex-boss had tricked him into protecting Gabriela from an unknown xenophobe, it had taken him less than a week to discover that her mentor and friend, suave and sophisticated Mr. Albert Heinige, had been the mad wacko who'd wanted them dead. If Gabriela had not pumped a clip's worth of lead into the arrogant bastard, their bleached bones would be fertilizing some gnarled umbrella pine tree in that wonderfully picturesque gorge of the Maritime Prealps.

Could someone now be trying to avenge the events of four years ago? The cold, clammy feeling in the pit of his stomach intensified at the possibility of this new scenario, one that hadn't occurred to him or to Maurice. Had they committed a tactical error by assuming the bastard didn't have any living relatives to take revenge?

"What do the police have to say about all this?" he inquired.

The priest's derisive sniff echoed with crystalline precision through the receiver. "The police are too busy with more important crimes than to be bothered with a silly priest's suspicions, especially when the accident appeared to be caused by an obvious brake failure. The policeman at the scene even intimated it was Gaby's fault the vehicle hadn't been in good driving condition. I realize it was the officer's duty, but under the circumstances, and after what I disclosed to him, he could have waited to issue her a citation."

"A ticket?" The humor of the situation did not escape Richard.

Father Ramirez sighed. "I know. But I'll tell you what I told the officer. Gaby had that car serviced two days before this happened. It wasn't her fault, nor was it negligence on the part of Mannie. That boy's been in charge of repairing her Beemer for three years, and I trust him when he claims there were no leaks in the brake fluid reservoir, nor any problems with the hoses or the master brake cylinder. Besides—"

"He wouldn't lie to you?" Richard supplied.

The priest ignored the jibe. "Mr. Harrison, my instincts tell me someone had to have tampered with her brakes. The timing was too convenient and too close for comfort. That's why I contacted your friend in hopes he'd find you."

"Has anyone found proof of tampering?" Richard asked.

"Mannie hasn't checked the car yet. At least, not thoroughly."

Richard paused, guessing the answer to his next query.

"Please humor me on this bit of curiosity on my part, Father Ramirez. Where is Roberto in all of this? Why hasn't he insisted on an investigation? Why isn't he doing something to protect his wife?" Richard didn't voice his thoughts about Roberto getting off his ass for once to take care of Gabriela…to protect her.

"Why call me?" Richard finished.

There was a long, uncomfortable pause. "Roberto can't help her," the priest finally answered. "And the police can't or won't help much at this stage, either. I've asked her to cancel things, but—"

"Excuse me for interrupting you once again, but I'm not getting all of this straight. You mean to tell me you know why she's being threatened?"

"Of course," the priest said simply.

"This has to be a joke." His patience disappeared, his eyes turning dark and violent like a storm.

"Let me be blunt," the priest said. "Gaby keeps dismissing the threats and our concerns. I've been at my wit's end, trying to figure out what to do. Then her manager, Jean-Louis, suggested I call your friend Maurice. He, in turn, suggested no one but you can convince Gaby of her predicament. You have undue influence over her, Maurice told me, more so than anyone in her family or myself."

Richard's smile was a deprecating one. Leave it to Maurice to put his two cents in and manipulate a forced reunion. However, the priest hadn't a clue about Richard and Gabriela's past. A tinge of smugness curled his lips wider. Undue influence? The priest wouldn't be contacting Richard if he had an inkling of the influence he could wield.

"I need you to convince Gaby the threats are real," Father Ramirez continued. "If she goes to England for that auction without selling her work to him, this cretin has threatened bodily harm. I believe him. But there is just no convincing her. Gaby may be sweet, but she's stubborn as an ox. And after her experience in France four years ago, nothing fazes or scares her. It's unnatural."

Not if you'd been there, Father. "Do you know the name of the person who is making these threats?" Richard asked.

"Certainly. The cretin doesn't even hide the fact," the man answered angrily, his tone rather vicious for a priest. "I hope he rots in hell for the agony he's put us through this past month."

"Father—"

"It's a man by the name of Wickeham. Arnold Wickeham."

For the second time that day, Richard was surprised. Wickeham. How on earth had Gabriela ever gotten involved with him? The man's reputation was dubious, at best, gossip hinting at illegal and coercive methods in obtaining his antique collections, at worse. He should know. He'd had a brush with the gentleman over a sought-after piece of antique furniture a year ago. Wickeham's tactics had been unscrupulous, to say the least, but against Richard, however, Wickeham had lost the coveted pieces. It simply had been a matter of who was the craftier bastard.

"About a month ago," the priest explained, "this man Wickeham called Gaby to offer her a deal for her illustrated medieval manuscript, *The Book of Hours*."

"What do you mean her manuscript? Isn't that volume part of the collection at the Uffizi or some such museum in Italy?"

The priest chuckled. "Gaby created her own version of the ancient tome using her own calligraphy and illustrations. Has always wanted to simulate the magnificence of those manuscripts and, by God she achieved it beyond anyone's expectations. Banking on her fame, she decided to auction it, the money from the sale funding a scholarship pool for the parish's poor children. It has taken us years to obtain the backing and approval from the powers that be, but we finally got the go-ahead."

Slides of memories flashed across Richard's brain. The lapis lazuli background, a one-dimensional figurine of a Madonna, gold paint accents, gorgeously convoluted script. He had seen the sketches on the desk in her workroom four years ago.

"So she finally finished it," Richard whispered, more to himself than to the priest.

"That's when the problems began."

"How so?"

"Mr. Wickeham called Gabriela barely a week after she had shipped out the volume. He claimed to have been present at the auction house when the manuscript arrived and was gushing with enthusiasm over the piece. He offered to buy it outright for a whopping two hundred and fifty thousand pounds. Gaby refused."

Typical of her, Richard thought, remembering the stubborn sparks in her amber eyes every time someone tried to manipulate her.

"At first," the priest continued, "the man was insistent, but pleasant. He thought Gaby was holding out on him to extract a higher price. But two weeks ago, he finally got the message Gaby was not giving in. That's when the threats began. When those had no effect, this accident happened. It was meant as a warning, you see. Early next morning, Wickeham called Gaby, regretting she'd suffered such an unfortunate mishap, as he politely put it. He then reissued his magnanimous offer."

"And let me guess," Richard supplied. "Gabriela refused, again."

"Yes, which made the man spitting mad." A heavy, tired sigh filtered through. "Son, the auction is barely days away. We've been working on this project for a long time and, by God's grace, we've accomplished a veritable miracle. But I'd rather take this man's offer than have her in any kind of danger. Please, Mr. Harrison, the help I'm asking for is simple. Call her. Ask her to compromise. Convince her to act like the logical woman she is and accept the man's offer before it's too late. It's not as much money as the Christie's manager promised the piece could fetch, but two hundred and fifty thousand pounds is still nothing to sneer at."

There was a long pause. From experience, Richard knew Gabriela wouldn't be convinced. She'd be even more stubborn now in auctioning the damn piece. It was her nature to resist coercion, to boldly crash into a wall if it meant going against evident manipulation and thievery. Richard knew it was useless to make her do otherwise.

"Allow me to offer a better solution," Richard countered. "I have some business deals to take care of by week's end in New York. I'll fly in to see Gabriela personally."

"You're coming?" the priest answered carefully. There was both hope and a healthy dose of caution in that phrase.

"I know Gabriela. It will take a personal meeting to convince her of what I have in mind. Don't worry, Father, my arguments will prevail. I have my ways." The priest didn't suspect the half of it. "Where are you located, exactly?"

"Gaby is in Monterey Bay. My parish is about ten miles northeast of the area."

"Let's say I meet you tomorrow afternoon at the San Francisco airport. We can then drive down to Monterey and try to convince Gabriela not to be obstinate for the second time in her life. If I can't convince her to sell, I will personally escort you both to London. My town house is well protected and big enough to accommodate you both, and my chauffeur-cum-bodyguard would be at your disposal whenever I'm called away on business. That way, she will be safer."

It didn't seem to occur to the priest to refuse Richard's suggestion, nor to reflect upon the consequences of his acceptance. Paramount in his mind, probably, was Gaby's protection, or so Richard surmised from the almost instantaneous agreement to his plan.

"Son, if you can achieve this, I will offer my daily mass in thanksgiving for an entire year. I've been so anxious, knowing the threat of harm hangs over her head. Not only that, but what kind of protection would she receive in a lonely hotel room with no one beside her but an old fool of a priest?"

Be careful what you wish for, Father. "Then consider it done," was all Richard said. "I'll have my assistant e-mail my flight information to you." Richard paused. "You do have e-mail, I presume?"

The priest rattled off his e-mail address. "You got that?"

Richard repeated what he'd written and received an affirmative grunt. "Oh, and Father?" he said, his voice turning into a silky murmur. "I trust you'll be very discreet about my forthcoming visit, won't you?"

He heard the priest swallow.

"Mr. Harrison, now that you'll help, it won't serve to warn Gaby of your impending arrival. I know that child better than she knows herself. Just to prove a point, she's capable of packing her bags right then and there and hopping over to England without a bodyguard beside her. I'm smart enough not to spoil things by throwing stumbling blocks into the path of the very person who's my only hope of changing her mind."

"Glad to hear I'm the answer to someone's prayer," Richard said.

"Never underestimate Divine Wisdom, son. Trust me."

Richard didn't bother to respond. He hung up and reclined in his chair.

Un-freaking believable. Here she went all over again. Of all the people Gabriela could bump into, she had to run head-on into this Wickeham creep. Hell. The woman still had a penchant for attracting the lunatic bastards, recalling their last encounter with Albert Heinige.

Wickeham, like Heinige, was another of these cocky egomaniacs who considered they deserved everything, including objects from which other people refused to part. Through personal contact, Richard knew Wickeham abhorred honest competition, choosing coercion and intimidation to achieve his goals. But, in his experience, Wickeham backed down in the face of fierce opposition. The question now was, why was Wickeham so determined? Why was he going beyond the extremes with Gabriela?

He paged his assistant. "Vivian? Get Jeremy up here ASAP."

"Yes, sir," she chirped. "Right away."

Richard grinned at her sudden eagerness, suspecting by her happy flutter around the office lately—and Jeremy's nightly absences from his rooms—they had recently become a couple.

Several minutes later, the thick body of Jeremy Hollis crammed the open door space. He entered confidently, his shoulder-length, champagne-colored hair drawn back into his habitually tight ponytail.

"What's up, guv'nor?"

Richard's lips curled into an amused smile. "Cut the cockney, Victorian bullshit and come sit down. I need your advice."

Jeremy grinned boyishly, his brown eyes crinkling with humor. He dropped his heavy bulk onto the chair across from Richard's desk and waited.

Three years ago, due to irreparable tendon damage to his legs, Jeremy had been forced to retire from Rugby Union. As luck would have it, Richard had approached him one month to the day he'd graduated from Executive Protection Training. Richard's offer was simple: pick up chauffeuring and bodyguard duties. Jeremy had accepted in a flash, to the amazed disbelief of friends and family. This sudden career change, and Jeremy's bloody cheerful enthusiasm at accepting Richard's offer, had left everyone baffled. After all, had a more unlikely working pair ever existed? Richard was sophisticated, worldly, intellectual, and well spoken. Jeremy's version of the Queen's English was interlaced with Rugby lingo. He had not gone beyond a secondary school level, was unsophisticated, and was, occasionally, rude. No one would ever understand why Jeremy preferred to hold down a job that didn't offer crippling injuries or require endless, daily fights against pain.

"Okay. So what's so urgent you wanted my bum up here *pronto?*" Jeremy asked, borrowing Richard's favorite phrase.

"Do you still have that friend at CID?"

"Yeah. Problem?"

"Not me. A friend. I want you to find out anything they have on a man named Wickeham. Arnold Wickeham."

Jeremy frowned, his chiseled features turning meaner. "Isn't that the bloke you had a ruck with about a year ago?"

Richard nodded. "The problem now is that he's using the bully treatment with another person—a woman this time. I never understood why dealing with Mr. Wickeham required evading his nasty intimidation tactics."

"Who's the woman?"

"Gabriela," he answered, a heavy dose of gratification lacing his words. "Gabriela Martinez."

Richard caught Jeremy's reaction to his possessive tone. The man before him might not have gone beyond secondary school, but intelligence was not something he lacked.

"The lady who painted that?" Jeremy asked in surprised awe, his right thumb pointing in the general direction of the *St. George.*

"The one and only," Richard answered.

"Why's Wickeham on her case?"

"Greed, possibly, or exclusivity in representation, perhaps. I'm not sure. But it has to do with her auctioning a manuscript she's been working on for the past four years. It's a unique book. An original from an original, if I remember her words correctly."

"And the bloke wants it?"

"Very badly. Remember our scuffle with him last year? That bastard doesn't like to risk losing what he covets in honest bidding. According to the priest, this manuscript can bring an elevated selling price for a charity Gabriela has set up. Mr. Wickeham offered to buy the book for two hundred and fifty thousand pounds before it goes up for auction, but Gabriela refused. He's becoming very insistent she sell, nastily so."

Jeremy's hefty whistle bounced around the office walls. "Two hundred and fifty thousand pounds, eh? Must be something, this manuscript." He rubbed the crescent moon scar over his left eyebrow, one of many souvenirs decorating his body, tattooed in by a well-placed opponent's kick on the rugby field. "I'll call Mike and see what he can come up with."

"Try to get an answer today, Jeremy, because we're going to the States tomorrow. After I talk to Gabriela, we hop to New York to close the Asian deal with the Hilton chain. She'll be joining us on the return leg to London," Richard said with certainty. "During the trip back and her stay at my town house, you'll be in charge of her safety when I'm not available."

"Nothing to it," Jeremy said.

"Wipe that cocky grin from your face," Richard said. "Gabriela is stubborn, pigheaded, and intelligent. You'll have to watch her closely because she can weasel from under your nose without you realizing it. And take my word for it, she's not easy to catch up with once she's into her mulish, evasive moods." His eyes, colder than a wintry sky, pierced Jeremy. "If you fail me in protecting her, Jeremy, I guarantee you won't like the consequences."

Jeremy nodded.

"We must do everything in our power so Wickeham doesn't get his greedy paws on her." Richard closed his eyes an instant. "She's special," he admitted, unable to block the raw need in his voice.

"How special is special?" Jeremy asked.

"Very." Curt, with no further explanations. "Pack your suitcase. I'll instruct Vivian to make reservations for our flight tomorrow. You'll get to meet Gabriela then."

"I'll get kickoff started," he said. "Anything else I should know?"

"No," Richard answered. "Nothing at all for the moment."

Jeremy nodded, recognizing Richard's silent dismissal. He left the comfort of his chair, the hundred questions he wanted answered, unasked. After seeing the fierceness in Richard's eyes but, especially, hearing the underlying possessiveness in his voice, Jeremy suspected it would be to his healthy benefit if he kept his mouth shut as tight as a scrum. He was too fond of his hide to appease his curiosity, even when he was bloody interested about the relationship between Richard and this Gabriela Martinez.

Well, damn, bloody curious.

Chapter Four

Monterey Bay, California

Blending like a ghost at the edge of the kidney-shaped expanse of her terrace, Gabriela bent over the balustrade and watched the dark waves caress the craggy shoreline beneath her home. She felt like a thief in the night, hiding from the roomful of guests—*her* roomful of guests. But, hell, she didn't really care right now. The need to ease the tension, humming through her like electricity, had been all-consuming. It had felt like an invisible hand squeezing hard enough to suffocate, and no thoughts of gross neglect or social faux pas could have prevented her escape. Not tonight.

Gabriela's golden eyes roamed over the breathtaking beauty of the sea. She raised her face and enjoyed the evening's soft breath caressing her hair as it playfully swirled the scents of pine and tangy sea around her. She snuggled within Nature's calm hold and thought that, for this stolen moment of peace, every raised eyebrow and condemning stare she'd receive later was worth it. She slowly moved her head in a tight circle. Tension finally freed its tenacious hold on her neck muscles.

God, she was edgy tonight, unusually so.

"What on earth are you doing, *ma chère?* It's freezing out here."

Gabriela barely turned. By the sound of her friend's voice, Jean-Louis was irritated with her again. She listened to his impatient strides as he moved closer and she smiled affectionately. Jean-Louis hated her disappearances from these tiresome, yet necessary, gatherings in her honor. He understood her shyness, her need to be alone, and was uncannily perceptive to her moods. It didn't necessarily mean he approved of her hiding.

"Don't exaggerate, Jean-Louis. It's barely fifty-eight," she said, shrugging. "Besides, I need a break from all this socializing."

He tsk-tsked and cocooned her shoulders in a silk wrap.

"*Ma chère,* I would have thought you'd be used to the fuss by now." He shrugged in habitual fastidiousness. "However, today I can sympathize with your need to get out of there. *Mon Dieu, chérie.* You Cubans can be soooo loud. That cousin of yours, Enrique. Really. He's a dream of a man, a genius CPA, but the way he screams his way into every conversation—" He sighed in exaggerated wistfulness. "*Pas chic.*"

Gabriela laughed and turned again to face the sound of the sea.

"Enrique has always been loud." She rested her elbows on the banister. "After thirty-six some-odd years of being bombarded with his voice, you sort of get used to it."

Jean-Louis harrumphed and imitated her stance on the banister. They remained in companionable silence, watching the moon tiptoe across the starry night, its light barely piercing the darkness of the surrounding coastal cliffs and the glittering sea.

"Beautiful, *n'est-ce pas?*" he whispered.

Gabriela's gaze swept over the horizon again, watching the by-play of tenuous moonlight and blanketing darkness there. "Yes, it always is," she answered, her mind and body in tune with the peaceful surroundings.

"But the view is not the only reason you're out here." Jean-Louis turned, scrutinizing his friend's delicately beautiful profile. "So, what's haunting you today? It's not your gorgeous cousin, nor the soirée, is it?"

Without taking her eyes from the horizon, she whispered, "No."

Jean-Louis sighed into the cool evening. "I have a feeling I'm not going to like the answer to this."

Her friend, and manager, was like a radio antenna, always tuned in to her current moods. Not surprising. They simply had experienced too much pain, shock, and turbulence in the aftermath of her near-death four years ago. During the chaos, Jean-Louis had remained her steadfast supporter, both in his friendship and in managing her career, guiding Gabriela at a moment in life when she would have thrown everything overboard. Jean-Louis had protected her aggressively from the paparazzi, the hungry press, and the loathsome curiosity seekers who had wanted a peek at the brave woman who had killed in self-defense. And because he'd been privy to all that turmoil, Jean-Louis and Gabriela shared that one secret, the secret that had turned her life into a living heaven despite a guilty hell.

Studying her expressive face and thinking she was about to give him an excuse, Jean-Louis chastised her.

"Please," he said before a whisper of breath slipped out of her mouth. "Don't you dare insult me by giving me a stupid answer. I will not have it."

Gabriela remained silent, studying the scenery beyond the terrace. Immediately contrite, Jean-Louis squeezed her shoulder affectionately, careful of her recent bruises.

"That was totally uncalled for," he apologized. "*Pardons moi,* my friend. I'm on edge myself. It's all this trouble with the *bourgeois cretin* that is making you nervous, no?"

She laughed huskily. "No. After what I've gone through, this little cretin doesn't make me nervous. It's just that . . . I don't know, I've had this feeling since the accident that I can't shake."

She shrugged slightly, trying to dismiss her uneasiness as not important. Yet the impression she needed to brace for an unseen onslaught persisted. Deep down, Gabriela suspected this sensation, despite its subtlety, would be close to cataclysmic. And she was tired of cataclysmic events. They ripped and clawed at her until she was exposed to her most vulnerable self, as vulnerable as she had been four years ago.

"I guess my thoughts are a haunting of sorts," she finally admitted. "But I can't seem to shake them off." She couldn't admit, either, the overpowering longings resurrected by this added complication to the current chaos of her life, one she couldn't deal with yet.

"Don't worry." Gabriela slipped an arm around her friend's waist and squeezed him briefly. "This black mood will pass. It always does, just like everything else."

"Not everything has passed," Jean-Louis said seriously. "And it can't continue this way."

Gabriela stepped away abruptly, leaving Jean-Louis to stare at her rigid back. "Leave well enough alone."

"*Ma chère,* you're carrying too many responsibilities on your slender shoulders," he said, concern and frustration clear in his tone. "You're not superwoman. You can't handle everything alone."

When she offered no response, he faced her, his feet planted apart like a sheriff facing a showdown.

"Gabriela, Roberto is lying comatose next door in your late mother-in-law's house." Jean-Louis made a quick sign of the cross. "God rest her soul. You are handling company business in his absence; you are finalizing this charity project with Father Ramirez, are up to your ears with your children's activities, your own work, and you're still confident you will handle this paranoiac and his veiled threats all by yourself? *Mon Dieu,* be realistic. You need help. We need help."

Gabriela locked gazes with Jean-Louis, her eyes glittering.

"I know the kind of help you want me to enlist." She rammed her hands through her hair. "It's not enough that Wickeham has been hounding me, but I have to put up with your hounding also?" She faced the sea and gripped the banister until her hands hurt. "I can't do it. I told you that a week ago, and every other day you have suggested it." She turned, her eyes heartrendingly vulnerable. "I can't do what you ask. Not yet. Besides, it's been four years of silence. He might not—"

She gulped and shook her head. Who was she kidding? Her choices, at the moment, were severely limited. Hell. She had none. Not the way her heart wanted to resolve them. If she could resolve them.

"Please, please, my friend. I need time."

Jean-Louis remained quiet, thinking about his foolish and proud friend, fighting the world and past demons all by herself. He cocooned her close within his arms and his heavy sigh floated in the breeze, its message part resignation and part frustration. If there was anyone who understood the reasons behind Gabriela's reluctance and vulnerability, it was he. But with events getting out of hand, especially after what had happened to her on the road two days ago, Jean-Louis also understood the need for immediate action. Hopefully, after his discussion with Father Ramirez, the good priest had taken matters into his own hands. Why should Gabriela shoulder this new threat alone when there was someone quite capable to assist her and, at the same time, bring her the long overdue happiness she deserved?

He mentally altered and discarded different strategies. If the priest hadn't done anything by tomorrow, he'd give Gabriela one more chance. Frankly, he was fed up with Gabriela's stoic and silent suffering. She deserved better.

"Okay," he said, outwardly capitulating to her wishes. "But, at least, hire additional bodyguards for the up-coming week."

Gabriela regarded him with little patience. "Aren't you overreacting a bit? This idiot is all bark and no bite."

Jean-Louis gave a disgusted snort. "And how do you explain this *cretin* knowing about your accident, making all kinds of innuendos about it, unless he staged it himself? Eh, eh? Explain that."

"You surprise me, *mon ami*, especially after what we went through in France. I would have been shocked if Mr. Wickeham hadn't known about my accident. Even before I arrived at the hospital, the tabloids certainly did." And had splattered her bruised face all over the front page. She shook her head, her burgundy-colored hair softly brushing her cheeks. "No. This man is just well informed and using this knowledge to his advantage. He is obsessive, but definitely not dangerous."

Jean-Louis was not convinced. He opened his mouth to blurt his opinion, but a blast of light and music spliced the darkness of the terrace, effectively cutting into their conversation.

"*Oye, prima,*" Enrique bellowed from the doorway leading into her living room. "What in hell are you doing hiding out here? You're supposed to be mingling, enjoying yourself. People are already wondering where on earth you've disappeared. And Henderson is leaving."

Latin music vibrated the air around the terrace, overpowering all conversation and laughter. Keeping pace with the percussive rhythm of the song, Enrique advanced on them, his compact, five-foot-ten frame displacing the darkness. Tonight, he looked elegant and sophisticated in his black, Italian silk suit, its dark color complementing Enrique's fair skin. As usual, the shirt collar was open casually to reveal Enrique's favorite gold chain resting thickly around his neck, while a matching, wider bracelet surrounded his right wrist. His favorite gold Rolex graced his left. With voice booming in harmony to the lyrics, Enrique continued his dance toward Gabriela, extending his arms. He drew her smoothly into them, hips swaying to the rhythm of the *guaracha*.

"Shame on you, *Juancito*," he said and threw a disarming smile at Jean-Louis, his brown eyes crinkling in wicked humor. "You're supposed to prevent these situations from happening, man. You know how much Gaby enjoys burrowing into her shell like a hermit crab."

Jean-Louis rolled his eyes. "*Mon Dieu*," he hissed. "Even here the man has to shout."

Gabriela smiled. "Now, Jean-Louis. Behave."

"Yeah, JL. Behave," quipped Enrique, twirling Gabriela in a tight circle. His soft brown hair, moussed to stiff perfection, remained unruffled by the evening breeze.

"You have absolutely no manners, Mr. Macho," Jean-Louis sniffed, the twinkle in his eyes negating the offended expression in his voice. "And it's Jean-Louis to you." He jammed his hands into his pants pockets and raised his chin in mock belligerence. "And we were having a very pleasant, quiet conversation until you blasted your way out here."

Enrique pivoted Gabriela in place, bent her backward into a dip, and held the position for three seconds. His protruding stomach, which Enrique jokingly claimed he'd earned through hard work and good food, bumped against Gabriela's torso.

"You're going to let this guy poke fun at me, *prima?*" he asked and swung her around in another tight pirouette.

Gabriela laughed. "Definitely. It serves you right for calling him Juancito, or JL."

Jean-Louis snickered. "It's inconceivable how you belong to this classy family, let alone how you snatched such a mild-mannered and well-educated wife with your lack of refinement, *Kique*."

Jean-Louis's use of Enrique's nickname sounded like an insult.

"Beatriz, mild-mannered?" Enrique's good-natured laughter drowned the music surrounding them. Gabriela winced. "Are we speaking of the same woman here? The one whose temper catches fire as quickly as a struck match?" Enrique laughed harder and pirouetted Gabriela to finish the dance.

Jean-Louis crossed his arms and shook a finger at Enrique. "Your wife might have a temper, but she definitely doesn't blare her way through a conversation. Well, no use trying to finish ours," he told Gabriela. "When your ears can't take any more of your cousin's loudness, come inside. I'll have most of your farewells done with Henderson before you see him off." He turned and headed for the doors.

"Bye, *Juancito*," Enrique shouted after him, unable to resist. Jean-Louis dismissed Enrique's parting shot with a rude hand gesture and rejoined the guests inside.

"When are you going to stop calling him that?" She playfully swatted Enrique's arm. "You know he hates the nicknames."

"I know," Enrique shrugged. "But I can't resist baiting that *maricón*. Hey," he complained when Gabriela's unexpected shove made him stumble.

"I've told you a thousand times not to describe Jean-Louis in that manner," she said, her angry eyes changing to a burnished gold.

"*Ay, prima*, lighten up. I like the guy. You know I don't mean anything by it."

She punched him with enough force to hurt.

"*Coño, chica*. You're no fun lately."

Gabriela raised an eyebrow and changed the subject.

"And you are here because?"

Enrique pressed his body against the banister and braced himself with both hands. His expression turned grave. "Henderson is at it again, Gaby."

"To go public?" Gabriela shook her head in disbelief. Henderson was crazy if he believed she'd go public just so he could gobble Roberto's company in a perfectly legal, hostile takeover. As long as the company remained private, she'd be able to pull things off.

Enrique shook his head, disgusted at the direction things were taking. "Hiroshi casually mentioned just now that Henderson, like the vulture he is, has been circling our top brass for the past two weeks. He is blitzing our executives, waving the carrot very casually and on the sly."

"I presume he found out when our board is meeting?" Gabriela said, deflated.

"Henderson knows you'll fight tooth and nail to stay private, so he's aiming guns at our execs. With Roberto incapacitated as he is, Henderson is betting he can pit our executives' personal ambitions against their company loyalty and outgun you." His fists pounded the railing in mounting frustration. "*Coño, prima*, he's setting us up and setting us up good. Unless Roberto can miraculously come out of his coma before the board meeting, I'm afraid we're screwed." Enrique shuddered in the cool evening. He didn't voice his fear of Roberto coming out like a vegetable and not whole.

Gabriela pressed her palms against her burning eyelids. Clint Henderson, the CEO of one of the most powerful petroleum and plastics firms in the US, wanted Roberto's company and wanted it badly. Like the predator he was, Henderson sensed something major was brewing—too many RGM lawyers working on a top-secret patent search. That meant Henderson had to cripple the foundering ship before Gabriela could safely move it to port, because if Gabriela successfully patented Roberto's newest invention, everyone in the industry would be left scrambling to catch up—if they ever did.

Gabriela heaved a tired sigh and snuggled deeper into the wrap's warmth, her eyes glued to the partly sunken silver moon. She wanted to scream, to cry, to hit and cause pain at the injustice of it. She was tired, desperate, disillusioned, and worried—way out of her league. Above all, she was scared, fearing she wouldn't be able to hold on to Roberto's company much longer. She closed her eyes. God, she needed time, more time than Henderson was allowing her, and she feared that if she didn't get the time, RGM Plastics, Inc., her husband's dream and his triumph, his legacy for the children's future, would slip through her fingers.

And she would never be free.

"Where do we stand?" she asked quietly.

"Hiroshi doesn't care one way or the other. He has given you and Roberto his loyalty from the word go. But Novell is vacillating. It's a matter of time before he's seduced by the lure of expansion. Lennox oozes company loyalty and support, but the bottom line is that he'll be the first one to sell out, if the offer is right."

"I know." Gabriela turned cynical eyes toward her cousin. "Lennox thinks he's got me fooled, but I pegged him for what he is months before Roberto even realized. He's like one of those thermal concealers—the real secret underneath will be revealed only if you touch it correctly." Gabriela's sigh overflowed with resignation. "Yes, he's greedy enough to defect to Henderson's side. Can't we sue him for breach of contract if he does?"

Enrique's sniff held a wealth of derision. "That'd be throwing away good money on legal fees and valuable time."

She pushed herself away from the banister. She paced, her heels clicking on the stone floor surface, echoing in restless, hollow snaps. "Any news from the lawyers on the patent?"

"No. But I'll get on their case first thing tomorrow morning. I'm pushing for results before this damn meeting is held."

Gabriela waved her hands in agitated denial. "Don't force them to rush, Enrique. The company can't afford to make a single mistake on that patent application and search. Too much is riding on it."

"Shit." Enrique rammed his hands into his suit's pockets. "If only we'd known about Roberto's plans earlier, we'd have Henderson writhing on his belly in death throes right now."

"It's my fault. I should have looked through Roberto's things sooner than I did."

"Hey, *prima,* it's okay." Enrique's arm offered comfort, precious little, he knew, but more than she had right now. Several months younger than Gabriela, he had always assumed the role of an older, protective brother. He had been the one to tease her constantly as they grew up, had taught her to play Monopoly and checkers, and had bluntly warned her about groping boys as teenagers. Now he shouldered half the responsibility of running Roberto's company—a company about which both knew practically nothing.

"Who could have guessed Roberto wouldn't recover quickly from his coma after the accident? Or that he had left work pending in his computer at home? Hell, you've worked miracles for someone in your situation. Even the family is amazed about how well you've rallied, and how quickly."

Gabriela smiled softly and rested her head against his shoulder. "Maybe I made a mistake in following Roberto's wishes. Maybe I should have let the board know about this new patent…about his condition."

He released her as suddenly as he had cradled her.

"Are you insane? If you let that egotistical blabbermouth Lennox know about the patent, everyone in the industry will know before the next coffee break." He grabbed her by the shoulders. "If you breathe a word of what is really happening to Roberto, everyone will defect. Don't flush your only ace down the toilet."

Gabriela placed her hands reassuringly over her cousin's. "I'm tempted, but I'll wait. Besides, you know what the lawyers warned us about—if we open our mouths, the patent information falls immediately under public domain. I definitely don't want to gift-wrap Roberto's invention for anyone to grab."

"Especially not that piranha Henderson. Let him stew in his own juices for the next seventeen years." He kissed her lightly on the cheek. "We'd better get back inside."

The terrace's French doors opened and Jean-Louis poked his head through, the volume of music and conversation now at a more tolerable level.

"Got the *mêlée* out the door, *ma chère.*" He waved her in impatiently. "Come, come, come."

Gabriela quickened her stride as Jean-Louis threw the doors wide open for her to step through. She blinked several times to adjust to the sudden glare of light and saw that, true to his word, the small group of associates and friends had already been herded out of her home.

"Mitchell is positively drooling at the chance you may accept their invitation for the summer exhibition," Jean-Louis murmured, careful not to bump against protruding plates and cocktail napkins on the center table.

"That desperate?"

Jean-Louis shrugged. "He's probably working under a considerable deficit after the flop he hosted at the museum. We should wait to give him an answer, negotiate a better deal."

Gabriela sighed. "*Merci, mon ami,*" she said, pointing to the closed door.

"*De rien,*" he nodded and smiled. In unison, they flopped on the sofa. She flicked off her shoes, splayed her arms across the sofa's back, dropped her head back onto the soft cushions, and gratefully closed her eyes. Like a hummingbird, Beatriz hovered, gathered, and scooted to every cup, dirty paper plate, fork, spoon, and crumpled napkin in the room. A grumpy Enrique trailed behind his wife with an open garbage bag so she could quickly dispose of the trash.

"Leave that, both of you, please," Gabriela said. "Lupe promised she'd help me clean the mess tomorrow."

"It's no problem." Beatriz's soft voice floated across the room. "We're almost done here anyway."

Gabriela smiled. Beatriz was the pause in a conversation, the relaxing Muzak in Enrique's life. She was soft gentility and delicate features, with thick lashes outlining gentle, puppy-shaped eyes. Her shoulder-length curls resembled chocolate-colored silk and framed her Raphaelite Madonna-like face. But Beatriz's floating gentleness hid a temper that, the rare moments when ignited, was furious enough to challenge an erupting Mt. St. Helens. Whenever she vented it, everyone in the family was smart enough to give her a wide berth—especially Enrique.

"Come on, Bea," Enrique complained as he followed his wife into the kitchen. "I'd like to get home before the sun rises."

"*Oui,* Beatriz," Jean-Louis shouted from his perch beside Gabriela. "Your husband needs his beauty sleep."

Enrique blurted out loudly, "*Cabroncito,*" while Beatriz calmly stated, "So do I." Gabriela jabbed Jean-Louis with her elbow.

"At what time did you plan to meet tomorrow?" she asked, rubbing one tired foot with the other. From the kitchen, Enrique's complaints to Beatriz escalated, their voices providing background noise.

"A bit after eleven. I need to finalize the latest changes in schedules."

Gabriela nodded and heard Enrique snap an order to Beatriz. Indignant spurts of 'fed up,' and 'troglodyte, macho bully' reached her. Gabriela winced.

"Bring the planner with you, okay? Might as well decide on a definite date for Mitchell. And tell Julien to give you the frame for the *Madonna & Child.* I want to see if the tones of gold finally match."

Jean-Louis nodded, gave her a quick peck on the cheek, and stood. "Get some rest, *ma chère.* You look done in."

She smiled weakly and stretched like a lazy cat. "I'll try," she said as Beatriz streaked through the living room like an irritated badger. Gabriela picked up her shoes, stood, and followed an amused Jean-Louis to the foyer.

"The woman is pissed," Enrique said and shrugged. His expression of outrage and put-upon, misunderstood male mirrored her three-year-old's.

Jean-Louis whacked him on the back. "Enjoy your ride home, *mon ami.*" His chuckle bubbled into a low roar. "*A demain.*" He laughed all the way to his car.

Beatriz reappeared, purse over her arm, her back up, her shoulders rigid. Gabriela hugged her affectionately.

"Even if the brute deserves it, leave some flesh on him, okay?"

"Men." Bea's eyes locked with Enrique's. They pitched shards of ice worthy of a glacier. "Testosterone on a rampage. I don't know why the hell we put up with them."

Immune to her frigid snips, Enrique folded her within his arms and nuzzled her neck. "Because you love us and can't resist our beautiful bods?"

"Conceited oaf," Beatriz snapped, but her eyes thawed.

"Out," Gabriela ordered and shooed them through her front door. "Out, both of you, before I puke."

Enrique chuckled and dragged his wife to their Lexus. "I'll give you a call tomorrow after I speak with the lawyers." He paused by the open car door. "Hopefully, they'll have good news for us. Either way, I'll let you know. Goodnight, *prima.*"

Not as optimistic as Enrique, Gabriela waved from her perch on the front steps and watched the car's taillights disappear in the inky night. A moment later, the evening hushed and the murmur of crashing waves against the coastline sang its lullaby to the night. She closed the door and locked it. One by one, the bands keeping her mask of competence in place snapped, baring her exhaustion.

She had one more ritual to perform, the hardest, the most draining.

Tired, she donned her flip-flops, took the secluded path from the pool house to the gate at the edge of her property, and jabbed the security code releasing the connecting gate to her mother-in-law's house. She crossed the driveway to a back entrance, procrastinated for a few seconds to gather her inner strength.

She knocked softly on the door.

"How's the graveyard shift treating you this week, Melanie?"

"Bo-oring," the night nurse whispered. "With everyone sleeping, we vampires have nothing to do but doze off." She sneezed and excused herself. "How come you came by tonight? I wasn't expecting you until tomorrow."

"Things wound down earlier than I thought and tomorrow I may not have time to visit. How's Roberto doing?"

"Oh, much the same. Olga gave him his bath today and dressed him up in his new jammies. He listened to an audiotape during his session with the physical therapist, and Sister Mary Margaret decorated the room with the new drawings you sent over from the children. Tomorrow, they'll have something extra to talk to their dad about, especially that scamp, Luis. I'm sure he'll give Roberto an earful and then some."

Gabriela grinned. Her toddler was a chatterbox, his speech going at a steady ninety miles an hour ever since the precocious age of two when Luisito had discovered the wide world of words outside his limited vocabulary of no. The rest, as someone had once said, was history.

"Listen," Gabriela asked. "I hate to do this to you so late at night but, would you mind very much if I talked to Roberto for a bit?"

"No problemo," she replied cheerfully.

"Thanks. I really appreciate this."

"Hey, don't mention it. This will help cut down on the ocean of caffeine I'll have to swallow tonight."

Gabriela followed the nurse to Roberto's room. The soft sigh of the artificial respirator, breathing in and out for Roberto, filled the air. Gabriela pulled a chair next to his bed, avoiding the sight of the obscene feeding tube protruding from Roberto's abdomen. She understood her imagination always ran rampant whenever she saw that plastic tubing, but she couldn't quite discard the image of a burrowing snake, ravenously eating away at Roberto's insides.

She looked at her husband's face as she sat down. Her eyes filled with pity, interlaced with a morsel of resentment, and a ton of regret. *You had to do this to me again, Roberto, didn't you?* her brain supplied, but her lips remained unmoving. *You had to mess up what bit of happiness I could have garnered after that morning.*

She sighed. A little late for recriminations. It was what it was, and no amount of wishful thinking would alter the past. But things would have been so different if Roberto had gone straight to work instead of going to see his lover that morning. For one, he would have avoided the six-car pile-up that day. He wouldn't have been catapulted under a sanitation truck by a carjacker fleeing the police. Roberto's brain wouldn't have been traumatized by the impact of bone against two tons of reinforced steel. His body wouldn't have been robbed of strength, his face of emotions. The high-speed chase that had ended with the felon trapped on the freeway with barely a scratch to his name had left her children with no gruff embraces, no teasing voice, no words of encouragement or advice. Day in and day out, Roberto lay impassive, his once strong and healthy body deteriorating a little more each week, his muscles contracting from disuse, twisting a fraction each day, tucking him slowly inward like a wilting flower.

Gabriela blinked, her eyes dry. Moot point. She knew the statistics and probabilities, what the doctors spewed out, at least those who kept pressuring her to make a decision about their brain-dead patient. They never lacked case histories to back up that ever-growing pressure, never omitting from their accounts the condition of the very few who recovered. They never refrained from singling out the high percentage of those few who did wake up, only to live no more than as human vegetables, with serious physical limitations.

She knew Roberto's condition was a deteriorating one, and she would be faced with another decision soon, one she was not yet ready to make. Hell, one she was still unwilling to make. It would be akin to murdering her husband. She simply could not do it.

So, like every day, and on occasion at night, she softly, patiently, recounted to Roberto her day's activities, as well as the children's. She outlined her plans for the next day, told him about Henderson, and described briefly the itinerary for the upcoming auction. Her voice droned on like a forgotten record, at times injected with humor, at others, with false enthusiasm. Only for the sake of her children did she keep talking to her husband, a man who now processed stimulus strictly on an input mode. Only faith kept a wispy flame flickering in her heart, hoping her husband would miraculously recover…hoping she'd be spared the final decision.

"Anything?" Melanie asked from the doorway.

"Nothing." She stepped out of the room. There was real regret in her voice.

"Hey, don't lose hope. You'll see. Roberto might surprise us one of these days. It's happened before."

Gabriela doubted she'd be that lucky.

God, she was tired, so very tired. She simply wanted to curl and hide in a quiet corner of oblivion to weep for the next hundred years. She felt beyond lost hope, anger, resentment, or guilt. She felt nothing but duty. For better or for worse. That would always remain and keep her trudging along until no choices were left.

Maybe tonight she'd be able to sleep, to escape her worries in REM doses. She opened the gate and headed home to rest, to sleep.

Time enough, tomorrow, to slay the dragons.

Chapter Five

London, England

A pensive Jeremy strolled leisurely over to Vivian's desk, his eyes crinkling in pleasure at sight of her. He dropped into a swiveling chair and started a pattern of semicircular swirls, remaining dutifully quiet as she jotted down phone instructions. Her long, carrot-colored hair hid her modest, pretty face.

"Hello, Miss Lindsay," he greeted, once she'd replaced the receiver. "And how are you on this damp, dreary morning?"

"As well as when you last saw me, Mr. Hollis," she answered, an amused twinkle in her sky-blue eyes. "When was it—four hours ago?"

A flash of recently shared pleasures made them both smile wider. Surprising what a fluke encounter in Piccadilly last month had accomplished, something working together for three years had not. It had been akin to a revelation. For Jeremy, the sight of the dumpy man with the horsy smile, holding Vivian possessively by the shoulders, had suddenly driven him crazy. Vivian, conversely, had taken great exception to the ugly Amazon sensually pawing Jeremy with greedy, beefy hands. The very next day, by mutual, enthusiastic consent, they had become very, very intimate.

"Did the boss give you the new instructions yet?"

"Just got off the phone with him. I should have the tickets late this afternoon." She motioned him closer with her finger. "What gives with the boss, Jem?" she asked. "The mysterious visitor from the Continent this morning, the sudden trip. Bizarre."

Jeremy eyed Vivian thoughtfully, debating how much he should divulge.

"Dunno, Viv," he answered finally, caressing her cheek with a callused finger. "I'll clue you in when I know what's going on." He'd better be certain before he fouled the boss, especially after seeing the emotions that had crossed Richard's usually impassive face.

"Unfortunately, the bizarre is turning into the disgusting," she said, her aqua eyes reflecting her words. "Honestly, Richard is not for the likes of that woman," Vivian finished with unusual brutal honesty.

Jeremy, thinking of Richard and Mrs. Martinez, was taken off guard.

"It's April," Vivian reacted to his look with an exasperated sigh.

Jeremy grimaced and conceded her point. April Cranfield was a young, beautiful creature, but spiteful and spoiled. No one in the office liked her. Sprinkle into the mixture an obviously selfish, conniving personality, and one wound up with a rather distasteful end result.

Still, those qualities weren't a handicap to enjoy a woman intimately. Jeremy had thought it awesome. April, like an animal in heat, was always all over Richard—in the car, in the house, and God knows where else. Had known only one instance, out of the hundreds, when Richard had succumbed. After that evening, however, April had been more desperate, offering more pleasurable extracurricular activities that would make a normal man salivate. Yet Richard had refused all her advances. No, it was more like he hadn't been tempted at all. His boss had remained impassive, definitely unmoved, and, on a rare occasion, Jeremy had glimpsed moments of disgust. Bloody hell, Jeremy hadn't understood that. He would have been all over April, his pecker relishing such an accommodating woman.

But the Richard he'd seen in the office moments back, the Richard who could murmur the name of a woman with a palpable, caressing sensuality, well, now, that Richard he could understand. For the first time, he understood the lack of enthusiasm for one certain catty Ms. Cranfield.

"Yes," Vivian continued, not pleased. "The one and only will shortly grant us the dubious pleasure of her presence. She's on her way up."

Jeremy raised an eyebrow and tried not to smile. "Did she rub you the wrong way, love?"

"Oh, bugger off, you hypocrite. I'm not the only one she brings out the worst in. You're always going on that she's rude, spoiled, selfish, bossy, obnoxious, and possessive of property that's not even hers yet."

"But simply gorgeous," Jeremy interrupted with a smirk.

Vivian casually flipped him the middle finger. "I'm telling you, Richard better watch his back with this one. I have a nose for trouble. There's something rather disturbing about her obsession with the boss, especially when it's obvious he's not interested."

The smoky glass doors, separating the main office from the executive suite, parted with a breezy whisper.

"Brace yourself. Here she comes."

A statuesque blonde floated through. A lush, black ermine coat cocooned her model's body all the way down to midcalf. Permed, blonde

Vivian, who had been smirking as she typed into the computer, pounded even faster at the keyboard, the perfect image of furious industriousness not wanting to be interrupted.

"That won't be necessary. Edmund is waiting for me downstairs." Under droopy eyelashes, she watched for Richard's reaction to this tidbit of information.

Richard merely stared, knowing her game. How did she expect him to feel any jealousy when no love existed for this capricious girl?

"Give Lord Cranfield my best, will you?" he said. "And tell Edmund to please be careful with his driving. Road conditions are a real mess today."

April's smile was stiff as she disappeared through the whispering doors.

***

Edmund Husher, rich by heritage and ancient surname, was not a peer of the realm, but was in love with one. Had been in love with April Cranfield ever since he'd seen her walking the runway at the charity fashion show three years back. Since then, he'd been following her like the lovesick spaniel he considered himself, offering friendship, solace, therapy, and substitution sex. He understood her well, accepted all her quirks, turned a blind eye to her occasional brutal narcissism, and loved her for who she was, faults and all. He wished, with pitiful desperation, his constant presence would lure her closer to him. He wanted permanency, even if it was à la April, but as things stood, he was having a damn time achieving it.

He waited for the light to turn and drove to the building's entrance, where he double-parked. April had rung him about five minutes ago, her voice an icicle worthy of a Swedish winter. She'd ordered him to move his ass and bring the automobile round the front. From her tone, Richard had either rebuffed her advances or embarrassed her in front of an audience, or both. Edmund sensed she was stewing. Certain as well that, by the time he arrived to pick her up, he'd be the target for her vindictiveness.

Weeks ago, Richard's rejections had oftentimes translated into April being left wanting and horny. Demanding. He hoped, today, at least, the aftermath would lead to a satisfying fuck rather than the awful moments of silence he'd experienced lately. Interspersed in between those, there had been merciless titillation, only for his libido to be brought down brutally moments later by demeaning jabs guaranteed to shrivel his manhood.

Almost as if he were the recipient of something that had been done recently to her.

Edmund was getting tired of playing the target for her bitchiness.

He grabbed the umbrella and ran to the lobby entrance. He was a tall man, who bore his height awkwardly due to a slim frame and muscles that looked stretched by a medieval rack. Comma-shaped curls hid some premature balding, and his skin, sensitive to the sun upon occasion, suffered from embarrassing acne flare-ups. A soft nose, pointed jaw, and light caramel eyes, gave him a cherubim-like amiability, which blended well with his affable personality. That drew in the ladies. Had drawn in April, once he'd gotten the courage to approach her. A blessing, at first, but the perceived physical softness, the unthreatening, the wholesome, the dependable in him, had become his curse the moment this Harrison chap had arrived on the scene. Edmund had been supplanted for the alpha Harrison the moment April had set eyes on the American. She had been panting for him like a bitch in heat ever since.

Lately, he very much minded having to pick up the other man's scraps.

He wanted to have his own.

But April had a way with her, and he was too desperate, too wanting. Mincemeat. He wished she desired him as much as he did her. He just didn't know how to lure her to him, yet.

"A bit more and I would have had to impose on strangers to take me home."

One look at her face told Edmund to stay quiet. Covering her well with the umbrella, he led her to the car and bundled her inside before the elements could bother her. He drove off once the roadway was clear of traffic.

The silence in the automobile grew. Edmund kept glancing at her from time to time, not quite grasping her mood. April seemed to be in a trance, eyes unfocused, staring ahead as if concentrating on an inner monologue available only to her.

"Are you all right?" he asked, a bit concerned.

April nodded and kept staring into space.

"Was Richard agreeable to your plan? Will he speak with this Mrs. Martinez about a possible event?"

"Somewhat."

Nothing else. After five more minutes of silence, Edmund gave up.

April, however, was furiously thinking and planning. There had been something different about Richard today. There was something...off. She'd gotten a glimpse of it when he'd wiped off her lipstick. Somewhere, on a very primitive gut level April suspected Richard was beyond losing interest in her. Had already lost it. But that was never going to happen.

She had other plans.

She had already cajoled her father's assistant to call Richard on her father's behalf this afternoon and invite him to dinner tomorrow. Lord Cranfield, however, would not attend. He was in York, on business, and would not return for several days.

Richard didn't need to know that today.

Of course, he would arrive at her home the next evening and see through her ruse. But she would concede she'd tricked him, bring up a few tears, look repentant, and beg for his forgiveness. She would offer him his favorite whisky, previously spiked with a very low dose of the MDMA one of her sleazy friends had supplied—and whose effects were guaranteed—and she would go all emotional.

April's nose scrunched up in distaste. No. Actually, that might turn him off faster than the required time for the chemical to work in his system. What she would do would be to express her feelings softly, regretful he did not feel the same. She could ask for more time, or perhaps for friendship? The concept might work if she included somewhere in her appeal the words *for the sake of Daddy*. Richard really cared for him, admired him. He might swallow her melodrama if she did that.

But once the drug took effect, she would draw him to her bedroom and let in the disreputable video photographer she'd hired. A corner of her lips lifted in satisfaction. For a week, she'd hounded her friend, Sara Sheffield, for a name. Sara, reluctantly, had supplied it, but had warned April she would blatantly deny she was the source of the scum's name. Too much was at stake, especially since Sara's show *Let's Talk About It!* was now the latest flavor-of-the-day talk show in Britain. April didn't care as long as the man recorded every romp with Richard, every orgasm, every deviancy she could supply. And she would ascertain every act was condomless. Her menses had ended a bit more than two weeks ago, so she was ripe.

She'd pretend outrage, guilt, and despair about the blackmail video received. April's lip curled. Imagination took over, supplying different scenarios in the confrontation with Richard. Her demeanor should alternate between remaining valiant in her despair, with angry moments at the injustice of it all. She should also pretend incredulity at the contents of the defamatory video. She would play the victim, the innocent woman trashed and injured by a feckless, scandal-mongering society.

The smile turned into a frown. What if the video did not persuade Richard to fall in line with her machinations? She'd better make sure, then, pregnancy became a definite.

She glanced at Edmund and considered.

Well, if the video and the pregnancy didn't force Richard's hand, then the tabloids would do the rest, if Richard proved stubborn.

advising Richard he would be at the town house in ten minutes, as soon as the stupid bobby gave the signal. Richard threatened to exclude him from all conversation if he did not make it in eight. Jeremy made it in six. In another twenty, they were walking into a mahogany-and-stained-glass-fronted pub, the inside bulging with naturally and artificially induced cheer and bonhomie. Jeremy, his bulk making a sizable opening in the milling crowd, led the way to a crowded corner where a slight man was holding court to two empty chairs, as promised.

"Hey, Mike," Jeremy roared above the din and waved his muscular arms. Richard grinned. Did Jeremy truly think that with the body of a two-hundred-fifty-pound linebacker, he'd go unnoticed?

The gentleman in question looked up in mild curiosity at the bellowing of his name. He stood, his slender frame made more so by the casual bagginess of his clothing.

Michael Morris turned out to be a surprise. For one, he was surprisingly young and preppie looking, his ash-colored hair stylishly cut, face unblemished by scars, pimples, or mustache. His teeth were big and orthodontically perfect, framed now to gleaming perfection by an easy, friendly smile. His grip, as he shook hands with Richard, was strong, assured; his keen blue eyes radiated intelligence, patience.

"Glad to meet you, Mr. Harrison."

Richard grinned. "Same here."

"Can I order you some ale?" Morris inquired politely as they all proceeded to sit.

Richard shook his head. "No, thanks. I still haven't gotten used to the taste of warm brew in my stomach. I'll take a whisky instead, neat. Why don't you go get us all a round, Jeremy?"

Jeremy started to protest.

Richard gave him a look. "You'll get to hear the entire juicy story when you get back. Git."

"Make mine a stout, will you, Jem?" Morris countered. "And do get my food order. My stomach is practically glued to my spinal column."

"Rough day?" Richard inquired politely.

Observant blue eyes regarded Richard with humor. "You can say that. Bogged down with reports and more research than I care to handle. How about you?"

Loaded question. "Same," Richard answered truthfully, nailing Morris with a penetrating stare. "I'm not known for my patience, you know?"

Morris nodded in understanding. "Understandable, although necessary when dealing with unknown variables." He cocked his head to the side, considering. "If I may be so bold as to ask—is your interest strictly business, personal, or both?"

"Personal. Yours?"

"Professional and personal, as you surmised already. In my case, unfortunately, the personal gets inconveniently in the way of the professional." He shrugged.

"So, let me fill in the rest," Richard supplied. "I waltz along and, presto, end your dilemma. Your personal interest in resolving things miraculously transforms into a professional priority demanding resolution. No more conflict of interest, correct?"

"Eminently so," Morris agreed candidly. Seemingly bored and doodling lightly on the table with his forefinger, he inquired all too casually. "If you'll pardon another slight indiscretion of mine, I'm rather curious as to why precisely you retired, Mr. Harrison. Or is it a moot point?"

"Richard, please. And, no, it's common enough knowledge. I almost got permanently retired from life by a bullet lodged too close to the heart."

Richard's hand automatically rubbed the scar tissue underneath his shirt, his eyes unfocused on the now, yet concentrated on a vivid past.

"By mutual consent," Richard continued, surfacing from his memories. "And to maintain the unparalleled reputation of my employer, my ex-boss and I decided it would be to our best interest if I quit. I, for one, am ecstatic."

"You seem to have pulled off the transition remarkably well. From what Jem tells me, you've built yourself quite a profitable little empire, together with a splendid reputation and impressive connections, especially among our noblest citizenry. Quite a feat, I might add."

"You've really done your homework today," Richard said. Amusement made his eyes crinkle.

"Quite," Morris agreed, a matching expression in his eyes. "However, it's been eminently satisfactory."

An oversized shadow blocked what little dim light existed in their corner.

"Here we go," Jeremy said and efficiently plopped the drinks in front of each corresponding person. Surprisingly enough, ale and whisky levels had arrived intact.

"Just drop that over there," Jeremy told the harried waiter as he pointed to a spot in front of Morris. The man neatly deposited a plate heavy with the thickest roast beef sandwich on which Richard had laid eyes. Framing it, in an overflowing, neat halo, were golden-colored chips. To further complement the fare in typical British fashion, Yorkshire pudding, bulging with roasted beef and gravy, rested on a second plate.

Richard contemplated the overflowing feast. He then turned speculative eyes on Morris.

Jeremy intercepted the look and laughed.

"Michael can pack it in like there's no tomorrow."

Morris looked from one to the other in resigned patience. "I fail to understand why everyone of my acquaintance ribs me about my eating habits, don't you know? After all, I must sustain my meager frame after putting in a hard day's work." Morris bit into the thick sandwich with gusto. "Intellectual sustenance," he said between munches, "requires quite a bit of material one."

His look of utter delight made the other two men grin. He wiped his mouth with the napkin and gave Richard his full attention. "Why, precisely, are you so interested in information about Mr. Wickeham?"

Richard's piercing eyes settled on Morris. "Today, I received a very interesting call from a priest who's very concerned about the safety of a mutual friend. It seems arrogant, son-of-a-bitch Wickeham is muscling into what can turn out to be very dangerous territory for him. I, in particular, am not amused with this turn of events. I don't like anyone threatening what's mine."

Morris chewed another mouthful in thoughtful patience. "I take it you've already met the gentleman in question?" he inquired.

"To his great misfortune," Richard replied, nasty satisfaction radiating from his eyes. "Gabriela and I go back a long way. Based on personal experience, I can tell you she's one hell of a stubborn woman. She despises any type of coercion or manipulation, and she has proven once again she'll fight against it when faced with a potentially dangerous situation. One reason she won't sell."

Morris raised an eyebrow. "So the lady in question refused Wickeham's offer?"

"Damn right," Richard said, his mouth twisting in a grimace. "I'm traveling to California tomorrow to convince her to accept my escort to London. Knowing her, I'm not even going to waste my time convincing her to sell. Once in London, she'll be staying at my home, which will somewhat guarantee her security. Additionally, Jeremy will back me up as bodyguard when I'm not available. However, I believe in being prepared. I despise surprises when facing my opponent, especially since I have to be at my very best behavior with the local authorities." The grimace turned into a nasty smile. "It's a damn shame I no longer have carte blanche to do as I please."

Morris took a long swig of his ale and wiped his mouth with polite fastidiousness. "This Gabriela...would she happen to be Gabriela Martinez, the illustrator? The one who's coming to London to auction a replica of a medieval manuscript?"

At Richard's sardonic look, Morris smiled. "I'm paraphrasing, you know, but *The Times* claims it is one of the most beautifully handcrafted pieces the modern world has ever seen. And, after seeing the manuscript in question, I have to agree with their assessment."

"You've seen it?" Jeremy asked.

Morris finished the last of his chips and drowned what was left in his mouth with a swig of ale. He next dug into the Yorkshire pudding with zeal, as if he hadn't eaten a sandwich that would provide the weakest man with a week's supply of energy.

"The management at Christie's contacted us last week to set up additional security on the day of the auction," he told the men. "The buzz is that the Royals might attend. The Duchess of York is a definite. Since it is a well-known fact my wife is an avid admirer of Mrs. Martinez's children's illustrations, my department assigned me to the project." He encompassed both men with his calm eyes. "It is really a most extraordinary piece of work, you know. The colors, the details, the calligraphy are exquisite, even beyond my descriptive powers. She's even been faithful in replicating the quality of ancient ink and vellum, or so the Christie's manager explained." He looked at Richard. "Have you seen it?"

Richard's eyes changed. "Part of it. In truth, I saw only the tentative, initial stages of the manuscript. It was, as you said, impressive."

Jeremy shook his head, his ponytail whipping around his neck in a repetitive dance. "No wonder the greedy bloke wants to get his grimy hands on this one piece before others do. He probably could get a fortune from a private collector."

"Actually, Jem, you're not too far off the mark. That is usually Mr. Wickeham's favorite MO."

Richard's gaze sharpened. "What do you mean?"

"Let me tell you a little story," Morris said, signaling the bartender for another round. "There was this little old couple—"

"Jeez, Mike. Cut this short, eh?" Jeremy interrupted. "We don't have the bleeding time this evening."

Morris grinned and quoted: "*But of all plagues, good Heaven, thy wrath can send; Save me, oh, save me from the candid friend.*"

"You and your bleeding quotations," Jeremy said, disgusted. He gave his friend a shove that could have felled a tree trunk.

"Well?" Richard's voice held a dangerous softness.

Morris considered Richard speculatively, his humor quickly fading. "As I was saying," he continued with calm decorum. "This older couple—very well liked, humble peers of the realm, may I add—had the misfortune to get acquainted with Mr. Wickeham at one social activity they attended. Unsuspecting of their new friend's predatory tendencies, they openly extended their friendship and home to him." He took a deep drink and pushed the finished plate to the center of the table. "As is Mr. Wickeham's wont, he already had a careful strategy plotted to get his hands on what he coveted and proceeded to study his victim for weaknesses and strengths, personal likes and dislikes."

"And any skeletons in the closet that could prove useful in his manipulative endeavors," Richard supplied, his expression cynical, knowing.

"Quite," Morris said.

"So what did the bastard want?" Jeremy asked, anger making his frown fiercer.

Morris's eyes became void of expression, his lips pressed as if he were swallowing disgusting medicine. "It was common knowledge the older gentleman's wife was the proud owner of a Rubens chalk sketch that had been in her family's possession for multiple generations. It was also understood it was unavailable."

"A word that doesn't seem to deter this man," Richard's disgust filtered through, remembering his past altercation with Mr. Wickeham.

Morris nodded and finished his ale. His eyes turned frighteningly cold.

"Since Mr. Wickeham's greedy eyes had already latched upon this drawing, he went about meticulously undermining his victim's life. You see, the older gent had two things going against him: his wife had been diagnosed with Alzheimer's a year past and was rapidly deteriorating, and he also occasionally liked to gamble on horseflesh. The latter had been somewhat curbed by his wife's illness, until Mr. W entered the scene.

"The gentleman was cajoled, then urged—very discreetly, I must add—to relieve the stress and frustrations of his unfortunate existence with the thrill of betting on horses. It was understood this little vice would be kept from the family. You know, a secret between good old chums and all that rot. Slowly, almost imperceptibly, the old man began accumulating debts—small ones, you know, easily covered by small loans from his bosom buddy, Mr. Wickeham."

"Hell, this old bloke didn't have the sense of a referee misjudging an illegal handing off call," Jeremy said.

Richard kept silent, the whisky glass kept warm by his continuously chafing palms. He knew the kind of scams unscrupulous types directed at defenseless, guileless older people, the members of society who always had the most to lose.

"When things started to get a tad hairy, the man's sense of honor arose. He could no longer keep asking Mr. Wickeham to bail him out, therefore—"

Jeremy interrupted. "More like his common sense finally won out."

Richard speared his chauffeur with one of his glacial stares. Jeremy shut up.

"Therefore," Morris continued, "this gentleman went out and mortgaged the family home. Went cold turkey for a while. Took care of his wife, refusing temptation, his family none the wiser until Mr. Wickeham called to invite him to a small get-together at Ascot. As you can presume, the gambling started all over again.

"Unfortunately, the debts accumulated higher and faster. When those reached more than a million pounds, in comes Mr. Wickeham for the kill. He showed up one day, aggrieved and apologetic, his pretense of not knowing what to do milked to the last drop."

"I'm sure not even a Shakespearean actor could have come up to snuff against his performance," Richard said.

Morris nodded. "Mr. Wickeham explained he was ever so sorry, but bad investments had forced his hand, therefore he needed to collect the almost million pounds owed. The older man was devastated. He pleaded and begged, asking for more time, for a chance to come up with the money."

"And Wickeham regretfully refused, pretending to be all broken up about this turn of events," Richard said.

"Not only that, but he subtly hinted if this gentleman didn't pay up, and soon, he would be forced to leak the events to the tabloids, who would devour the old gent alive. The news would cause a horrible social scandal and terrible grief for him and his family. However, Mr. Wickeham suggested there might be a solution to the current dilemma."

"Let me guess," Jeremy said. "If this cove parted with the Rubens gratis, that would dispatch the loan to the goal line."

"Precisely. However, Wickeham never expected the gent to turn the tables on him. The poor chap was so excited when he heard Wickeham's idea he began making plans to sell the piece to the higher bidder. Wickeham had other plans."

Richard and Jeremy exchanged knowing glances. They had witnessed these tactics from Wickeham before, a year back.

"But the tale gets even better," Morris continued. His expression turned ugly.

"When Wickeham understood what the old chap wanted, the bastard helped with the plans, suggested contacts, took photos, and even made appointments with different art dealers for consultation. But the very day the old gent visited one of those dealers, Wickeham went to see the wife. He solicitously gave the harried nurse companion a break in her duties, remarking he would have a nice visit with the old man's wife. The nurse didn't even question the request. After all, Wickeham was a frequent visitor and friend of the family."

"I'm sure he counted on that," Richard said.

"He took the woman for a stroll through the gardens," Morris continued. "Once out of sight, his bruiser went to work on the poor thing. According to the nurse, the old woman came back from her stroll so hysterical, everyone thought she'd had a brutal psychotic episode, you know, part of her dementia and all that. She spent a week in hospital, but the damage had already been done."

"What do you mean, precisely?" Richard asked.

"The bruising came out first, around her torso. There were burns around her belly as well. Wickeham's persuasive methods, I'm sure, entrusted to his thug. We presume he tortured her until she finally signed a binding bill of sale for the Rubens."

"Son of a bitch," Richard said.

Morris nodded. "So, that very afternoon, Mr. Wickeham became the legal owner of a Rubens sketch that, incidentally, brought more than triple the amount owed him from its sale to a private collector. It was the coup of coups for Wickeham: no taxes owed, a discreet cash wire transfer to an account in a tax-haven paradise in the South Pacific, and more than one hundred percent profit."

"Shit," Jeremy breathed. "Some set up." He paused briefly then added as an afterthought. "Whatever happened to the old gent, Mike?"

"He committed suicide a week later, after an anonymous source divulged, very discreetly, may I add, the man's gambling habit and how he had placed his entire family, especially his ailing wife, in financial bankruptcy. Photos of his debauchery were also published side-by-side with ones of his demented wife. Unfortunately, he took his life under the mistaken delusion life insurance monies would guarantee the care of his wife of forty years."

"Not in those cases," Richard commented.

"Yes." Morris's voice was flat. "Now Megan has to work two jobs, admit tours on the property, and rent it out as well in order to keep up the private nursing care the old woman requires, not to mention the inheritance taxes slapped on the family home."

"Megan?" Jeremy hissed. "Your cousin, Megan?" At Morris's nod, Jeremy blurted. "Bloody hell." He was horrified.

"Your cousin's parents?" Richard asked.

"No. Her aunt and uncle, but it's as if they had been. Megan's parents died when she was thirteen. Her aunt took over then."

"I see," Richard commented and studied this young man with the calm yet jaded eyes. Yes, he understood the silent request only too well. And knowing Gabriela as he did, she would be gung-ho to get the bastard.

"I offer no guarantees, except I will speak to Gabriela and present your case. It's been four years since I last saw her. The only promise I'll give you is that I'll try. She will either help you in nailing this bastard, or she won't."

Morris nodded. "That is all I ask, for the moment. However, let me warn you about Mr. Wickeham. Although he does not belong to the documented criminal element in our society, rumor has it he employs those who are. Unfortunately, all of this is hearsay, you know."

"As in all complaints or evidence dramatically vanish?" Richard asked.

"Precisely. Not everyone has the fortitude to choose between an extended hospital stay, death, or silence. If given the choice, even I would choose the latter. In any case," Morris continued, "regardless of what my personal desires are and my wish to see this cancerous sore behind bars, I must give you fair warning. Bait and capture must be done legally. Mr. Wickeham is a slippery eel. There is not a dent in his hardware as far as the department is concerned. If the case is not carefully and scrupulously documented per proper departmental procedures, the judge will laugh in our mucked-up faces."

"I did mention I would be on my best behavior."

"Just as long as you know the rules."

"Understood," Richard said. "However, I return the favor and warn you in turn, if this bastard so much as makes a wrong move or makes good on his threats, I don't care about your rules. As far as I'm concerned, Mr. W becomes fair game. And like fair game, I will hunt him down by every means available—legal or not."

"I cannot be a good chap and turn a blind eye on any illegalities, Richard," Morris warned.

"Who said there would be any for you to see?" Richard said, his stony gaze underlining his meaning.

Jeremy rubbed his hands, shifting a gleeful gaze from one man to the other. "Am I ever going to be happy to rub the bleeding cove's face in the dirt. I haven't brained a bastard since we played against Cardiff."

"Bloodthirsty devil, aren't you, Jem?"

He laughed. "Just fond memories, Mike."

"Well, I hate to break up this party," Morris began while doing another popping body stretch. "But I'm excessively tired and my wife will have my hide if I don't show up at the cottage soon. Besides, I'm looking forward to dessert."

"How are Caroline and the twins?" Jeremy asked.

"The twins couldn't be better. It's Caroline who is at tether's end." His face broke out in a fond smile. "Those cheeky little devils are a parent's worst nightmare. It is astounding where stubby four-year-old legs can roam and what busy little hands can dig up. Yesterday, the twins tore through the garden and ripped Caro's prized petunias from their pots to decorate their room, dirt and all. Caroline almost had apoplexy."

"Why the flowers?" Jeremy asked.

"They were playing Alice in Wonderland and needed the petunias to complete the scenario at the garden," Morris supplied. "Told their mum they couldn't sing to paper flowers. They wouldn't listen if not real." He chuckled. "Anyway, it's time to go enjoy my wife and children."

All three rose simultaneously. Extending his hand, Morris shook Richard's. "I'll be anxious to hear your news."

"Can we drop you off anywhere?" Richard offered.

"My car is parked by the door. A small privilege given to a humble public servant." He smiled broadly.

"Come on, Jeremy," Richard shoved him into motion. "It's time we turn in ourselves, if not, Vivian will have your hide."

Morris eyed his friend with humor. "What's this? Is love afoot?"

Jeremy turned a dull red. "Well, we have discussed linking up a bit," he murmured to his chest, his face turning redder.

"Good God," Mike exclaimed, scrutinizing his friend's embarrassed face and enjoying it. "Cupid's arrow has struck at last. I must meet the woman who has felled the mighty, immovable hulk."

"Actually," Richard cut in, amused at Jeremy's growing discomfiture. "She's a pretty little redhead, with a temper to match, but loyal, intelligent, and efficient. A good woman, all around."

Jeremy's mouth slacked into an astonished O. Richard was not one to praise indiscriminately. Wait till he told Vivian.

"In that case, why don't you both come over for supper when you return, Jem? Caro will be thrilled to meet her."

"At least she'll stop trying to match me with every girl in the bloody district," he grumbled.

"That's my sweet Caro. The unrelenting romantic."

Richard smiled and passed Jeremy as he held the pub door open for them. The cold April evening pelted their faces with rain. Tonight, the raindrops had the quality of darts.

"Blasted weather," Morris grumbled and hunched into his raincoat. Without further words, he ducked his head into his body, waved a quick good-bye, and ran the last few steps to his parked car. Jeremy and Richard imitated him quickly.

"What do you want to do now?" Jeremy asked as he slammed the limousine door shut. He shook his head like a wet spaniel.

"Home. My workshop."

Jeremy's gaze bumped into Richard's in the rearview mirror. "Came up with a new furniture idea?"

Richard rubbed his face, his emotional weariness reflected in the slow movement of his hands. "No," he finally answered and searched the night outside the limo windows. "I want to work on a gift."

Silence followed as they drove through the busy streets of London. After some time, the car glided through the gate and headed to the back door. "Anything else?" Jeremy asked, braking the car smoothly.

"Go to your rooms. I'm sure Vivian is waiting impatiently."

"Ah, boss. Ease off."

Richard laughed. "Nighty night, Jeremy. Don't let the bed bugs bite."

Jeremy's disgusted mumbling about friends and employers quoting the bleeding Royal library was lost as he drove the car into the garage.

Richard turned slowly and entered a spacious room, meticulously organized with carpentry tools tiered in symmetrical precision upon pegged walls. The bulkier machinery was spaced evenly between tables and benches. Richard paused in the middle and breathed in the familiar scent of his workshop. When he had bought this house, he'd chosen this room to convert into any carpenter's dream. It was his haven. It had kept him sane. Here, he gave form to whatever ideas his mind concocted. Here, he came to relax, or brainstorm, or simply build things that gave him pleasure. Here, the aromatic scent of pine, cedar, and maple blended with the harsh ones of turpentine, glue, stains, and paints. The aromas were like old friends: homey, recognizable, familiar.

Richard dropped his raincoat carelessly onto a chair and straddled the work stool, rummaging among the wood scraps inside a box. He chose a flawless piece of maple. As Richard caressed the wood's rough surface, his mind already whittling, routing, and shaping the breathing wood, his heart somersaulted within his chest. He automatically rubbed his old wound, wishing the discomfort away and selected a router bit, his mind already busy with the shape of the toy. What he was about to create needed concentration, a special touch, imagination, and skilled fingers. He had to make this special. He would be making it for the son of the woman he loved; making it for a yet-unknown little boy...his own.

Chapter Seven

Out on the terrace Gabriela placed her latest work, a Byzantine-like rendition of a Madonna and Child, beside the picture frame Jean-Louis had uncovered moments ago. The Madonna stared solemnly back at them with eyes reflecting patience, holiness, wisdom, and a weary, painful acceptance of a destiny that rent at the soul.

"What do you think?" Gabriela asked.

The noon sunlight shimmered down onto their small corner, daring Gabriela to overlook flaws or imperfections as she stepped back to survey both painting and frame.

"I think that the dusting of copper Julien added to the gold leaf on the frame did the trick." Jean-Louis slanted his head. "The tonality of the gold is slightly off, but hardly noticeable."

Gabriela nodded in agreement. "The nuances are subtle. I don't think anyone will see the differences." She walked over to the chair and carefully placed the frame over the canvas. "It looks good, doesn't it?"

"*Incroyable,*" Jean-Louis agreed. "My Julien has done it again."

Gabriela smiled and lovingly ran her fingers over the frame's curves and planes. Julien, Jean-Louis's gallery partner and lover, had come through once more. The textures of Julien's craftsmanship pushed against her fingertips, warm and full. Her smile widened. "I think so, too."

"You know, *ma belle.*" A crafty gleam lit Jean-Louis's eyes. "Instead of exhibiting this at the gallery as we planned, why don't we give it to Mitchell for his showing at the Arts Center?"

While Gabriela considered, Jean-Louis pressed on. "*Chérie,* Mitchell will positively salivate over the prospect. Imagine: His biggest draw not only agreed to exhibit her works this summer, but she'll honor him with her latest and most beautiful work."

"A world premiere?" Gabriela bit her lip to contain her amusement.

"With free promotion and advertising. Think of all the money you'll save."

Gabriela laughed in delight. "You are precious, my friend. What would I do without you?"

"Remain a popular, barely renowned *artiste*, no doubt," Jean-Louis answered, a mischievous smile quirking his lips. He sidestepped Gabriela, carefully lifted the frame, rested it gingerly on top of his sneakers, and grabbed one of the protective canvas bags Julien had supplied. He covered the expensive frame lovingly.

"And speaking of exhibitions—" Jean-Louis reclined the delicate frame against the lounge chair. He reached for the painting to repeat the process. "We need to come up with a date."

Gabriela stretched her hand backward and retrieved her thick organizer from the chair. Nowadays, with the juggling of her schedule and Roberto's, it was never far from her. With quick movements she riffled some pages and studied her summer work calendar for a moment.

"How about two months from now, on June 25th?" She looked at Jean-Louis for confirmation. "That's a week after we return from my exhibition in Monaco, and two days after the children begin their summer camp. As for RGM Plastics, July is always a slow month. I shouldn't have anything to interfere from that day on."

"I'll call Mitchell this afternoon and get that out of the way. We can decide which items to ship to San Francisco later on. If I give Cristina and Alex a list of them before we leave for Monaco, they can pack and ship everything while we're there."

"Sounds good."

Jean-Louis stretched, his joints popping. "By the way—"

"*Mami*," a voice squealed from inside the house. Gabriela and Jean-Louis looked at each other and grinned.

"The little monster has arrived," Jean-Louis said fondly and chuckled.

Gabriela pivoted in time to see her toddler skid to a halt beyond the open French doors connecting the living room and terrace. Her children's constant shadow, William Washington III, better known as Spike for his hairdo preference, followed sedately behind. Gabriela smiled, crouched, braced herself, and opened her arms. Her son spotted her and immediately bolted though the terrace doors, targeting her like a ballistic missile. He catapulted into her welcoming arms. "*Mami. Mami.* I'm home."

Jean-Louis laughed and tousled Luisito's burgundy-colored hair, a replica of his mother's. "You positively have to do something about the screaming men in your life, *ma belle*."

Gabriela chuckled and hugged her son. She stood and twirled him around, tickling his neck with her nose. Luisito dissolved into giggles.

"Good afternoon, Mr. Washington," she said, her eyes flicking toward her sons' bodyguard as he approached. Her eyes offered the same blanketing warmth that permeated her voice. For four years this man had guaranteed her children's welfare with a protective instinct as fierce as a mother bear with her cubs. She'd been lucky to find him. She knew it. She never forgot.

"Afternoon, ma'am," Spike answered courteously, professionally, always in awe and just a bit in love with this woman who emanated warmth and fire. He shook hands with Jean-Louis. "Sir."

Gabriela stopped twirling and focused on her son's face, barely an inch away from her own. His gold-speckled gray eyes were brimming with happiness, excitement, and secrets to tell. She watched, always a bit stunned by the resemblance of his eyes to another set of eyes—cynical, world-weary eyes whose glances had once caressed, possessed, until reason had fled, until—

Ignoring the pain nipping at her heart and the renewed hunger in her body, she sat on the nearest chair. Her son was definitely getting heavier. "How was school today?" she asked.

Never one to need much prodding, Luisito prattled on about his teacher being sick that morning, about the Crayola incident where Stephie had hit David—he had refused to give back her scented marker. "And I traced my whole name without help," Luisito announced proudly.

"Wow, Squirt." Gabriela hugged her son. "You are so smart."

Luisito nodded in agreement. "And I painted like you, *Mami*. With my hands. It was smooshee. I liked that. Can I do it here? And Allison did *pipi* in her panties."

"*Mon Dieu*," quipped Jean-Louis. "What a disaster."

"*Mami*, I'm hungry. Can I eat now? Can I feed Zip? He needs a bath, too. He's smelly."

"Only after you've eaten your lunch," she agreed.

Her son's whoop of delight made Gabriela wince. She deposited him on the floor but held him in place before he could scoot off. "Put on your bathing suit before you wash Zip. No bathing suit, no bath for Zip. Understood?" Gabriela waited for her son's nod of confirmation and asked him to repeat what she'd just requested. When he rattled off her instructions, she gave his cheek a quick peck. "Good. Now, run along to the kitchen. Lupe should have your lunch ready."

Luisito squiggled out of her grasp and bolted toward the kitchen. "Lupe. Lupe. I'm home." His little voice carried enough decibels to pierce even the neighbor's ears.

"Don't forget to say please and thank you," she reminded him loudly, but in typical three-year-old impatience, he disappeared through the kitchen doorway, oblivious to his mother's instructions. Gabriela watched Lupe come into view, snatch Luisito up in her arms, and deposit his wiggling body on the kitchen counter chair.

Gabriela sighed. To be so carefree, so wrapped up in one's world so as to not feel reality, she thought wistfully. She turned to face the men. Her smile disappeared.

Seeing her expression, Jean-Louis braced himself. He knew what her look meant. Spike simply waited.

"I'm glad you're both here," Gabriela began. "I'm getting tired of this creep. I saw this morning on the caller ID that Wickeham rang last night while the get-together was in full swing. I still believe the man is all hot air and no substance, but I can't dismiss his impertinence any longer."

"About time," Jean-Louis murmured. He started to pace the terrace in an effort to control the terrible foreboding the mention of this man always brought.

"Did he leave any messages, ma'am? Any threats?" Spike asked, his professional demeanor hiding his outrage. He admired this client of his, with her wine-colored hair and sunshine eyes, her dignity and her love of others. Such a private, talented, but especially good person, shouldn't have been cursed with the trials of Job.

"No, for which I am grateful," she said. Had Wickeham ever issued threats? Not really. Innuendos, veiled phrases, impertinent remarks, yes. "Harassment. That's really what he's doing. Can you find out what's required to tape this man's telephone conversations? I think it's time to take his snobbish British behind to court."

"I'll find out what the new legal procedures are," Spike said and quickly scribbled a note in his organizer. "But I suggest you start taping his conversations. Warn him first."

"What's the point?" Jean-Louis asked.

"Admissible evidence in court," Spike said.

"Frankly, I'm getting tired of Wickeham's shenanigans," Gabriela said. "I don't care if he's warned. Maybe it'll force him to back off."

Jean-Louis stopped his pacing and faced her. His worried eyes spoke volumes, silently telegraphing an old fear, but especially a growing dread a similar situation, one they had faced before, was brewing.

"And what if he doesn't, Gabriela?"

Gabriela turned away from her friend's knowing eyes. "Mr. Washington, could you arrange to stay with the children around the clock, starting tomorrow? I'll pay your usual overtime."

"What about you, Mrs. Martinez? I should arrange a twenty-four hour escort for you, especially so close to the auction."

"He's right, *ma belle*," Jean-Louis said. "Herb Bryce is again on the hunt."

"Nice to meet you, Father." Jeremy shook hands with Father Ramirez. "Don't worry about the boss. Richard's always a shocker the first time you meet him."

Father Ramirez gazed from one man to the other like a drunkard whose reality shifts with each drink. A shocker. How appropriate, but not for the reasons this man believed.

"Rein in your runaway mouth, Jeremy," Richard said, studying the priest. Inches shorter than Richard, with a face carved by time, worries, and smiles. Eyes as black as the pit of hell, with hairline receding like an eroding coastline back toward the priest's ears. He was chunky, his skin sagging in places where age and gravity had won the battle.

Studying Father Ramirez, Richard could appreciate the man's reaction to his presence. The priest probably understood now the can of nasty worms he had opened. *Be careful what you ask for.* Richard's eyes didn't waver. His smile turned a few degrees cooler.

"I'd love to stay and chitchat, Father, but I believe we have more pressing matters to attend to." Richard quickly scanned the hallway and turned in the direction of the vehicle rentals. "Shall we?"

They began navigating the crowded hallways, deftly avoiding hurrying tourists, golf carts rushing employees to work, and strolling window shoppers.

"How was your trip?" Father Ramirez asked, not keen to exchange polite conversation, but common courtesy demanding he do. He lengthened his gait to match the other men's. His initial shock was altering slowly to outraged anger at Gabriela. For four years she'd been lying—by omission, granted—but it was still deceit. How dare she not have confided in him?

"Uneventful, but long," Richard replied. "Anything new since we last talked?"

"My very words to Gabriela this morning. Her reply was, 'Not exactly,'" Father Ramirez said.

"What kind of a half-assed answer is that?" Richard blurted. He stepped off the people mover with the men and headed for the limousine rentals. He pinned the priest with another stare.

"At least, she's now considering round-the-clock protection for the children," Father Ramirez explained.

"And for herself?" Richard asked.

"I doubt it," the priest answered in disgust.

Jeremy rushed ahead to deal with their reservations.

Richard grunted, understanding the priest's frustrations only too well. She'd done this to him four years ago.

"Well, we'll just have to change her mind. Won't we, Father?"

Father Ramirez gulped. The hardness in Richard's tone, the certainty was unmistakable, and he knew now what Richard's weapon of choice would be to guarantee Gabriela's cooperation. *Oh, Christ. What have I done?*

"I checked on the limo," Jeremy announced. "It's out and waiting."

"My car's in the parking lot," Father Ramirez protested. "You don't need to dish out for a rental."

Jeremy gave Richard an amused smile. Ignoring the priest, he hefted Richard's bag onto his shoulder, then picked up his own. He disappeared through the automatic doors.

"Let me explain something, Father Ramirez," Richard said, following Jeremy. "My limo is not a frivolity. It's a necessity. Because of my previous line of work, and the success I've garnered in my present, I've stepped on a few toes."

Richard motioned for the priest to precede him through the whispering doors.

"This baby is customized for comfort and equipped with sophisticated safety improvements," Richard said, pointing to the glossy, black limousine into which Jeremy was loading their luggage. "Wherever I travel overseas, I ask for one. At home, I have my own."

Richard opened the back door for the priest. Father Ramirez glimpsed spaciousness and silky leather. It beckoned.

"Hop in, Father. We'll drive you to your car, then follow you to Gabriela's house." It wasn't a request. It was an order.

Father Ramirez reluctantly stepped in and began to pray.

***

Herb Bryce was pissed—not that anyone would notice. With patience and care, he unwrapped the turkey sandwich his wife had prepared for him that morning, deliberately keeping his breathing under control. His fingers worked the aluminum foil until it finally flattened against his slacks in symmetrical perfection.

Bryce took careful bites off the sandwich, his silence absolute, even rude. He felt no shame. He knew he lacked manners. He didn't give a damn. He simply kept ignoring the pimply-faced rookie to whom he'd been ball-chained for the past week. Why should he bother with niceties when the little shit sat not two feet away from him, guzzling down food like a poorly trained animal, unaware he'd ruined two good hours of surveillance because of his gluttony?

Bryce kept chewing, seemingly unconcerned, but, mentally, he hurled curses at his boss hundreds of miles away. He still couldn't understand why Johnson had stuck him with this asshole, nor the reasons for his decision.

"Teach Marvin the ropes," Johnson's cajoling voice reverberated in Bryce's brain. "You're the best in the field . . . guide him. The kid's got potential."

Potential, my ass. The acid in Bryce's mind churned the acid in his stomach. This kid didn't have a clue, bored easily, and was pathetically unprepared for surveillance work to boot. This afternoon was a prime example of the kid's ineptitude. They had wasted precious observation time while hunting down food for this idiot. The little prick had known for two days they would camp out at Mrs. Martinez's house today, and that once in position, Bryce would not leave his post—if he'd been alone. But this jerk would never understand the patience and sacrifices required to gain lucrative front-page photos even if they hit him in the face. No. Marvin, The Bullshitter, was trigger-happy, possessed no sense of timing, no finesse, and would never stop singing his own praises long enough to look away from his image in the mirror. He would never notice anything worthwhile.

Translated, it meant Marvin didn't have the instinct. He would have, at best, a mediocre future as a paparazzo. But that would be the rookie's problem. As of this evening, the asshole would be out of his life and assigned somewhere else by morning.

Bryce adjusted his Padres baseball cap over his thinning hair and took another slow bite off the meaty sandwich. He chewed slowly, methodically, and patiently, flushing his carefully chewed food with a few sips of lemon tea. He adjusted his weight on the hood of his beat-up Mercedes and concentrated on the view framed in one of his mounted cameras. It was better than watching Marvin, The Animal, alternately tear greasy chunks off his fried chicken and gulp them down with disgusting slobbers of root beer.

Bryce wiped his fingers on a paper napkin before adjusting the focus of the telephoto lens. The view of Gabriela's partially hidden driveway and front door, the only things visible though the iron gates and strategically placed trees and shrubs, sharpened. No activity yet. Good. With any luck he hadn't missed anything important while wasting time for Marvin, The Guzzler.

Bryce swallowed more tea, took another bite off his sandwich, and turned to his other camera, the one focused on the approaching road. With a patience born from his training as a sniper in the force, he focused on the job, on the hunt. Back in his army days, he'd stalked an enemy who was just as patient and predatory as he. Now his quarries were celebrities, harmless people who thankfully didn't shoot back—except through their lawyers.

Bryce mentally shrugged. Those minor inconveniences were the hazard of the trade. At least, staking out Gabriela Martinez at her home was always a sweet deal. Out here he could walk, stretch his legs, enjoy the scenery, the quiet, the privacy. Except for—

"Man, I've got to pee," whined the bane of his thoughts.

Without bothering to turn, Bryce pointed to a bush not three yards away. "There's your bathroom."

"Shit. You've got to be kidding," Marvin said when he looked at the area to which Bryce had pointed.

"If you keep close to the bush and aim right, no one will know but us."

"You're putting me on."

Bryce shrugged and narrowed his eyes at an approaching car. It sped away, up another road. "Suit yourself. Either lose your modesty or pee in your pants. Your choice."

Hesitating only briefly, Marvin decided the call of nature was stronger than modesty. He scrambled to his feet and grumbled all the way to Nature's potty.

"This is bullshit," Marvin complained as he unzipped his pants. "A total, fucking waste of my time. We should be in LA, chasing after real meat, not in the middle of fucking nowhere, chasing a goddamn shadow woman."

Bryce knew his sarcasm would go unnoticed, but he couldn't resist. "Yeah. Such a waste of your talents, right?"

He pinned his sights on another approaching car. In the now fading afternoon light, it was still too far away for him to identify the driver, but the forest green of a functional Saturn sedan was vaguely familiar. As it slowed down, Bryce tuned out Marvin's constant bitching. A second later, recognition hit—the priest's car. Then his instincts went into overdrive. A second car, a limousine, followed the priest like a toddler with his mother. Bryce dropped the remnants of his lunch on top of the car's hood and focused the camera's sights on the approaching limousine. Generic license plates, he saw. He'd check on those later. He shifted his focus to the driver but could barely make out the face due to the heavily tinted glass. He didn't waste time with the passenger who would be well guarded behind a wall of the same, impenetrable black tint.

With stomach clenching and breath hiking, Bryce focused and pressed, the triggered camera shutter making constant, purring clicks. His experienced fingers kept at this synchronized dance until, in a matter of seconds, he'd captured license plate, limo, blurry driver, and priest's face. He kept clicking away as the cars stopped at Gabriela's front gate.

"Marvin. Take your camera; knock on that limousine's windows. See if you can get a reaction."

For once, Marvin offered no suggestions and gave him no lip.

Bryce kept shooting away, gauging the results of Marvin's actions. There was no reaction from the limo. His heart somersaulted in delight when he saw Gabriela's bodyguard sprint toward the gate. William Washington III never did gate duty unless absolutely necessary.

Bryce smiled in delight, snapping picture after picture of the receding cars, of Washington closing the gate, of him warning Marvin to step back, of his sprint back to the house. Bryce shifted cameras, focused. Both cars rolled to a stop, but no one made a move. Bryce kept shooting as Washington spoke quickly to the limo's driver, blocking Bryce's view of the chauffeur's face. He took more pictures as Washington pointed to the side and of the cars rolling quietly behind a solid wall of green. He stopped when they disappeared from view.

Bryce smiled, satisfied. The notorious Martinez had a guest, and he or she was being ushered through a private side entrance. That meant only one thing—she wanted this visit kept secret.

Bryce rubbed his hands in delight. Something important was going down, and he had just captured every detail of it on his camera.

Despite the asshole, he'd struck gold. Again.

Chapter Eight

The expression on Richard's face as he climbed out of the limousine could only be construed as stormy. With deliberate steps he approached Father Ramirez, his eyes never wavering from the priest. Neither did he acknowledge the hulk of a man who stood next to him.

"Well, *padre*," Richard said softly. "It seems that all details were not forthcoming when we last spoke. Care to elaborate on what the hell that was about?"

The priest shrugged. "Oh, he's the least of our problems. You've just made the acquaintance of our resident pest, Herb Bryce." Father Ramirez turned to Spike, who had shifted to cautious mode next to him. "You can let your guard down, Mr. Washington. This is Richard Harrison, the man who saved Gabriela's life four years ago."

Spike's eyes raked Richard in quick appraisal, a speculative gleam lighting them up. So this was the man who had risked his life for Mrs. Martinez's. Everyone in her family had something to say about his help, his courage—everyone except Gabriela. For the first time in his four years of employ, Spike finally understood the underlying sadness lodged in Gabriela's eyes. Richard Harrison's eyes told the rest.

"Actually, she saved mine," Richard said. He centered his gaze on this six-foot-two mass of muscle. The man was fit and mean, his hair cropped spiky and short, but neat. He radiated confidence, an efficiency radius about him that signaled 'lethal if riled.' Richard gave up his scrutiny and guessed, "Marines?"

"SEALs," Spike replied. "You?"

"Intelligence."

Spike nodded. "Figures."

"So who's the jerk outside?" Richard asked.

"Paparazzo," Spike volunteered. "Tabloids."

Jeremy stopped beside the men. "Told you I have a nose for those guys. Bleeding paparazzo."

Shit. Richard would've wished for anything but a journalistic leech to complicate matters. "And he's outside because?"

"Morbid curiosity," blurted Father Ramirez.

Spike's look was level. "Profit," he told Richard and extended his hand. "William Washington III. Spike for short. Bodyguard to the Martinez household."

Richard shook hands with Spike, glad Gabriela had hired a competent bodyguard to protect the family. He turned to Jeremy. "This is Jeremy Hollis, your counterpart in my employ." Richard looked at the two men, priest and bodyguard, who, for the past four years, knew more about Gabriela's life than he did. A fierce pang of envy sliced through him. "You've explained who. Can you explain why?"

"That man in Europe, the one who died. What was his name?" Father Ramirez asked.

"Heinige. Albert Heinige," Richard supplied.

The priest nodded and continued his explanation. "That man's death vaulted Gabriela to the status of celebrity. Somehow the news she'd been with this Heinige when he was killed leaked out. Reporters from tabloids and every press corps in Europe hunted her down for pictures, interviews. They couldn't get enough of her, like they'd discovered the modern version of Joan of Arc, detractors and all." The priest shuddered. "They were months of hell. For over two months, Gabriela's face was splattered across the front pages of every tabloid and gossip magazine in Europe. The rag Bryce worked for nicknamed Gaby 'The Notorious Martinez.' The name stuck, and here we are."

Richard was appalled. Gossip magazines? Of all the places he had looked for information about Gabriela, those had not been it. Shit. And tabloids? He never, ever, read tabloid filth and would, not for a moment, have imagined Gabriela as tabloid fodder. Maurice had definitely not mentioned any of this when he'd visited Richard at the hospital a year later. And his bastard of a former boss? Seldon had kept him so busy, Richard's stays in the US had become shorter and shorter. He had been halfway between the jungles of Colombia and Ecuador when this seemed to have happened. Why hadn't Maurice kept everything under wraps and protected Gabriela in Richard's absence?

A sudden image of her lovely face flashed in his mind, her eyes soaked in pain and despair, her face battered from the savagery of Heinige's brutality, her voice pleading, "Don't leave me." The acid of his leaving her bore through him.

"Herb Bryce was one of the herd of paparazzi popping up like weeds near Gabriela," Father Ramirez continued, disgust and sadness lacing his voice. "His inventiveness got him the best pictures. Gabriela's face made his reputation and fattened his pension fund quite adequately."

"And even if she's a private citizen, she's well enough known that Bryce can skate outside the fringes of harassment," Spike told Richard. "And when there's an important event coming up, this guy shows up like a herpes flare-up."

Father Ramirez cleared his throat, embarrassed. "Well, to make a long story short, other photographers left, hunting other stories, other faces. Unfortunately, Herb Bryce didn't. Now that the auction is close, he's set up camp outside Gaby's doorstep and won't miss a blink until this is all over."

"It's a shame the Heaven's Gate fiasco is no longer front-page news," Spike said. "We had a short reprieve because of them. Let me show you in."

Spike walked over to a seven-foot pruned hedge, sliced in the center and plugged with a wrought-iron gate. Spike opened it and gestured for them to enter. "Is Mrs. Martinez expecting you?"

Richard's gaze hooked onto the priest's. "No, she's not. This is a surprise."

Father Ramirez gulped. This wasn't a surprise. It was an execution.

Spike closed the gate while Father Ramirez took the lead. "I'll take you to the kitchen first. You must be hungry after that long flight."

Richard's lips pressed into a grim line. Hungry. Such an appropriate adjective and yet falling short in defining his desire, his craving to see, touch, possess this woman. "If you don't mind, I'd like some privacy. It's our first meeting in four years."

Father Ramirez agreed with a curt nod. He recognized his response for what it was, cowardice. He didn't want any part of the fireworks when they exploded. And explode they would. His fault.

"Ah, boss," lamented Jeremy. "I'm peckish."

Richard chuckled. "You would be hungry."

"Last I saw Mrs. Martinez," Spike said, catching up to them. "She was working on the terrace."

Spike led the group across a manicured lawn that extended short of a half an acre toward the horizon. Richard did a quick survey of the surrounding property. Flowering weeping willows, wisteria, cherry, jacarandas, dogwood, and other trees he couldn't identify, peppered the lawn, the riot of colorful blooms complementing the canvas of lush green lawn and blue sky in clumps and spatters. At the edge of the property, a stone barrier bisected the horizon. Birds and seagulls sang counterpoint to the quiet, and in the background Richard could hear the murmur of the sea as it ceaselessly pounded the shoreline.

Spike stopped by a French door on his right and opened it. "You can access the terrace from the kitchen. Through here."

Following the priest closely, Richard entered a huge rectangular kitchen made up of earth-tone tiles, blond wood, stainless steel, and sunshine. A split-level island decorated the center of the kitchen, sink and counter on one side, tall stools on the other; a halo of wrought iron dangled myriad pots and pans at its center. Wooden beams framed the three wide skylights in the ceiling, and colorful clay pots, holding all varieties of spices, hugged the windowsills.

A woman, chopping vegetables at the counter, stopped at the intrusion of so many people in what was clearly her territory. Petite, with ebony hair thick and straight as a line, she studied the newcomers with curious chocolate-colored eyes, pinched upward at the corners. She smiled at Father Ramirez as he approached, her teeth defining pearly white.

"Hi, Lupe," he greeted her, snatching at a perfectly sliced carrot stick. "Can we crash for lunch?"

Lupe swatted his hand. "This is dinner," she said. "If you want lunch, Padre, I have some leftover enchiladas that I can warm for you."

Crunching loudly on his carrot stick, Father Ramirez turned and extended an arm toward Richard. "Lupe, this is Richard Harrison, an old friend of Gaby's. Richard, Lupe Serrano. The best cook west of the Mississippi." He winked.

Richard shook hands. Jeremy, not to be left behind, especially when this woman would be his source for food, reached forward. "Jeremy Hollis, ma'am. At your service." As he shook hands, his stomach growled. "Can I have some of your enchiladas, too?"

Lupe chuckled and pointed to the stools facing her. "Have a seat. You, too, Mr. Harrison. Padre. I'll have the enchiladas heated in no time."

Richard shook his head. "I'll pass for now."

"She's at the edge of the terrace, working. We'll be here if you need us."

Spike watched as Richard did another quick scan of the room before focusing on the open terrace doors. He saw his body still, very much like a predatory cat when it catches the scent of prey, its senses sharpened, adrenaline pumping but controlled. Experience had taught Spike to gauge both man and circumstance quickly. Right now it warned him they had a situation here—a major situation. Conversely, his instincts also whispered maybe Richard was the catalyst this household needed, what Mrs. Martinez needed—a champion.

Slowly, like a man walking toward an uncertain destiny, Richard stepped over the threshold, walking in the general direction Spike had pointed. His heart shuddered from the tension, and he rubbed his thumb over his scar in a pacifying gesture. He scanned the terrace, hardly absorbing details. His senses suddenly sharpened when he caught movement on the far right. There. There she was, at the far corner near the railing, her back to him, concentrating as she dabbed at a canvas with a brush thick with oil paint. She was wearing baggy carpenter dungarees, a soft-blue Madras shirt that floated carelessly in the breeze and covered her white spandex tube top. She was slimmer than he remembered, her rich Burgundy-hued hair even longer, held carelessly in a ponytail, feathery wisps escaping the clip to tickle her face.

He stepped closer, hearing the music hovering over the terrace, her husky alto humming in tandem with the Latin American artist singing soulfully from a CD. The kick in the gut was swift, brutal. Talk about déjà vu. Like the first time they'd met, he thought, and yet so different. Unlike their first encounter, he now had the flavor of her imprinted on his DNA. His memory, once more, effortlessly supplied the scent of her, the smoothness of her skin, her mouth, and her body, the feel of her silken hair on his chest. Like a sleepwalker, Richard silently crossed over the flagstones, practically devouring the sight of her. And as he shortened the distance between them, Richard had his final answer. He would never be able to sate his thirst for this woman. She offered light to his darkness, fullness to his emptiness, her saving grace for his battered, lost soul. His face altered, thinking back to the years wasted. He'd never make the same mistake again. This time he wouldn't step aside like the altruistic hero he'd played four years back. He'd get downright mean and dirty in his fight for her. The stakes were no longer the same.

Gabriela stepped back from her work and brushed back the tendrils of hair around her face with her arm. Richard smiled at the impatience of her move, as if her hair was a nuisance keeping her from concentrating on her work.

He waited for a pause between the singing voices.

"Gabriela."

Gabriela's body stilled at the soft sound of her name. For a moment, she stood listening, then shook her head like a wet dog shaking off water. *You are such a fool,* her mind supplied. Disgusted, she stabbed at the cerulean blue on her palette. Her mind had deceived her yet again. She slobbered the paint on the canvas, realized what she had done, and hissed. Since agreeing with Jean-Louis to call Maurice later that evening, she'd been a nervous wreck. Throughout the noon hour, her brain had staged all sorts of encounters with one infuriating, unforgettable man. Like a dutiful stage manager, her mind had supervised every possible scene, every possible emotion under its tutelage. She'd jumped from rage, to indifference, to haughtiness, but longing had finally won, hands down. No matter how hard she tried to avoid it, she could never escape the terrible need she felt for him, a need that went deeper than the instinct to breathe.

The lyrics from the song she'd impulsively put on swirled around her, teased her. The singer, in his soulful tenor voice, sang about the moment of encounter with his beloved, anticipation heating his blood, nerves tingling in expectation of the seduction. His words mimicked her own guilty longings, her desires. *Oh, God. How would she ever get through this day? How would she find the courage to do what must be done?*

"Gabriela."

This time the voice penetrated, took form. It called out to her, familiar and unmistakably real, a living entity that caressed her skin and raised goose bumps on her warm flesh. This was no figment of her imagination, no mistake. She felt him, her nerve endings suddenly electrified, awareness shaking her. Panic sent her heart scurrying. Hope and love made her turn around slowly, ever so slowly.

She blinked, thinking her eyes were deceiving her, but Richard's tall frame stood static before her, his chestnut hair combed by the soft breeze, his eyes intense, pinning her and caressing her all at once. The embers of irrational hope fanned to life like a conflagration. For an unguarded moment, her eyes reflected her hope, her joy, but especially her hopeless love for him.

Richard watched those powerful emotions play across her face and relief slammed him. Gotcha. She'd always had such an expressive, beautiful face. Now, no matter what she did, but especially said, he would know the truth. The love was there, and it flared like a beacon.

"Hello, Gabriela."

"Richard." Her voice snagged with emotion. "Richard," she repeated like a moron, choking on his name this time, a fist lodged in her throat. Memories exploded around her. Hurt, anger, need, betrayal shattered within her. Love that consumed and burned suffocated her. Her entire body began to shiver, her muscles trembling like a spastic, her fingers tightening on the palette like a vise. She wanted to run, to hurl herself into his arms, to weep four years' worth of anguish and pain; to kiss him, to meld with him; to hit him with something, anything until he hurt as much as she had hurt.

Instead, she did nothing, frozen like a doe about to meet its doom.

Richard's gaze bored into her, mesmerizing, speculative, in a look she knew well. In self-preservation, Gabriela's face became a mask of indifference. One thing she had learned well from this man—one must never show vulnerability. Richard would pounce on it and use it to his advantage.

"Hello, Gabriela," Richard repeated and closed the gap between them. Familiar scents, such as oil paint and turpentine, surrounded Gabriela like a misty fog and teased his nostrils. His eyes never left her face and, for once, he was unable to read the emotions behind her golden eyes. He didn't like it; didn't like the way she had slammed the door through which he had always been able to read her soul. In a deliberate move, he reached between them and pried her fingers off the palette she held in front of her like a shield. He carefully deposited her colorful kaleidoscope of colors on a chair nearby and moved closer.

"Is this the kind of welcome you give me, sweetheart?" He needed to rattle her, break the mask that worked as efficiently as a wall between them. Richard leaned closer, his lips quirking, his intent obvious.

Gabriela gasped and jumped back. Was he nuts? Did he think he could waltz in here like four years had not happened, like nothing had changed?

"What the hell do you think you're doing?"

He smiled like the predator he felt. Good. Caution. Her eyes burned with it. He'd rather be scorched than have to slam against the emptiness of her blank stare.

"Greeting you appropriately. Even I say hello with a peck, love."

"Don't call me that." She had once believed him, trusted him. But he had left her, disappeared from the face of the earth for four silent years. Could she trust him again?

He read the acrid message written in her eyes and felt it latch and tear at his heart. He deserved no better. But now that opportunity had come knocking, he wasn't about to flinch from it, or turn away, never again. Especially after seeing the love in her eyes.

"What are you doing here?" she asked, wary now. She took a step back, placing her easel between them like a barrier.

"I was invited." Richard smiled, rattling her further.

Her eyes narrowed. If this afternoon had all been a bogus performance by her sneaky manager in order to get approval for a fait accompli, she'd strangle him.

"Not by you, I'm sad to say." Richard moved near her again, in pretense of studying her painting. Strong blues and sharp greens jumped out of her canvas as they vied for supremacy with the frantic reds. He cocked his head, considering. This chaos wasn't her usual style. There was desperation here, and also something not quite defined.

Gabriela took another step back, disliking and mistrusting Richard's scrutiny of her work. He was too intelligent, too empathic—had always been where she was concerned.

"Who?" She spoke as rudely as she could, in order to divert his attention. "Was it Jean-Louis?"

Richard turned slightly. "Why didn't you call me, Gabriela?"

"What?"

"If my memory serves me, I once told you to contact me if you ever needed me. Why didn't you?"

Gabriela's heart skidded to a stop, only to thunder out of control. Those words. God, those words from his letter four years ago. "Who says I need you?"

Richard leaned forward until their faces were mere inches apart. Gabriela scooted back, only to bump into the railing. Richard followed, effectively cutting off any means of escape by caging her with both arms against the railing.

"Why didn't you call me? You're under attack—again. From what I've heard, you're way out of your league—again. You need my help to get out of this mess—again. What I don't understand is why I had to hear of your predicament from Father Ramirez."

"Father Ramirez?" Gabriela echoed, surprised. And here she thought Jean-Louis had betrayed her. "He called you?"

"Maurice. He, in turn, contacted me. Imagine my surprise when I discovered you were in danger, again."

"I'm not in danger," she scoffed, then revised the pronouncement. She was in danger all right, but not from Wickeham. The man facing her was the real danger.

"I beg to differ. After Father Ramirez explained what's been going on, I did a little investigating of my own. The answers I got were not encouraging. Wickeham might not be in the same league as Heinige, but he's got a record of getting violent if he is thwarted."

"What crap." She pushed against his chest, unwilling to stay trapped a moment longer. Richard obliged her by moving, for now. "This man is all hot air. Besides, I'm not the naïve, vulnerable woman I was before. I have a formidable bodyguard who handles my family's security and well-being."

"I've met him." Richard smiled his approval. "Good choice."

"Well, I'm so happy you approve," she said, her voice dripping with sarcasm. With as much nonchalance as she could muster, she reached around him, picked up her palette, and stabbed at the colors she held. With similar staccato movements, she dabbed at the scenery she'd begun that morning. "So, as you can see, you came out here for nothing. Give your boss my thanks, but he needn't have sent out his best man for the job, again. I no longer need government protection. I supply my own."

With a swiftness she remembered all too well, Richard clasped her hand and stilled her movements. She didn't bother to snatch her hand away. It would be impossible. She waited for his next move, staring blankly at her painting.

"Gabriela." The humor in his voice caught her by surprise. Her eyes locked onto his, and she couldn't understand how he always managed to look amused and serious at the same time. "I no longer report to Seldon. Haven't in the past three years. I'm a free agent."

She gasped. "You're a mercenary now?"

This time Richard's amusement was full-blown. His eyes crinkled and laughter rumbled deep in his throat. With a smile that made his eyes dance, he slowly turned her to face him, removed the palette from her hand, took the brush from her fingers, and deposited everything back in its proper place. She snatched her hands away, before he got any other ideas.

"Retired, Gabriela. Retired." He chuckled at her expression. She was blushing in embarrassment. At least, that hadn't changed. "I still deal in antiques, but now I also manufacture imitation antique furniture for exclusive hotels and businesses. Quite a lucrative career, I might add."

"Then, why—"

"Because Father Ramirez asked me, and because I've had dealings with cauliflower-nosed Wickeham. I can personally guarantee he's a tenacious bastard."

Gabriela looked her surprise. Richard forestalled her next question. "A year ago we butted heads over the acquisition of two Restoration period chairs. Wickeham had approached the owner of a small antique shop two months before I entered the picture. During that time, the shop owner was burglarized, his creditors banged on his doors, and he suffered an accident at the underground. There's still no proof Wickeham was involved with the shop owner's mishaps, but after speaking with Morris—"

"Who's Morris?"

"A friend of my chauffeur. CID." At her perplexed look, he supplied, "British police."

"Figures." She walked to the edge of her terrace. She turned her back to the Pacific, pressed her palms against the warm railing and lounged back. "What happened to the shop owner?"

"I happened," he smiled as he stopped beside her. "By the time Wickeham realized I was in the picture, the shop owner had a hefty money advance to calm his creditors, held a binding contract, and had already packed and shipped the pieces to my buyers."

Gabriela smiled. She just couldn't help it. It was so good to hear Wickeham had gotten slapped and beaten. "Good for you."

"Which brings me to why I'm here. Father Ramirez wanted me to persuade you to sell—"

Gabriela leaned forward, her eyes fierce. "I'm not going to sell my manuscript to that sleazeball, especially after I offered to create a folio or two for him as a substitute."

"You did?"

"Of course I did. I'm not a moron. But he turned me down flat. He became mean, insulting, actually. He wants this one and none other. Well, screw him. I won't shortchange the kids from the money due them from this auction. And I'm not creating another manuscript like it, ever."

"I know. I didn't come here to dissuade you."

"Then why did you come?"

"To escort you back."

She jerked. "What?"

"For the duration of this auction, you will be my guest, at my home. At the hotel you'll be easily recognizable and vulnerable. At my home, you won't be. I'll escort you to whatever functions you need to attend, and my bodyguard will accompany you in my stead when I'm not available."

Gabriela stared at Richard, stupefaction turning into something ineffable, laced with a serious dose of caution. "Are you out of your mind? I'm not going to your home. Period." She began to pace, but immediately whirled to confront him. "Who do you think you are? You have some gall waltzing in here to propose and dispose as if you have a right to."

"Ah, honey. You really don't want to go there."

Gabriela's body suddenly stilled. Richard's gaze hinted at a shared secret, his smile one of satisfaction, his look issuing a challenge. *Jesus. He couldn't know, could he? No, no, no. Not yet. Oh, please, God, not yet.* Gabriela began to sweat, but she didn't back down. "I'm not altering my plans, Richard, regardless of what you might wish. You don't dictate how I run my life."

Richard's smile widened. Before he could voice his thoughts, however, an ear-splitting screech rent the air. In an instinctive move, Richard shoved Gabriela behind him, pinning her between the railing and his body. He tensed, alert, ready, scanning the terrace for danger or threats. It was empty. His eyes scanned the kitchen entrance, but saw nothing amiss. Spike was relaxed, having a brisk conversation with Jeremy. Father Ramirez stood calmly beside Jeremy's stool, an amused expression lightening his features as he listened on. Everybody was eating.

Gabriela tried to shove the human wall before her. She had recognized the squeal. "Richard, move."

Richard didn't pay any attention, keeping her effectively pinned. Could that high-pitched noise have been a seagull? He did a quick search of the sky. No birds gliding overhead.

"Richard." Gabriela shoved. "Move."

Another piercing squeal erupted, closer this time.

"Get out of my way." She shoved harder this time, her mind cursing and praying things couldn't be happening like this.

Richard heard the squeals get more frequent and closer. They were followed by a very masculine bellow of "*Viens ici, petit monstre!*" and excited barks. Barks? "What the hell?"

At the edge of the terrace, in a direct line opposite them, a compact human cannonball exploded into view, little legs pumping in so rapid a succession Richard thought the small child would trip any minute. Beside this little whirlwind, a golden retriever hopped and barked, its tongue drooling in ecstasy and its tail whipping the air in joy. Behind and gaining ground, a man, crouched, arms raised above his head in mock menace, kept chanting, "*Viens ici. Viens ici.*"

Richard stood transfixed, watching man and dog chase the little boy, whose delighted squeals still ripped the air. His body suddenly hummed in expectation, in thrall.

Gabriela closed her eyes. Leave it to their son to make such a dramatic entrance, dog, et al. It was also uncanny how she could still sense mood changes in this man who stood so motionless in front of her. Moments before he had been alert against threat, now there was a different feel to his vigilance. Expectation. She pushed her way from behind Richard, thinking to escape, wishing for the ground to open and swallow her, but especially wanting to be anywhere, anywhere but here.

Richard reached out and captured Gabriela's forearm, ruining her escape. His eyes never left the little boy or his animated antics around the terrace. The man pursuing kept at his monster imitation, his arms still high above his head, weaving after the laughing boy like a drunken orangutan.

Gabriela's heart stopped at Richard's touch. She closed her eyes and fought hard against the emotions churning inside her. "Let me go," she pleaded softly.

Richard's gaze shifted. Slowly, caressing her skin like a master sculptor exploring for flaws, he lowered his hand until he could weave his fingers through hers. He felt her tremors and heard Gabriela's breath hitch. Her eyes reluctantly traveled from their locked fingers to his face. He absorbed the turmoil in her body and the pain reflected in her whisky eyes and couldn't help but be thrilled that his touch still created such havoc within her. It still created mayhem in him.

"Please," she begged.

"No. Never again."

"*Mami,* why is this big man holding your hand?"

Gabriela jerked as if hit. She looked down at her toddler, not two feet in front of her, his eyes staring fixedly at their locked hands. Zip woofed, his tail whipping faster than a mixer as he paced from the transfixed little boy to the transfixed adults, nudging Gabriela with his wet nose first, then later wedging himself between Richard's free hand and leg, begging for a caress. He obliged while Gabriela tugged, trying to free her hand, but the stubborn man tightened his hold, drawing her ever closer to him.

By this time, Jean-Louis realized the man standing so close to Gabriela was not anyone from her household. He skidded to a halt and focused.

"*Putain,*" he gasped when he recognized Richard Harrison, all six-feet-four dangerous hunk from Gabriela's past, who stood unmoving next to Gabriela. He blinked in stupefaction. "*Putain.*"

Zip barked again excitedly. Luisito kept staring at his mother's discreet, but futile attempts at extricating her hand from Richard's hold.

By now, Gabriela felt a bubble of hysteria clawing its way to the surface, shaking her muscles, hitching her breath. Never, in her wildest dreams or nightmares, had she envisioned a situation such as the one she faced. She felt like howling to the wind like a demented cartoon character, while simultaneously tearing at her hair and screaming at the injustice of it all until she was hoarse.

"Well, as I live and breathe," Richard said, amusement underscoring his sarcasm. "Heinige's gallery manager, isn't it?" He raked Jean-Louis with cold assessment. "Jean-Louis. Correct?"

"He's my manager now." She again tried to pry her hand from his grip but failed.

Richard glanced from Gabriela's dismayed face to Jean-Louis's stupefied one. "Interesting, wouldn't you say, Gabriela? It seems as if the old pawns from the previous endgame have assembled for another match." Richard glanced toward the kitchen where four faces peered out with different degrees of curiosity and anxiety. He cocked an eyebrow and smiled. "Plus a few new players to boot," he amended.

Luisito, in typical three-year-old fashion, and oblivious to the tension surrounding the adults, lodged himself between Richard and his mother, tugging at their clasped hands in jealous self-centeredness. Every time his mother's attention shifted from him to another, Luisito would poke, tug, or interrupt until he was the center of attention once more. With resolution, he dislodged his mother's hand from this big stranger's and replaced it with one of his own. He then grabbed the stranger's hand with his other little one, and began a series of squeezes and tugs until the adults focused on him.

"*Mami, Mami.* Swing. Swing."

He giggled in anticipation as he hung like a limp noodle between them, his chubby legs bent, knees almost kissing the ground. He immediately shot up and did a barrage of staccato jumps and bounces in an obvious attempt to force the adults into playing his favorite game. For the next couple of seconds he alternated from dead weight to acrobat, his high-pitched squeals echoing his demands of, "Swing. Swing."

Richard stared in fascination at the diminutive dynamo who jerked his hand in increasing demand. He felt the little palm, vibrant with warmth and life against his own, and felt his lungs burn and his chest compress. He was drowning, if one could drown in a sea of emotion in the middle of a scented California afternoon. His fingers curled around Luisito's tiny hand with the awe and care of a mother cradling her newborn; his eyes stared in wonder at this miracle of life demanding their attention, one minute limp between Gabriela and himself, the next bouncing like a spring. He stared, mesmerized, his eyes processing significant details about this child: the hair, a soft down of burgundy so much like his mother's; lips, baby full and smiling in innocence, reminded him of the woman who stood so stiffly beside him. He took in the healthy glow of the excited face, first turned his mother's way then to his, and the mischievous smile, so like his own. Even more remarkable, Richard saw eyes identical to his, laughing back at him in innocent expectation, speckled with gold dust inherited from his mother's eyes and lacking the cold cynicism of his.

Fascination turned to pride, and pride into a fierce and consuming possessiveness. This child, this miracle was *theirs*—his and Gabriela's. He wouldn't have needed his DNA checked out to prove it. His gut proved it. The child's eyes proved it. Luisito was *his.* The knowledge unleashed another wave of savage possessiveness unlike any he'd ever experienced, except with Gabriela. His eyes lifted and hooked on to hers with a brutal triumph that was difficult to conceal.

Gabriela swallowed and suffered another jerk from her son. *Oh, God. Oh, God.* She wasn't misreading the message in Richard's eyes. He suspected...hell, whom was she kidding? On a gut level, and Richard's gut was practically infallible, he knew. The only thing he needed was confirmation on her part, but that was a mere formality.

"*Mami,*" Luisito whined. "Swing."

Gabriela broke eye contact and looked at their son. "Luis—"

"What does he mean by swing?"

Richard's question generated a smile of motherly resignation from Gabriela. "He wants us to lift him off the floor and swing him back and forth. Just like a swing. Whenever he gets two adults in this position, the squirt never misses an opportunity to play his favorite game."

"Then let's not disappoint our little fellow." Before she could prepare herself, Richard lifted Luisito's arm in readiness. She quickly imitated him and held the squiggling toddler aloft between them. Luisito's delighted laughter bounced around the terrace. "At the count of three?"

Gabriela nodded, her heart thumping, melting. How many times had she visualized this moment? Guiltily fantasized, really, about Richard sharing playtime with their son? As they began swinging Luisito back and forth between them, Gabriela covertly watched this man, who had unwittingly caused such havoc, joy, passion, and pain in her life, handle their son with care, his typically cynical gaze reflecting such wonder it was painful. Richard, whom she still loved, acted as if he'd been born to actively participate in family life. It was as if the cold and brutal world he had navigated through most of his adult life had been erased at sight of their child.

Gabriela closed her eyes against the wonderful tableaux she and Richard made as they swung Luisito back and forth between them. This image might be what she hungered for in her heart, but it was a fantasy.

"Okay, Squirt. Enough." She signaled for Richard to lower his arm and knelt beside her son as they deposited him on the ground. "Now, Luisito," she affectionately rumpled his hair. "I've got work to finish up. Say thank you to Richard."

Luisito stepped closer to his mother, his eyes locked on this stranger invading his home turf. "Do I have to give him my hand?" he asked in a loud whisper.

Richard crouched so he'd be at eye level with the child, his child, he reminded himself. Shit. He was still in shock. "Not unless you want to," he said and waited.

Luisito studied Richard for a second or two, his face a poem of serious consideration. Then, quicker than a blink, he blurted, "Hi," and smiled. He shoved his little hand forward like he'd seen his father, brothers, and mother do countless of times with strangers. Richard took it and let his arm be pumped up and down with childish vigor.

"Who are you? I'm Luisito. Have you met Zip?" He pointed to Jean-Louis, who was still reeling from the shock of finding Richard in their midst. "That's my friend. He's silly. Do you like to paint? I like dinosaurs. Do you want to see them?"

Richard started laughing, amused at not being able to put in a word edgewise. Beside him, Gabriela sighed in resignation.

"Okay, Mr. Motor Mouth." She hugged her son to stop his chattering and avoided Richard's eyes. "Now scoot along to the kitchen so Lupe can give you a snack." Gabriela turned him toward the kitchen entrance and patted him on the bottom. "And take Zip with you."

At the promise of a snack, Luisito forgot the adults. Without further prodding, and with Zip woofing close behind, he quickly covered the distance between his mother and Lupe, who stood sandwiched between Spike and Father Ramirez in the kitchen doorframe. A man Gabriela didn't recognize craned his neck behind them, not missing a single thing.

"Some things never change," Richard whispered to her.

Gabriela turned, her eyebrow lifting in a silent query.

"Food," he said, chuckling. "At the mention of anything edible, everyone pounces."

Gabriela didn't respond. She waved to the men standing like petrified salt effigies in the kitchen doorway to step forward. They remained rooted to their places. Her next wave was more emphatic, even a little desperate. Not only did she want the unpleasant topic which had brought Richard back into her life discussed and gotten rid of, but she also needed the men as a shield against Richard's proximity. This scenario was too intimate, too dangerous for her.

Richard's smile as he stood next to her clearly showed he wasn't fooled with her tactics.

Jean-Louis finally broke his inertia and moved quickly toward Gabriela and Richard. He wasn't sure whether to smile in relief or cry for his friend.

"Oh, no." She backed away, waving her hands in negative emphasis. "You're not going to trap me in that again. I'm not changing my lodgings, itinerary, or security arrangements. Uh-uh."

All hell broke loose on the terrace, with everyone except Richard arguing or persuading. Gabriela's face turned mutinous, a look with which Richard was only too familiar. Jeremy was the only one who stood bewildered within the *mêlée*.

"Stop it. Stop it," she said, her voice laced with exasperation. "Nothing you say will change my mind." She crossed her arms to stress her point.

"But, *ma belle*," persisted Jean-Louis. "You haven't even heard what Monsieur Harrison has dug up on this cretin."

"That's right, Mrs. Martinez," Spike added. "His information could be critical, forcing us to change plans and security strategies."

"Well?" She looked at Father Ramirez. "Everyone seems to have an opinion. Let's hear yours."

"I only want your safety." His face was thunderous. "Whatever it takes."

"Christ," she said.

had probably not even remembered what Richard looked like, he'd been that engrossed in his pet project back in France.

"That's not really important now," she said and saw the struggle for resolution between the priest and the outraged cousin. She squeezed his forearm and her eyes turned sad.

"I know I am a sinner in your eyes, but I don't regret my son with Richard. I will never regret what happened between us."

Father Ramirez sighed. He squeezed her hand and shook his head.

"However, right now we have a more pressing problem," she said. "You've got to promise me you will say nothing of Roberto's real condition to Richard. Nothing at all," she finished.

Jean-Louis searched her face and frowned. "Why not?" he asked, suspicious of her answer. "He needs to know what is going on."

Gabriela shook her head in forceful denial. "No, he does not. Trust me."

"Then what the hell are we supposed to say," her cousin's truculence was evident in his forceful use of hell.

"We stick to what we have told everyone: Roberto had an accident and he is currently in rehab next door. Nothing more, nothing less."

"But, *chérie*—"

Gabriela saw movement at the edge of her terrace and watched Richard leading the vanguard toward her office, his face determined, his mouth set.

"Too many things are at risk here, especially the patent," she said, her nerves jittering, knowing the other men would arrive soon. More importantly, she knew Richard. He could smell deceit or omissions a mile away. "We cannot say anything. Not until the lawyers have that patent search done and the application secured." She looked from one man to the other. "You've got to promise me," she repeated, more insistent this time.

"What about your children, Enrique, Julien?" Jean-Louis asked.

"We tell them Richard doesn't need to know the extent of Roberto's condition, just like we have done with everyone else. The children are used to that. I'll handle Richard."

Mentally, she crossed her fingers and hoped to God the statement proved true.

The men had almost reached the door.

"Promise me, guys." She waited a heartbeat. "Promise." The last was said vehemently, with a tinge of desperation.

Both men nodded, but they were not happy with their agreement. Gabriela's stomach unclenched. One more catastrophe averted, she hoped. She turned to her desk, her back to the door, composing her features as the men entered.

Richard surveyed the tableau in front of him. Like thieves plotting a heist, he thought. Some happy with the plan, others not.

"Finished plotting?" he asked, his tone neutral but knowing.

Gabriela looked up from tinkering with the paraphernalia on the desk and her heart skipped a beat. Jesus, seeing Richard at last, vibrant, vital, made her realize how much she'd missed him. He looked, looked...good enough to eat. She'd always thought that, even the first time she had seen him shirtless in her guest room in France and at the safe house. Her face exploded from the heat in her cheeks and she lowered her eyes quickly. She did not want Richard to see her want, her need.

"Why don't you tell us about what you know of this guy?" She rounded the desk, sat, gestured for all to sit, and waited.

Richard opted for sitting near her, at the edge of her desk, and recounted all he knew about Wickeham. When he'd finished, the silence in the room was heavy.

"*Merde.*" Jean-Louis's expletive was heartfelt.

"Succinct and accurate," Richard told him.

"When the heck did I become a magnet for the wackos?" Gabriela shook her head in disbelief. She should serialize her life like a soap opera—ridiculous, but true.

"Does he hire out as well, or does he use his lackey exclusively?" Spike asked. Richard's account had changed everything. They needed to revisit every security measure as of today.

"From what Morris told us, he does both," Richard answered. "I'd do the same: use my goon on local stuff and hire out for the rest. Expedient and cost-effective."

"You think he hired local talent to create my accident?" she asked.

"Probable, but it is mere speculation, at least not until evidence proves otherwise."

"Jesus, Mary, and Joseph," Father Ramirez said, his hand rubbing his face, his expression incredulous.

Gabriela looked at Richard. "But that's not all, is it? What does this CID guy want from me?"

Smart of her to have tuned in to what remained unsaid. He turned to Gabriela but didn't smile. "He wants you as bait to set a trap for Wickeham."

"Well, that's blunt," she said.

Gabriela ignored the ruckus erupting in her office, all except for Richard. His expression seemed to be saying he was not wholeheartedly behind the request, but would accept her answer.

"And if I accept?"

"Then we're back to where we were four years ago," Richard answered.

"Only this time we actually know what we're up against," she replied.

"In a nutshell."

Yep, back to square one. But years ago, she didn't know what was at stake. Now she knew, and there was much more to lose.

"Well, that alters a few things," she voiced her thought out loud.

Jean-Louis narrowed his eyes. "You are not seriously considering the idea, are you?" he asked Gabriela. His eyes widened in disbelief at what he read on her face. "You are, *n'est-ce-pas?*" He slammed the chair arms as he sprung up from his seat.

Gabriela waved her manager back into his chair. "Considering is not a fait accompli." She had to consider many things.

"Even if we don't find any evidence," Richard said to the room at large. "I agree security measures have to be changed on the off chance, because if he really wants your work…"

"Trust me," Gabriela interrupted, remembering Wickeham's conversations, his insistence, and his suppressed anger at her refusals. "He does. Badly."

"As soon as I return with the boys," Spike cut in. "I'll start working on a new security plan."

"I'll bounce off a few ideas with you on our way to see the mechanic," Richard added. "Jeremy, get the lay of the land, see what you can suggest. We can also help implement any additional suggestions you want here, just in case you're short-handed."

"Does he always take over this way?" her cousin whispered to her.

"And then some," Gabriela answered.

***

Mannie snapped the last photographs of the braking system with his small Podunk camera. At first glance, with his sun-bleached hair and his tie-dyed, oil-stained T-shirt, he resembled a surfer boy who should be catching waves at Big Sur rather than tinkering with motors and wheels. Always cheerful, nothing bothered him much. Years ago, he'd been told he had the disposition of a 60s love child, where nothing rattled or disturbed him…where everything was peace and love and a mellow whatever directed at life.

But today, he was pissed. His reputation was on the line and someone wanted to screw him over.

He threw the camera on the bottom tray of his tool cart, dumped the oil rag he'd used to clean the brake area over it, and rummaged in the top tray for his flare-nut wrench and Vise-Grips. He knew he had checked Mrs. Martinez's car from the A-arms to the trailing arms. He had meticulously checked caliper pressure in case of clogging. He had verified and insured this inspection because the rubber there had a tendency to bubble, expand, or break down due to normal wear and tear. But the small pinpricks he thought he'd seen on closer view told him her brake failure had not been happenstance.

Some prick had sabotaged his baby.

Mannie jammed the flare-nut wrench into the back pocket of his jeans, positioned the Vise-Grips at a bitch angle, and locked it to loosen the spring clip at one end of the brake line.

He never saw the blow coming, just slumped on the ground like a wilting jellyfish.

Chapter Ten

Gabriela had won the argument. Amend that. Richard had let her win the argument about accompanying him to Mannie's garage. What his reasons were, she could come up with a few scenarios, but the one she would choose, hands down, was the one that kept her within his vicinity for close surveillance.

"Will you please move over?" she hissed under her breath.

Spike was driving the rented limo. Jeremy sat next to him, listening with interest as Spike talked about his security stint at the house, the children. Richard, on the other hand, who had use of an ample, cavernous back seat, had opted, since leaving her house, to glue his entire left side to her right: shoulder, hips, and leg.

He was crowding her on purpose.

He knew it.

She knew it.

His proximity and his inconspicuous caresses were creating havoc with her nervous system.

She knew it.

He did as well.

Case in point. For the past three minutes, his fingers kept touching her thigh, his strokes bare whispers on her skin. Was he doing it on purpose, to wear down her defenses? Or was he doing it unconsciously, wanting to keep contact, to make sure she was real, very much like how she felt? Every time he touched, she wanted to lean in.

The cynical in her thought Richard was using a tactical maneuver. He knew she wanted to keep him at arm's-length. She knew he had recognized her signals back at the terrace. She also remembered the message in his eyes: undermine her resolve. If the latter was his purpose, it was working. Her nerve endings were on fire. Physical contact with Richard had always made for an effective, undermining weapon, and he knew she was no match for it.

"Nervous?" he asked without even looking her way.

"You wish," she answered.

But two could play this game as well, she thought with vindictive glee. Throwing caution to the wind, Gabriela leaned into her need. She placed her hand over his knee and let it meander ever so softly up his inner thigh. His tremors satisfied her at a very deep, feminine level. The look in his eyes pleased her no end. A few precious seconds later, however, reason surfaced. She was playing with fire and, right now, she could not afford to get devoured. Not yet.

"Move." She softly jabbed him in the stomach with her elbow. "It's not going to work."

Richard moved to face her. How on earth did he do that without breaking contact? His shin was now pressed against her thigh and his attention fully centered on her face. Gabriela did not know what position was more dangerous.

A quirked eyebrow posed his question.

"What you want," she supplied and tried to move away from him, but her other side was plastered against the car door. Not much maneuverability.

Richard studied her for a few moments then leaned in. "If you really knew what I wanted," he whispered into her ear. "You would be blushing and definitely not in this car."

Her cheeks exploded with color and Richard softly skimmed the rushing blood with his forefinger. "I know you don't want to discuss things, but we will. We have to." He shifted, finally giving her the space she needed. "But not now. Later."

Gabriela closed her eyes briefly and hoped she'd be ready for his later.

"I'm bringing in Matthews and Rivers tomorrow, Mrs. Martinez," Spike interrupted her thoughts. "They'll keep tabs on the boys while I keep mine on the squirt."

"That's good. The kids know them and feel comfortable around them." She glanced at Spike through the rearview mirror. "Notify school security first thing tomorrow morning, and I'll let Principal Sandowski know what's going on as well. Make sure you warn Coach Phillips and his staff about what's going on. They will keep a sharp eye on all the boys and make sure no one who shouldn't be there approaches them. I'll call my mother tonight and let her know the kids will arrive by Friday."

Gabriela heard Richard chuckle.

"What?"

"I like this new take-charge facet of you."

"I've had to do a lot of that since you left," she said simply.

Truth never settles well. That bitter taste flavored his senses as her matter-of-fact statement jabbed at his heart. He should have known better than to leave her with a man he knew, from experience, had always placed her as second best. Forcing her hand and making her stay with Roberto four years ago may have been altruistic and noble on his part, but now he understood he should never have allowed this span of separation to happen.

"Where is Roberto in all of this, Gabriela?" Richard asked. He scanned her face, wanting to understand. "Why is he still leaving you alone to cope?"

Spike suddenly hooked eyes with Gabriela through the rearview mirror, waiting to catch his cues from her.

Gabriela inhaled deeply. Might as well take the plunge.

"Roberto can't help me at the moment," she said. "He's recovering from a recent car pile-up at my late mother-in-law's house next door."

Of all the excuses Richard had expected to hear, this was definitely not the one. A memory of this afternoon flashed across his mind. Richard understood now why everyone had frozen earlier at the mention of her husband. Maybe this time around, he should give Roberto the benefit of the doubt. After all, four years had gone by, and they had all changed, in one way or another. But Roberto's transformation, in that respect, remained a bit difficult to swallow as far as he was concerned. Something about a leopard not being able to change spots. Roberto's incapacitation, however, put a dent in things and might very well work against Richard's plans. He knew Gabriela. With Roberto playing victim, her husband would keep her anchored to him until he recuperated. Could this be the reason she wanted to keep her distance? It was her nature to protect and help. Damn. He shook himself mentally. Richard was not going to allow Roberto's condition to alter his endgame. A change of tactics might be called for. He needed to reassess.

"Why next door?" he asked.

Gabriela shrugged. "It was that or a rehab center. He didn't want the latter, and since his mom's death, the house has been empty. It had space for the special bed and gadgets Roberto needed. The children and I can visit him every day, if we want, and he can do what he needs to improve without disrupting our routine."

Richard opened his mouth, but Gabriela forestalled him.

"I'd rather you didn't."

Her emphatic statement, so in opposition to what he'd been thinking, caught Richard by surprise. Suspicion replaced it.

"Why not?"

Gabriela simply added to her previous lie. Well, not quite another bold-faced lie. There was some truth in what she was going to say next.

"I need to break the news that you are back in our lives slowly. The doctors don't want anything to upset Roberto because he needs to heal with no stress. So, right now, I'm not telling him. Please respect my wishes." She turned her head to avoid any further conversation and watched as Spike drove the car off Cabrillo Highway, down to Del Monte, and into a small industrial area bordering the Pacific.

Richard was less than satisfied with that answer, but he would get around her barriers somehow. He had to. "Where are we?" he asked.

Spike turned into Ramona Avenue.

"Industrial park. Mannie's place is coming up." Spike turned left. "Here we are."

The car stopped in front of a flat, gray-colored, one-storied building that receded from the attached back wall of another business on the right. The asphalt in front of Mannie's place was old and well-used, with gravel showing as whitish blemishes on the off-black, gridless surface. On the left of the building, a tow truck that had seen brighter days stood next to a battered blue pickup. Behind these, a small area was surrounded by a chain-link fence, which was topped with spiky barbed wire. Behind the barrier, several cars were locked up for the night. Next to this section, an open-ended alleyway, spanning a width of a few feet, ran perpendicular to the street before touching the business wall next door.

Richard took stock of the flat structure as they all stepped out of the car. A battered office door faced him on the left, with a hangar-wide opening on the right. Wide enough to fit two cars, the area was currently closed. Above the rolling bay doors, the name of the business was splattered clearly across its entire width: *Mannie's Place – Your Complete Auto and Collision Solution*. On the remaining free space, a placard showed the address of the business. Underneath, another sign displayed the establishment met the usual state-authorized licensee credentials. On Richard's right, and hugging the wall all the way to the street, a hodgepodge of debris, cones, street blockers, and a trash bin cluttered the area. One lonely security camera was mounted above the front door.

That door now stood ajar, a slice of light brightening the asphalt a couple of feet into the night.

"That's strange," Gabriela said, catching sight of the door. She pointed.

The reaction was immediate, almost orchestrated. The three men changed from relaxed to alert, surrounding her as one, with Richard and Jeremy flanking her sides while Spike protected her front.

"Get in the car, Mrs. Martinez." Spike reached for his gun. "And lock the door behind you."

Gabriela shook her head. "Not on your life. I'm sticking with you guys."

Richard grabbed her arm and began retreating.

She began to resist. "No, Richard. I've always been safer around you."

"Shit. Come here."

Richard opened the back limo door, embraced her, crouched, and placed himself, the car, and the open door as shields.

"Jeremy." Richard pointed his chin in the direction of Spike.

"Right, boss."

"I won't let anything happen to you," Richard vowed.

"I know," she answered with devastating trust and burrowed into him as though it were a homecoming.

When she settled deeper into Richard's scent, his strength, and his protection, she realized she'd missed him. Terribly. How long had it been since she'd been held like this, surrounded by strength, protection, and love? If she were honest, she couldn't say she had been bereft of caring these four years. But Roberto had expected her to hold everything together, to cope with all problems, to be the strong one because his energy, his focus, and his continued absences were centered on building his company. *And, let's face it.* For many years, Roberto hadn't bothered to understand how she had changed or what she needed, either. And, frankly, she was getting tired of being alone, of shouldering everything. This reprieve in Richard's arms was like a godsend, even if it turned out to be an ephemeral moment.

"On your six," Jeremy said to Spike.

With backs hugging the wall on either side of the front door, Spike and Jeremy paused and listened. Their moves seemed choreographed, rehearsed, as if they'd been working together for years. Jeremy grabbed the doorknob. Spike nodded. Training took over, and each man moved on instinct. In an explosive motion, Jeremy wrenched the door open and Spike charged in, gun raised, shifting his body and line of sight right and left as he scanned the interior of the small reception area.

After a brief pause that felt like a lifetime, both men shouted an all clear. Richard lifted her, slammed the limo door shut, forced her into a crouched position, and pushed her forward at a fast pace until they were inside the building. He shut the door and locked it.

Whipping around, Richard grabbed Gabriela and plastered her back against the brick wall, using his body as a shield in front. He scanned Mannie's reception quickly. It was small, and the furniture looked as tired and grungy as the gray walls. A small counter bisected the area two-thirds in, blocking customers from accessing the office behind. A small computer rested on the bottom tier of the counter while a scruffy phone stood directly on the top. A tiny holder of business cards rested next to an empty used oilcan filled with pens. To the right, where Spike and Jeremy were doing exactly the same routine as outside, a door with clear glass halfway down was closed. The area behind was brightly lit and Richard could see a banged-up BMW perched on the hydraulic lift.

"Office is empty," Spike said, when he saw Richard enter. "Nothing touched. Stay here while we clear the work area." Spike stepped to the connecting door and took a quick peek through the glass. The scan showed him feet on the floor that were not moving.

"Man down," Spike said.

Gabriela huddled closer to Richard. "Mannie?"

Spike's face was hard. "Looks like his work boots."

Jeremy and Spike entered the garage bay area. Gabriela slithered out of Richard's arms and rushed toward the door. She had almost reached it when Richard held her back.

"No."

"But—"

Richard shook his head and clung hard. "Let them do their job. Wait."

From their vantage point near the door, they could both see work boots on the ground. Gabriela's breath hitched. The position of those feet demonstrated the man lying on the ground was either unconscious or dead. Tears welled up. She hoped the former was the case, if not, she would never be able to live with herself.

The men, almost like a bizarre dancing couple, reconnoitered the area, ignoring the body lying so helplessly on the floor. When the word clear left their lips, Gabriela zipped across the threshold and rushed to where Spike and Jeremy knelt beside Mannie. Spike's relief was clear.

"He's alive," he told them. "Nasty blow to the head."

"I'll call 911," Gabriela said as she pivoted and beelined it to the phone in reception.

Richard joined the men. "Any other injuries?"

"Won't know until rescue comes. I'm not moving him until they give the okay."

Richard nodded and turned to the BMW as Jeremy joined him.

"Someone blindsided him while he was looking into this," Richard said and pointed to the brake area. Jeremy peered in closely and pointed to the Vise-Grip.

"Section cut clean," he said and walked to the other side. "Here, too." He looked at Richard. "There goes any evidence."

"Cleanup crew, definitely," Richard said to the men. He took a step back and studied the car.

Horror gripped him as he took a good look at the driver side of the BMW. The metal on the fender, as well as the entire driver side, was scrunched in as if a giant fist had pummeled the side in repeated brutal punches. Horizontal gouges had stripped the car's paint to such a degree that, in many places, the raw metal shone through. The driver-side window looked like cracked ice. Richard thought if he blew on it like the big bad wolf, the entire thing would shatter without resistance. The side view mirror had been wrenched out, the wires within exposed like spaghetti left out to dry.

"How did she survive this?"

"Some training and a shitload of luck," Spike said.

"When Mrs. Martinez first arrived in California, she was adamant about taking self-defense classes and defensive driving. She told me she never wanted to be clueless as to what to do in case her life was ever in danger again. It paid off."

Mannie grunted and began to stir. Gabriela, like a homing bird, appeared as if by magic. She knelt beside the young man, holding one of Mannie's rags bulging with ice. She had twisted everything to create an impromptu ice bag.

"Rescue and the police are on their way," she said and threaded her fingers through Mannie's hair. She gingerly felt around until she found the bump on his scalp and softly pressed the ice there.

Mannie groaned once more and tried to open his eyes.

"Don't move," she told him, squeezing his shoulder in a comforting move. "You have a nasty bruise on your head," she finished. *God knew what other injuries he'd suffered.* From his position, he'd probably fallen forward, so his face might have taken the brunt of the fall first. That could mean all types of facial fractures.

"God, Richard." Her eyes were pained and, at the same time, incredulous. "How could this be happening again?" Her fingers caressed Mannie's head, avoiding the clump of dried blood near the impromptu ice pack. "He didn't deserve this."

"You didn't deserve that, either," Richard said, pointing to the car.

Gabriela shivered at the memory.

"This bastard is toast," Richard said, his features taking on an expression Gabriela had seen four years ago. "Evidence or no evidence, my gut says Wickeham is responsible for this. The gloves are officially off."

"But, boss," Jeremy interjected. "Remember what Michael warned us about."

Jeremy took an involuntary step back when Richard turned to face him. He had never seen his employer with such depth of anger and ferocity in his gaze. It was definitely an eyepopper.

"Frankly, I don't give a rat's ass whether Morris wants things done above board. This isn't above board." Richard gestured to the car first, then at Mannie. "If we're dealt poisoned apples, we'll counter with grenades."

"How do you propose we do this?" Gabriela asked, and shifted the now soggy rag to another section of Mannie's bump.

"Not we," Richard stated coldly. "I."

"Oh, no, you are not shoving me aside on this one, Richard Harrison." Gabriela stared Richard down despite the storminess in his eyes. "Whether you like it or not, I am involved." She pointed to the car. "Have been involved from the beginning. This cretin wants my work. Has been harassing me since day one. You need me to bring this man down."

"Gabriela," Richard began, his voice low and fierce.

"Richard," she interjected, not fazed at his growing anger and frustration. "I'm no longer as defenseless or as naïve as I was four years ago. You'll need me, and you know it. We simply have to come up with a foolproof plan that will throw Mr. Wickeham's sorry ass in jail."

Jeremy was in awe. He had never seen anyone push back at his boss when in this mood. Bugger it. He'd never seen Richard in this mood and would not have tempted the bull, at least, not without a hefty dose of caution and fear. Mrs. Martinez, however, not only stood her ground, but she also shoved back hard. His admiration for her grew.

Spike was also fascinated by this interchange. He had never seen Mrs. Martinez in this light. It was a revelation.

Gabriela continued to stare at Richard. From experience, he knew she would not back down, and the look in her eyes confirmed it.

"Shit," Richard mumbled.

"Glad you agree," she said.

Sirens echoed in the distance.

"What do we tell the police?" Spike asked.

"Let them come to their own conclusions," Richard said. "I'm not volunteering information."

Gabriela agreed silently. She understood about not volunteering information only too well. As things stood, she definitely did not want the police to butt into her life. Too many things needed to stay hidden.

Mannie groaned and his eyes flickered.

"Why don't we let him do the talking," Gabriela said, and soothed the young man once more. "I'm sure he'll have plenty to say once he comes around. It won't keep us completely out of the limelight—"

"—but it will keep the focus off us," Richard finished for her.

Spike's eyes shifted from Gabriela to Richard. These two, apart from the obvious electric sparks that flew off each other when in proximity, were now finishing each other's sentences. Fascinating. He hoped, one day, he'd be privy to what had really happened to those two in France four years ago. Had to be one hell of a story.

The blaring sirens bellowed close by.

"Let's get the show started," Spike said and left the area to allow the paramedics access.

Chapter Eleven

Mannie lay on a stretcher, waiting to be transported to the hospital. The blood on his face had been wiped clean. His forehead served now as anchor to a wide strip of gauze that held a flat ice pack stationary to his now less swollen bump. His face was bruised but, according to the paramedics, he'd been lucky. He had landed on his arm first rather than the concrete floor. Yes, he'd banged his face on the ground, but on the rebound. He'd suffered no fractures, his nose was not broken, just the bump, as far as they could tell. The hospital would verify if he'd suffered a concussion or anything else that could not be diagnosed on this triage. He'd be held for observation and, if everything turned out well, he'd be discharged in a day.

"My head hurts," Mannie complained.

Gabriela commiserated with her mechanic. She knew about physical pain, having experienced a similar situation before. She stroked the hand she held in a soothing gesture. She was so grateful he was okay. So, so grateful.

"The paramedics gave you something for it. You should feel better soon."

"Not with all this crap noise around me," Mannie complained.

She smiled. Although the garage area, both outside and in, was a beehive of activity, the noise decibel was low, with policemen, crime unit workers, and detectives speaking at a decent level. But every time someone slammed a car door, or yelled to nosy bystanders to move behind the yellow crime tape, Mannie would wince.

"It's the headache," Richard said. "Amplifies everything."

"Woo-hoo for me," Mannie said, snappishly.

"Do you remember anything else?" Gabriela asked softly.

Her mechanic started to shake his head, winced, and lay still. "Like I said to the detective, I don't remember much after I was brained. Just that I took some pics of the brake line before I started dismantling it. I never got around to it." He looked at Gabriela. "Sorry."

"Pictures?" Richard asked.

Mannie let go of Gabriela's hand and pointed back to the inside garage. "I left the camera on the bottom work tray over there," he said. "Don't know if the bastard took it." He realized what he had just said out loud and blushed. "Sorry, Mrs. Martinez."

Gabriela had to smile. "I've used that choice word myself on occasion. No harm."

Richard looked at Spike.

"I'm on it," he said and sprinted to the detectives in the work area.

"I knew the brake line was in good shape when I checked your car, Mrs. Martinez," Mannie continued. "I knew things didn't fail through my fault. Someone drilled three small holes in the system so the brake fluid would leak out slowly. I'm sorry you had that scare."

And now, there's no longer any proof to show for it, Richard thought, disgusted.

"Mannie, forget the brakes," Gabriela said. "I'm just glad you're okay. Nothing else matters."

Spike returned, but not alone. The lead detective investigating the assault followed close behind. He shook hands all around and introduced himself as Detective Correia from the Monterey PD.

"We found the camera," Detective Correia began. "We'll develop the photos and get back to you."

"It's not a high resolution camera," Spike said to Richard. "The images may not show what he saw."

"The photographs, plus this attack," Richard commented, "will hopefully prove someone did not want the car closely examined."

Detective Correia turned his attention to Gabriela and poised his pen over his notepad.

"When did you report brake tampering, Mrs. Martinez?"

"I didn't," she said. "Thought it was an accident. At least, until now."

"We'll need to reopen your accident report," Correia told Gabriela. "What is not clear is why you thought this inspection was necessary." Correia paused. "Now."

Richard cut in before Gabriela could say anything. "Wouldn't you?" He looked at the detective with his most benevolent expression. "You have brake failure a week after your mechanic tells you nothing is wrong with your car. If it had been me, I would have dragged the car over here the minute after the accident, demanding to know why."

No mention of Wickeham, Gabriela thought, grateful to Richard for diverting the attention of the detective. For how long could they keep Wickeham's name under wraps, she didn't know. Hopefully, long enough.

"I know I checked those brakes before I returned the car to Mrs. Martinez," Mannie said, his voice reflecting his mounting anger. "It's my reputation and livelihood on the line. Can't let anyone screw me over."

A paramedic interrupted, asking if they could finally remove the patient to the hospital.

Detective Correia nodded.

"I'll keep you posted on the photos," Correia told Mannie as he was lifted into the ambulance. The detective reverted his attention back to Gabriela.

"I have a final question for you."

Gabriela stiffened, ready to be blindsided at any minute by this seemingly innocuous detective. Richard, whose arm was draped over her shoulders, gathered her protectively into him.

Correia's hard gaze pinned her. "Do you, or your husband, have any enemies? I understand he recently suffered an accident as well."

"None that I know of," she lied. "But my husband is in a very competitive and lucrative business. So am I. Anything is possible." She shrugged.

Correia studied her face a moment longer. "I'll keep in touch if I have any more questions." He closed his notebook.

"Mrs. Martinez is leaving in a couple of days on business," Spike told the detective. He fished out his wallet, opened it, and took a business card from it.

As the detective scrutinized Spike's business card, Gabriela added. "Mr. Washington will remain here with my children and can answer any of your questions. He can also reach me at any time while I am overseas."

The detective, in turn, handed his business card to Gabriela. "Call if you think of anything else. I'll be in touch."

With a curt nod to their group, he returned to his crime scene, relaying his order to allow them through to the officer near the crime scene tape.

"This is our cue to exit," Richard said, "before he can think of anything else to ask."

Still holding on to her shoulders, he turned and headed to the waiting car.

Gabriela shivered in the cool night. This evening had brought back too many memories of her time in France with the police. She was grateful, however. Detective Correia was a sweetheart in comparison to her prior experience with the French cops. Back then, the *gendarmes* had been relentless in their questioning, in their skepticism she'd killed in self-defense. "*Madame, really?*" they'd asked over and over. The evidence of Albert's brutality had still been evident on her face, on her body, but they'd turned a blind eye to that. Monsieur Heinige was their most upstanding citizen: a true philanthropist, famous, rich, influential, politically connected, and generous to a fault. She, on the other hand, was a stranger—a guest in their country, an American living under the forbearance of the French. It had not been until Maurice had unearthed the damning videos from the clearing, and released one for the police to see, that they had finally believed her.

Then all hell had broken loose.

Jeremy held open the limousine's back door for them to climb inside.

Richard leaned into her. He had felt her tremors.

"Are you all right?"

When she shrugged and didn't look at him, he stopped shy of the opening and turned her. He scanned her face, her averted eyes. She was not telling him something. He placed a wisp of hair behind her ear and cradled her face in his hands, his thumbs warm, caressing.

"What's wrong?"

Gabriela finally looked up. Her eyes spoke of unpleasant shadows, laced with a world of suppressed pain.

A flash illuminated the night.

"Mrs. Martinez, over here."

Another blast of light hit the night.

"Shit," all three men said in unison.

The whirr of the camera, snapping picture after picture, made Gabriela cringe. She ducked into the limo, hiding her face from the man whose voice she'd recognized, her relentless shadow, Herb Bryce. Richard was not a second behind her, his face set, his jaw clenched.

Jeremy slammed the door, sprinted to his side, and practically dived in. Spike had the limo already gunned and ready to run. Within seconds, they backed out. The camera flash kept flaring, the inside of the limo blinking as if strobe lights had lit the night. Over the hum of the motor, Gabriela heard Bryce yell, "Hey, buddy, I'm press. Lay off."

"Where the hell did this guy come from?" Richard exploded.

Spike glanced at him through the rearview mirror. "Told you," he said, and then mouthed h-e-r-p-e-s silently.

"Must be listening to a police scanner," Gabriela said, her voice resigned. She pressed her fingers to her forehead and began massaging the tension there. "That's how he found me at the hospital after the accident." She shuddered. Just what she needed, her picture splattered all over the seven o'clock local news, at the scene of a crime, not with her husband, but with Richard. "Christ."

"Is there any way we can stop the pictures from getting printed?" Richard asked Spike.

The laughter that came out of Gabriela was cynical. "Only if you were still working for your ex-boss, you might," Gabriela said. "But not now.

Even with the injunction I slapped him with years ago, he's still press and can have access to my person at any time he wants."

Richard folded her hand in his. "How long has this been going on?" he asked.

He caressed her cheek. Such a simple, feathery gesture, she thought, with such a world of comfort behind it. She closed her eyes and leaned into the caress. Now she understood what she'd been missing all these years at her husband's side—his lack of support. Richard had always offered his, without question. She'd had to search for, even demand, Roberto's. Now, to receive support again, without her having to ask or plead for it, felt alien.

"Sweetheart?" Richard whispered. "Has it always been this way, this bad?"

The look in her eyes pierced his heart. "Oh, it's been worse. Much, much worse, especially after I left the hospital in France. Herb Bryce?" She nodded back in the general direction of the garage. "He's a harmless puppy in comparison to the jackals in Europe. Thankfully, they went after other tasty meat soon after, but it took the release of one of Albert's videos to the police for the journalists and the police to leave me alone. I have to thank Maurice for that reprieve."

"The only misfortune," Spike cut in, "is that Herb Bryce didn't go away, and he'll sell whatever he got back there to the local news stations tonight and publish everything in his own rag by tomorrow."

"My face will be splattered all over the evening news and the next edition of the tabloids." Her entire body quivered. "Jesus."

For once Richard did not know what to say, what to do. This was alien territory for him. He'd always had control of the situation while he was working for Seldon. Now, he didn't. And he hated not being in control. He wrapped her in his arms and whispered, "We'll figure things out, sweetheart. I won't let you face this alone."

Gabriela nodded and burrowed deeper into his arms. Richard's heart lifted. At least, she still trusted him to protect her—to fight for her. It was a beginning, of sorts.

Chapter Twelve

The daily ritual to check her children before retiring was as old as her firstborn and as necessary as air. She rounded the corner and tiptoed into Robertico's room. The comforter covered her son's lank body up to his nose, his bed as unruffled as his sleeping habits. She cocooned him tighter still, caressed his hair, and kissed his cheek. He mumbled in his sleep, surfacing from dreamland long enough to hear her soft 'Love you,' and murmur something unintelligible in return.

She crossed through the connecting door into Gustavito's room. She evaded the obstacle course of toys, drawing pads, pencils, and clothes littering the floor. Unlike his brother, Tavi sprawled face down on a bed that looked like it had seen a recent skirmish. The comforter, crumpled and half resting on the floor barely covered his gangly leg as it protruded from the mattress like a flagpole. Inches from the floor, his left arm cradled his pillow against the mattress. Gabriela chuckled, tucked his leg in, wrapped him in the comforter once more, placed the pillow under his head, kissed him, and gave him her love without him so much as moving a muscle.

Her last stop was the baby's room. Over the wood railing that acted like a surrounding barrier reef to the bed, she could see his bottom sticking out. He loved to sleep on his tummy, knees tucked under him, rump in the air. She caressed the baby-soft hair, so like her own in color and consistency, and felt the usual tightening in her heart. She kissed the downy cheek and took in the recent, subtle changes in his cherubic face, changes that showed uncanny similarities to his father's striking, chiseled features. Carefully, Gabriela skimmed two fingers across his cheek in a feathery caress. She, who had once claimed she would never live a lie, stared at the little boy who everyday made a mockery of her arrogance.

Her son—God's bittersweet joke on her.

And, now, his father was here, in the flesh, reminding her of other moments, other yearnings.

She sighed. After the debacle at Mannie's, she thought the rest of the evening had gone well, at least, most of it. Before dinner, the boys had had a satisfying game of hoop with Spike, Jeremy, and Richard, with her sons' good-natured ribbing at Jeremy's clumsiness with the basketball. That had turned into a bet, followed by an impromptu game of tag football, with Jeremy trouncing everyone's behind. By the time dinner was announced, everyone was dirty, scraped, happy, and laughing all around.

Boys.

The best part of the evening, hands down, had been dinner, with the dining room full of noise, warmth, conversation, tempting aromas, complaints, and laughter. It had brought a moment of pity for her husband, for his absence. Roberto would have enjoyed the evening, despite his shortcomings. Even Jeremy, who had sat between her two oldest sons, had blended in, talking to them with the enthusiasm of an eleven-year-old about his favorite characters and episodes in the *Dragon Ball Z* series. That short interval had felt sane, except for the insanity currently surrounding her. The shadow of threat was never far away. It was reflected on the moments of waiting stillness, by the adults, each time the phone rang, as well as in the pauses in conversation the instant some noise outside reached them.

Gabriela took Richard's toy from their son's grip. Placed it on top of the commode and tiptoed out of the room, a smile on her face.

Luisito hadn't let go of the duck all evening. Her older sons had not stopped playing their music CDs, either. Richard had surprised them all at dinner by distributing his gifts to the children. She chuckled. Robertico and Gustavito had been elated, gloating over the fact they had music none of their friends had. They had become even more enthusiastic when Jeremy had explained the bands he'd chosen were the hottest groups in England. Her sons had closed ranks immediately, discussing to whom and how they could brag about this at school.

Luisito's gift had been a delight: a duck that, as you pulled the string, rolled with you while it slapped its silly oversized rubber feet at each roll. She sighed. Even now, she was hard pressed not to cry. The joy in their son's eyes was hard to describe. So was the pride and joy reflected in Richard's. And when she had heard he had created it with his own hands, Gabriela had escaped to the kitchen to help Lupe serve the food, if not, she would have broken down in front of everyone, blubbering like an infant.

Richard, as well, had enjoyed the evening. Ever in tune to him, she'd chosen Luisito's seating arrangement on purpose, sensing he would appreciate the nearness to their son, this little bundle of life so similar to himself. She'd been right, although it had been painful at times to witness how Richard absorbed every movement of their child, every smile, every whine, every breath, as if to make up for the three years he'd missed of their son's life. He'd clumsily helped Luisito with his food, cutting food for him;

had helped him with the fork upon occasion, picking up the debris Luisito dropped on the table. Zip had taken care of what had landed on the floor.

Now the evening had wound down, all in all an extremely satisfying one. It had gone without a hitch or secrets divulged—until her cousin Enrique arrived with Bea, just in time for after-dinner drinks.

Enrique had barged in, as was his style, all excited. He had spoken to Father Ramirez and had been told about Richard's arrival. To finally meet and personally thank the man who had saved Gabriela's life four years ago was a wish he'd harbored in his heart. But that enthusiasm had turned from confusion at first, to slight shock second. That had finally been replaced by simmering anger the more he watched Richard's and Luisito's faces. More often than not, he would glance her way, his eyes brimming with recrimination.

Beatriz had put two and two together very quickly, throwing surreptitious glances from Richard to Gabriela then back to her husband, her eyes huge. Knowing her husband well, she had kept her questions innocuous, asking the men about their flight, about London and their jobs, anything and everything to avoid the explosion she knew would come.

Well, at least her cousin's anger had not detonated in front of Richard. Enrique had snapped, "We need to talk. Privately," and had stalked away toward her office, Bea in tow. Gabriela had excused herself calmly from her visitors as well, under the guise of giving Luisito his bath, and during the next hour or so, she had left her cousin to stew in the office while she finished her nightly routine with the children, with Lupe, and the dog.

She headed from Luisito's room to her office. The house was quiet now. No muted echoes of Spike's or Jeremy's voices floating in the air; no interjection of Richard's voice to keep her company while she had futzed around throughout the evening.

Gabriela grabbed the doorknob but did not turn it. Well, she couldn't delay the inevitable any longer. Things were rolling downhill at a derailing pace. *Denouement.* She smirked. It had finally caught up to her, and, this time, she would not escape the consequences.

She took a deep, steadying breath, not looking forward to this showdown. Not that she feared this confrontation with her cousin. Actually, she was glad things were finally being placed out in the open. Her only wish was to get this over quickly. She was tired, still had to make her nightly visit to Roberto, and hoped Richard wouldn't waylay her before she retired for the night. Despite the fact his body had been in a different time zone this morning, and was probably suffering from a generous portion of jet lag as well, he had looked alert, more like wired she would say. She could bet, and win that bet, he would corner her tonight. Now *that* conversation was the only one she actually dreaded.

She opened the door and got hit by the blast of recrimination.

"Que carajo hace tu amante en esta casa? Your lover... here," Enrique sputtered.

Gabriela closed the door softly.

***

"Her schedule is the most flexible," Spike said. "Thanks for taking over that duty. I can now work with my men to give the children our maximum protection."

"Just leave us a map of the area," Richard said. "Gabriela can guide us for the rest. The GPS unit in the car is really useless."

Spike grinned. "New technology is always a bitch. Never works when you want it to."

"And the bugger freezes every few seconds," Jeremy put in, remembering how excited he'd been about using the new gadget. It had been a waste of his time.

"Jeremy's good at memorizing areas quickly. We'll come up with some getaway moves." He saw Jeremy hide a yawn. "Go get some rest. You're working on fumes."

"So are you." Jeremy's next yawn was wider and deeper. "I don't know how you keep up."

Spike handed a printout to Richard. "That's more or less the rundown of her day tomorrow. Things can change, especially if the lawyers get involved."

Lawyers? "About?" Richard asked, way too casually.

"Patent search for Roberto's company. All super-secret, hush-hush. Mrs. Martinez has been handling things for her husband since the accident and, last I heard, they were almost done. She's waiting for word." His gaze shifted to the office area. Wishful thinking made him want to believe the discussion in the office would be about that, but Spike doubted it. He knew Richard wouldn't believe it, either.

"What about this Bryce fellow," Jeremy asked. "He may become a serious security issue."

"I would usually say no," Spike said. "This time, you may have a point."

"Meaning?" Richard asked.

"This is just my gut talking." Spike's eyes turned serious. "Bryce is no fool. Things are not normal, at least not the normal he expects from Mrs. Martinez. With this latest fiasco at Mannie's, his reporter antennae will be screaming exclusive, especially after he digs into the story a little deeper."

"What else do you know about him?" Richard asked.

"Did a background on him a while back. Army sniper. Studied photojournalism under a VA program after his army stint, and has worked for the same tabloid since '90."

"Family? Children?"

Spike shook his head. "No children. Married to the same woman for fifteen years."

Richard voiced his disgust. "I can call in a few favors, but I bet if we put pressure not to publish, he'd grab the bone even tighter." Not that Gabriela was a bone, but Bryce would stick to her as if she were.

Spike nodded, his thoughts paralleling Richard's. "He'd be more in our faces than ever." And Mrs. Martinez did not need a relentless bloodhound asking impertinent questions and digging up more dirt on her, especially about her husband.

"That'll change in London."

"Michael's good at keeping tabloid scum away," Jeremy cut in. "He'll make sure no one gets near the flat."

The look Spike gave Richard was clear—don't mess with my employer, or else. Richard was glad, and jealous at the same time, Gabriela had another advocate.

"I have yet to press that point on Gabriela," Richard said, his eyes acknowledging and relaying he had different dibs on this woman first and would do everything to protect her. "She's going to fight it, but she would be better protected at my place."

"She could also be more isolated. Riskier," Spike shot back. "Hotel is more public. More people. Connecting room doors with Jean-Louis, Julien, and Father Ramirez in case of emergency."

"But more hallways and stairwells where one can hide, abduct, or attack." Richard shook his head. "No. She'll fare better at my place."

Spike wasn't that sure.

Jeremy stood and stretched. "Well, gents. I'm off. Can't keep my bloody eyelids open."

Spike rose as well. "Coming?" he asked Richard.

"No. I'll hang around a bit."

Spike slapped Jeremy on the back. "Come on, Jeremy. Try not to pass out on your feet. Hate to have to shoulder-heft you." He assessed the bulk. "What—two, two-ten?"

"Fifteen stone."

Spike shook his head. Whatever. Brits had a funny way of measuring things anyway.

"That's two hundred and ten pounds to us," Richard translated, his grin wide.

Calm descended when the men left. The muted voices of Enrique and Bea ebbed and flowed from the office area as Richard kept adding mental notes to the situation. Once more, he was amazed and worried. What more would Gabriela take on? How long could she take this level of stress? Granted, this time she had several people willing to help her—Jean Louis, Spike. But Richard could guarantee they could only help so much—she would take the bulk of the problems onto herself. And what good did that ever do for her, her family, even to that asshole of a husband who kept adding to her woes without much care, it seemed? At least Roberto still behaved with familiar constancy. More importantly, how to handle this new Gabriela, this woman who seemed not to depend on anyone or anything? He had told her the truth earlier about his liking this new take-charge woman, but would she listen to him? In France, she'd been a handful.

Richard was bone-tired, but he couldn't rest. The whisky he was drinking now might help him relax eventually, although he doubted its effect would strike soon. Something was driving him, the adrenaline at a level he'd not experienced in years. Part of it was due to the gift of spending time with his son. He wanted so much for that child, for them. He also wanted Gabriela: her joys, her sorrows, her anger, her family, her smiles, her caresses, her love, and her body—all of her. He needed her with a yearning that was painful. But he wanted answers as well, needed them, and waiting for a moment of privacy with Gabriela had been frustrating, especially when her house here resembled hers back in France—a damn circus, with people butting in when he least expected it. He hated to have to sit tight until he could get her alone. Patience was not one of his virtues.

He was also antsy, and that really bothered him. He'd felt the same way in France, at Maurice's headquarters. Call it premonition, call it experience, call it whatever you like, he felt as if the cosmos was holding its breath, certain in the knowledge all hell would break loose soon. Maybe the conversation about security here at the house, security for the kids at school, and security for Gabriela here and at the auction was triggering this hair-raising mode. He wanted Gabriela and their son far away from any possible harm. Hell, he wanted them out of there now, wishing them somewhere safe, somewhere where they could never be reached, could never be touched. This Wickeham was willing to go the extra mile to get Gabriela's work in his greedy hands. The car was evidence of how badly. They needed to put this bastard away fast, either through legal channels, like Morris wanted, or, preferably, permanently, like Richard wanted. And, damn it, Gabriela was right, also. Despite the fact he was not keen on the idea, they needed her to set the trap.

Something else bothered him—no, not bothered. Pissed him off. Enrique, with wife in tow, had barged in as if this was his own house despite the fact it was late in the evening. As time elapsed, Enrique's mood had turned from enthusiastic at meeting him, to morose, to downright rude. Richard knew why and, frankly, he didn't give a shit. He would not put up with anyone berating Gabriela for what they had shared. He would screw Enrique from here to the end of the universe if that happened, and he'd do it with a smile. So he kept an ear open to Gabriela's movements. He would know the moment she went to the office, and he would follow right behind.

"Screw this," he said and downed the remainder of the whisky. He dumped the empty tumbler on the coffee table, stood, got his bearings, and stretched the kinks in his body. Waiting was driving him insane, his thought processes turning to that of a blubbering asshole. He'd had enough. Itching for a showdown, his thoughts reverted to Enrique. Her cousin had looked like he'd wanted to punch him out. Good. He might just give him the excuse, because Richard was eager for a fight.

He turned into the hallway and saw Gabriela pause before opening the door. Her cousin's contained rancorous undertone reached him before she closed the door.

He quickened his pace.

***

"Keep your voice down," Gabriela admonished. "Everyone's asleep." Her icy look hooked onto her cousin's. "And what Richard is to me is none of your business."

"Beg to differ, *prima*." The anger he felt, the disappointment was brutal. His image of the sweet innocent cousin, of the beleaguered, brave woman who had stood up to life with her head high had died a fiery death. Gabriela, his cousin, had had an affair four years ago with a stranger, under the nose of Roberto. Worse, she had passed her bastard as Roberto's.

"You are *not* dragging our family through the dirt."

"You don't dictate to me, Enrique. Roberto did, and he never really cared one way or another."

Richard entered the room silently. Standing by the desk, facing each other and fully absorbed in their own skirmish, Enrique and Gabriela did not notice his entrance. Beatriz did, but then, she was facing the door.

"You lied to him, to us." He couldn't believe he'd been played for a patsy.

"Gaby. Enrique." Bea cleared her throat. Richard's face was a controlled mask. For the first time, she feared her husband was in danger of getting the beating of his life.

"Get rid of him," Enrique nearly shouted. "Get rid of your lover now. If not…"

"What? You'll throw him out?" Gabriela's smile was cynical. Richard would have Enrique on his ass quicker than a blink. "May I remind you this is my house? He is a guest here and the father of my child. I can't and I won't tell him to leave."

Richard felt a savage satisfaction at her answer.

"If he won't, I will. I'll drop everything and resign tomorrow."

Gabriela shrugged, hurt by her cousin's behavior, but not surprised by it. She didn't back down, however. "I'm used to being abandoned, Enrique. It won't be the first time, nor the last."

Richard saw Beatriz frown at that statement, turning speculative eyes on Gabriela. No one knew the degree of abandonment she had suffered—no one, except him.

"Didn't realize you had turned into such a *cabrona*."

"Enrique." This time Bea's voice held an angry edge to it at the way her husband was addressing his cousin.

"Don't butt in," Enrique warned his wife, his eyes still centered on his cousin's face. He closed the gap between them, his eyes narrowed, his demeanor suddenly changing from angry to speculative.

"I get it. Now that Roberto is next door, incapable of preventing anything, or defending his own, you're taking advantage."

Gabriela's back stiffened.

"You have an itch, *prima?*" His body leaned into her, his tone pejorative.

"You're disgusting and way beyond insulting."

"You need—"

"Shut up." Gabriela took a step closer and raised her chin belligerently, her eyes burning with rage.

"—to scratch it?"

The slap brought a stunned silence. Gabriela had used such force behind the blow, Enrique's face began to mar with the welt.

"*Comemierda*," she blasted. "You'd never understand. Never."

"Your lover—"

"Shut up." She almost raised her hand once more, but decided against it. Her palm was throbbing and itching from the blow. "I'm sick and tired of being lambasted and blamed for everything. I didn't do anything wrong. I don't regret anything, least of all my child."

"You screwed Roberto over," her cousin, still angry, pressed on.

"Roberto, the saint." She spat the words out. "Roberto, the poor maligned husband. What a joke."

She jabbed one finger into her cousin's chest. "We wouldn't be in this mess if not for Roberto." She stabbed a bit harder, with mounting outrage and frustration. "If he had driven to his office first instead of, how did you crassly put it, to scratch his mistress's itch that morning, the accident would never have happened."

Gabriela slammed a hand over her mouth to stifle her sudden gasp, one that had come simultaneously with Bea's. She looked at her cousin's wife. *Oh, my God.* What had she let out? She saw shock battle it out with sadness in Bea's eyes.

Enrique backed up as if hit. Had he heard right? "What?"

But Gabriela was no longer paying attention to her cousin. All her nerve endings screamed Richard was in the room and had witnessed everything.

"Roberto took a mistress?"

Richard's words confirmed her fears. She closed her eyes, thinking her life definitely outdid a soap opera in grand proportions. She turned to face him.

"That son of a bitch," Richard said too softly. Gabriela knew, by his voice and expression, if Roberto had been present, well, Roberto would be at a distinct disadvantage, if not beaten to a pulp.

"Oh, Gaby," Bea said softly. "I'm...this is...when?" She was on the verge of tears.

"He admitted it the morning of the accident." Gabriela looked at her cousin. "He'd been sleeping with the woman for months."

Gabriela saw and read Enrique's expression accurately: Roberto took a mistress in response to her own faithlessness. A tit-for-her-tat. Joy. Suddenly, the room suffocated her. She needed to get out before she imploded, and she didn't want to implode in front of her cousin and, least of all, Richard.

"I'm going next door," she announced in general, opened the terrace door nearest her, and blended with the night.

Richard stood paralyzed for an instant. She was going to see the scumbag after all this? *No way.*

"Gabriela, wait."

Enrique blocked his path. "Listen, buddy—"

He never got to finish the sentence. In an instant, Enrique's upper body was slammed against the desk, his face plastered against the blotter, his eyes level with the stapler. Enrique couldn't move. Richard held him down by the neck, with Enrique's right arm twisted behind his back.

"Listen, *buddy,*" Richard said. "You get in my face again, you'll get real up close and personal with a hospital bed." His voice turned meaner, colder. "And if I ever, ever hear you denigrating Gabriela again, your life will be worth dick."

"Mr. Harrison," Bea pleaded, a soft hand on his shoulder. "Please."

Richard pressed Enrique into the desk and leaned in. "You don't know shit about Gabriela, what happened, what she suffered."

Bea leaned forward, her face inches from Richard's, her eyes seeking, trying to assimilate what had not been divulged.

"Make us understand," she asked softly.

Richard released Enrique and faced his wife. "It's not my story to tell."

He turned to follow Gabriela, but paused. His gaze raked Enrique.

"Your cousin is not a whore. She is the mother of my child and the woman I love. Never forget that. I'll move heaven and earth to protect and avenge her. Even from you."

Richard followed her into the night.

Chapter Thirteen

Gabriela's visit with Roberto had not been a good one for her. One look at her husband's face as she had entered the sick room had slammed emotions within her to such a degree she was blindsided by their intensity. She had wanted to slap Roberto into consciousness; shake him until he opened his eyes. She had wanted to rail at him, to skewer him with her pain. For what? What satisfaction was there in venting to a man who still would not have heard her words, nor would have understood her meaning? Who, before the accident, really hadn't cared beyond how things affected his work or himself? Who, for years, had berated her silently with a look, its message one of irritation at having to deal with female histrionics? It was pointless. Everything was pointless now.

She bid the night nurse a goodnight and walked to the connecting gate.

The coolness of the night braced her. The cloudless sky beckoned observation. The soft sounds of the lapping ocean on the shore whispered to her over the ficus fence dividing the two properties. Her hand gripped the iron rail of the connecting gate to steady her body as she took a calming breath, closed her eyes, and dropped her head back.

Richard would be waiting for her, she knew. She'd heard his demand back at the office, but had ignored it. Knowing Richard, especially after what he'd heard her reveal, he'd be fuming, not to mention be incredulous about her visit to Roberto tonight.

Her next breath was deeper, more calming. She exhaled and opened her eyes to the universe, its stars hazily dotting the cosmic ceiling above her. A wisp of white mist floated from her mouth and hovered playfully over her nose. She inhaled deeply once more, straightened, and rotated her neck, releasing small pops of tension. Time for the next showdown, she told herself, her fingers punching the code to release the lock on the gate. Would Richard understand? She pulled the gate open. Would he support her current position? Would he be willing to wait for her once more?

The slam was brutal and efficient. Her entire body was smashed into the shrub barrier, her back pressed into leaf and bark, lacerating clothes and flesh. A merciless hand squeezed her cheek and covered her mouth so brutally it swallowed her surprised shriek. A thick frame of muscle pressed against her front, effectively pinning her. She tried to struggle, but could barely move. The pressure on her face intensified and a knife blade came into focus as it rested on her cheek.

At first, Gabriela thought her attacker wore a mask, like those caricature ones worn by 1960s Mexican wrestlers. But as her eyes focused, she realized she was wrong. Tattoos in patterns, script, and shadows practically covered the entire face, shaved head, and exposed neck, revealing only miniscule patches of paler skin to the night.

Gang.

Panic set in. She began to struggle in earnest, but was body-shoved deeper into the ficus fence. She felt twigs break and others dig deeper into her flesh and break skin. The knife shifted from cheek to left eye.

She got the message. She froze.

Body odor, ripe with sweat and musk, assailed her nostrils. So did the stale scent of jalapeños and tecate when he whispered. "I have a message for you, bitch."

She tried to concentrate. His hold on her cheek and mouth had not abated; her breathing was somewhat impeded. Her teeth began to scrape the soft flesh inside her lips with each labored breath. She needed to get out of this. Needed to protect her family. Needed to warn Richard. *Think. Think.* Her brain, however, refused to function. At the moment, her thoughts didn't stretch beyond the knife tip held so casually near her eye. Her body trembled and a stifled whimper escaped her throat.

The son of a bitch smiled when he heard. Fear suddenly transformed into a fury she had not felt in four years. She narrowed her eyes and stayed still.

"*El jefe* is not pleased," he said. "You are making his very good client very angry."

She didn't answer or cower, she simply waited for the message while she looked at him, unmoving and unblinking. The lack of response on her part, it seemed, did not settle well with the goon. He pricked her cheek with the knife. She felt something warm slide down her skin.

"Are you listening, *puta?*"

Gabriela's eyes narrowed even more, but the only sign she gave the bastard was a small nod. Her mind was frantic, trying to remember the lessons she'd learned from her defense trainer. She needed this asshole to feel he was in control, that he had the power. Who the hell was she kidding? Right now, he *had* all the power. She closed her eyes for a fraction of a second, and thought of Richard. If only he could hear her screaming mind.

"Your actions forced *el jefe* to dispose of a good *vato*."

A euphemism, Gabriela was sure, for the permanent removal of said *vato*. Had he been the one who'd sabotaged her car? If they had gotten rid of him, definitely. He'd botched the job, so he was no longer useful to them. Somehow, she didn't feel any pity for the riddance of scum, especially one who had almost gotten her killed.

"My *jefe's* client wants your guarantee you will sell," the man continued. "No more games. Do you understand?"

Gabriela nodded.

"The man wants an answer now or your beautiful children will be relocated—" The man paused, smiled, and caressed her face with the flattened blade. "Elsewhere."

Gabriela's rage at this threat of abduction of her children reverberated throughout her body in small spasms. She needed her mouth freed. She needed to relay her danger to the men not fifty feet away. She needed a gun. No, her hands would do, if she could get them around his neck. Threaten her family, her children? She'd kill the bastard or die trying before he touched a hair on their heads.

She squirmed, vying for a better position in which to attack this scumbag, and grunted as loud as she could. Maybe the men would hear the rustle, her throaty complaints.

"*El jefe* doesn't care what I do with you. His client doesn't, either." The man shifted. He plastered his body against hers and shifted his knife arm to a position across her throat. He poised the knife next to her jugular.

"Gabriela?"

"Mrs. Martinez?"

The men's voices were never so welcome, but they sounded far away. The knife jerked against her throat and Gabriela didn't think she could meld into the greenery even farther, but she somehow managed to move her head back. The movement slackened the gap between her and the man, releasing one of her arms.

White teeth glared at her through the night.

"I've been watching you, *mamacita*," he whispered next to her ear. "Always surrounded by men. Always smiling, touching." The man jerked his head toward her house and began to grind his pelvis against her. "Two men waiting. It seems you like *pito*, bitch." His smile widened and a salacious breath escaped his mouth as he ground into her with more force. "Maybe I can get first dibs, huh?"

Gabriela's stomach roiled and she almost gagged. *Wait. Wait,* her mind screamed. Make him loosen more of his hold, make him believe she was too afraid to fight, to strike. She needed her mouth freed. Needed to sink her teeth into the bastard. But how the hell was she going to accomplish that?

The goon removed his hand from her mouth. Gabriela gulped in air, expanding grateful lungs for this respite, but froze when she felt the scum begin to fondle her, squeezing her breast painfully.

Something snapped within her.

"You son of a bitch."

She rammed her forehead against the bastard's nose and heard a soft crack. Pain shot through her forehead but she ignored it. Something hot spattered against her face, hair, and neck the same instant she sunk her teeth into the soft flesh of his forearm. Caught unawares, the man jerked away, cursing, and she shoulder-shoved him with a strength she never thought she possessed.

She ran toward the path leading to the house and screamed like a banshee.

"Richard!" Her voice rent the night. "Richard!"

Two seconds later she was tackled to the ground. Her body bounced and scraped earth, grass, and flagstone. She somehow shifted, facing her attacker. The man tried to pin her with his body. Her body became a blur of movement as she bit, scratched, and kicked her assailant. She gouged his eyes at the same time his fist grazed her ear with a punch. She punched his bloody nose. He released her, but not before she heard the man's yowl of pain. She crawled away from her attacker like a crab. Her hands clutched the grass, and she tried to get up.

"*Puta cabrona*," he cursed and made a grab for her feet, clutched one.

She kicked out with the other. Missed his face, but got his shoulder. She tried to roll and get up. Saw him gather for a pounce, knife still at the ready. How the hell did he still hold that knife? He was too close, too damn close, but she was not going out without a fight. Somehow she managed another ear-piercing scream worthy of a fire engine, clutched some dirt from the ground, and threw it at his face before the man could slash her.

***

Richard had been pacing the terrace in front of the pool for what seemed to him hours. He couldn't believe Gabriela had gone to visit that asshole of a husband. He wanted to ram his fist against Roberto's face, break something, anything. He needed to vent by tearing something apart, and that desire was growing exponentially.

Spike, sprawled on one of the lounge chairs next to the grill, kept a keen eye on Richard while he alternated sips of beer with subtle grins. He doubted the man would lay a finger on Mrs. Martinez, but, at the moment,

Richard looked as if he could tear up the flagstones with his bare hands and do a good job of it. Always the good bodyguard, Spike lounged out here and kept a wary eye on this human pressure cooker. He needed to supervise Richard's spurt of angst just in case things got out of hand.

He swigged more of the beer, his lounging body cool almost at the level of discomfort. His gut instinct had been on the money this morning. Richard had played the catalyst—an explosive one at that. Patching events together from Richard's angry outbursts, things were definitely hopping, so much so it was difficult to keep up. Spike was secretly glad. Mrs. Martinez had long needed a champion, and Spike liked the guy. He liked the message 'This woman is mine. Don't touch' in Richard's eyes. Not something he'd seen much in this household since he'd been employed. Spike only hoped Richard would find a way to release his frustration soon, preferably before she came into view. If not, he would have to intervene, and Spike did not relish having to kick Richard's ass while getting his own kicked. Not this late into the evening.

"Where the hell is she?" Richard fumed. He glanced at his watch.

If it had been colder, Spike would have seen Richard's breath hang in the cold air. The pressure cooker image popped to mind and he grinned, despite the situation.

"Time's not going to move faster just because you want it," Spike said.

The man was right. Only three minutes had passed since he'd last looked at the time. But it felt like an eternity. Richard stopped and lifted his face, begging the night for patience. He gulped a huge breath of the cold air, held it for several seconds, and released it slowly. His brain kept processing the information he'd heard, trying to understand how Gabriela had not kicked her asshole husband out the door, why she had not divorced him the moment she'd found out he'd cheated on her, and why she hadn't come back to him.

He opened his eyes. He felt as if he would explode at any minute, and he didn't want to do it with her. He resumed his pacing, his jaw clenched. Why? Why? Why? Why was she staying? Why was she still loyal to a man who had clearly betrayed her, damn it? Roberto's actions had been intentional. Deliberate. A sudden picture of Enrique's expression at the office came to mind right after Gabriela's unwitting revelation. He had read the message clearly, so had Gabriela. But Enrique was wrong. Dead wrong. Richard and Gabriela had not planned what had happened in the safe house. Hell, they had tried to avoid falling into each other's arms since the beginning. Shit. He'd even sacrificed years without her for the sake of her marriage, for the asshole next door.

"Fuck."

Spike took pity. "She never stays more than fifteen minutes. Twenty, tops." He looked at his own watch. "She should be coming through soon."

As if on cue, Richard heard the soft tones of Gabriela wishing someone a goodnight. Roberto? His anger seethed. He veered in the direction of the sound. Took a step.

"I would hold off for a minute," Spike cautioned. He met Richard's eye, saw the warning, and ignored it.

"Give her space, time. She's had a bitch of a ride lately." *More like four years.*

Richard glared.

Spike shrugged. "Don't give a shit. I'm butting in anyway." His look was even. "My job is to protect. She does pay my exorbitant fees."

Richard took a deep breath, then another, and another. "You're right," he admitted. "She doesn't deserve the brunt of my anger. It's Roberto I want to pummel into the ground."

Spike didn't say he might never get the chance, but that was the only thing he would not reveal about his employer. It was not his job to come clean. It was hers.

"Glad to hear it," he said.

Relax. Give her time. Calm down. It's not her fault she was a generous woman. It was one of the reasons he had fallen in love with her—her humanity. He chided his impatience, his need.

He tensed. "Did you hear that?"

Spike sat up, placed the beer bottle on the floor.

"What?"

Richard shook his head for the other man to be quiet and strained to hear the sounds of the night. He thought he heard a grunt.

"Gabriela?"

No answer.

"Mrs. Martinez?" Spike echoed.

Not a peep, just some rustling. Could she have bumped into something? Why didn't she answer?

"I don't like this," Richard said. Spike wasted no time. He was beside Richard, listening as well.

The prickly sensation he'd had before became a burning burr on his butt now. Richard angled his head. There it was again, that rustling sound and—was that a hoarse whisper?

Something was wrong.

Richard sprinted toward the sound. By the time he reached the path between the two properties, he heard her vicious insult. By the time he heard her scream his name, he was running full tilt, Spike not far behind.

***

Herb Bryce sat in his car, camera on his lap, his eyes watching the display screen but not really focusing on what was captured there. He was still at the crime scene, the night dark and silent in stark contrast to hours before. Police, rescue, bystanders, his photo quarry, everyone was gone. *Everyone, except yours truly.* So, why was he still here, going over the photographs he'd taken, looking but not processing what he saw, like a newbie asshole? Why hadn't he gone home and sent out the photos to his editor and to the news media?

Because something was not right, his brain kept supplying. Something felt wrong, incomplete. There was much more to this story and he was missing a critical piece of the puzzle. That royally pissed him. He hated to be left in the dark. He hated for the narrative to be incomplete. That meant he might miss an opportunity for a bigger payoff, a bigger story.

He shook his head, the static of the police scanner occasionally jabbing at the silence of the night. He flicked to the next photograph. He didn't recognize the John Doe with Mrs. Martinez, but he recognized the limo. This man had probably been the one hiding behind the tinted windows this afternoon, the one whose identity Mrs. Martinez's bodyguard had so zealously protected.

He zoomed into the frame. Profiles became sharp. He had never seen this man. Didn't know who he was or how he tied in to Mrs. Martinez. He focused on their image as he brought the camera closer to his eyes. Shifted to the next photograph. There it was again, that ineffable message he got from the body language of these two. His was protective, caring. Herb would even go so far as to speculate, what, possessive? Hers, well, she was leaning into that safekeeping, almost with need? Herb would bet his next paycheck he was not wrong. There was familiarity there, electricity between them. These two shared a history, or he'd volunteer to babysit Gulper Marvin for a whole month.

"—copy unit 45," the scanner squawked.

Herb clicked to the next image and the next. The man's moves were smooth, practiced. He'd blocked Herb's view of Mrs. Martinez and placed her in that limo in less than five seconds flat.

"—a four-fifty-nine reported with a possible two-forty-five."

Herb was used to her evasive moves, but this? This was professional. Who the hell was this guy? Another thing, where was her husband? It was as if he'd fallen from the earth and disappeared. He usually wasn't around much, but lately, he'd been almost MIA.

"Four-fifty-nine. Copy. Has an eleven-forty-nine been dispatched?"

And the accident, Herb thought. From what he'd gathered from his interview with the police, they were checking into her car accident once more. He couldn't get much from them after that.

"Affirmative. Canyon Road and Mariposa. Copy."

There was something here he was not getting. This was not normal. *What? What?* His head snapped up as the address over the scanner sank in. That was Martinez's neighborhood. *What the hell?*

He reached for the knob of the scanner and spiked the volume.

"Copy. Four-fifty-nine, with possible two-forty-five at Canyon and Mariposa. Five minutes."

"Roger, 45."

Herb threw the camera onto the passenger seat of his car and pumped the gas. If he hurried, he'd have front row tickets to robbery, with a possible assault with a deadly weapon.

Herb Bryce smiled. His boss was going to get an orgasm from tonight's revenues. His smile widened. Best part was he was solo. Didn't have to share dick with asshole Marvin.

This woman's life was his fucking gold mine.

***

It took a second for Richard to assess the situation. Gabriela, on the ground, her face and shirtfront bloodied, was frantically scooting upward, trying to get some sort of purchase to flee her attacker. The goon was crouched at her scrambling feet, spitting dirt out of his mouth and using his forearm to get rid of the excess from his eyes. His foul curses filled the surrounding air like toxic fumes, his knife slicing the air like a pendulum.

Seeing Gabriela's bloody face unhinged Richard. He pointed in her direction and yelled to Spike, "Get her out of here. Now!" He followed words with action less than half a second later.

Richard rammed into the intruder, capsizing him in a direction opposite to Gabriela. Using his own momentum, he rolled, sprang up, and faced his attacker, whose lithe movements had landed him on his feet with the instinct and speed of a freaking cat. This was no amateur, Richard thought. This was an experienced street goon who knew how to fight dirty.

Now, halfway crouched, and still spitting dirt from his bloodied mouth, the man jabbed the knife at Richard in staccato movements, circling as he went. They sidestepped each other in this macabre dance for a minute, the man closing the circle with each forward stab. Richard waited, allowing the goon to think he was gaining ground, that he had the upper hand. The moment he stabbed forward again, trying to slice Richard's gut this time, Richard grabbed the wrist, jerked the arm forward, and jammed his knee into the elbow. He heard a pop. Without waiting for a reaction, and satisfied with the scream of pain reverberating in his ears, Richard followed with a vicious punch to the chin.

The asshole went down, squirming in pain, more filthy invectives jettisoned into the air.

Richard straddled the man, grabbed the front of his T-shirt, and slammed his fist into the goon's face once more. The man grunted, but stayed just above consciousness. Richard lifted and hit until he beat the man senseless.

Then he shook his hand as the pain hit.

"Shit," was all he said, and smiled.

Chapter Fourteen

"That was an effective way to release pressure," Richard commented, the irony of the situation not escaping him. Minutes before, he'd wanted to pummel Roberto's face until he'd flattened it. Now, he'd not only punched the cretin who'd attacked Gabriela to unconsciousness, but he'd also broken the cretin's knife arm as well. Very satisfying.

Spike jerked his head toward the goon now writhing on the ground next to the pool. The obscenities uttered, in two languages no less, were the best case of potty mouth Spike had heard in a long time.

"You know he'll accuse you of using excessive force, right? But, who's bitching?"

Richard smiled and nursed his lip with the ice Gabriela had brought for his battered knuckles. The prick had elbowed him when Richard had taken him down. Lucky punch. After that, the creep hadn't been so lucky.

"Nice take down, boss," Jeremy said, delivering a quick kick to the man on the ground. "It usually isn't this lively back home."

Richard answered Jeremy's grin with his own. "Welcome to my world with Gabriela."

"Funny," she quipped, not amused at all. Accurate, but not humorous.

She pivoted and paced back the way she had come. She should really paint this tableaux, one truly worthy of a Greuze. All the adults now sat or lay around the pool area, in various degrees of agitation, anger, shock, and bitchiness, waiting for the police to arrive. She'd passed Jeremy God knows how many times in the past five minutes, unable to stop herself, and wishing she could jab the occasional foot into her attacker's kidney, just like Jeremy was doing at the moment.

She glanced at Richard's bodyguard. Poor Jeremy. He'd been woken up by his boss and behaved like a trooper. Without being asked, he had taken control of the insensate piece of refuse who'd attacked her, trussed him up like a rodeo steer, and now stood guard over him like a quiet sentinel in the night. Probably had not slept much. He looked disheveled, with jogging pants and T-shirt hastily donned for propriety's sake, she was sure.

Enrique, with Bea in tow, had wanted one last word with her and had appeared at the pool house just in time to see Richard and Spike drag her knocked-out attacker into the area. They now sat next to each other on the outdoor chaise longue, hands clasped, various degrees of disbelief stamped on their faces. Her cousin kept shaking his head. Bea kept squeezing his hand, more for her own reassurance than for his.

Well, welcome to my world, Gabriela thought rather unkindly. They were getting a smidgeon of what she had faced before and with what she was confronted now.

As she passed in front of her cousin's wife, Beatriz offered, for the fifth time, comfort. Gabriela, for the last time, she hoped, refused her aid. She couldn't stand anyone but Richard touching her at the moment. She was filthy, felt grungy, was horrified and pissed all in a neat package, and wanted to keep the evidence of her attack untouched. Her skin felt tight and uncomfortable from the blood caking on her face, neck, hair, and shirt; the bruises on her arms, knees, and back were burning. She wanted to be held by Richard, to be comforted, but her body couldn't stay still, either. If she stopped, she would break down, and she needed to relay Wickeham's latest message to Richard and Spike. Needed to get her children out of the house immediately. Wanted to inflict more pain on the bastard writhing on the floor. Realized, if her attacker was really a gang member, her life had gotten even more complicated than before. These gangs didn't usually take kindly to attacks on one of their own. Retaliation could be swift and brutal.

Richard gently clasped her forearm and brought her to a full stop. He leaned forward, looking deeply into her eyes.

"Sweetheart. Stop."

"I can't," she said, her eyes relaying how she felt. "And we need to talk." Her gaze flitted between her attacker and Richard. "He said…" But she couldn't finish.

"We'll strategize later." Richard caressed her face, wanting to lean in, to kiss, and to envelop her in his arms. He'd almost had a heart attack when he'd seen her fighting for her life, the goon almost on her, his knife ready to slice her. He'd gone crazy then.

Approaching sirens sliced the tranquility of the night.

"After the police leave," he finished.

"About time," Enrique said. It was a welcome sound.

"Mr. Washington. Can you show them through the gate next door?" Gabriela requested, a tired hue tinting her voice. "I don't want the children disturbed. Warn the night nurse as well."

"On it," he said and sprinted toward the approaching sound.

Several minutes later, Spike led two patrol officers to the area, followed closely by the same EMTs who'd worked the scene at Mannie's garage.

One of the technicians scanned their faces. Recognition lit the man's eyes. "Busy night."

Hell. A comedian, Richard thought. "Yeah," he answered sarcastically and pointed to the yelling garbage on the ground. "Arm's broken."

"I broke his nose, too, I think," Gabriela put in.

The tech looked from the supposed victim to her bloody face and cuts. "Ma'am, you need to get treated."

Gabriela dismissed his concern with a wave. "It's mostly his," she answered and stepped to the nearest policeman to give her statement.

The next hours were a nightmare. On the heels of the squad car and ambulance, Detective Correia, all disheveled and none too happy with what was going on, entered the scene with the crime scene unit in tow. Gabriela led the detective to where she'd been assaulted. Richard followed her around like a constant shadow, listening to her account of the attack with deceptive silence. Glancing at him upon occasion, Gabriela judged he wanted to pulverize the bastard again.

After that things became a bit of a blur. The police took multiple photos of her face, arms, back, and front, cataloging her injuries. They snapped others of Richard's swollen knuckles and broken lip. They processed the scene where she'd been attacked in such minute detail, she doubted a speck of dust involved in the assault had not been processed and collected. They collected the goon's bloodied knife and her shirt. Her face had been Q-tipped for evidence, cleaned, and the cut covered with wound closure tape. They collected detailed statements about Richard's involvement and from Spike. The criminal had been read his rights, told he would remain in custody at the hospital, and was transported there by ambulance. Detective Correia followed close behind.

It was now after two o'clock. Gabriela gratefully sank down on the sofa and looked around at all the faces, some marred with fatigue, others with fear, and all depicting levels of concern.

Richard knelt in front of her and took one of her hands in his. Gabriela looked at him. His bottom lip was less puffy, and his clothing was scruffy, wrinkled, and torn from his fight with her attacker. She looked at his swollen and abraded knuckles, accentuated by the fierce hold of his hands, and her breath hitched.

His knuckles had to hurt. She freed her hand carefully, cradled his, and began to caress his injury ever so softly. She couldn't bear seeing him hurt because of her. Not anymore.

"I'm so sorry," she said softly. "I always seem to put you in harm's way."

Richard pressed her roving hand still. He leaned in, waited until her beautiful eyes focused on him. "No." He combed back her hair with his fingers. His forefingers stroked her jaw, his touch feathery gentle. "It's not your fault, love."

The fleeting smile was whimsical. "I guess it's too late to ask you to stop calling me that?"

He smiled, not widely because stretching the cut on his bottom lip burned like a bitch.

"Four years too late," he admitted.

Well, bollocks, Jeremy thought. He felt equal parts excluded, awed, awkward, and embarrassed at witnessing this very deep and personal scene. What these two had was similar to a slow burn—blanketing warmth enveloping every pore of your being, with a simmering passion waiting to be fanned into a conflagration. Theirs was something ineffable, almost intangible, yet fierce.

"What the hell's going on, Gaby?" Enrique asked. He looked uncomfortable, as if he did not want to know the answer.

God, when would Enrique and Bea leave? She wanted a hot shower to rinse all signs of the attack from her body; needed near-scalding water to take off a figurative layer of skin, to erase the touch of the attacker, to revive her cold body, which seemed to have grown colder and colder as time lapsed. The effects of adrenaline withdrawal were imminent and she needed to divulge the information she had not given the detective. They needed a plan of attack.

"The goon delivered a message," she said to all in general. The pained look Gabriela gave Richard next almost did him in. "He threatened…" She stopped and swallowed.

Richard waited.

Gabriela's eyes kept steady on his. "To kidnap and dispose of the children if I didn't agree to sell the manuscript to Wickeham right now."

"Son of a bitch," Richard exploded.

"Said he'd been watching the house," she added. "Hinted he's been at it for a couple of days."

Richard stared at Gabriela with eyes similar to fathomless pools of ice. If eyes could kill, she thought. If he'd known what he knew now, Gabriela was sure her attacker would be dead, and his body thrown into the Pacific rather than injured and at the hospital.

"We need to get everyone out of here, quickly," Richard said softly.

"Yes," she answered, her breath hitching on suppressed tears.

"Correia gave the usual can't divulge bullshit," Spike added. "But he reluctantly confirmed the asshole who attacked you was gang."

Enrique looked horrified. "Gang? Here? Jesus freaking Christ." He turned to Gabriela, his gaze incredulous. "Who the hell is this guy that can hire gang members? What the hell have you gotten the family into?"

Welcome to my messed-up world.

"Local?" Richard asked.

Spike shook his head. "More like LA. Word is new muscle has recently been trying to encroach onto established territories and activities around the Bay area."

"We need to work on strategy," Richard told her.

"Mr. Washington developed an emergency plan four years ago for such a case," Gabriela said. "We need to implement it."

Spike nodded. "Bits have to be altered, though."

"This is seriously fucked up," Enrique blasted.

"The children need to be moved to safety tomorrow. They can't go to school," Richard said. He looked at Gabriela. "Your mother and father will need to be removed as well."

She nodded, understanding the need to protect.

"Can everything be done incognito?" Richard asked Spike.

He nodded. "Part of the plan. We'll camouflage our exit better, though. Leave the area before taking final transport. We'll need to move the parents in the same manner as well. Convene at our prearranged meet."

"What about Roberto?" Richard asked.

"Roberto?" Enrique looked incredulous. "Roberto doesn't need protection. He's—"

"Enrique," Gabriela and Bea warned at the same time.

"*We* need protection…Bea, myself."

"I'll call Jean-Louis and Julien tomorrow… I mean today," Gabriela said. "They'll need to rework security at the gallery, at the event. Get prepared."

"The event?" Enrique said, his voice a bit incredulous. "You need to cancel it. Sell the piece."

"I'm not canceling anything," Gabriela said, her eyes disdainful.

"Are you crazy?" Enrique railed. "This guy won't stop until he gets what he wants."

"So we stop him," Richard said. "In London. It's the only way." He turned to Jeremy. "Call Morris later on, give him details, and relay everyone's contact numbers. See if he can come up with suggestions."

"This is insane," Enrique repeated.

"Go home, Enrique." She held her palm up to stop what she knew was another harangue and got up. "There is nothing much we can do now. Besides, I'm tired, filthy, and want to get some sleep." Her gaze swept across all the faces. "So does everyone else. What time should we meet?" she asked Spike.

"Six. Matthews and Rivers are on their way in. We'll start grinding all the details and work on prelims."

"I'm taking a shower." She turned around and disappeared in the direction of her bathroom.

***

Bryce was finally heading home. The level of satisfaction he felt was indescribable, his cupidity well met. As soon as he arrived at his house, he would cull the best photographs for publication and send those out immediately. His editor would prepare everything for publication and print his work by the next edition.

Headlines flitted through his brain, paired with the record of the night.

Crime Spree at Mannie's Garage – ka-ching.

Notorious Martinez's Mystery Man…Where Is Her Husband?

Nah. He didn't like that one.

Notorious Martinez Dumps Husband for Mystery Man. Now that had possibilities.

Better yet, *Martinez Love Triangle,* tagged with a small caption stating: *illustrator Gabriela Martinez torn between husband and hunk mystery man.* More ka-ching.

But the pièce de résistance was what he'd recorded at her house.

Gabriela Martinez's Gang Member Stalker Revealed – Gets Sent to Hospital. That didn't quite satisfy, but he'd think of something before he turned in for the night.

Herb drove into his driveway, a smug smile plastered on his face.

Ka-ching.

Chapter Fifteen

Gabriela stood in the middle of the bathroom, telling herself she needed to get on with things. It felt as if eons had passed since she'd stood like an automaton under the hot shower spray, rubbing shampoo with small, mechanized movements on her hair, face, and body, her brain desensitized to any thoughts, letting the water run over her body like a steaming salve. Her movements afterward were as robotic: she'd automatically donned her nightgown and covered that with a bathrobe, her brain outside herself. The bathrobe's heaviness and warmth had made her skin burn, so she had taken it off. More like dumped. The thing still lay on the floor like a disjointed form, much as she felt.

Her eyes viewed her reflection with detachment. Somewhere in the recesses of her mind, she knew she was probably suffering from delayed shock, but her brain refused to care. She should weep, yet her eyes stayed dry. She needed to put salve on her scraped and broken skin, but her hands would not move. She should go to bed. She didn't. She just stayed riveted in place, her reflection gazing blankly back, her body like a car permanently set in neutral.

Slight tremors vibrated along her nerve endings and muscles. Her body felt tight to her, as if compressed, held wound to such a degree that, if what was holding her in place snapped, she would explode like a supernova. *Sit down, sit down before you faint,* her mind screamed. But the sound echoed faintly inside her, as if coming from an abyss. Maybe she was frozen in time, unable to break that stasis? She blinked and saw her reflection blink. Her eyes roamed down her body, saw her hand clutching something, and raised it. Moisturizer, she read. With slightly trembling hands, she placed the glass container very carefully on the counter top and slid it out of reach with her forefinger.

Her breath hitched. She closed her eyes, splayed her arms to grab the counter's edge, and leaned forward. She needed to anchor herself to something tangible. She felt disoriented and her legs had a rubbery feel to them now. Like a somnambulist, she straightened, glanced around, and retreated to sit at the tub's edge, but slid to the tile floor instead. She bent her legs, hugged them, and dropped her head on her knees.

How could this be happening to her once more? How could her life be in such chaos again? What had she done in life to deserve this?

Her position suddenly shifted. Gabriela's body and brain registered things simultaneously: someone sat next to her, and a strong, warm arm embraced her shoulders, pressing her body against heat and strength.

Richard.

Gabriela slanted her head and her eyes collided with Richard's intensely concerned ones. His hair was wet like hers, his gray T-shirt deepening his eyes to a smoky color. He trapped a wet strand of hair behind her ear and cupped her chin with his palm.

Raised her face.

Slowly leaned in.

The kiss was soft, offering consolation rather than passion. Gabriela instinctively gravitated toward its succor, its warmth. He continued the gentle assault again, and again. Nibbled at her lower lip. Explored her mouth slowly like a wine aficionado extracting all the flavors and bouquet of what was tasted.

He retreated.

Gabriela fisted her hands on his T-shirt and whimpered, bereft at this loss. He pressed her face into his shoulder, placed a whisper of a kiss on her head, and began a hypnotic caress of her face.

"Shh," he whispered. "It's all right. I'll take care of you."

Gabriela choked, imploded. Tears gathered and began to flow—round, wet drops that fell without touching skin. Her body heaved. She was suffocating on her own emotions and her lungs tried to expand every few seconds to gather air. She was drowning, and only Richard's arms tethered her from getting lost in the storm of her own making.

Richard felt her tremors and her tears, and wanted to howl in anger. He gathered her in even closer. He wanted to erase the memories, the hurt, and the nightmare of the attack. He'd rather she were ranting and raving, cursing from here to the end of the galaxy. He'd prefer her violence rather than this controlled, desperately silent weeping.

He began rocking her until his back muscles screamed in complaint. He realized they needed to get up from the cold tile floor, or they would be even worse messes in a couple of hours.

He gathered himself, ground his teeth, and lifted her in his arms. Her body vibrated against his own, wracked with spasms. Richard stood. He had spotted a very comfortable-looking wing chair in a small niche offset to the right of her bed when he had come into her bedroom. He headed in that direction and sat with her on his lap, at all times keeping to his comforting whispers, cradling her like a child, wanting to absorb her tremors, to stop the flow of hurt.

"Don't cry, sweetheart," he repeated over and over, caressing her face. "Please don't cry. You know I hate to see you cry."

He cradled her, breathed in her scent, and felt her warmth. He loved this woman so much he felt overwhelmed by it. And despite their years of separation, that love had not abated, but grown. How could that be even possible? Realization dawned that it had everything to do with the knowledge Gabriela was the mother of his child. This sensation was alien to him, and yet, it was as real as breathing. How exactly could he define it? Was it a sense of fulfillment he felt? No, not quite. It was more a sense of completeness.

Richard lost track of time. Gabriela's body began to relax. Her shivers receded. He gathered her closer and leaned his head on the chair's left wing. He closed his eyes and began to sink into welcome slumber.

"Why didn't you answer?"

The whisper penetrated and he was shocked awake.

"What?"

"Why didn't you? I wrote. Twice."

Richard tensed as if hit. "What are you talking about?"

"At first, I only asked for a word here and there from you. A postcard," she whispered, a world of remembered pain etched on her voice. "To keep in touch, even if sporadically, until I could figure things out. I didn't ask for more."

"Did Maurice know of this?"

Gabriela shook her head. "Mailed them directly to your office. Never returned. The world seemed to have swallowed you up. Didn't know if you had been killed." She gulped and cuddled closer to his warmth.

Richard couldn't speak. She had contacted him. He hadn't really imagined she'd actually reach out immediately to touch base with him, to keep some line of communication open and alive between them. He should have expected it, even when he'd asked her not to in his letter, at least not until her marriage had failed of its own accord. Now he understood her initial reticence, her reaction to his presence yesterday, her lack of trust.

"My last one...I...well...when I...you know...my pregnancy...such silence. I assumed the worst."

What could possibly be worse, he thought, than her believing he was dead?

"Assumed what?" he asked her quietly.

She didn't respond.

He squeezed her shoulder and urged, "Gabriela?"

"That you had abandoned me," she stated from the vicinity of his chest, her voice muffled. Her breath hitched. "That you had moved on, found someone else."

At this moment, Richard wanted to tear chunk by despicable chunk off his former boss until only a bloody mass of pulp remained. He tried to focus on Gabriela rather than on this raw urge to eviscerate Jack Seldon. What had he expected from his bastard of a former boss? Seldon would have read and ditched her letters, ignored her pleas. He squeezed his eyes shut, trying to regain control from this overwhelming need to lash out and destroy. He was an ass. Isn't that what everyone said about those who assumed? He'd assumed many things, particularly placing his trust in a man who thought about the mission first rather than the personal needs of his agents. Assumed she would contact Maurice rather than Jack. Assumed she would not reach out before she had come to a decision about her marriage, as he had asked.

"Look at me."

It broke his heart to see her eyes overflowing with tears, some of which had meandered across her cheeks. He breathed deeply and dried one with his thumb. Anger battled it out with love and determination.

"I never received your letters."

"Never?"

The brief doubt he saw telegraphed there hurt him deeply.

"Damn it," he lashed out. "How could you believe I would ever abandon you?"

"You disappeared the very day you promised to stay at my side."

"Shit," he voiced in exasperation. "I had to debrief. Had no choice. I told you—"

"I know what you said," she said testily, her own anger growing. "Believe me, the contents of your letter are forever etched in my brain."

"But I explained—"

She took a deep, steadying breath.

"That was unfair," she said and squeezed him to relay her apology. Reproaching Richard was not the answer.

"You were right, you know. I had to give my marriage a chance. The regrets, otherwise, would have destroyed me...us. So I honored your request, but I couldn't your silence. I only wanted a sign of life, of caring." She shrugged. "Was I selfish?"

"No," he said and kissed her forehead. How could love still grow for this woman? He rubbed his cheek against her hair. "No. Just human."

"Who intercepted my letters?" she said.

"My boss." Richard spit out the words as if they were acid.

"Why? What was so wrong about them?"

"Sweetheart, my ex-boss was and still is a bastard of the highest caliber. Probably knew I'd skip whatever mission I was working on as soon as I heard from you."

Some humor brimmed in her eyes. "You mean you'd have arrived unannounced at my door to claim me?"

"Damn right," he said. He splayed his hands in her hair, anchored her head, and kissed her with all the passion, love, and desire he'd held back. There was no apology, either, for the underlying carnality of his need.

Richard's emotions were like a devastating vortex dragging her into the furnace of his need, and she returned his kiss with an abandon not in her nature—at least, not with anyone but Richard. If she had been standing, she would have melted through his arms and landed like a boneless puddle on the floor.

A lifetime passed. They surfaced for air and stared at one another. Hunger and need. Gabriela attempted to control her wayward mind and body. This was not the time, nor the place to make reckless love. The children were near. It would be wrong now, in her home. Her marriage was still not dissolved, although that issue would not have stopped her now. But the children...

She placed her hand on his chest in, what? Appeasement? A promise?

"We can't," she whispered and kissed him softly. "Not here. Not yet. More so now than ever."

Richard begged his brain and body for control.

"I know," he acknowledged and gave her one last ravenous kiss before he pulled back.

Her sigh was deep and shaky as she dropped her head back on his shoulder. She could hear the chaotic beating of his heart, one that resembled her own so much. Felt his hand splay against her flat abdomen, press there.

"Was it difficult?" He tried to imagine their child growing there, moving, kicking. Life. His life linked and burgeoning within her. So much he had missed. His chest ached.

"No," she whispered. "No complications. Quick labor. Hurt like the dickens, as usual."

"Cursed me, huh?"

"More than you'd care to know." Her smile was soft.

Richard shifted their bodies, made them more comfortable on the chair. For a brief span of time, silence became their blankets.

"Does he know?"

Gabriela knew what he meant. "No. He's been a good father, Richard. Despite his flaws, Roberto loves our children and would do anything for them."

Richard bent his head and kissed her softly. "Thank you."

Her eyes, a bit bewildered, asked the question her lips did not.

"Another would have terminated or given away our child. Been abusive," Richard said, his voice suddenly dry, toneless. "But you gifted me with Luisito. He's beautiful, happy, content." For a moment, Richard thought of his own sterile childhood. "Loved," he finished.

"Oh, Richard." Her voice broke. She understood his past only too well. Four years ago, his recounting of it had broken her heart. It still did.

"I can't stay away now, Gabriela. I need him…hell I need both of you permanently back in my life." He made eye contact. "Will you deny me?"

"No." She took the plunge. "I already asked Roberto for a divorce," she admitted. "I was going to contact Maurice the day Roberto suffered the accident."

Richard kissed her. He couldn't help it. She'd finally made her choice, and he was that choice. Something in him expanded and settled. She was his.

Richard released her lips and pressed her face against his heaving chest. He'd better stop that. His body hurt and ached for her, and the bed was so conveniently close. He needed another shower—this time a very, very cold one.

"What now?" she whispered. "The children need to be protected. I won't allow them to witness anything inappropriate between us. Everything must stay under wraps until the divorce is finalized. And that's not happening any time soon."

"Why don't you tell me, then, what is really going on with Roberto?"

The sudden, utter stillness in her body and breathing confirmed what he'd suspected.

"Enough of the runaround, sweetheart. What are you not telling me? Why does everyone freeze and tiptoe around you at the first mention of your soon to be ex-husband?"

Jesus. Richard and his gut. Who needed a lie detector test? Still, it was difficult to open up. Gabriela was not accustomed to sharing, to being the open book she once had been.

"Well?" His tone remained unyielding.

"Because no one knows I asked Roberto for a divorce and, after the accident, things got complicated."

"I know, but that's not all," Richard stated with conviction.

"Weeks before he was injured, Roberto finalized a new process for plastics that would revolutionize the industry, but he had not filed for a patent yet. Then the crash happened. I didn't know what he'd planned until I went over his notes. Thankfully, he'd completed the patent applications before his injuries. From then on it was a scramble: the lawyers setting up the POA, Enrique running the day-to-day minutiae in the office, keeping Roberto's condition from his executives, rushing the patent search. Our most critical problem was the preliminary search with the Patent Trademark Office. The lawyers warned, in no uncertain terms, if we divulged what we were doing, we could lose everything. No one can breathe a word until the patent has been approved, and I can't divorce him until then."

Richard didn't say anything, digesting the information. Something still didn't add up. He knew very well, since he'd dealt with lawyers most of his life, what a POA meant. Why the hell would Gabriela need power of attorney? Why the hell did she need to wait to get divorced?

"Sorry, sweetheart, but I'm still confused. Isn't Roberto next door, handling business from there? Why are you so engaged in his company, in his troubles? Why bring your cousin into the picture? Why are you still not divorced?"

"He's incapacitated," Gabriela said. "He's in—"

The phone screamed.

Her body jerked, and she jackknifed off Richard's lap with the agility of an acrobat. *Oh, God. Oh, God.* Had something happened to Roberto, she thought frantically, her heart beating in a crescendo inside her throat. Before she reached for the receiver, Richard stopped her.

"My bet is on Wickeham. Put him on speaker."

She nodded, took slow breaths to calm her racing heart, picked up the receiver, and pressed the speaker and record button of the phone simultaneously.

"Hello?" she croaked.

"Good morning, Mrs. Martinez," the cultured voice of Wickeham invaded her room. "I hope I have not disturbed your slumber?"

Gabriela gritted her teeth. Richard's gut scored once more. It was the cultured bastard. She should have guessed it'd be him. Why should tonight be any different?

"Oh, no, Mr. Wickeham," she answered snidely. "I cavort every day till dawn just so that I'm awake to take your calls."

There was a chuckle at the other end. Could a chuckle sound cold? Gabriela swore she felt this man's chilly breath slither through the receiver. Richard tensed beside her, but kept quiet.

"Dear Madam. Your wry humor never ceases to impress me."

"Then cease to be amazed and come to the point. What do you want now?"

"Mrs. Martinez," he chided. "I thought I'd made that quite plain. Must I repeat myself? How tedious."

"And how many times must I repeat myself? It's rather tiresome to constantly inform you that I'm not interested in selling to you or anyone else before the auction. Why can't my refusal finally sink into that thick skull of yours?"

"Really, Madam. There is no need to be so uncivilized over this issue. My offer, after all, is quite reasonable and lucrative. It would be extremely wise, and healthy, if you accept it. I do so hate it when I'm forced to switch my persuasive methods to more, shall I say, aggressive techniques? I thought you would be more agreeable to my suggestion after this evening. Your persistent refusal in this game is rather bothersome."

Richard made a grab for the receiver. Gabriela evaded him, swatting at his hand and shaking her head.

"I fail to see this as a game. I may be an artist, but a fool, I'm not. And I'm fed up with your harassment and innuendoes. You want my work? Very well. Fork over the money at the auction like everyone else will. I won't cheat the parish children out of their future on your whim and overly inflated ego." She waited for that to sink in before she added, "Oh, and by the way. Thank you for the message, but it's been denied. Your messenger is currently under arrest at the hospital where he is suffering, shall I say, multiple injuries?"

If silence could slap, she'd be knocked down on the floor. When Wickeham spoke, his voice was cutting, brittle, like cracked ice.

"I regret you have not understood me clearly on this point, Madam. You will eventually sell your *Book of Hours* to me, and to none other. It is lamentable you're so obstinate and require further convincing."

"Don't hold your breath," she said with impatience. "I'm not going to change my mind."

"We'll see," Wickeham began, but Gabriela didn't let him finish. She rammed the receiver back in its cradle before Wickeham said anything else. In the same movement, she reached over and unplugged the phone. If an emergency arose, the nurses would reach her through her cellular.

Richard hugged her and gave her a swift kiss. "Bravo. Thought the son of a bitch would have an apoplexy when he heard his latest goon was arrested."

"So did I." Gabriela saw the savage pleasure in Richard's eyes.

"Vindictive, aren't we?" she asked.

"To the max."

He grinned.

She grinned back.

Chapter Sixteen

Gabriela stared at the Pacific. She stood at the edge of the rock outcropping beneath her terrace; the sea, restless, its waters a forbidding, murky gray-blue reflected her mood to a T. Miles to the west a storm was brewing, but she guaranteed the low front arriving in the late afternoon would be a tame one in comparison to the imminent whirlwind that would soon hit her life.

This was her moment of respite, with her thoughts in sync with the sea, gathering strength and peace in any way she could.

Since dawn, the house had been a plethora of activity, with all the adults scrambling to get things done. She had escaped here, not from the commotion inside her house, or from the ton of people demanding her attention in one way or another, but from maintaining an excited façade for the children. All she had wanted was a private moment to allow the sadness to envelop her. Spike wanted to leave with the children before the forecasted storm hit, preferably within the next half hour.

Thank you, Action News 8, for predicting the local weather so accurately.

Unfair, unfair, unfair. The urgency to remove the children from her vicinity was, well, urgent, she thought, especially after yesterday's attack. Their departure could not be derailed and must be done before anyone else got wind of what was happening, especially Herb Bryce. Her face scrunched up in disgust. How the man had shown up at her house last night was still a mystery. What was appalling to her was how carelessly intrusive he'd become last night, snapping pictures of the police, ambulance, goon, and everything else he could record. He'd tried to sneak into her yard as well, but Spike had prevented it. This morning, everyone had conceded nothing would stop Mr. Bryce from appearing on her doorstep later in the day to document her moves, the children's. Possibly follow Spike. The trick was to avoid him at all costs.

Ergo, the rush to remove the children was of paramount importance, with her, Richard, and Jeremy disappearing at a close second.

Well, the children were packed and ready to go, enthused at this surprise vacation with *Abuelo* and *Abuela*. She was packed, thanks to the help of Jean-Louis earlier. Richard and Jeremy were packed, basically because they hadn't had time to unpack. Spike was packed. Everyone was packed, packed, she thought inanely.

Gabriela hugged her stomach in a protective move. Matthews and Rivers would arrive soon with the rentals to pick up Spike and the children. She felt guilty at disrupting her sons' lives, at placing them in danger through no fault of their own. Her body quivered as if she were shaking off dust. *Be fair,* she admonished. Things weren't her fault, either. What kind of man would go to such extremes to obtain one of her works? This just didn't happen in real life, damn it. What were the odds of facing another lunatic who was out for blood? Her blood?

Gabriela shook her head. The point was moot. The possibility of harm to her children was not. She saw no other way out of this mess but to implement the protective measures on which they'd decided. She could handle anything directed her way, but it would be a hotter day in hell before she allowed anyone, *anyone,* to touch a hair on her children, or abduct them, or hold them for ransom. And this maniac had no scruples and showed no signs of aborting his plans, so she needed to stop him; she needed to sell that manuscript quickly. Richard had suggested, once the piece left their hands, Wickeham's focus on her would vanish. Somehow, she doubted it. From her conversations, and her own gut, this man was probably a vindictive bastard. Even if Jeremy's friend, this Morris, came up with a foolproof plan to incriminate this idiot and bury him in jail, her instincts assured her Wickeham would get even from prison. Let's hope, she thought, Richard was correct: selling her work and landing the cretin in jail would end everything. Then, maybe, she could get her life back on track, finalize the divorce when the patent went through, and begin a new life with Richard.

Richard.

The smile that touched her face lifted the heaviness around her. They'd had their first tug of war a couple of hours before dawn. She'd wanted him to return to the pool house and sleep there. He had adamantly refused, hunkering down on the wing chair, covering his body with a blanket any which way. He'd told her, point-blank, he wasn't budging. That she'd better get used to it. Gabriela thought it was pointless and told him so. After a whispered back and forth, she gave up, flopped face down on the bed and slept the sleep of the dead until her dog decided to bark his greeting, front paws on the bed and snout near her ear, Richard's laughter harmonizing in the background.

She had exploded with energy after waking. Richard's doing, she knew. Getting everything out of her system was also another reason her adrenaline was flowing. She smirked in self-deprecation. *Ha,* her brain scoffed. Her reaction to Richard was the real culprit for the excess in productivity. She smiled, remembering the wild kisses. *Wow.* Had that been her? Her body reacted to the memory. *Yeah.* It also felt liberating Richard knew about Roberto, that he understood the stakes and was willing to stick it out, and that he had her back. That she was no longer alone.

Maybe, now, she could have a future.

Maybe Roberto could have one as well.

She sighed. Not for the first time, she fervently prayed her husband would come out of the coma. Despite their personal problems, despite the fact they had grown apart and now only shared their love for the children, Roberto was a good man. He deserved happiness, even when, this time, Fate had dealt him a crappy card during the last shuffle. In spite of everything, Gabriela didn't want her children to grow up without their father. It was not fair.

She sighed, looked at her watch, and decided she could give herself another five minutes. Nature had always been her soothing balm. Waves, riled up by the wind, crashed against the boulders near her, spraying foam and water into the air. She inhaled the salty wind. If only she could literally throw her troubles into the Pacific and have the turbulent sea chomp up, swallow, and digest her woes at the bottom of the ocean. But life was never that easy.

She should know.

***

Richard kept an eye on the terrace area where wooden stairs angled toward the shoreline at the edge of Gabriela's property. Ten minutes ago, he'd watched her escape through the French doors of the living room to disappear down the steps there at a fast clip. She had always done that in moments of need, he remembered. Solitude regrouped her thoughts, helped her to gather herself. It was her way to cope, juggle, and settle everything, so as to regain some control of her emotions. He didn't blame her. Right now she needed the distance. He'd seen her struggle with her feelings since early this morning. Seen her battle unhappiness as they had discussed last-minute details, including finalizing alterations to her travel plans to Europe and increasing security measures at the gallery and at the event. But, during the past hour especially, her gaze had turned downright distressed at the imminent departure of her sons. He was surprised the house wasn't vibrating with the bleak overtones to some turbulent classical orchestral piece. She had blasted his eardrums with one in France, playing it at a moment of anguish.

Richard checked the terrace once more. He'd give her another five to ten minutes. The first part of the plan, the children's safety, needed implementation, the quicker the better. Therein lay his restlessness, one derived from the visceral necessity to protect the children, get them out of harm's way immediately. The more they delayed, the better the chances of things going wrong, of someone following, of anyone interfering.

Especially Herb Bryce.

The man was a sadistic leech, turning up to suck as much of Gabriela's misery as he could profit from.

His gaze shifted to his son, a little whirlwind of activity without a pause button. He had zipped here and there since he had woken up this morning, the dog faithfully following behind in excited adoration. Richard thought fleetingly about the dog's name. Was it somehow an acknowledgment honoring the animal's faithful mimicry of their son? He zeroed in on his son's latest antics. Luisito kept butting two dinosaurs in a gloriously loud and convoluted battle royal, sound effects and all. He was also all over the living room, circling the place God knew how many times, often standing, oblivious to all, in front of the television set where his two brothers were having a different battle with a very loud video game. During those moments, the adults would know the exact position of Luisito by the occasional, frustrated eruptions from his older brothers of, "Shut up, Luisito," or the, "Get out of the way." Richard didn't know how Gabriela kept up. He was exhausted from watching all the boys, from answering the occasional, but repetitive demands from Luisito's active brain, and dizzy from keeping tabs on him. The craziness would need some getting used to if he wanted to remain a sane parent.

The thought floored him for an instant. He was a parent, a dad. He had created this child together with Gabriela.

He closed his eyes briefly, remembering the early morning. Emotions swirled through his blood and he savored the pleasure coursing within. He rubbed at the puckered scar on his chest. These daily doses of Gabriela, something so simple, so mundane to others, had generated fulfillment at such a scale he was blindsided by it. The depth of gratification when he'd brought her face forward and kissed her deeply had vibrated him like a rocket blast. The normal, what he'd wanted and hungered for years, especially with this woman, was taken for granted by many.

But not by him. He could have that now, he thought, once they got rid of Wickeham.

"Any sign of her yet?" Spike asked.

Luisito decided to bring his dinosaur war next to the adults. The dog barked and jumped, trying to get at the plastic animals.

"No. I was going to give her another five." Richard opened the French doors and ushered both boy and canine out. "Okay, my little dynamo. Out. You can run to your heart's content out there."

Richard watched as his son ran around the terrace like a madman. Within seconds, he finally settled down next to the balustraded retaining wall, dinosaurs ambling jerkily at its top, and Zip looking on rapturously, tail wagging like helicopter blades on steroids.

Jeremy joined the men. "Reservations are set for New York, with same day to London." He smiled knowingly. "Babysitter and all."

Richard scowled. He was not pleased at the latest wrinkle to his objective of getting Gabriela all to himself. An hour after Jean-Louis had arrived to help out, her cousins had descended on the house. Upon hearing their finalized plans, the good *padre* had altered his own travel schedule, since Enrique and Bea couldn't leave to attend the auction.

"Screw you," Richard said. "Meeting with the execs on track?"

"Vivian confirmed, as well as your lunch reservations at Le Bernardin." Jeremy didn't divulge the extreme blitz defense he'd had to use against Vivian's curiosity and pointed questions.

"Parents on the way?" Richard asked Spike.

"Left several hours ago. Should make their flight with no problems."

"Let us know the moment you arrive at the destination." Richard saw Luisito drop the dinosaurs on the ground and disappear down the stairs with the dog. That should get Gabriela moving. He glanced at his watch. Time to leave.

"What about the scumbag who attacked Gabriela?"

"According to Correia, processed and booked. LA wants to claim dibs on the asshole, though, and that is pissing the good detective. Seems the jerk riddled a competitor down there a few months ago. Three .45 slugs in the gut." Spike sniffed, disgusted. "The dude is a real pisser."

"Did you relay we're making ourselves scarce?"

"That pissed Correia off, as well." Spike grinned. "But he can't stop us."

"Would have wanted to be a fly on his wall after you informed him you'd be incommunicado."

Jeremy chuckled. "Wait until Michael calls him. He'll really sound off."

"Frankly, I don't give a shit," Richard said. "As long as Correia doesn't butt in until we're done with Wickeham, I'll be happy."

The dog banged a paw against the glass, startling the men. The animal had returned, sans Luisito, and now stared at them from the other side of the French doors.

"Is this his way of knocking?" Richard asked, amused.

"Yeah," Spike replied. "He's a pain in the ass when he wants to come in."

The dog banged the glass once more. Well, the animal was insistent, Richard had to give him that. He cracked open the door just enough so that Zip could squeeze through.

But the dog refused to come in. Zip began to pace, agitated, whimpering and looking toward the terrace stairs.

"What the hell is wrong with him?" Spike asked. "Stupid animal. Come."

But the dog wouldn't budge. Zip began to bark, front paws splayed, head thrust forward, looking at the men. Richard stared, thinking the animal meant business. The dog turned in the direction of the stairs, came back, and whined. The quality of those whimpers was different from those of regular playfulness.

"Something's wrong," Richard said and ran.

***

"*Mami.*"

Gabriela turned, smiling as the cacophony of footsteps and nail clicks reached her. As was his habit, Luisito had barreled down the steps, Zip not missing a beat behind.

She bent at the waist, grabbed her son in midstride, raised him, and hugged him tightly. She knew she'd need to stay one step ahead of Zip, who always enthusiastically welcomed any participation in hug fests. If that happened, she'd have a seventy-pound fuzz ball on top of her. She didn't relish landing on her butt on top of this granite.

Luis pushed his upper torso away from his mother and looked at her.

"What are you doing?" he began, and then there was no stopping him afterward. "When are we leaving? Can I take more dinosaurs? Why can't Zip come with us? I'm hungry."

He framed her face with his chubby hands. "*Mami,* Tico and Tavi told me to shut up."

Gabriela grinned. "Did they?"

He bobbed his head up and down several times. "Can we go now? I want to see Abo and Aba. They'll like my new duck. Will it take long? Where are we going?"

Gabriela closed her eyes. If her heart were an orange, it would be pulp at the moment. She didn't know where Spike was taking them. That had been a nonnegotiable in the plan from the very beginning. Richard had fumed at that. But he'd understood the need as well. If any one of them were captured or tortured, the location of the children could never be divulged. Nor would she be able to give a phone number. Spike was using what he called a burner phone. Whenever they moved location, he would type in a prearranged code letting her know everything was going according to plan. If he didn't get back her own modified, alternating code answering his A-okay, he'd go to plan B immediately.

"Abo and Aba want to surprise you, but I'm sure you and your brothers will have a wonderful time."

"*Mami,* I want to take Zip."

She hugged her son. "Zip will be fine at Lupe's. You don't want him to get cold or sad in a cage on an airplane, do you?"

He shook his head, his eyes huge, a teary film in them shifting their shape and color.

Gabriela placed him on the ground. "Time to go, Squirt." She began tickling him.

Luisito giggled and darted here and there from her outstretched hands, trying to avoid her wiggly hands, but not quite achieving it.

Gabriela laughed, following him around, her fingers tickling neck, sides, and belly. It helped her more than her son when she made a game of their departure. Zip kept pace, jumping into the action, barking, snout-butting them, and running in circles.

She guided him to the stairs. There, the going up was much more of a chore for Luisito's chubby legs than the coming down. With his little hand in her own, she lifted her son as he jumped on top of every step, each hop counted like the Count from Sesame Street. Once on the middle deck, she chased him a bit more. He grabbed her leg, placed his little feet on top of her sneakers. She dragged him around a bit like a spastic Frankenstein monster.

"Okay, my little koala, let's go." She lifted his body and twirled. By the time she finished, breathless, they were both giggling uncontrollably.

"More, *Mami.* More."

She pressed his face on her shoulder, squeezed, and breathed in his scent. Oftentimes she wished Robertico and Gustavito were still this old. There was always something special about your child's entire, small body pressed intimately to yours. Their irrepressible life, hope, and love vibrated through to your every pore. Robertico's and Gustavito's hugs were now different. Not lacking. Just different. Every embrace already had the quality of an older, more settled, growing-up love. The already independent, trying-to-keep-your-distance-but-we-still-love-you love. This loving with such recklessly abandoned hugs still just melted your heart.

She lost her balance, swayed, and corrected her stance. She must be dizzier than she thought.

"Up," she ordered the dog. She took a step and the platform swayed.

Gabriela stilled.

"*Mami?*"

The swaying was minimal, but she felt it. Earthquake?

"Shh. Stay still."

Nothing. She took another step, felt a board shift beneath her. She tiptoed onto the next board and didn't move.

The dog turned back to join them. There was more movement, a small tremor from the soles of her feet reaching her arms.

"No, Zip. Up. Stay."

She stared at the next stage of stairs. Did they look a bit lopsided? She inched closer, grabbed the railing with her left hand, but instead of feeling strength, she felt it give way. She let go, compensated backward, felt the deck shift beneath her, sway farther, quiver, and settle. Something cracked, dropped, and settled.

"*Mami.*" Voice edged with fear, Luisito grabbed his mother, arms squeezing her neck, cheek pressed to her own.

"Don't move, sweetie. Hold on to Mami. It's a little earthquake."

But was it?

Zip was whining, his fur trembling from the quiver in his muscles. He wanted to be with them, but was obedient. *Good dog,* she thought inanely. She shuffled slowly to the railing close to the wall. With every slight move, the platform shifted. The deck was now her own personal balance board, with her and her son as disproportionate weights to destabilize it.

Gabriela looked at her dog. Knew the command that would draw attention.

"Zip…fetch."

This wasn't an earthquake. Son of a bitch Wickeham had struck again.

***

Richard and the dog came to a stop at the stair opening. The sight greeting him was not what he had expected. Gabriela was standing stock-still, their son holding fiercely to her neck, looking up at him when he appeared. *What the hell?*

Richard scanned the surrounding area, but saw no threat. Spike and Jeremy flanked him. They looked equally perplexed.

The dog kept whining.

"Stupid dog." Richard negated his scold with a caress on the dog's head as he focused on Gabriela's face. Fear and anger reflected from her eyes by turns. Something was not right. He stepped forward.

"Don't," came the guttural whisper.

Richard froze. Waited.

Her eyes tried to project so many words and emotions. Would Richard read her cues? What would alert them without frightening Luisito?

"Earthquake," she said.

The men looked at each other.

"But, Mrs. Martinez," Spike began, "there's no…"

Gabriela shook her head, but the movement was so careful, ponderous, and slow, she resembled a security camera set to capture every pixel in its arc range. It telegraphed her anxiety more effectively than if she had done it with a swift careless shake.

Richard's words attempted at nonchalant, but the tension seeped through. "Explain."

Gabriela raised her free hand and, mimicking her head movement of seconds before, pointed to the stairs, railing, and especially the platform, enumerating silently the problem spots by dipping her fingers. Then she moved her entire hand in a movement resembling the waves of the ocean. Her lips pressed together in her effort to remain as still as possible. Circulating blood drained.

She brought her hand to caress her son's head slowly.

The platform shifted. Gabriela, fraction by fraction, spread her legs, trying to get better purchase and balance for what she needed to show Richard. She hooked her hand underneath Luisito's armpit, and made a slow motion to heave up, her body straining upward, looking at the wall, inching her feet closer and closer to it. She needed a good angle to pass her son over to safety, and hoped to God her meaning was understood.

Luisito, feeling the body separation, whimpered and clung harder to his mother's neck.

"Rope?" Richard asked.

"Nothing that would hold them," Spike answered over Gabriela's choked mewl.

Richard gauged the distance to maneuver without placing anyone in danger. Picked the most reasonable spot and bent over the retaining wall.

"Spike. Jeremy."

The men didn't need any prodding or explanation. Spike positioned himself between Richard's legs, grabbed his shins, and anchored them against his body with his elbows. He bent forward slowly, carrying Richard downward like a wheelbarrow. Jeremy grabbed Spike's waist, pasted his feet against the bottom angle between wall and ground, dropped his butt, and hung on as counterweight.

Gabriela watched Richard slide down slowly. She again soothed her son, caressing his hair with her cheek and hand, spreading small kisses on top of his head.

"Sweetheart, Richard is going to grab you, okay?" She angled her face to look into his eyes, smiling softly so as not to scare him, making him believe this was normal, adventurous.

"When I tell you, lift your arms."

Luisito shook his head. He wasn't buying it. He clung harder to her neck.

Gabriela filled her lungs with patience. Of all the times for her son to turn stubborn. "It's a new swing game. It's going to be fun."

Luisito looked up and saw Richard stretching his arms to reach him. He giggled and looked at his mother. "He looks like a monkey." He laughed louder, delighted, and reached up without being told. His fingers barely grazed Richard's.

Gabriela tried to steady them from the renewed wobble of the platform, moving her body in counterpoint to its direction. *Please, God. I don't care if something happens to me. But don't let anything happen to my little baby. Please. Please. Please. I'll do anything. Promise anything. Let him get to safety.*

Without looking away from Gabriela and Luisito, Richard ordered Spike to lower him more.

"Raise your arms real high, sweetie. Mami will raise you."

Carefully, Gabriela shifted and raised her son at the same moment Richard reached down. She felt as if she'd grabbed a car and tried to hoist it barehanded like Superwoman. Richard reached, grabbed the little extended wrists, and locked his hands with enough pressure to hold the boy securely but not enough to squeeze with the intensity of the fear drag racing through his veins.

"Okay." Richard smiled at his son and made a silly face to divert his attention. How could a little body weigh so much? "Pull, guys."

Inch by slow inch, the men dragged Richard. His shirt rode up his torso and he felt the rough stone rasp at his skin. He ignored the burn.

Gabriela kept hold of her son, guiding his small body to prevent further swinging. But as her hands slid down his legs, the platform shifted away from them. She instinctively grabbed Luisito's ankles. Wood groaned beneath her. Their three bodies became a taut line, almost as if she was the guide, her son the string, and Richard the kite. Their holds became rigid. Luisito whimpered. Gabriela knew if she didn't do something quickly, she would place too much pressure on Richard's hold and they could all tumble to the rocks below.

Richard read the message in Gabriela's eyes, saw her hands twitch, and enunciated the next words with cold emphasis.

"Don't. You. Dare. Shit. Hold on."

Their son's breath hitched. "He said the S word." His tone sounded similar to an adult's scold. "*Mami,*" he looked down at her. "He said the S word."

Gabriela tried to smile, but her mouth turned down in a lopsided grimace.

"I'll give Richard a time out later."

Richard's gaze connected with hers. *You want to give me a time out?* His imagination flooded with scenarios in which he could indulge.

Gabriela understood the telegram and blushed.

Richard concentrated on their current problem, glad his son's outrage had alleviated the tension. He arm-curled Luisito upward and thanked whatever gods looking after them he kept in shape. Hoped to eternity the men would also keep hold. He'd heard Spike's choice expletives mix with Jeremy's grunts from keeping him balanced and anchored. Those two might be a burly duo, but a dead weight was still no easy task, no matter how much brawn, especially when improvising.

Gabriela saw the curl and felt the tug. She imagined standing on a swing. Thought transferred to action. She bent her knees and elbows slightly and pushed forward, bringing the deck back with her. It bumped against the retaining wall.

Shuddered.

Rattled.

Vibrated and shifted.

She released her son, seized the railing affixed to the wall, flattened face and body to the brick, and held on. The platform settled, but for how long?

Her diaphragm heaved while her heart thumped, ramming muscled walls against the constraining bars of her rib cage.

"Spike. Jeremy. Hustle."

Richard disappeared with her son over the retaining wall. *Thank God. Thank God.* Luisito was safe. Her son was safe. A few milliseconds afterward she heard Richard's voice, "Don't you dare move. Back in a jiff."

Moments became sound bites—she heard her son's excited voice, Zip's bark, the men's fake enthusiasm to Luisito's recounting of the ordeal; door opening; Richard's call for Lupe over loud video game sound effects. Whispered voices. In the meantime, her fingers curled tighter on the railing, her position really precarious. She pep-talked herself for what seemed ages, inanely thinking she was a gecko, her fingerprints and pores tiny Velcro hairs plastering her to the wood and wall.

Richard's head came into view seconds later. He measured distance, angles. Was probably calculating her weight. Would he be able to hold her? She wasn't fat, but she was no lightweight, either. Her body would probably feel like hefting a sand bag with your fingertips. She imagined-slapped herself suddenly. Really? Was she an idiot? How could she be thinking about her weight right now?

The balancing act became more difficult, the sway more pronounced. She wanted to scream but her words came out as a croak. "Hurry. Please?"

Richard's body slanted downward. Stopped. Reached. Gabriela slowly rose in a *relevé*, lifted her right arm, but barely grazed Richard's fingers.

"Sweetheart." His voice, soft at the outset, turned into a clipped one when he saw panic mount in her eyes.

"Look at me, Gabriela." He waited. Got her attention. "You need to jump. I'll grab you."

Gabriela swallowed, even when there wasn't much spittle left in her mouth.

"Trust me," he said, reading the hesitation.

She gathered herself. Thought a thousand ways this could go wrong. Chose the only option. Bent her knees, raised her arms, and launched.

The impetus shoved the deck outward. Gabriela heard wood groan, felt Richard's grip handcuff her forearms. She couldn't help it. She squealed in harmony to Richard's groan and curse. Her legs swung, found nothing but air. Gravity pulled. Her body sank, sliding her downward centimeter by centimeter. Forearms gave way to wrists. Richard tightened his hold. So did she. Her body played a wimpy Ping-Pong with the wall, but the downward motion braked. Settled.

Stopped.

The men heaved. She heard their straining efforts in the wind. Gabriela stared ahead, afraid to look up and squirm, or down and cringe. With every jerk upward, she noticed green-black moss filling microscopic cracks and imperfections in the mortar. Lichen was replaced with nuances in the brick color. More mortar. A less weathered running bond brick pattern rolled by next. A sliced view of the house and terrace popped into view at the balustrade railing. She was dragged on top of it. Spike and Jeremy sprawled to the ground near her, heaving. She released one of her arms from Richard's grip. Grabbed the inside edge of the balustrade, hoisted belly and a knee on top of it. Richard, feet now solidly on the ground, searched, found, and laced two fingers into her jean's belt loop and pulled, dragging her over and on top of him.

Set her down.

He clutched her body against his, his shoulders concaved, and his head pressed against her neck, his breathing tortured.

"Shit. Shit. Shit."

Succinct and apt, Gabriela thought, trying to suppress her own shivers. She simply clung to his strength, joined his fears, and shared his relief.

"Our baby." Her eyes became two shimmering suns about to weep. "Christ, Richard. Our baby." An irascible, unstoppable monster replaced her tension, rampaging through her body.

"I'm going to kill that son of a bitch."

"Not if I kill him first."

"That'll be a long queue," Jeremy added. He offered Spike a hand and pulled him up from the ground. Both men massaged their abused muscles.

Richard grabbed her shoulders and pushed her slightly away. His face closed in, almost making her cross-eyed.

"If you ever," he began. "I never. I swear I'll smack you if I ever glimpse again what I read in your eyes today."

"As if." Gabriela's eyebrow arched, her expression challenging him on his smacking statement.

"Leave the damn self-sacrificing to saints." He shook her slightly and crushed her against him the next moment. It never paid to bluff this woman who knew him so well.

"I'll throw myself in front of a tank to save my sons." She tried to push him away, but he would have none of it.

"Shit. Don't you think I know? But consider things before you act, damn it." He squeezed her harder. He wanted his voice to rattle her brain, to blast her eardrums with his *I can't lose you now.* "Don't react first and think later. That will get you killed."

"Whatever needs to be done," she said.

"Not while I'm around." He looked at her. "You're not alone anymore. I'll protect you. I'll protect them."

"Or die trying." She finished what had remained unsaid. "Just like me."

"We are a hell of a pair." He hugged her fiercely. "A pair that needs to get out of Dodge fast." He glanced at the men. "Got your wind back?"

"Damn," Spike said. "Knew things would be hopping around here when you popped up. Didn't expect a boatload of shit to explode in my face. Damn need to keep up." He flexed his muscles to relax them.

"Never to bore is our motto," Richard answered.

"Crap. I just want normal," she said. "Do you think we'll ever get normal?"

"Three's the charm." Richard enumerated with his fingers. "Heinige. Wickeham. Us. Right now, however," he added, "we all need to get the hell out of here."

Richard grabbed her hand and pulled her toward the French doors.

***

Wickeham considered himself a pugilist. That sweet science, which was spurned by current bleeding hearts in their spineless society, kept him in shape. It was his great mood equalizer, as well. Frustrations vanished, pacified the instant his fist transmitted energy to the heavy bag. The satisfaction was immediate as taped knuckles felt the initial resistance at impact. The pleasure escalated when the leather succumbed to his will, with the ever so slight inward collapse seconds later. His endorphins, like his body, set to work.

The ramming today, however, was different. Today, rage fueled his punches. Seething anger. No one, not any one of his bloody marks had ever balked the way this woman had, or evaded his countermoves with such efficacy. He leaned his shoulder in for the next punch. Amend that. Last year he'd lost two pieces. Outmaneuvered by some asshole from America. Minor interest on his part. Minor glitch to his life. No second thoughts. But this, this lack of cooperation, this failure to attain what he craved more than money, was simply unacceptable. He landed three brutal jabs in a row. He remained stupefied at the manner in which she had disdained his efforts at coercion. Overly angered by her mockery.

Earlier, Bogdan had scrambled to verify if the incompetent twit his LA contact had hired was, indeed, in custody at hospital. He visualized the compacted sand within the leather bag as the prat's body. Excellent. Jabbed with his right. Fantasized cracked ribs at the onslaught, sharp bone puncturing spleen. He waited for the bag to stabilize. Hit it with two rapid punches, leaning in with his shoulder, transferring more power to fists. Imagined body parts fracturing, eyes swelling, nose breaking. Excessive bleeding. The images electrified and satisfied him at a deep, almost orgasmic level.

Sweat pooled on his brow, skin, and elbows, but he ignored the dampness. Either Mrs. Martinez had the most unbelievable luck, or someone was aiding her. Her bodyguard? If her claims proved true, Bogdan had orders to execute his second plan immediately. Utmost cooperation would be guaranteed then, once the children were in his grip. But time zones were mucking his game. At present, things were at an impasse. Distance was screwing, as well, with the control he always desired, demanded, and exerted in any situation.

He brutalized the bag with a rapid volley. Never give a job to a second party. Golden rule. Lack of control was unacceptable. Possibilities for fuck-ups abounded when someone else held the reins, someone who did not have a vested interest in the outcome.

His arms began to quiver and his muscles burned, but Wickeham ignored the signals of the onset of fatigue. He kept at the barrage of fists on leather until his enforcer returned and stood silently facing him, awaiting acknowledgment. Bogdan knew better than to interrupt him when he was in this mood.

"News?" Wickeham stabilized and embraced the heavy bag almost lovingly, allowing himself a moment of respite. Reached over and drank from the mineral water with which he always hydrated.

"Confirmed." Bogdan's voice grated the air like sandpaper. "Man in hospital."

Wickeham paused in his drinking.

"Plan B executed?"

Bogdan shook his head. "Boys not in school. Home empty. Not even dog."

Wickeham lowered the bottle slowly, placed it carefully back on the stool. Excessive blinking telegraphed his intense displeasure at the situation, evidence of his attempt at controlling his fury.

"Where is she?" His voice held a trembling edge to it.

Bogdan shrugged and his hands mimicked a small explosion. "It's like, poof. Everyone gone."

Wickeham signaled Bogdan to hold the bag in place. He jabbed and jabbed, punishing the bag as well his enforcer's body. He had trusted him to find an efficient messenger. Bogdan had failed him. The auction was days away.

"Find her." He followed with a battery of jabs, ending in a cross, and felt the impact catapult from wrist to shoulder in even ripples.

Time. He was running out of time.

Chapter Seventeen

"Are you ready?"

Gabriela turned her attention from the snarl of traffic that was London to Richard, who stood next to her by the window. His stance was relaxed, his hands clasped casually behind him. His eyes, however, never missed anything as he followed the activity out on the street below the seventh floor of the New Scotland Yard building. They were waiting for Michael Morris to appear.

"As ready as anyone can ever be in this kind of mess, I guess." Her eyes did another quick catalog of Morris's office. Not big, a bit cramped with furniture, file cabinets, but bright, organized, like an overstuffed sandwich, the walls dry-board slices trying to contain everything within.

"How's Spike holding up?"

"Barely."

Richard chuckled. "If he had longer hair, he would probably be tearing at it. Those three can be a handful. Your parents?"

"Scared." Four years ago, their worry had been slight when Seldon had sent bodyguards to their house. Kidnapping threats to the executives in Mexico, at the same company where Roberto had worked at the time, had been the excuse for their presence. Normal, for the time. Doubtful it would ever occur in the US or Europe, but caution never hurt, one simply dealt with a few minor inconveniences. After the events in France, however, her parents would never be as blasé as before.

"Concerned and angry in turns about my not selling the manuscript to this man."

"How are you holding up?"

She shrugged. It was difficult not talking to the children, not listening to their banter. Theirs was the need to blurt everything, a desire to share every little detail of their adventure. Any conversations, she knew, would divulge their destination. Knowledge she could not have until the manuscript was sold.

The silence spoke volumes for her.

"Come here." Richard drew her into his arms and held her. "This will be over soon."

She filled her lungs with his essence, surrendered to the pleasure of burrowing into his warmth and strength for a bit, for a moment, before disengaging herself softly.

He let her go, for now.

"Any ideas on the plan of attack?"

Richard shrugged and leaned against the windowsill facing Morris's desk. "An inkling, but I don't want to get ahead on this. Let's wait to find out. By the way, you were closeted with the specialist for close to a half hour after your meeting. Is everything okay with the event?"

"Paperwork. Signatures. You know how it is. Will you be able to work around my schedule?"

"I'll figure everything out with my assistant once we get to the office." He straightened when he saw Morris weaving his way to the office.

"So sorry to keep you."

Gabriela faced a young man with regular features whose eyes betrayed any notion of softness. An almost jaded look to his gaze was backed with a piercing awareness. She thought many would underestimate this detective to their detriment.

"Mrs. Martinez, this is indeed a pleasure," he said and extended his hand. "Christie's sent over your itinerary for the next couple of days. Wanted the fax in hand before we discussed anything."

"No formalities, please." Gabriela shook a hand whose grip was strong and determined. "Simply Gabriela." She smiled.

Morris took a moment to study these two briefly. Richard's moves had been interesting—the protective guiding to the chair, the reassuring squeeze of the shoulder, his body touching, but not overpowering. There was restraint in their proximity, as if hiding from others signals of an established intimacy. His gaze turned speculative.

"I have spoken to my superintendent about your situation," Morris began. "He has agreed to open a preliminary investigation, rather reluctantly, I may add, since the case now stands more as a she said / he said snit. I reminded him of the previous fizzled-out accusations and investigations. Called to mind we finally have a witness willing to cooperate. Your personal attacks. We can build a solid case. Attain proof to convict. He changed his mind."

"Farsighted, your boss," Richard said, his lips twitching in a cynical smirk.

Morris's eyes crinkled at the edges. "A political animal. Realizes this capture would greatly improve his curriculum vitae. Rumors abound he's aiming for the Director Generalship of the new NCS division to be launched next year."

"You'll be spearheading Gabriela's case now, I hope?" Richard asked.

"Since I'm already involved with security—"

"Glad to hear it."

"The escalation of threats, particularly, concerns me. The Christie's event is garnering more international attention by the second. I can't afford a botched-up event on my watch." Morris scanned the fax and grimaced. "Your schedule, Mrs. Martinez—"

"Is a logistics nightmare," supplied Richard. "But look at it on the bright side. The window of opportunity for attack has been diminished greatly simply because of the publicity and activity."

"But it narrows the opportunity to garner proof." Morris shook his head. "Hell. Mr. Wickeham may not even take the risk now things are so visible."

"Oh, he will," Gabriela said, quite certain on that point. Why was she so convinced? She thought back to her first interchange with Wickeham and tried to explain to this man her reasons.

"You weren't there for his first phone calls," she said. "I'm sorry I didn't record the conversations back then, but I never thought…never mind. Wickeham's excitement over the manuscript held a disturbing edge to it, something akin to zealotry. Life altering. He held no doubts I would sell."

"Strangely similar words describing Wickeham by the antique dealer I did business with last year," Richard said. "Chances are Mr. W thought the adulation would seal the deal. His offer was quick and magnanimous."

Gabriela shivered. Knowledge was a frightful thing. She had not known the beast before, but she did now, and the image was frightening.

"When I didn't budge, he honestly believed I was haggling for more money. At that moment, his interest altered to a compulsion, like a child's. The moment he realized I meant what I said, his attitude became darker. Colder. When I offered to reproduce a few folios…"

"A consolation prize, sort of?" Morris asked.

"Something like that. Anyway, Wickeham lost it then. He became more threatening." Not that she'd believed his threats, at first. Stupid of her.

"Jeremy mentioned you have a recording to that fact?"

Gabriela nodded and reached into one of her attaché case's zippered pockets. She retrieved the cassette tape from her answering machine and handed it over to Morris's eager hands.

"There's really no flat-out threat to his words," Richard told him. "But when you start adding up the brake tampering, the assault, the deck incident, and the innuendoes, you may have the elements to a stronger case."

"Circumstantial, at best, for now." Morris tapped the schedule for emphasis. "With this itinerary, however, openings for coercion will be brief. Hate to be repetitive, but he may retreat, not wanting to sully his reputation in the UK or abroad."

"Not Wickeham," Richard and Gabriela said simultaneously.

"He'll find a way," Richard stated. "I know his type. Can't risk losing the piece to a higher bidder. He can't stop, not now so near the auction."

"I spoke to your Detective Correia, by the by," Morris said. "I apprised him of the situation, as well as the probability of criminal malfeasance. He's faxing your mechanic's photographs together with his reports and his investigation of the deck incident. He will redirect his interrogation of the suspect toward that end before the man is transferred to face attempted murder charges in Los Angeles." He looked at both of them, his gaze a bit critical. "You should have been more forthcoming, you know."

"Couldn't risk it," Richard said. "Secrecy was crucial in the protection of the children, especially with the journalistic leech we have on our backs."

Morris's gaze sharpened and waited for an explanation.

"Herb Bryce, my very own personal stalkerazzo extraordinaire for the past four years." Gabriela sighed. "The moment the auction was announced, he camped outside my home and has been clicking to his heart's content ever since."

"He's recorded the aftermath of the attacks on the mechanic and at her house," Richard added. "You may want to collect those photos as well."

"His timing is always impeccable. I expect the headlines should hit the tabloids by tonight's edition, if they haven't been printed already to coincide with my visit here." Her words ended on a disgusted note.

"We were able to weasel from under his radar by doing things quickly and secretly. The fact I had Vivian do all reservations, change in itineraries and flights bought us some time," Richard said.

Gabriela pointed to the fax on Morris's desk. "That schedule of events was distributed to all media, patrons, and bidders an hour ago. Invitations distributed. I saw Wickeham's and Bryce's names on the list. Everyone will know where to find me from now until the auction."

"Bryce is probably extra pissed we gave him the slip," Richard added. "He'll redouble his efforts to track Gabriela here. That means her whereabouts in my home will come out into the open, as well."

Morris leaned back to digest this bit of information.

"You know," Morris said, understanding the irony of his next statement. "This may not be such a negative. Another person following and capturing all your moves, Mrs. Martinez, may very well work to our benefit."

Gabriela didn't say a word. She didn't think Bryce was such a positive in her life. On the contrary, he could hamper and complicate things.

"Would you be agreeable to be body-wired, Mrs. Martinez?" He glanced at her itinerary and sighed. There were so many opportunities there for Wickeham to strike without warning. "We may need to do so every day."

"Maybe not. Let me see your schedule again, Gabriela."

Once she extracted her copy, Richard leaned in, grabbed the opposite edge of the paper, and held it steady. Shoulder to shoulder, they studied the long list of activities, the final product of the morning meeting with the Christie's specialist, their publicity coordinator, Jean-Louis, Julien, and herself.

"He'll have two windows of opportunity to corner her," Richard said. "And even then, she will be surrounded not only by her own people, but also by Jeremy and myself." He scanned the list quickly. "Here, at the formal publicity bash tonight and here, at the informal cocktail gathering at the hotel tomorrow evening. He may be able to waylay her for a moment when everyone else is otherwise occupied."

Morris studied his own copy of her agenda. "Agreed. In the meantime, one officer will be assigned to your detail."

"Shifts?" Richard asked.

"Every six hours."

"I want a mugshot of the officer *du jour* on the off chance someone wants to do some creative substitutions."

"Gave Jeremy the GSC 100 this morning for that purpose. Set up for e-mail. The gadget will help us record and trace your moves anywhere in London, as well, even throughout the UK for that matter."

Morris opened a desk drawer, lifted a small cell phone, and pushed it across his desk toward Gabriela. "For you. It must never leave your person."

"God, another phone. Those things follow me better than mosquitoes in Florida." Her disgust showed on her face. "Must I?"

"It is what you use from now on. Has recording capacity, triangulates, and handoffs as needed without interference. I've programmed speed dial for emergencies."

"Codes?" asked Richard.

"The number One patches her to you."

"Why One to him?" she asked.

"From what Jeremy suggested, Richard will be the first person you'll think of calling if anything goes wrong."

Gabriela stared.

Richard grinned.

"Conceited oaf," she mumbled, seeing Richard's reaction.

"But accurate."

"You wish."

Definitely something was up with these two.

"Two links to my cell. Three to the office here at the Yard. Four connects to Jeremy's cell. Nine-nine-nine is police dispatch."

"So," Gabriela put words to action. "If I press Two for a couple of seconds—"

Nothing sounded. No annoying beeps or clicks, yet Morris's phone began vibrating.

"Security of the witness comes first," Morris explained, declining the call. "No audible sound bytes while you press numbers may save your life. My suggestion is that you practice blind recognition of the keypad."

"How will you work the body wire?" Richard asked.

"Anir, my tech, will be at your flat this p.m."

Gabriela shook her head. "I'll be at the hotel this afternoon, preparing for the event. We leave directly from there to the auction house." She rattled the room number where she'd be with Jean-Louis and Julien.

"I'll have my man meet you there, then."

"What other security measures do you have in mind?' Richard asked.

Morris reached for a file and opened it. "Let me show you."

***

Edmund Husher walked toward the back sunroom of the Cranfield home.

With an edge to his grip and gleeful spite in his heart, he held the tabloid he'd purchased. This could be the turnabout for which he'd been hankering, the advantage for which he so longed. Edmund was fed up with his hankie persona, conveniently forgotten by April until the onset of sniffles. His jealousy dragon now rampaged out of control.

Edmund glanced at the paper rod he'd created from the tabloid, smiled, and stepped into the enclosed sunroom, bright for a change on that spring day.

April sat sipping tea, the finished dregs of her breakfast littering the small linen-covered table. Her body was ensconced in a silk, floral print in corals and blues, the upper bodice open negligently, revealing the inside of a plump smooth breast. She glanced up, saw Edmund, and returned to her bored examination of the expansive backyard.

Edmund leaned down and kissed her in clumsy strength.

"My, my," she said, ending the kiss with a not so gentle push on his chest. "Aren't we overly stimulated this morning?"

Edmund controlled the hurt and sat facing her, slapping the newsprint into his open palm with staccato impatience.

"Brought you the rag you read. Don't know how you can stand all that nonsense." He unrolled it, stared at the headline, glanced at the photograph and its caption, and smiled.

April frowned. Her abrupt dismissal of Edmund usually brought on a puppy-dog pout and hurt to his eyes. There was no other way to describe it. Oftentimes, she was sorry and would treat him kindly for the rest of the day. Sometimes she profited by a stimulating romp in bed, riding him hard and frantic, controlling. At others, however, she didn't give a damn. Today was one of those times—she had Richard on her mind. Unmovable, untouchable Richard. Not controllable Richard. She was still ticked off by his surprise trip to America, by his derailing her plans, but his pain-in-the-ass assistant had reluctantly admitted he'd be back today. Time to implement her campaign to get that ring on her finger.

Her eyebrow shot up as she extended her hand for the local news rag. Edmund's smile did not change one iota. He never smiled when rejected, nor did he when bringing over the tabloids she loved to read.

"Only one?"

The only one you will need to see. "You'll like this one." He passed it to her with an enthusiasm not normal to his usual manner.

The headline hit her first.

SCANDAL!
Love Triangle: Notorious Martinez and Mystery Lover?

Ooh, scrumptious! April smiled. Naughty tidbits on the woman she was about to meet. Once Richard introduced...

The contents of the photograph slapped her next. The smile disappeared.

"Isn't that Harrison on the cover?" Edmund's question fluttered innocently around her, but rammed her with the force of a bus.

Richard was in profile. So was the woman. Another would have perused the photo as a curiosity, but April honed in on the suggestive elements Herb Bryce had recognized nights before, tangible and inescapable to a woman whose goal in life was to have the man of her dreams submit to her will. April leaned forward, focused on Richard's face. She'd never seen that look before, and definitely not directed at her.

"Seems those two go way back," Edmund said. "Cozy, even intimate. At least, as it stands out from that shot." He leaned back and smiled wider. "Now we know why he didn't include you in his plans."

This couldn't be happening to her. She'd always gotten what she wanted from a man. Richard had been a challenge, yes, but April believed she'd eventually manipulate him into submission. Assumed she would eventually reel him in.

Her eyes latched on the image once more. Read the caption over and over.

Mystery man comforts artist Gabriela Martinez after attack on her mechanic. Where is her husband?

This…this was catastrophic. The bitch. The bitch. Now she understood Edmund's smile. Never thought he had it in him. Ever since she'd seen Richard, Edmund had yearned for her to fail in her quest. She pinned her focus on the photograph once more, wanting to evaporate what was there. This, like nothing else, proved her so-called control over Richard was delusional.

The guttural scream clawed its way out of her, releasing the savagery burning through her veins. She tore the front page, balled it, and threw it at Edmund.

"The bastard," she said. "Get out. I have things to do."

"I'll drive you."

Her scathing look didn't rile Edmund, for a change. She pivoted and ran to her bedroom.

She'd had enough. Her push to capture Richard suddenly notched up into high gear.

***

Wickeham was in the process of perusing the Martinez list of events, when Bogdan entered the study.

"Woman in England. Not at hotel." He placed two tabloids on his desk, directly in Wickeham's line of sight, and tapped the photo on his right for emphasis. "May have problem."

Wickeham's eyebrow shot up in silent questioning and released the newsprint from underneath Bogdan's meaty finger. He read the newsprint's banner and the derision in his sniff carried over to the manner in which he held the local rag.

"Look man over," Bogdan suggested with a thrust of his chin. "Same one last year, I'm sure."

Wickeham disregarded the clamor in the headline and concentrated on the photograph. He recognized Mrs. Martinez immediately from every picture over which he had mulled. He concentrated on the man leaning toward her, protective and caring. He grabbed his magnifying glass and held it over the image. The snapshot expanded, came into sharper focus. Wickeham tensed.

He'd wondered who had been helping the woman not long ago.

Finally, he had his answer.

Chapter Eighteen

It was after lunch, and Jeremy had left them in front of Richard's office door in search of Vivian. Gabriela had yet to meet the love of Jeremy's life, the redhead dynamo on whom Richard depended to run his office.

Gabriela was still trying to process all she'd seen the moment they had stepped into Richard's world. Reception had been a big, bold, semicircular yet contained area, which encased a colorful aquarium opposite an elegant receptionist's desk. All working areas in the main office sported a mix of leather, glass, metal, and warm mahogany that was inviting, despite the partitions. Ceiling-high, automatic glass doors held center stage and separated the executive suite from the main office. Everything reflected Richard's personality and tastes.

"What do you think?"

He'd been watching her every reaction. She seemed to be fielding several emotions, but the pleasure surfacing above all others satisfied him deeply.

"*Provençal, Inc.*?" she asked. She traced the elegant script of the company's name etched on the coppery plaque riveted to his office door.

Richard gestured for her to precede him into his inner sanctum. "Named it after the region where I met you," he admitted, following her through his office door. "Has served me well as a marketing strategy. Anything *à la Francaise* attracts business."

Gabriela stared at him. He had named his business with her in mind?

Richard closed the door, cocooning them in his office. He reached out, enfolded her in his arms, and kissed her. He imparted all his hunger, all his desire in that kiss, releasing the reins to his famished need for her since California, the flight home, and that morning's chaos.

"Been wanting to do that for hours." He anchored her back to the door, pressed in, and inhaled. She always smelled of jasmine.

"Damned hell of a protective armada you have as an entourage." He nibbled at her lower lip; assuaged the nip with a roving tongue. Captured, explored, tasted every inch of her face and neck.

Gabriela throbbed in harmony to his assault, and the heat pulsating through her body felt like neon signs screaming: danger...more... danger...more. Would she ever get used to Richard's sensual assaults? Get used to this constant hunger for him, from him? Or was his passion a phase that would fizz out after a bit?

Now, where the hell had that thought come from?

"What did you expect?" she said, trying to stay afloat. The hum of a workplace coming alive after a pause began to filter through the door. "Two male cousins, one a priest. An eagle-eyed chaperone for a cousin-in-law, and two mother-hen managers. In their eyes, my virtue violator meter needs to remain untouched."

The noises from the outside office became more evident.

"At least I'll only have to worry about three here in London."

She captured his face to stop his roving mouth, and gazed at him steadily.

"Behave," she whispered, but her lips curled in a soft smile.

"Damn."

He breathed. Saw a smudge of lipstick close to the edge of her mouth and swiped at it with his thumb. Slanted his head, considering, before Jeremy's voice blended with Vivian's near the door.

He fished a handkerchief from the back pocket of his pants and wiped his lips with a tinge of regret. He was tempted, really tempted, to leave evidence of her lips on his own, but they did need to be circumspect. He had to protect her image, the children's. As far as his own image went, well, he didn't give much of a damn.

Richard rested his forehead on hers. He wanted to indulge so badly, but privacy and time were not to be had, not yet. And he needed to find it. In the subconscious recesses of his brain a warning clamored, an urgency to reconnect physically with this woman. Imperative, now that he had recaptured the emotional. Richard believed if body mated with the spiritual, their bond would resolidify into a more powerful one than four years ago, which no one, nor anything, could sever ever again.

Gabriela, on the other hand, attempted to curb the Dantean vortex she was riding. As the hours passed in Richard's proximity, she gave less and less of a damn what others wanted of her, hoped for, or demanded. The temptation to throw away all her chains and not be the responsible one for once was tearing at her. It was the image of her children that kept her tethered in reality and her emotions tempered. But she was tired of holding back. Of renouncing her wants, when all she desired was to be caged in by Richard.

Richard kissed her forehead.

She rose on the tip of her toes and unmanned him with the softest, most caressing kiss he had ever experienced.

"Now you behave." His beautiful eyes crinkled in a smile.

"I love you," she murmured.

Unexpected. Whispered simply, and simply devastating.

Richard stared, dazed after her confession.

Gabriela studied him. Usually he was the one extracting the words from her. She had surprised herself. She hadn't uttered those words in four years. But the intensity of what she'd felt in the past held no comparison with what she felt at the moment.

She held her breath.

Waited.

Richard remained speechless.

With cheeks like two miniature furnaces of embarrassment, she wriggled out from behind the pressure of his body. *Calm down, calm down.* Her ears, however, throbbed in violent rhythm with her elevated blood pressure. *Relax. Do something mundane.*

"Magnificent workspace," she said, and walked farther into the office, taking in his desk, the glass windows overlooking the city. She never saw him reach and fail to catch her.

"You must be so proud of what you've accomplished. It's truly incredible." Her eyes rested on the only framed artwork hugging the wall and stopped. She gaped. Her eyes were not deceiving her. There rested her *St. George*, proudly displayed over an elegant credenza.

Richard reached her side, his hand caressing the small of her back in comfort and possessiveness. He'd been gifted with the three words that carried the weight of gold in his world. Hadn't expected them. Would later hold her to them.

"I thought this had been destroyed, or confiscated."

"Maurice, the sly bastard, sneaked it out of Albert's house after we confronted that murdering maniac. Left it a year later at my apartment stateside while I was recovering at the hospital."

She glanced at his profile. He was studying her work with the same intensity as he sometimes studied her. He began to rub his shirt around the vicinity of his heart in absentminded circles. It had not been the first time she'd seen him do this. Was this a new habit or was it something he had always done? The pragmatic in her understood she knew so little about Richard, the man. Why the certainty, without fail, there was very little new to learn?

He glanced her way. "Do you mind?"

"Not at all," she said, truthfully. She would have hated, despite the unpleasant memories, if it had been destroyed. "I'm glad you own it rather than anyone else."

She meandered away from her illustration toward the bank of windows at the edge of the office, glanced down at the street view from there, ambled back to his desk, saw a photograph next to his phone, and picked it up curiously. Another surprise hit. This was her family on the day of Luisito's baptism.

"Seldon's lackey took that one." He watched her intently, waiting.

"You knew?" she asked, a bit breathless. It turned out more of an accusation than a question.

"Suspected, yes." He didn't say suspicion had turned to certainty thanks to Maurice. He had delivered precious data together with the photograph and her painting. Data he verified with his own blood as soon as he left Seldon's employment three years ago.

When he saw her wince, he walked over to face her. "I was waiting for you to contact me."

"That's right, the letters that never arrived." She placed the picture frame on the desk in the exact manner she'd found it. He'd suspected, and yet he'd stayed away.

"We would not be having this conversation otherwise, sweetheart." He held her shoulders. "You know it."

Yes, she did and was about to tell him so when all hell broke loose, and her world exploded in a way she would never have predicted.

The muffled "Wait," came first, followed by the office door bursting open. Gabriela turned toward the commotion. Outlined inside the mahogany door's frame, stood a tall, slender woman. Beautifully coifed, flowing blond hair haloed her face, and her statuesque figure remained frozen in fashion model perfection. It seemed she was posing, announcing to everyone, "Here I am. Gaze upon this wonder." An open-shouldered, striped dress of white on black hugged her slender frame provocatively, the wide lines embracing her curves in candy cane fashion. But what caught Gabriela's attention was her age. The woman looked young. Really, really young. Flawless in muscle tone and skin's luster. Mid-twenties? Not even?

A pretty redhead stood close on the woman's heels, her expression in turns angry, horrified, and distressed. Jeremy's Vivian? Must be. Both Jeremy and Richard had described her as petite, with red hair. Jeremy stood to her right, a fur coat in his arms. He stared at the blonde apparition at the door with a look of outraged disgust. Another man, a few steps behind him, appeared to be smirking at them all.

"I'm so sorry, Mr. Harrison," the redhead said. "She just barged in, sir. There was no way of stopping her."

For an instant, the vision at the door turned disdainful eyes to the woman behind her, only to refocus with calculation on Richard immediately after.

"Darling." Her voice was husky, savoring Richard's name like a honeyed treat. Her next move, however, surprised everyone. She ran and threw herself at Richard.

"You're back."

"What the hell?" Richard tried to balance and fend her off all at once.

Ever the opportunistic animal, April grabbed his face and gave Richard an open-mouth kiss, her tongue roving his mouth in familiar pleasure, making sure everything, everything, was visible to everyone. She didn't care if he wasn't cooperating.

Gabriela froze, her insides solidifying into a burning mass like Lot's wife when zapped by the force of God's retribution. This woman, this really young-looking, beautiful woman was Richard's girlfriend? She had never expected this curveball.

Shock and dismay transformed into eviscerating pain. Had he lied to her? Had all the care and the shows of affection from him been a sham? Or was she simply unfinished business he needed to expunge out of his system? Her fears, now pounding cymbals in rhythm with her blood, deafened her. She was sure she was on point. Familiarity and intimacy were there in the kiss, as well as in the body language.

Her fears took hold. Richard had a woman in his life. He'd moved on, until circumstances had dutifully forced him into her chaotic life once more.

And you confessed your love for him not two minutes ago, like a juvenile idiot. No wonder he had said nothing.

Oh, God.

Crushing embarrassment replaced the hurt. Richard lusted after her but had not admitted he loved her.

Eyelids shuttered her distress. What a fool. She tamped down her emotions into a fortified panic room in a familiar corner of her heart, replaced it with nothing, and turned her back on him, on them.

Richard saw the change in Gabriela and wanted to kill this thoughtless woman who'd jumped him as if she had a right.

All the work he'd done to crumble Gabriela's guard, to lower her defenses, evaporated in an instant. Her trust had been replaced with a flash of such deep hurt he would have sold his body to all the demons in hell to avoid witnessing. Now shutters had clamped down, her face expressionless. He could no longer read her.

Richard's fists clenched and unclenched, controlling an urge to slap April like he'd slapped Silvie, Albert's mistress, years back.

"Get away from me," he whispered. His hold on her forearm was merciless as he kept her from further touching him. His eyes changed to a tempered steel never before seen by April.

She licked her lips sensuously at the possibility of sexual dominance, her eyes igniting with arousal.

Richard saw the reaction to his treatment and the disgust on his face was palpable.

It was that disgust that made April back away.

"Gabriela—"

But Gabriela, her back stiff, ignored him and walked over to the crowded doorway. She directed her next words at Jeremy and smiled. "Is this Vivian?"

"Yes, Mrs. Martinez." Jeremy's voice was gravelly, as if he were trying to control his own anger.

Gabriela turned to Vivian, whose eyes darted here and there like furtive rabbits trying to hide in the best lair, and whose cheeks were stained red banners of embarrassment.

"So sorry about this," Vivian said, shaking her hand with too much enthusiasm.

Gabriela glanced at the man hovering behind Jeremy. He was no longer smirking. Rather he looked unsettled, but she liked what she saw: tall, good-looking, a bit too slim, with a personable aura about him.

She raised an eyebrow. "And you are?"

The man shook his head as if coming out of a trance. "Edmund Husher, Ma'am."

His voice was deep, cultured.

Gabriela laughed. Edmund did a double take.

"Good Lord, you make me sound ancient." The smile in the statement reached her eyes as she extended her hand. "Don't ma'am me, please," she said. "I'm Gabriela."

He shook hands and would have made it last if not for catching sight of Richard's face. He backed off as if he'd been physically pushed back.

Gabriela, intrigued, followed the direction of Edmund's gaze. His eyes were fixed on Richard. Conversely, the maddening man was staring Edmund down, in a downright threatening manner, to boot. Figures. Subliminal intimidation. Some nerve.

"Do you work for Mr. Harrison?"

"He does not," Richard answered, clipping the words for more emphasis.

Gabriela's eyebrow arched.

"He's Miss Cranfield's...friend." He'd almost blurted out boy toy.

April, never one to lose the advantage over another woman, grabbed Richard's arm in both of her own. She leaned in, establishing her territory, ignoring the tensing of his muscles.

"This is so like you, Richard," she said, her voice smooth, like silk. She nudged his arm with her breasts and kept clinging.

She turned sultry eyes to Gabriela. "I'm April Cranfield. Didn't he speak to you about us? About our plans?"

Gabriela's emotions rounded the corner of hurt and accelerated toward the straightaway of indignation. The wanting the earth to swallow her whole became an eagerness to wallop Richard and give him a bloody nose. Maybe even tear a few blond hair roots from his bimbo, as well. She kept a straight face instead.

"And that would be?" she inquired softly.

"Your auction, of course. We were so excited you were coming. Richard knows how much I admire your works, don't you, darling?"

Richard must have accurately read what he saw on Gabriela's face because his eyes narrowed.

She needed to get out of there. If she didn't get the hell away in two seconds, a scene of major proportions would be unleashed, involving bruised knuckles and broken fingernails. And she wouldn't give him the pleasure of witnessing her lack of control. Wouldn't give the bimbo the pleasure, either.

"I really must get back to the hotel. Meetings. Can't delay things further."

"Need a lift?" offered Edmund with surprising bravado.

"Gabriela." Richard's warning rang clear.

She ignored him.

"How sweet of you...Edmund, isn't it?" At his nod and smile, she continued. "But no. I already arranged for Mr. Hollis to take me." She smiled. "Maybe next time."

"I'll take you down." Richard stepped forward, but she raised her arm, palm up.

"Don't bother," she said, her voice a honeycomb of dripping politeness. "Nice to have met you all. Thank you so much for the tour, Mr. Harrison. It's been...instructive. Maybe I'll see you and your Ms. Cranfield at the event this evening?"

And like a Shakespearean actress, Gabriela walked regally toward the elevators and the exit.

Jeremy's expression, when he turned toward Richard, was equal parts appalled, distressed, and concerned. Bugger the bitch and the atomic scrummage April had planted in their midst, it seemed to be saying.

Richard jerked his chin in Gabriela's direction.

Jeremy didn't need any prodding. He shoved April's coat into Edmund's chest and disappeared in Gabriela's huffy wake.

"Vivian, could you get me some coffee, please?" Richard nodded in the direction of the break room. He turned his attention to Edmund next. "Get your car. You're leaving."

Vivian made herself scarce in less than a second. Edmund followed in Gabriela's wake. He was equally glad and uncomfortable about what April would witness. Couldn't say she did not deserve it.

"Listen carefully." Richard faced the woman who'd messed with his life for the last time. His soft words raised gooseflesh more effectively than stepping into a freezer.

"Don't ever pull that stunt on me again. Despite what your fevered mind may have concocted, you do not have carte blanche over my time or my person."

"And this married woman does?"

The vibrations emanating from Richard transformed from chilly to arctic.

"Tread very carefully, April. Poke me again the wrong way and not even the respect I hold for your father will prevent a nasty backlash. Now take your boy toy and get out of my office. Don't come back."

He didn't wait for her to obey. He turned and dialed Jeremy.

***

Gabriela had almost reached the security station at the lobby when Jeremy's voice stopped her.

"Mrs. Martinez, please," Jeremy pleaded. "Hold off."

Gabriela waited for him.

"What you saw upstairs was not at all what it looked like. There's nothing between Richard and April."

Yeah, right. And I'm Bambi. Men and their little protect-the-guys club.

"As soon as you drop me off at the hotel, Jeremy, I want you to retrieve my suitcases from Mr. Harrison's house. Drop them off at my manager's hotel room."

"The boss is not going to like this."

"Your boss doesn't own me. Now, are you going to drop me off or do I need to get a cab?"

Jeremy gestured to the elevators at the same moment his phone rang.

"Did you catch up to her?" Richard asked.

"Yes."

Gabriela cocked her head, her eyes knowing.

Jeremy blushed. He hated to be the hooker to these two props, especially two very angry props.

Richard sighed into the telephone. "Be careful and take good care of her until I get there."

"Will do."

"Keeping tabs on me?" Gabriela asked.

"Ah, Mrs. Martinez. Don't."

She placed a hand on his arm. "Sorry. Don't mean to take it out on you."

The elevator dinged its arrival. Jeremy held the door open while Gabriela walked inside.

***

Bogdan arrived at the lobby and walked to the building's directory as if he had a right to be there. He always did the beginning reconnoiter, but left surveillance to others less conspicuous than he. His operating window in these cases was slight. Because of his physique, people would begin to notice his lurking within ten minutes. Within less, security would start asking questions or escort him off the premises.

Today, he was here to confirm the information given to his boss. Check out if man's business was listed in building. Verify floor. Go to parking garage. Reconnoiter some more. Move out. Pass orders to one of his *siledzijas* to continue to watch, follow discreetly.

Knowing your enemy simplified things and helped focus plans of action, attacks, or abductions, whichever worked better. Opportunity was getting shorter, timing critical to get woman to agree, according to boss. Now that she was here, on his territory, he would not fail.

Quickly, Bogdan verified this Harrison man's business was on the seventeenth floor. His simian eyes wandered around the lobby area and located the exit staircase leading to the underground garage. He was on his way there, practically level with the elevator banks, when a very angry woman stepped across his path directly ahead. Bogdan was good with faces. It was the woman, the one giving his boss grief, and she was alone.

Bogdan was close, but not close enough to snatch her without alerting security and the few people loitering around the lobby. If he'd had his favorite toy in his pocket, the one releasing four milliamps of pure, debilitating, painful energy, he'd have risked it. She'd have been putty in his arms.

He was debating whether to follow when a man, who looked and smelled like a bodyguard, stepped out from another lift and rushed in the woman's direction, calling out her name. Bogdan studied the pair. He caught snippets of car and hotel as he pivoted and headed toward the staircase leading to the garage. By the time they went down, Bogdan would be in place, waiting for them. He would observe from there.

***

Herb Bryce raised his fourth cup of what the British thought was coffee and sipped the tepid, pissy-strength flavored water left there. He should be grateful. At least, when in London, the office staff made an effort to supply him with some brew. More often than not, he wished they didn't. But, damn it, lack of sleep, on top of jet lag, always fucked with his body and brain, and it was either drink this swill or settle for their milky tea, which made him want to puke. So he got his caffeine kick with this shit. At least, it kept the contents of his stomach where they belonged.

He shifted his butt, angling his body so the edge of the desk he'd been temporarily assigned didn't cut more circulation. Finally, his quarry was back in his crosshairs, thanks to the fax sent by the Christie's press office. But, shit, he was pissed. For several days, he'd gotten nowhere, the woman, her family, the bodyguard, her mystery guest, even the freaking dog, had disappeared like a cloud with no humidity. That meant no revenue in his bank account. The Monterey police hadn't helped, either. They'd transferred the perp to LA, and the mechanic was suddenly incommunicado. Not even his press credentials had made a dent. Frustrating. On top of everything else, the office staff here had also proved useless. No one had recognized the man in his photographs. And from a pic with a grainy profile, even less. Bunch of ineffective dweebs.

The familiar noises of rapid-fire keyboard clicks, loud conversation, constant phone rings, equipment hum, and occasional shouts within the bustling newspaper room surrounded him. He tuned them out to concentrate on the fax. The woman's itinerary was a freaking nightmare. He would have to do some very creative hustling to keep up.

"Got a map handy, Jones?"

The reporter two desks across didn't look up from his typing. "Second drawer on my right."

Bryce retrieved the map and reacquainted himself with the grid. "Mind if I write on this?"

"You muck up my map, you replace it."

"You're a real wanker."

Without pause to his typing, Jones lifted his right hand and flipped him the bird.

"Highlighter?"

With middle finger still extended, Jones pointed it to his right, at a cup overflowing with pens, pencils, highlighters, and permanent markers.

Bryce laughed, flicked him back the same hand gesture as thanks, and lifted a red marker and a highlighter. Back at his desk, he began to mark routes, circle tube stations near the events, and jot down kilometers between venues and his hotel. He'd have to convert the fucking metric system back to the yards and miles with which he was familiar. Go taxi or tube, maybe even foot, depending on traffic. What a pain in the ass.

"Bryce!"

The shout materialized from somewhere around the vicinity of the break room. He ignored the summons.

"Visitor," the same person shouted again.

Bryce looked up. A royally pissed-off Anglo goddess marched his way, followed by what seemed like a less royally pissed-off acolyte dogging her footsteps. He squinted. No, the man was not so much pissed off as unhappy with the situation and trying to be vocally persuasive about it. Bryce's eyes flicked back to the woman wrapped in fur, barging in his direction, and sized her up in a photographer's click. Used to getting her way. Probably the woman traded on her looks to get what she wanted, plying sex as her emasculating tool du jour. However, by the driven I'm-going-to-get-even expression written all over her face, it seemed she was not getting what she wanted this time. Bryce's eyes focused on the man following in miserable dejection. Poor fucker. Didn't know how to handle this type of dynamo.

The woman threw a newspaper on top of the desk and pointed a blood red, perfectly manicured claw to it.

Appropriate color to the mood, he thought. Wondered what she wanted with him.

"You shoot that?"

No introductions. Right to the point. Murder in her eyes. He scanned the banner and the photograph. Interest heightened and became the smell of the chase.

"Do you know who he is?"

"Know him?" Corked fury erupted from her mouth. Her volume increased. "He's my lover and that bitch is plotting to snatch him away."

The chaotic decibels of before, fell to barely discernible whispers around the office area. Some work simply stopped. Bryce could feel all ears cocking their way, journalistic radar antennas zeroing in on a juicy headline. No fucking way. The story was his.

Bryce picked up the discarded newspaper, grabbed a pen, his flip notebook, and motioned to his left.

"Let's find some privacy."

He smiled. He could just see sleighs of dollar bills jingle-belling toward his account.

Chapter Nineteen

"That big, good-for-nothing liar."

Jean-Louis sighed beside her.

Gabriela tramped to the next display.

About ten minutes ago, she had entered the elegant auction house in St. James's with Jean-Louis and Julien flanking her. She always enjoyed entering this elegant building, its façade a melange of Regency and Georgian architectural styles. Tonight, dressed up for the occasion, guests were welcomed with a red canopy stretched out to street level, imprinted with the auction house logo. Unlike earlier that morning, barricades now framed a dedicated periphery for curious passersby and journalists alike. A few of the latter, cameras in hand, perched behind the wooden blockade and flashed away at every person entering the venue. Upon arrival, Gabriela had dutifully pasted on a smile, turned here and there under Julien's guidance as they'd done hundreds of times in prior events, and beamed fatuously at the photographers, including Herb Bryce, who kept shouting her name over and over again to capture her attention.

Once inside, the coordinator of the event had brought them to a dedicated display room, empty for now, and had immediately made her excuses, disappearing the way they had come.

The spacious area had been outfitted for the evening with an open bar at the far right of the high-ceilinged, open floor plan. At its other end, a buffet area displayed a myriad hors d'oeuvres to please any palate. The arrangement had been the brain child of Julien, who wanted all guests desiring either drink or food forced to traverse the entire length of the room, where photographs of selected manuscript pages, enlarged to body-length size, hung from the ceiling, filling the softly lit walls in between. It was a beauty to behold.

Gabriela adjusted her dress once more. The transmitter taped on her thigh by the CID tech guy, and now resting between her pantyhose and skin, was chafing her. She fervently hoped the sharp edges, blunted with some tape, would not poke a hole in her hose before the event started. She didn't have an extra pair.

Her cocktail dress, as well, designed for this occasion by her friend Christian Harel, had not been created with bulgy equipment in mind. It felt inordinately tight. Then again, if she had known she needed to play stool pigeon on a man who wanted to physically harm her in order to get his hands on her work, she would have replaced the asymmetric chiffon sheath dress with a more comfortable one with pockets. She shrugged. At least, at waist level, an excess of ruched material fanned down the side of the dress, affording great camouflage. But the transmitter was warm and, therefore, a nuisance she'd have to deal with this evening, similar to another annoying, deceitful…

"Jerk."

"*Ma chère*," Jean-Louis said, placing his hands over his ears in exasperation. "Not again, please. *Ça suffit.* Let's move on, *s'il te plaît.*"

But she couldn't. Her emotions played within her like a psychotic pendulum, one minute hurt, another minute miserable. The occasional vocal lambasting of one specific man about his duplicity helped vent some of her emotions.

"*Gabrielle*," the soft voice of Julien cut through the drama. "Jean-Louis is right. Besides, you haven't even listened to Monsieur Harrison's side yet. I'm wondering, *chérie*, whether you're upset because he slept with this woman, or whether you are angry because she is so young?"

Both, she thought, but wouldn't admit it.

"I just feel so betrayed." *And I shouldn't.*

She sighed.

The expression on Jean-Louis's face was a bit incredulous. "*Mon Dieu, chérie*, it's not as if you had exclusivity over his person before today."

They worked their way to the buffet table. Jean-Louis did a quick eeny-meeny-miny-moe selection of some choice morsels and deposited them on a small plate he held. He skewered a kiwi fruit slice with a purple toothpick and chewed.

"Think about how he's felt about you sleeping with Roberto these past four years."

Gabriela didn't say a thing. No one knew she hadn't slept with Roberto for a long, long time.

"He's my husband. Big difference."

"Really? How so? Richard is an M-A-N. He's got needs, *chérie*."

Julien reached over Jean-Louis and pierced a strawberry from his plate. Her manager caressed Julien's forearm as if in apology for the next statement.

"What do you expect from an unattached drool fest like Harrison? Key word. Unattached. Such eye candy always has the bees buzzing."

"My point," Julien said. "He hasn't done anything unexpected."

That was the issue tying her into little knots of misery. What if she was messing up his opportunity at happiness? Worse. What if Richard felt obligated to be with her because of what happened four years ago? Had she become his duty, his yoke, like Roberto was hers?

"He should have said something. Warned me."

Jean-Louis huffed. "Really? When? While the goon attacked you? When your deck collapsed and you were hanging from the wall like a demented lizard? While he was trying to save both Luisito and you?"

In typical skeptical mode, Jean-Louis faced her completely, his eyebrow quirked.

"While you've been like an iceberg of rage after you caught a glimpse of the two tabloids at the hairdresser? While you've been hiding under our skirts at the hotel for the past three hours?"

"I haven't been hiding."

When his eyebrow reached St. Louis arch proportions, she capitulated.

"Okay. So sue me. But we had a day of peace and quiet while in New York and on the plane. He should have said something then."

"Are you for real, *chérie*? Your cousin surrounded you like a chastity belt, and once I arrived for the flight, Harrison couldn't get near enough to touch you with a finger. If he hadn't bamboozled Jeremy to switch seats with you on the flight over, you wouldn't even have gotten the good sleep you did."

She remembered. With head on his shoulder, she had slept like a newborn, safe and protected in their first-class cocoon, and only woken at two intervals to eat dinner and breakfast. It had been an unexpected reprieve.

"Besides," Julien interrupted. "You put down the discretion parameters for him, which, may I remind you, he has patiently observed."

Jean-Louis plopped a kiwi fruit slice into his mouth and moved to another image.

"By the way, I positively love the tonality of the lapis lazuli you used on this vellum."

Gabriela rolled her eyes. Leave it to Jean-Louis to have work on his brain as well. Why couldn't she?

"Concentrate on his actions, *ma belle*. If he didn't have feelings for you, he would not have dropped everything and crossed an ocean..."

"Plus a continent..." Julien added.

"To be with you and protect you."

"After four years," Julien finished, his jaw working right and left as he munched on another strawberry.

"You know how difficult it is to move heaven and earth to alter business schedules. Not only did Harrison do this to rush to your side, but he also did it with no questions asked. And you moan about a *petite liaison?* For all you know this woman is a regular *Marie-couche-toi-là.* Not the type your Richard…"

"Or any man…" Julien interrupted once more.

"Would be serious about."

A grin lifted the edge of her lips. A loose woman. How utterly Victorian of Jean-Louis. But, Jesus. What a mess. Not that the term couldn't be applied to her as well.

"There she goes," Jean-Louis told Julien, pointing the toothpick her way. "Look at her. She's already raking her soul over the coals of guilt. *Merde.*"

"He could have felt it his duty to help."

And therein lay her quandary. She wanted his love, not his duty. The picture she'd been shown on the front page of the tabloid showed a smiling Richard very much up close and personal with a vibrant and young April. The headline told the rest of the story.

Julien squeezed her hand and waited until her attention was fully on him.

"*Gabrielle.* Give yourself a break, as you Americans are so fond of saying. You gave Roberto and your marriage your all. It didn't work. *Tant pis.* Second chances are rare, *ma belle,* yet the universe just gifted you with one. Don't risk it because of petty jealousy, self-doubts, or fear."

"You love your Richard deeply," Jean-Louis said. "I'm sure he loves you deeply as well."

Suspicion was a bitch, she thought.

"Oh, pooh. Wipe that doubt from your face, woman. I've seen Harrison look at you with eyes that could burn demons in hell. And wait until he sees you in this outfit." The one-shoulder dress, with the ruffle beading at waist level, transformed her into a divine vision in gold.

"We recognize those looks, don't we?" He raised Julien's hand and placed a kiss on it, his eyes crinkling in a knowing smile.

"*Oui.* The kind that explodes the surrounding air with sexual energy." Julien fanned himself with his hand. "*Oh, là.*"

But was wanting enough to last a lifetime?

Her thoughts and their little *tête-à-tête* were interrupted, however, by the arrival of Inspector Morris. Anir, the tech guy, and a woman officer followed in tow.

Gabriela introduced Morris to her managers. Morris reciprocated by telling her the policewoman, Sergeant Hollister, would be her assigned detail for the evening.

"Great job, Anir," Morris said, inspecting her. "Didn't have much to work with for camouflage."

"It took some finagling, but I managed."

"And my thigh keeps complaining." Gabriela squirmed inside her skirt once more.

"Audio?"

"Good for now," Anir said. "Once the event starts, I'll need to adjust for ambient noise. We'll begin recording then. Any issues and I'll send someone from the van to support."

When Morris nodded, clearly satisfied, Anir took that as his signal to depart.

"Mrs. Martinez, make certain you stay within Officer Hollister's visual periphery, preferably in and around the center of the room at all times, especially if Wickeham makes contact. I encourage a one-to-one with him, but warn us of any problems."

Gabriela nodded.

"If you need to go to anywhere, even the loo," Hollister added, "come and get me. I'll secure the area."

"We'll relieve you of the transmitter before you leave for Mr. Harrison's home to retire for the evening."

"I won't be there."

Morris, who had been about to retrieve a folded paper from inside his jacket pocket, stopped and stared.

"Should I be worried now about unexpected complications?" Morris asked, scanning her face slowly. When her cheeks flushed red and her eyes skittered downward, he asked point-blank.

"Did something happen between the two of you since our meeting this morning?"

Embarrassed silence on her part.

"Changes this late in the game can muck up all the security measures we've already taken," Morris said. "We would need to start fresh with some. Delays or alterations without much thought can mess everything and place you in jeopardy."

Gabriela felt reprimanded, which was Morris's purpose, she was certain. Unfortunately, whether she liked it or not, he had a valid point. Today, she'd acted like a recalcitrant child, not a woman in danger. Her guard was down. The mundane, the days without threat, had relaxed her, decreased her vigilance. The jealousy, she had to admit, kept her focused on one theme, instead of on what was really important. She needed to regain her wariness, her edge. Too much was in the balance. Richard...well, she would handle Richard, even if she had to barricade the door against him with a dresser, or whatever. Maybe she should ask Frank to sleep in her room.

Something in her expression must have reassured him, because Morris looked satisfied as he handed over the sheet of paper.

"I've already sent this out to Mr. Harrison and Jeremy."

Once she unfolded the Xeroxed copy of two enlarged identification cards, Morris pointed to the image on the left first.

"Hays will take first shift tomorrow." He pointed to the image on the right as he included everyone with a quick sweep of his eyes. "Trinder will take the second, six hours later. If anyone other than those two show up without my prior notification, we have a problem."

Gabriela scrutinized the faces and handed the sheet to Jean-Louis, who then passed it on to Julien.

"They have instructions to report to each of you personally. Mr. Harrison wanted me to show you this because their shifts will overlap after you're finished with your interview spots at the telly tomorrow."

"What about Wickeham?" Jean-Louis asked. "What should we do when he comes tonight?"

"Give him room to approach Mrs. Martinez," Hollister said. "But be aware if he begins to maneuver her into a precarious situation."

Morris nodded. "React as you've always done with any admirer of Mrs. Martinez's work. See if you can get him to admit involvement with your previous mishaps, Mrs. Martinez. What does the proverb say—give him rope?"

"Yeah, to hang himself. What if he doesn't bite?"

"We'll take one instance at a time."

Julien spotted the coordinator waving at them. When she'd captured their attention, she pivoted and disappeared once more.

"That's our cue," Julien said. "They're opening the doors."

"If you need anything, Mrs. Martinez, remember, go to Hollister, come to me, or ask for help. We have ears on you and we'll also be working the room all night."

Jean-Louis looked at her. "Ready?"

As ready as I will ever be, Gabriela thought. And so the curtain rises. Let the show begin.

***

Richard arrived half an hour after the event was in full swing. Once Jeremy announced Morris's security flotilla had arrived at the hotel and would relieve him of bodyguard duties, Richard had been able to relax some, catch up with a few pending issues, rearrange a few others in his agenda to match Gabriela's commitments, and gotten ahead with others.

He was led to the second floor where animated vocalizations overshot the constant hum of human conversation. The area, although huge, was packed. His eyes did a quick sweep, catching sight of Father Ramirez in conversation with two other priests close to the buffet table. Morris was weaving every which way. Next to the open bar, at the edge of the room directly across his line of vision, he spotted April beside her father and Edmund.

Richard blended discreetly with the crowd, heading toward Hollister, who had positioned herself near one of the displays. Gabriela should be somewhere nearby.

He spotted Gabriela next to Jean-Louis and another man he didn't know. Julien, maybe?

He focused.

Christ.

Draped in gold fabric, Gabriela looked as Helen must have looked to Paris—irresistible, desirable, gorgeous, and sexy as hell. She was his siren, luring him, captivating him, and fascinating him equally. Her shoulders were bare, a wide strap discreetly hiding most of the scar on her left shoulder—that ugly memento of her experience four years ago. The rest of her creamy shoulder was partially hidden by her Bordeaux hair, which curtained her shoulders and back like an undulating silk river.

Richard stopped. He wanted so many things at that moment—to feel the vibrant warmth of her hair, kiss any anger from those lips, caress her scarred shoulder and brush a healing touch over her bruised skin. He wanted to whisper he ached because she'd been hurt by the scene with April, wanted to tell her he deserved her anger for not warning her, but not her scorn.

Jeremy appeared beside him, like a genie uncorked. His eyes forever shifted, observed.

"Anything?" Richard asked.

"No, sir," Jeremy answered after sweeping the entire room once more. "No sign of him yet."

"Keep a sharp eye and warn me if he arrives."

Jeremy nodded and made himself scarce, working the room in similar fashion to Morris and Hollister.

Richard ambled toward Gabriela and saw Jean-Louis tap her cheek playfully. As he stopped behind her, Richard caught the tail end of their conversation.

"I am still not convinced, *chérie*," Jean-Louis said. "Besides, you have enough problems as it is to let this *pétasse* get the better of you."

"Who is the bitch?" As if he didn't know.

Gabriela turned.

Of course, it had to be Richard.

Her lungs couldn't capture enough oxygen. He was breathtaking in his elegant, black silk suit, every inch of it filled with his warm muscle and strength. The suit's color also intensified his eyes, turning them into a sexy, smoky gray.

As Jean-Louis had said earlier, the man was a drool fest.

Unfortunately, an image of April's hungry lips, consuming Richard's, superimposed itself over the reality facing her.

Gabriela tried. Really, really tried to curb her wayward mouth. Petulance, unfortunately for her decorum, went on a rampage. She lifted her chin and pointed it in the direction where April stood with Edmund and a gaggle of other men she did not know.

"Your girlfriend back at the office. The one who jumped your bones and practically ate you."

"*Dieu*," Jean-Louis whispered.

Richard, who'd had a bitch of an afternoon, tamped down the urge to drag her somewhere private to have the mother of all showdowns.

"Sweetheart, didn't know you'd replaced your Uzi submachine for a bazooka launcher."

Jean-Louis cleared his throat, but his eyes danced in devilish amusement. Gabriela wanted to throw her small purse at her friend.

"Actually, I was thinking more in terms of ballistic missiles."

Julien almost choked on the wine he was sipping

"I've had a pisser of a day," Richard said. "If you hadn't rushed out and hidden behind these two for hours, I would have explained—"

"Actually, as I recall, your explanation was rather clear and to the point this afternoon. Actions do scream louder than words."

"It's not what you think."

Pride, rather than heart, spoke. "Isn't it?"

Richard had had enough. His eyes raked her entourage.

"Give me two minutes...alone."

Jean-Louis studied him for a second. "Let's find the photographer for a publicity shot."

Julien nodded. "Two minutes," he warned and turned to follow.

Richard pulled her to a secluded corner near the emergency exit. He turned to face her, leaned closer, and spoke into her shoulder. "You, too, guys. Mic off. Two minutes."

Gabriela knew she was blushing, but her defenses bristled. She turned to leave, but his hand prevented it.

"Oh, no, you don't."

When he was in this mood, Gabriela knew it would be impossible to escape. He wanted a showdown? Well a showdown he would have. She leaned forward, bristling, her words contained.

"You've got a hell of a nerve."

"With you, yes."

"Stay away from me. Go back to your Lolita. The tabloids said you were happy lovers until I waltzed along."

"Damn it to hell." His whispered words indicated a fierceness she'd witnessed before. "Do you believe every vile word written in those shit rags?"

"And are you telling me it's not true you've slept with her?" She lowered her voice. Several people had looked at them curiously.

He caged her even more. "No, I don't deny it and will never deny it. I did. Once. It was enough."

"Famous last words."

"Gabriela…"

"What? You want me to believe you greet friends in your office with the enthusiasm of a horny toad?"

He stared, incredulous. "You believe I'd trade you for another version of Silvie?"

That got her attention. Damn the man. Of all the examples he could have used, he'd have to pick Silvie. Heinige's lover had been a vapid, vacuous woman, mercenary as hell, who wouldn't have thought twice about wrapping her naked body around any man if it was to her advantage. Expediency had always trumped love for Silvie.

Richard saw the change in her eyes and pressed his advantage.

"I don't want a petty, selfish girl. I don't want a body to satisfy my occasional sex drive. I want a woman to share my life. An equal. Emotional fulfillment is what I crave. April can't give me anything, except boring sex."

He pulled Gabriela so close she felt his warm breath on her lips.

"No one can fulfill me the way you do. No one."

Gabriela's eyes became two swimming pools of distress.

"Damn." Every emotion colored that one word. Capitulation. Forgiveness. Frustration. Anger.

"Why didn't you tell me? Warn me, damn it. Finding out in such a manner the two of you were lovers hurt…a lot."

Richard wouldn't call what he had experienced with April satisfying enough to label them lovers.

"How do you think I felt every time I knew Roberto was touching you, loving you? Supernova doesn't begin to describe my viciousness and my pain. The walls in my apartment, or at the dumps I stayed in often, carried the wounds of my frustration. So did my hands."

"I almost gave you a bloody nose, you know," she admitted. Not to mention the fact she'd had to rein in the urge to rake her short nails across April's face.

"Jealousy is a bitch. Why didn't you?"

"Wasn't too keen about bruising my knuckles, and I didn't bring my rolling pin."

"Shit. You still have that thing?"

"Handy weapon."

Richard chuckled and framed her face with his hands.

"We have a ton of things working against us at the moment, none of which is more important than getting Wickeham off your back."

"Don't forget Herb Bryce."

"That, too. But he's contained outdoors. Thank you Christie's."

"What about your spring chicken over there?"

"April?" He glanced in the direction Gabriela had last seen her. "She's a self-absorbed virago. She'll try her damnedest to upset you, to manipulate things to pull us apart. Be prepared."

"Set a bullseye on you, huh?"

"You've no idea. Tried every trick in the book to make us a couple. Hasn't got me to bite, although I have to commend her on effort."

"You did give her reason."

"Never."

"Never? You did the moment you chucked your clothes with her, you know. Why on earth get involved with a woman like that?" She didn't say young.

"Convenience."

That was harsh. Gabriela never, ever wanted to hear such an apathetic tone of dismissal directed at her. She began to feel sorry for this April…but not too much.

"Don't let anyone screw us out of a future, Gabriela. You are the mother of my child. I will never let you go again or allow anyone to come between us. I know it sounds like I'm a selfish bastard. I am when it comes to you. But I gave you up four years ago. I can't anymore. Keep that at the forefront. Everything else will fall into place."

He leaned forward to kiss her lips when a tap on his shoulder interrupted.

Timing for them, as usual, sucked.

"Your two minutes are over, Monsieur." Jean-Louis took Gabriela by the hand and, without apology, led her to where the official photographer for the event waited with Julien.

"Let's take a photo in front of this piece."

She turned to face the elderly photographer, her cheeks burning with embarrassment. Why was it she forgot everything when Richard was around? He had almost kissed her in public and she would have let him. She didn't say another word.

"Here, Mr. Harrison." Jean-Louis pulled Richard forward and sandwiched him between himself and Gabriela with the finesse of an elephant going through brush. He told the photographer to wait a second while he waved Julien to Gabriela's other side.

"Think of the sales, *chérie*," Jean-Louis said. "Think of recouping, *tout de suite*, the money spent on the tons of gold foil you used in the manuscript. Smile."

Richard heard her chuckle and then her nervous intake of breath as he took advantage of this conspicuous setup by her manager. He drew her closer, ascertaining her body was pressed to his from feet to shoulder, enjoying the warmth of her body, the feel of her waist in his palm, and the small tremors undulating through her.

He smiled.

As soon as the barrage of flashes ended, Jean-Louis, together with his partner, shepherded the photographer away like a well-oiled machine. Jean-Louis, in typical fashion, talked nonstop.

"Who is the tall man next to your manager?"

Gabriela chuckled, remembering Richard had not met Julien during the fiasco four years ago, or at her home recently. His description of Julien was apropos. Slim, with a sleek swimmer's body, Julien stood a lean head's worth over Jean-Louis's own. Shy by nature, he was the soothing balm to her manager's outrageous and colorful personality. A good blend, much like an award-winning rosé.

"Julien. The Laurel to his Hardy. Partners in business and life. He manages the financial, security, and administrative aspects of the galleries and my career. He's a gifted artist himself. A dear, dear friend as well."

The warmth and love emanating from her voice caught Richard's attention. Gabriela answered the question in his eyes.

"Apart from Maurice, who tried to shield me, but had a hornet's nest of incredible proportions in his hands, these two protected me furiously, especially from the paparazzi who were out for blood four years ago. They took over my career at a moment when I was about to give it up. They encouraged me, promoted me, kept my secrets, and have been my selfless cheerleaders from day one. I owe a lot to them."

"Will you show me your work?" He paused. "Forgive me?"

Gabriela's heart melted. She turned, trying not to show how her eyes spoke of her emotions, trying not to make things too easy for him.

"This vellum copy," she began, "is my reproduction of a psalm page on the original Visconti Hours manuscript." She expanded her descriptions, explaining the Latin script, the allusions of the falcons perched on stylized oaks. She glossed over the embellishments and the trefoil, what method she'd applied in creating the colors, the gilding of the page, and how Julien had pitched in by obtaining the vellum. All the while Richard's hand, warm against her back, moved in wide, concentric circles, roaming from her waist to underneath her hair, and back down again.

She was about to explain another exhibit when a voice floated over her shoulders like bad news.

She recognized it, to her detriment.

La pétasse. The bitch.

"Richard." Breathless in its delivery. "Love." Exaggerated in her emotion.

April, in iridescent black lamé to complement her blonde hair and pale skin, was close. She held Edmund's hand with her right hand. Her other arm stayed snuggled within the crooked arm of an elderly man Gabriela didn't recognize.

The woman was smiling too brightly. Gabriela narrowed her eyes. She didn't like the message written in that face.

April let go of the two men simultaneously, grabbed Richard's arm, and pulled him away from Gabriela, positioning herself as replacement. Gabriela was left with no other option but to step aside.

If Richard didn't do something about this, and soon, well, it wouldn't bode well for him. He'd better make his choice clear, or else.

"A wonderful event, Mrs. Martinez," April said, without even glancing her way.

Gabriela caught the deliberate emphasis on her married status and the silent, forced elbowing to get her out of the picture.

She narrowed her eyes into slits.

With a smile on her lips and cattiness in her eyes, April caressed Richard's chin with nimble fingers and kissed his cheek before he could step away. Then, for the benefit of her audience, she laughed in delight, making a point of erasing the lipstick from Richard's face with what looked to Gabriela like a sensual massage.

"I'm always doing this. Shame on me."

Richard moved his face away from further touch and, with a firm hand, forced April away from his proximity.

Edmund, catching the undercurrents and one to avoid unpleasant rows, extended his hand to Gabriela in gentlemanly greeting.

"Nice to see you again, Mrs. Martinez." His voice held warmth and admiration. "Congratulations. Splendid work."

"Indeed," the older gentleman said and slapped Richard's shoulder in a warm welcome. "Glad you are back. We've missed you." His glance oscillated between Richard and April. "Well, someone has."

"You are so sweet," April said and gave her father a quick hug. "My father, everyone, is always so circumspect." She laughed. "No need to be, Daddy. Everyone knows I missed Richard terribly. Right, darling?"

Gabriela stared. Daddy? How old was this woman? Was she for real?

Richard, however, was not amused, especially when April kept coming back to hang onto him like a leech, despite his attempts at removing her. It was obvious she had dismissed, with the ease of a two-year-old, his earlier warning.

Enough was enough. He was fed up.

"Second warning." His whisper was forceful, his hands rougher than usual as he pressed her away from him. The final, deliberate rebuff, however, occurred when he turned his back on her and extended his hand toward Gabriela.

He hoped Gabriela had read his body language accurately. Her eyes turned speculative. The snub he'd given April was as in your face as he was going to give, at least here in a room full of people. He wouldn't do anything else, either, not in front of April's father. Lord Cranfield did not deserve to witness the treatment he really wanted to dish out to his daughter.

Richard held his breath and his hand steady. *Your choice.*

It felt like an eternity before Gabriela placed her hand in his. He captured it, cradled it in the crook of his arm, and pulled her near and forward.

"Lord Cranfield, this is Mrs. Martinez, the honoree of the event and a very, very special friend."

No one, not even April could mistake the fierce and pleased inflection in his voice.

Chapter Twenty

Stealth, tonight, had generated for Wickeham a wealth of information. He'd entered the event one hour after it had begun and was delaying greeting business acquaintances and former patrons, keeping to the fringes of the room. He'd targeted his quarry immediately and was certain her bodyguards had spotted him as well while doing their rounds. He persisted on his nonchalant approach and merged from display to display with gawkers around him oohing and aahing over her work.

His property...soon.

"Magnificent, isn't it?" said an elderly woman somewhere around his right shoulder. He glanced over and saw more jewelry worn than the queen at a state dinner.

His eyes returned to roam over the enlarged manuscript page, slowing and absorbing details: the fashionable Renaissance courtiers singing from a scroll, the convoluted arabesques, the foliate forms resembling fireworks. The leaves, the flowers, the petals in gold, blue, and soft pink. He read part of the explanatory marker of the Latin beneath the grid: *Domino canticum novum*...Sing ye to the Lord.

The folios he'd first perused several weeks ago had not come close to capturing the soul and beauty of her entire work. Now, here, with the magnitude of her work in full display, Wickeham realized gaining ownership of the piece was as vital as the throbbing within his veins, the oxygen to his lungs. His need to possess had been ratcheted to inordinate proportions, similar to a drug addict's need.

"Breathtaking," he answered. "Will you be bidding?"

"Most definitely, especially after seeing this," the woman answered.

"I hear bidding will be intense," Wickeham commented calmly, while inside he was vibrating.

"Rumor is the Princess is interested. Charities are always near and dear to her."

Wickeham bent his head in acknowledgment of the admiration in the woman's voice.

"Diana is truly many a charity's champion."

"If she does make an appearance, expect a shark frenzy."

That will never happen.

Without excusing himself, Wickeham worked his way to the open bar, asked for white wine, and received what he considered cheap Zinfandel for the occasion.

He, on the other hand, would have served the finest champagne.

He listened to more commentary while ambling from stunning display to stunning display, his need metamorphosed to a craving so deep his muscles contracted until he could barely breathe. He wet his lips with what he still considered inferior wine and forced his body to relax while he observed. He needed to seize the right opportunity to approach her. In the meantime, he kept garnering interesting information, a fortune's worth to achieve his goal.

He subjugated a shiver of pleasure. He felt almost ridiculously old-fashioned, a voyeur in a ballroom, witnessing the development of a delicious scandal that, by evening's end, would become the latest on dit.

It always paid to be inconspicuous.

Always paid to be a silent observer.

And definitely paid to study your opponent while their guard was down.

First, she was better protected than expected tonight. Apart from the two obvious bodyguards, one roaming, the other stationary near her, the same people kept gathering around her. Their actions brought to mind dragonflies hovering and darting over the ground. Two people within that group appeared to be her promoters, posing her for publicity photos and leading her from group to group of admirers, patrons, and bidders. But protectors would not deter him from speaking with her personally. This would be his last cajole. His last civilized warning, so to speak.

He chuckled.

Second, the tabloid filth he'd read this afternoon had gotten something correct. This Harrison chap had feelings for Mrs. Martinez, with a possessiveness bordering on the animalistic, if the man's body language and expressions—gentle when touching her, sensual in its roaming, and brutal in its defensiveness—were any indication. The other headline he'd read, with photographs showing the other woman clinging to Harrison? Worthless, when faced with the reality of these two together.

From Mrs. Martinez he was getting rather mixed signals. He'd captured anger mixed with wariness and an occasional loving body-language Freudian slip. These two had a history and a link—a powerful one he could use to his advantage.

Another element on which to ponder this evening.

Third, and most interesting, was the invisible slap Mr. Harrison had given the other woman, a little over five minutes ago. In her obvious, carnal desire for him, she kept ignoring the glaring signals of rejection, the many rebuffs. And from the way Harrison had often clenched his jaw and dislodged her greedy hands, it appeared he found the woman's nearness distasteful. An interesting dichotomy after seeing the photograph of those two in the tabloid. The turning of his back and the extending of the hand to Mrs. Martinez had brought the final, humiliating realization. The woman's face was worth studying now, her cheeks flashing alternately red from anger and embarrassment. Retribution burned in their depths as well, an emotion with which Wickeham was eminently familiar.

His lips curled. Spurning a woman who thought herself desirable and irresistible to the opposite sex, in a public venue no less, and in front of a competitor for Harrison's affections, was a death knell and a gross miscalculation on Mr. Harrison's part. Everyone who dealt with narcissistic personalities, especially self-serving women as the blonde there, should tread warily. Heaven did have no rage like love turned to hatred, nor hell such a fury as a woman scorned.

Mr. Congreve had gotten it correct.

Mr. Harrison's loss.

Wickeham's gain.

He would use it to his advantage later this very evening.

Now, however, he simply waited for the appropriate moment to approach his prey.

***

For the first time Gabriela found herself alone. Milling humanity surrounded her, but it ebbed and flowed like a current in the ocean, skirting her as an unwanted piece of flotsam as she stood in the middle of the room.

Morris's plan.

He'd warned everyone, a while back, her quarry had entered the building, and requested they all give her room to be approached. Richard had dutifully disappeared a minute ago to get her a club soda with a lemon wedge, while Jeremy and Morris resembled two penguins with ADHD, roaming the periphery of the room as if she were a fixture of no importance. Hollister, her police shadow, did her thing, while Frank and her managers fluttered around like an invisible boundary.

Gabriela knew the need, but was not looking forward to any confrontation, and the waiting to be approached by this man made her skin tingle. *Focus on the positive,* she thought, about how well the exhibition was going, about how much excitement her work was generating. Frank was ecstatic. So was she. The event promised to bring in even more money for the schoolchildren than they had anticipated.

That was a good thing.

On another positive, a much bigger one than tonight's event, she'd spoken to Spike and her parents earlier in the evening while dressing at the hotel. The children's excited voices and squeals of delight in the background had expanded her heart with joy. It had made up for the unpleasantness of the afternoon in Richard's office with... *Okay. Let's not go there again.* She wanted pleasant, not pissed.

Her eyes roamed around the room, pride and pleasure filling her lungs. Gratification did not even begin to explain how she felt. The completed, polished images captured and displayed here tonight would never divulge the years of toil, of trials and errors, of tears shed, nor reveal the sacrifices suffered to bring this work to fruition. She counted herself proud of what she had achieved and felt truly satisfied with the conclusion.

If only her private life could come to the same satisfying fruition as well soon.

A whisper, a small something stirred her senses. An electric frisson sensitized the skin at the nape of her neck and shoulders. *Good grief,* frisson? *Really? Why on earth was she coming up with this vocabulary?*

But, there it was again, that unpleasant shiver.

She angled her head toward her left. A man approached on an interception course with her, his steps deliberate and his eyes two pinpoints of penetrating focus. A big nose, in appearance similar to a bulbous, cratered lava rock, was set on a flat face. There was something about the intensity of this man's gaze, the accuracy of his aim on her that made her feel like a living bullseye.

Something wicked this way comes...

Good Lord, now she was quoting Shakespeare. But the sense of nasty did not diminish. She was certain this was her nemesis, Wickeham.

And she was alone, as planned.

Lucky her.

Next to the man, Gabriela recognized an auction house employee from his uniform, name badge, and monogrammed logo on his jacket. Why was he there, escorting Wickeham of all people? Vaguely, a thought slithered through her brain about someone showing Wickeham the manuscript when it had arrived. Could this be the man's contact?

"Mrs. Martinez?"

Gabriela placed her most gracious smile on her face.

"Yes?"

"Lloyd Werner, junior specialist for Christie's."

She shook hands and hoped Morris made a note of this man's name.

"For what department do you work?"

"Furniture, sculpture, and works of art of the 19th century."

"Ah," she said as if the mysteries of the world had just been revealed. She turned, knowing full well what would be said next.

"And this is?"

"We've already met, Mrs. Martinez, but through different means." Wickeham turned to the junior specialist. "Thank you, Lloyd. That will be all."

Well, hell. As dismissive, arrogant, and forceful as over the phone.

"Mr. Wickeham?"

He nodded.

Gabriela did not offer her hand, but neither did he. And even if he had, she would have been hard-pressed to touch it. It would have felt like touching cooties, as her children were fond of saying.

They faced each other silently for a moment, almost assessing, and she wondered who would shoot first.

"I must congratulate you on a most instructive display this evening."

First innocuous volley—Wickeham.

"Always good business to motivate benefactors with a taste of what they'll possess."

Wickeham tensed. Her choice of words did not please.

"My offer remains, although you've been quite an imaginative opponent. Nevertheless, I must insist you accept my offer tonight. It will be my last. After this evening…"

"All bets are off?"

His face was a rather interesting gauge of his internal emotional pressure. He did not like to be interrupted, either.

"Mr. Wickeham, how dull. Really." Gabriela raised her hands, palms up. She spread them in front of her as though she were opening a handheld fan. Her gesture encompassed the entire room.

"Look around. Does it look as if I were interested in your pitiful offer? Before the ten minute mark goes by at auction, I will have raised more than twice the amount you proposed."

She stopped smiling. Gloves off.

"I won't ever sell my work to you now. Bid like a good man on Thursday." Her eyes moved up and down in an insulting assessment, returning to his face as if he had come up wanting.

"I'm wondering now if your insistence on my selling is because you don't have the money to dish out?"

Even though she was prepared, Wickeham's action surprised her. He grabbed her, his hand a manacle on her forearm. He reduced the gap between them.

"Don't provoke me, Mrs. Martinez."

"Or what?" Her voice dripped with a disdain difficult to overlook.

"Unfortunate things do happen on occasion."

She laced her next words with humor, although she was far from feeling it. "Is that another threat?"

The chuckle following her words triggered something ugly. His face distorted, his grip tightened further, and she could feel the anger vibrating his sinews.

"A warning."

"Like your warnings in the States?" She laughed this time. "How pathetic."

He reeled her in, his voice pleasant and low, in stark contrast to the message reflected in his eyes. She would have preferred a shouting match to this controlled purpose and menace. *Where the hell was Richard?* Things were decidedly not getting any pleasanter.

"Different territory. No more incompetents or mistakes."

"Really? Are you planning another ambush?"

"You will sell to me and to none other."

"How positively one-track minded. The answer is still no. Bid for it during auction."

His hand became a tourniquet.

"You'll soon change your mind."

That crushing of her forearm, the demands, the cruelty shining from the eyes, brought back memories of the clearing in France where Albert had brutalized her. It triggered a visceral response, a hatred of being manhandled by psychopaths.

She leaned farther in, surprising him.

"You don't scare me. I've dealt with your type before. I've even killed your type before. Your methods honestly don't impress me."

Gabriela did not try to dislodge herself. She simply looked down at the hand holding her prisoner and then up at him.

"Now, if you don't want me to create a scene by giving you a bloody nose in front of this group, you will remove your hand from my person, immediately."

"I suggest you do what the lady asks, Wickeham." The frigid tone fell between them like ice to skin.

Richard.

She had been so attuned to her foe, she had not realized Richard, Jeremy, and her managers were practically surrounding her. Morris and Hollister were watching, waiting, speaking softly into the microphones on their wrists. Father Ramirez hovered around the periphery of the group.

"Better take what the lady says at face value," Richard said. "Trust me. Tonight, she's bitchy enough to do as she promises. I, on the other hand, wouldn't have warned you."

"Americans. Always so crass."

"But accurate," Richard told him.

"Can I shoot him?" Gabriela countered.

Wickeham started.

Richard's smile was nasty. "Taught her myself. She's good." He looked at her. "Maybe later."

Once more, Gabriela looked at the imprisoning hand.

"Two seconds. If you don't release me, you're on your own."

Wickeham seemed to reconsider, understanding he was outmaneuvered and definitely outmuscled when he glanced around her.

Worse than a reluctant octopus unwilling to release its suckers from a victim, Wickeham's fingers relinquished their hold. His eyes, however, promised retribution.

"Certainty oftentimes is deceiving," Wickeham told her, bowing his head slightly in acknowledgment of her upper hand. "You may regret your choice."

Wickeham exited in the direction of the open bar.

The movement was swift, as if silent stage directions had been issued. Everyone surrounded her at once.

"Are you okay?" Richard was not happy.

Gabriela shuddered and hugged herself. "I'm fine, just feel as if some filth attached itself to me."

"*Mon dieu, chérie,* a minute more and I would have slapped the man silly," Jean-Louis said. "But Monsieur Morris gave orders to back off, to give this nasty man, what was it he said?"

"Rope," Gabriela supplied.

"That was awful," Julien said. "I wanted to scratch his eyes out."

Melodramatic, she thought, *but accurate.*

"Did he hurt you?" Richard asked, his touch on her forearm soothing.

She shook her head.

"*Cretino hijo de puta,*" Father Ramirez's tone resembled the look in his eyes, which followed Wickeham's path to the open bar very closely. He crossed himself. "He's also really creepy."

"Guys, I'm fine."

"Will he try that again?" Jean-Louis's whisper floated next to her ear.

"I think this was his final pleasant overture," Richard said. "From now on, however, we have to be at our wariest."

Father Ramirez squeezed her hand. "Incredible, Gaby. How did you keep your cool?"

She shrugged. She didn't know how, either.

"You made him lose control, sweetheart," Richard said. "I'm impressed."

"You heard?"

"Behind you all the time, once the bastard approached."

He always had her back.

"Not quite a confession though."

"His words crossed beyond the range of innuendo tonight. Morris should be more than pleased. Evidence, even circumstantial, is mounting, and Wickeham didn't deny your allegations he was behind your attacks."

"Might as well return to normal," Jeremy suggested. "We don't want to tip our play."

Gabriela studied Wickeham's stiff figure at the bar. He sandwiched himself between April and another patron and stared at Gabriela. Richard veered her in the opposite direction, his purpose to blend with the crowd.

"The man does not like being ignored," Gabriela commented, revisiting the conversation with Wickeham.

"Delusions of grandeur, possibly," Richard said.

"And then some. He'll destroy everything and everyone in his path to get what he wants. I saw it, felt it."

"A modern Nero."

"Let's just hope he'll destroy himself before he destroys anyone else."

Especially me, she thought. She hated parties.

***

"Such a striking couple, don't you think?" Wickeham said to the air in general. He'd wedged himself between the bar and the woman ten minutes ago, gauging her mood, biding his time, watching her down two glasses of wine during the time he'd stood there.

"Although, I must say, Mrs. Martinez's husband is a trifle on the overprotective side."

Wickeham waited.

The woman took the bait. Anger fueled her gaze.

"He is *not* her husband."

"April, please." Edmund tried snatching the wine glass from her hand.

She rounded on him, spilling drops on the floor as the liquid splashed over the rim of her glass.

"Defending her?" Her words were spit out with syllabic preciseness and could have chipped brick. "Never pegged you for a prick, Edmund."

"And you are drunk beyond bitchiness."

She glared at him with eyes gauging the choice morsels of flesh where she would skewer him.

"Should have known you would fall under the bitch's spell in under two minutes."

"Are you certain of this?" Wickeham interrupted. His voice held enough naïveté to ensure she'd react. "The way they react, lean into each other, gaze at one another, shouts intimacy."

Wickeham let his last words sink and simmer.

"He's *my* lover. Mine."

Any more emphasis on those words and they would have been ground to a pulp.

"Oh, dear. Wouldn't have pegged Mrs. Martinez as a femme fatale. She's touted as such a moral individual, so above board, so respectable."

"She's a conniving bitch."

"April, stop," Edmund said, more emphatic than he'd ever been. "You're spewing rumors."

"Isn't she being interviewed in *Let's Talk About It!* tomorrow morning?" Wickeham continued as if these two weren't bitch-slapping each other. "Wonder if they'll mention this."

Everything in April stilled.

Wickeham smiled into his wine glass. He did not sip from the now warm liquid.

"You mean Sara Sheffield's chat show?" A crafty look took over her stillness.

"You wouldn't stoop so low," Edmund said, knowing perfectly well how her mind worked.

"Wouldn't I?"

"There were rumors buzzing some time ago, about her killing a man, as well."

Another stillness, this time from both.

Wickeham pasted his most innocent look on his face.

"Around four years ago, I think. Something to do with a mentor and friend of hers who was killed. If memory serves, Mrs. Martinez was not directly linked to the killing, but her name was bandied about some." He shrugged. "Vitriolic speculation, I'm sure."

He waited, a predator cat waiting for the quail to rise.

April slammed the glass on the bar. "Excuse me."

"April, don't." Edmund rushed after her.

Wickeham, smiling, watched the two leave the premises. If anyone decided to scrutinize him closely, some feathers should have been visible between his gleaming teeth.

Chapter Twenty-One

Gabriela stepped out of the bathroom massaging her leg. About an hour ago, Anir had unburdened her of the annoying transmitter fixed to her thigh, but the tape had left a welt on her skin. She still itched.

Her nose wrinkled. It had been one hell of a long evening, ending with more fizzle than bang. Wickeham had not approached her after their confrontation; then again, Richard had made sure of that. Christie's was ecstatic about the success of the publicity bash. So was Frank. And Inspector Morris had turned all Cheshire cat with what he'd gotten on tape. Not long after, following a quick discussion of tomorrow's agenda, they had all filed out—Jean-Louis and Julien to their hotel; her, to be driven to Richard's flat with Herb Bryce bringing up the rear. The ride had been a quiet one, with her sandwiched between Richard and Frank.

Upon arrival, however, Frank had turned strict Cuban chaperone, staying in her room, talking inanities until he thought Richard had retired for the night. He'd rushed taking his own shower. When she had gone to take hers, Frank had waited in her room until she was done, keeping a sharp eye out for Richard's possible wiles, she was sure, and inconveniencing her.

He'd finally left her alone a minute ago.

She walked to the window overlooking the street and lifted a corner of the blind. She squinted through the small opening there. Bryce had finally left. He would return tomorrow, she was certain, before she even stepped outside Richard's door. He was on the hunt once more, with flash after satisfied flash as they had exited the limo, and everywhere else.

The bed beckoned, with its fluffy and downy bedspread and thick mattress. But she was wired, despite her weariness and exhaustion.

She turned, stretching. She would not get much sleep tonight. Might as well make the usual call of the evening.

She sat on the bed, dialed the number quickly, spoke softly to Roberto while the nurse pressed the phone to his ear. By the time she hung up, her heart ached.

A soft knock came from the connecting bathroom door. Her cousin peeked in.

"I overheard when I brushed my teeth. What's going on?" he asked.

"Roberto's vitals fluttered all day today, but he recovered."

Father Ramirez walked into the room and stood by her. "How are you holding up?"

Gabriela shrugged.

"Don't despair, Gaby." He squeezed her shoulder and placed a kind kiss on her forehead. "Have faith. Things may yet work out."

Gabriela didn't respond, knowing her cousin still hoped for a miracle. But not many had come her way, and she didn't think any would be bestowed on her husband's condition.

"I'll pray a rosary for him before I go to sleep," he said.

She squeezed his hand. "Thanks, Frank. Sleep well."

At the connecting door, he stopped and looked at her. Sadness permeated his eyes. "Will you be all right? Do you want company?"

She shook her head.

"Remember, a day at a time," he whispered and disappeared through the bathroom, leaving the connecting door slightly ajar. Gabriela stood, closed it softly, and locked it.

The muted, droning recitations of Our Fathers and Ave Marias filtering from his room through the bathroom in-between did not lull her to sleep, as she had hoped. The hiccupy snores that followed did not help, either. For an hour, she kept tossing and turning, staring at the clock, compelling the numbers to change at will. By two o'clock, however, silence finally reigned, and her limbs relaxed. She drifted into sleep.

Drifted into dreams.

Drifted into impressions, strokes.

Heat.

Hardness.

Softness.

Sighs.

Her eyes fluttered. Opened wider.

"Shh," Richard whispered.

Caressing lips from ear to nape followed sound.

"Let me love you."

A soft kiss on one eyelid.

"Complete you."

A touch on the lips.

"Love you."

A kiss to end all kisses.

Her insides curled. A holocaust kindled both body and heart.

Gabriela learned quickly that intensity did not require noise. The lovemaking, the rediscovery of skin against skin, touch over touch, hands caressing in blind exploration, enhanced by the silence, exploded sensations, created a completeness where inhibitions fled and exquisite passion scalded.

She never believed skin could burn, but hers did as Richard slowly slid fabric over her skin. When knowing hands replaced her nightgown, her nerve endings ignited. Touch became a tasting as Richard's lips explored and pressed soft kisses on her torso, breasts, and as his mouth swallowed the soft moans wrenched out of her. Her own hands and lips roamed over him, reveling in his tremors, his pleasurable intakes of breath. Lovemaking became a revelation. As their bodies joined, Gabriela almost came apart. Skin to skin, heat to heat, movement became a glorious, rapturous ride to an apex of pleasure. More of her whimpers were masked by Richard's mouth and blended with his fulfilling groans. She drowned in every inner caress, in every kiss, in every pressure; drowned with every stroke over her body, in her body, in every pause within her fullness.

Drowned softly.

Slowly.

Gloriously.

Satiation exploded without sound, but with blinding intensity. It shook them. Lifted them. Froze them. Released them in united, wordless love.

Richard stirred. Rolled onto his back with her snugly wrapped in his arms.

Damn, but he loved this woman. And, shit, he'd forgotten how making love to her shook the foundations of his soul.

He breathed deeply and delighted in the silent aftermath of primal pleasure. This was surely a taste of heaven.

"I love you." His words grazed her ear in an intimate whisper.

She raised her head and kissed his cheek.

"I love you more," she whispered back.

His chest vibrated with a satisfied rumble, while his hand fondled her soft back from shoulder to backside. His fingertips tingled. This...now this could last a lifetime and be as satisfying every single time, every single way.

Since the earlier debacle in his office, he'd waited patiently until he'd felt satisfied the priest was in deep La-La Land before coming to her, before loving her. He'd needed to tell her, show her how precious she was. Had needed to reinforce in her mind that April was insignificant in the scope of his life.

"You are a devious man, Richard Harrison."

"Mm."

"Frank thought he'd outwitted you."

"I've had more practice."

He felt the tremble of her laugh. Felt the tingle of her exploration, pined for more the moment her fingers paused near his heart. She examined the puckered scar there.

"Bullet," he whispered.

"When?"

"Three years ago."

"How?"

"Distracted."

He could almost hear her brain calculating, putting facts together, understanding, perhaps, his carelessness, his despair.

Her breath hitched. "You almost died."

"Close enough."

He touched her scar, the keloid tissue not yet smoothed by time. "So did you."

"Almost."

"We're a hell of a pair."

"One day we'll compare notes." He felt her lips move into a smile.

Her explorations continued.

His breath spiked.

He rolled over with her and began another languorous assault on her body. Discovered new textures. Never would he have thought there could be another, even more towering dimension to passion, of hunger, and deep satisfaction.

He was proven wrong.

He didn't get much sleep that night. He didn't let her sleep much, either. Too many years of thirst. Too many years of want.

This marked their new beginning. A lifetime worth of joinings.

And before the fingers of dawn caressed the canvas of the sky, he finally left her in decorous satisfaction.

Chapter Twenty-Two

Gabriela was being bugged once more, but this time with a wired lavalier for the interview.

The show was currently on an advert break, she'd been told. The floor manager of the segment verified the microphone on her lapel was properly clipped and that the battery pack was secure on her skirt's waistband. His movements were rushed, and to Gabriela's view more like frantic, as he assured no wires showed on the blue silk blouse or anywhere around the collar of her contrasting black jacket.

The associate director, Jennifer Cady, or call-me-Jenni, took over.

"Sara will introduce the segment first," Jennifer said, guiding Gabriela to the set. "Show music. Clap, clap. Segment intro. We'll cut to a taped video of the exhibition, fade in and pan live to Sara when done. She'll introduce you and your project, and follow with the interview questions."

They stepped over wires, dodged crew and staff, and skirted two stationary cameras. Gabriela was led to a couch next to where the host was seated. Jennifer's expert eye did a quick, final assessment of Gabriela, turned and yelled, "One minute, people."

The host of the chat show, a slim woman, with washed-out blue eyes and a pixie haircut in blonde tones, leaned over from her chair to greet Gabriela.

"Very pleased to meet you, Mrs. Martinez. I'm Sara Sheffield." Her grip was strong and her manner businesslike. "Think of this as a friendly conversation. Relax, smile, and you'll be fine."

Gabriela swallowed. Did she look as panicky as she felt? Probably, if Sara felt obligated to reassure her. The issue, however, was why. This, after all, was her third interview of the morning and the show's format was similar to the previous two, with only one exception—there was no audience, thankfully. This time around, she simply needed to concentrate on the host, her questions, answer cordially, and leave on the next hard break.

But she couldn't get rid of this onset of jitters. Maybe a glimpse of her friends would get her mind off the ants crawling all over her nerve endings. Her gaze shifted to the live feed monitor of the Blue room and found them. Jean-Louis and Julien were facing the camera over their own monitor, giving her thumbs up and impromptu, soundless kisses as they watched her on set. She smiled. Jean-Louis looked like a prim spinster, positively ridiculous with her purse hanging from his bent arm, while Julien alternately tapped and squeezed Jean-Louis's shoulder in order to soothe his nerves, which were usually worse than hers.

Her eyes shifted to the bodyguard, standing on set in the background, behind the cameras—far enough not to be underfoot and close enough for any emergency. Another pair of watchful eyes when added to the dozen people on set and in the control room.

Gabriela breathed long and deep, paused for a couple of seconds, and exhaled slowly. A deep longing, a wishing Richard were here overwhelmed her. Where was he? Had something happened? He'd promised to be here in time for the taping. Afterward, for once, they would have the afternoon to themselves. Her armada was giving them a much-desired breather due to prior commitments. Frank was meeting some friends for lunch. Jean-Louis and Julien were going shopping for kilts. When she'd asked why on earth they wanted Scottish garments when they were French, Jean-Louis, in his unique, blasé manner had answered, "*Chérie*, who cares. It's the freedom that counts."

Christ.

"Thirty seconds," boomed a voice from the darkened bowels of the studio.

Gabriela made a mental review of people she needed to thank. Her brain refused to work. A moment of immobility revealed a blank void inside her data bank. What the hell was wrong with her today? She felt like an unprepared Oscar winner ready to blab nonsense due to nerves. Would taking out her notes inside her jacket pocket look unprofessional? Maybe. Texting Jean-Louis with the cell phone tucked away in her skirt pocket certainly would.

Think pleasant thoughts…pleasant thoughts. Think last night. No, no, no, not last night. Jesus. That was the last thing she needed to really scatter her brainwaves.

But the feel of warm, languorous lips, roaming, tasting, capturing her own galloped across her thoughts and fired up her mind into sensory overload.

Yikes. Was she an idiot? Her body temperature felt like it spiked a good ten degrees hotter than normal. Her brain refused direction, supplying vivid images of Richard's heat against her own, of his consuming mouth and of his knowing hands, squeezing, pressing, and driving her crazy with want, fulfillment, satiation, her body merged to his to a degree where their contours blended into no discernible separation. It had been gratifying beyond anything she had experienced yet, or recreated still. And it had left her wanting him badly.

He had left the room wanting her badly, as well, he'd whispered before he'd dropped her off at the first interview this morning.

The floor manager cued them to action in fifteen.

She began to sweat. *Good grief.* Looking around the studio, she hoped they would blame the perspiration pooling on her forehead on the hot studio lights.

"Live in ten, nine..."

Gabriela started. Deep breath, deep breath. She watched the TV host gather her cue cards, tap them neatly into a perfectly aligned stack, and focus on the teleprompter under camera 1.

Well, there was something to be said for being hot and bothered. Miraculously, Gabriela's brain functioned once more, spewing out the names she could not recall earlier. The jitters had disappeared.

Music blared from the overhead speakers, the silent, three-second cue flashed from the floor manager's fingers, and Sara plastered a smile on her face.

Show theme finished. Canned applause. The host welcomed back her viewers and immediately segued into the taped segment, visible on the monitors. Another cue, cut to Sara and Gabriela, brief introductions, platitudes, more fake canned applause, smiling nods both ways.

The interview began.

Gabriela reacted to the cordial and friendly questions with graciousness and ease. Her answers, on-point, detailed her work, the exhibition, and the purpose for the charity auction. Folios faded in and out of the monitor near her. She explained the images when prompted, and talked about the colors, symbols, and imagery used, how long it had taken to create it. In the back of her mind, she was pleased and impressed at the research from the production team.

A fifth folio photograph faded out.

"The exhibition is open to the public today and tomorrow at the Christie's showroom on King Street. Phone the number on screen for exhibition hours and information. Remember, all proceeds will go to the St. Francis Bay Area Charity for Children."

Gabriela nodded and smiled into the camera, waiting for the final 'cut' cue that never came.

"Before we go on commercial break, Mrs. Martinez, I do want to finish on a more personal note," Sara said, her smile bland and generic, her eyes intent.

Gabriela smiled and nodded. Interviewers always asked about her children, how she balanced her career and motherhood, and how she juggled the latter with marriage as well.

"Can we get the next photo up on the monitor, please?"

Gabriela watched the blue screen blend into a photograph of Albert. Her body froze. She saw her own shock on the monitors.

"Four years ago, you were embroiled in the murder scandal of Albert Heinige. Back then no one could confirm your involvement. A source has recently stepped forward, claiming your complicity was greater than was led to believe. Is it true you were the killer?"

Gabriela tried to speak but nothing came out.

"Numerous sources linked you to his murder, but nothing was corroborated. Doors to information were slammed shut." Sara's voice pounded into her. "Could we get a statement from you on this issue?"

When Gabriela didn't answer, the interviewer asked for the next photograph. Gabriela's subconscious barely registered what the monitor displayed when she was blindsided by the next question. Shock increased. She recognized the grainy photograph.

"Is this your current lover?"

"What?"

"Another private source informed me you've cozied up quite nicely to…" Sara looked down at her cue cards, "to a Mr. Richard Harrison. When did you start the affair? Can you verify when the two of you met?"

Gabriela could only stare. Every second became a lifetime, every question a rock thrown her way. Stoned woman came to mind, unprepared, defenseless, not knowing from where the next killing blow would come.

"Oh, come now. Silence as denial?" Sara looked somewhere toward the bowels of the studio and back at her.

A close-up of Gabriela's pale face filled the monitor, replaced instantly by the photo taken in Mannie's garage, only to shift once more to another photograph. She recognized it as the one plastering the front page of the tabloids yesterday. It had been taken at some social function hosted by Lord Cranfield, showing a smiling April sandwiched between Richard and her father.

Gabriela blinked to keep from crying. Her eyes, still riveted on the images on the monitor, watched as all the images shuffled—first her face, then Albert's face, followed by Richard and her at Mannie's, to finally end with April's face. Again, and again, and again.

Gabriela quivered. Her body became a tight braid of muscles, her mind in disbelief at what was happening.

"No comment?" Sara asked. "Surely you have something to say?"

Gabriela choked on her own words, incoherent snippets finally emerging from her mouth.

"This is...I'm not...Richard is a friend."

"My source disagrees," Sara cut in. "I've been told Mr. Harrison is the fiancé of a Miss Cranfield."

Gabriela couldn't believe this was happening.

"Didn't your husband have a recent accident which incapacitated him as well?" Sara kept up her attacks. "Is that when you began your affair with Mr. Harrison? Will you be divorcing your husband now?"

More hits. Horror struck. The children. The children would be watching this interview when it aired.

Battered on all fronts—the heart, the head, the groin, her eyes blurring with the tears she refused to shed—Gabriela stood. Wobbled. She needed to get out of there.

"I didn't come here to be insulted. This interview is over."

Without much care for the equipment, Gabriela ripped the lavaliere off her body and, with trembling hands, dropped everything on the chair she had just vacated.

Her lungs labored. Breaths came sporadically, not enough oxygen. She needed to get out. Her stomach muscles cramped. She felt suffocated. She needed to get out. She needed to get out.

Tears blurred her vision. She skirted cameras, crew, the snickers from some, the commiseration from others, and avoided the cables on the floor. She slapped at hands and told everyone to leave her alone.

But before she could make her escape, someone blocked her way. Glancing up, Gabriela received the third shock of the day. April Cranfield stood a few inches away. Looking into the woman's eyes, Gabriela read irrational hate and deranged fixation.

"Did you really believe I would let you interfere?" Her voice was soft, almost childlike, giving Gabriela the creeps. "He's mine." April's lips curled. "You shan't have him."

"Ma'am, step aside."

April ignored the bodyguard who had stepped forward. She bent even closer to Gabriela and whispered, "I'll destroy you first."

Gabriela turned to Hays. "Get this woman away from me. She's crazy."

Hays took April's forearm. "Ma'am, I must insist."

Gabriela did not wait for the bodyguard to remove April. She beelined it to the recording studio exit behind the set, to the door leading to a hallway, which led to the Blue waiting room and her friends. Her refuge.

"Come with me."

The accent threw her. Strong arms pulled her shoulders into brick muscle. Audible, static electricity crackled near the vicinity of her waist.

What the hell...

Legs gave way, brainwaves scattered. Something fried her synaptic circuits. Dazed for mere seconds, Gabriela discovered she was being led, unresisting, to an exit opposite the studio and people. *When did that happen?*

"Don't make fuss."

Her wits returned, but not as fast as she would have liked. Despite her disorientation, however, she realized something was wrong.

Get someone. Let someone know.

She opened her mouth to scream.

Crackle.

Pop.

Another shock, longer this time. The pain hit with a slight burning sensation, her muscles convulsed and tensed, jerking to escape the tormentor. Her thoughts fled, scattering in every direction, similar to a struck anthill. She couldn't figure out what was wrong, only that someone was practically carrying her now, carting her away down a stairway to God knows where, a someone who did not look familiar at all.

She tried to struggle, certain she'd sent out the order to fight. Only a pitiful, half-hearted grunt emerged somewhere deep in her throat followed by pathetic Jello wobbles from her limbs.

Somewhere, in the vagaries of her scattered brain, the echo of a name beckoned.

Richard.

A car.

I can't get in. I can't get in.

Panic must have increased her struggles and strength because she heard another crackle. Felt another, very long zap. Dizziness and nausea overtook her and she didn't give a damn where she was going, just as long as the zapping stopped.

Chapter Twenty-Three

"Where is she? Where the hell is she?"

Richard bellowed the words as he barged into the studio with little regard for anyone, his face full of lightning and a dark, tempestuous anger.

He wanted to kill, painfully, slowly. Wanted to rip people apart, tear through drywall, and pummel faces in order to allay the fear savagely tearing at his insides. Wanted to eviscerate the asshole Edmund, who'd delayed him for more than half an hour by cornering him in his office to berate him about Richard's treatment of April.

Now, Gabriela was missing.

The room exploded into chaos.

Jeremy tried to pull him back. "Boss, calm down."

Some of the crew tried to grab him, lead him out of the recording studio.

"You can't be in here."

"Sir, please."

"Get that man out of my recording studio," the overhead microphone bellowed. "Get security."

Richard swiped away all attempts to control him like annoying mosquitoes on his skin.

"Mr. Harrison," the floor manager grabbed and held on like a limpet. "We've set up a room. Security is there. The Yard should be there soon."

Eyes, promising painful retribution, glared.

The floor manager swallowed.

Rigid with tensed muscles, Richard tore the floor manager's hand from his arm and followed him to a secluded room a fair distance from the studio. A watchful Jeremy followed close behind.

Richard entered a secondary control room, with enough equipment to function well for smaller recordings and shows.

His evaluation of the area took mere moments. A man sat behind a console, fidgeting with dials and buttons, looking at the various television screens wallpapering the wall in front of him. Jean-Louis paced the room's periphery, a caged animal throwing French expletives into the air in a continuous angry stream. Julien sat on a chair by the raised second layer of electronic controls and chairs set in parallel line behind the sound engineer. He was stroking a purse he'd set on top of his knees, his motion purposeless, his expression forlorn as well as despairing.

The bodyguard in charge walked in a seemingly aimless pattern, talking into his cell phone, his voice low, information spoken in rapid-fire spurts. His rambling steps, however, served their purpose to cage in April, creating an invisible fence around where she sat in the far corner.

April looked at him. Her lips curled slightly.

The room almost faded to black, the rage roaring through him blinding him for an instant. A visceral, animalistic urge to kill overwhelmed him. Deep in his gut, he knew April had set him up, had sicced her spineless sex toy on him earlier, in order to delay him. Richard stepped forward, but Jeremy blocked his way. He recognized Richard's Stygian mood. Saw the flexing of muscles, the preparation to lunge.

"No, boss," he whispered. Jeremy faced him, his hand pressed hard on Richard's shoulder in warning and commiseration.

"She's not worth it."

Richard closed his eyes in an attempt to control the savage beast roaring and tearing his insides. Losing it would not help Gabriela, and getting her back safe was his priority.

He had to get her back.

His breath came out in a whoosh as he scanned the room once more. There were two other women present there as well. One stood near the engineer, talking into a headset. Richard didn't recognize her, but he did the other one—the host of the interview show, Sara Sheffield. Together with April, she was the other asshole responsible for the current chaos, for Gabriela's disappearance. She sat in the same row as Julien, several seats apart, her back stiff, jaw tight, expression daring. Their eyes clashed. He saw recognition, speculation, and satisfaction all at once in her crafty eyes. She stood, her intent obvious.

Viciousness tore through him once more. He saw the bitch jerk and pause in her goal to intercept him. He knew if she uttered a word or approached him now, he would not be responsible for his actions.

He concentrated on the bodyguard instead.

"What the fuck happened? Why the hell was no one with her?"

"Sir," Hays said. "I was taking proper measures to remove this woman after she threatened Mrs. Martinez."

"How the hell did *she* sneak past everyone?" Richard pointed to April.

"Ms. Cranfield was my guest," Sara interrupted, coming to a stop by his side, making herself part of the conversation. "Now, Mr. Harrison…"

"Get out of my face," Richard said, his voice a low vibrating threat. "I'll deal with you later."

"Mr. Harrison, is it?" the other woman rushed over. "I'm Jennifer Cady, the assistant director of the show."

"Where the hell is Morris?" Richard asked Jeremy.

"Ignore me if you want," Sara began, "but I want to know…"

"You." Richard rounded on her. His eyes revealed hell had indeed frozen over. Jean-Louis had briefed Richard by phone on what this woman had done. "You don't need to know shit."

"May I remind you I'm press? News…"

"You, lady, are filth. A bottom feeder of scum." He turned to face Jennifer Cady. "If you and your producer don't want a libel suit of immense proportions, I expect the personal attacks in that interview to be edited out by the next airing, and an apology plastered, on screen, every hour on the hour, in those regions where it already aired."

"My source…" Sara interrupted.

Richard's eyes bored into April. "Is a jealous, petty, spoiled, manipulating bitch, who lies through her teeth with the ease of applying Vaseline on skin."

April, at that ferocious appraisal, narrowed her eyes. She stood, the innocent air transmitted by the white froth she wore a sharp contrast to the canny, malicious expression on her face.

Richard turned to Jeremy.

"Get rid of her." His expression telegraphed exactly what he wanted to do to April. "I'm sure her boy toy is somewhere nearby. Drop her in his lap with my compliments. I don't want her filth near me again."

"Bastard," April said.

"You started it."

"You'll regret this."

"I've regretted it since you opened your legs and humped me."

"Really," Sara huffed.

Richard focused on Morris's man. "Where's Bryce?"

"Saw him loitering in the lobby," Jeremy answered as he neared April, more careful than approaching a cobra.

"Get him up here. See if he snapped anything that may help."

Jeremy pulled a stiff and resisting April to the exit, desperate to escort her out before Richard exploded. He made sure he circumvented him by a wide berth.

"You'll regret this," April repeated, her voice a low hiss.

Richard didn't answer. His eyes simply roamed over April, his revulsion and rage open for all to see.

"Now see here, Mr. Harrison," Jennifer Cady's insulted tone did not escape him. "This is a professional news agency—"

But Richard was not having it. "Lady, what you did was not professional and definitely not news. It was tabloid filth, damaging innuendo at its best. You didn't even vet your sources before you went on air with your self-serving rumor mill bullshit. Didn't verify your source is a bitch in heat with neither brains nor humanity. Retract and apologize."

"Or else what, Mr. Harrison?" Sara smirked.

A familiar voice answered from the doorway.

"Or your station will be charged with aiding and abetting a criminal in an ongoing police investigation. Definitely kidnapping charges. Obstruction as well," Morris said, ambling into the center of the storm, his ID raised high, like a flag for all to see.

"Need I go on?" Morris stopped. Waited for his words to sink in. "Detective Inspector Morris. CID."

He stared at the two women, his lips a thin line of displeasure. "I've spoken to your director and my superior has spoken to the news division president. They've offered full cooperation." He turned to Richard. "And retractions."

Morris ignored the outraged blubbering in the room. "Tapes from building security already cued here?"

"Whenever you're ready, sir," the engineer said.

"Anything else taped before, during, and after the interview, I need sent to my office immediately." He looked at Richard. "We're on high alert, monitoring everything."

Richard nodded, his jaw tight, his fingers massaging his chest. Morris squeezed his shoulder in commiseration.

"We'll find her."

"Shall we start?" the engineer asked.

Richard looked at the women in the room.

"Out." He walked to the door and jerked it open.

The blubbering and outrage was identical.

"If you're not out of here in five seconds, I'll throw you out."

"Now see here..." Sara sputtered.

"One..."

"Beyond rude..." Jennifer said.

"Two..."

"We have a right..." Both women said together.

Morris saw the narrowing of Richard's eyes, the downright glacial, I don't give a shit, I'll tear you apart look. He cleared his throat.

"Ladies, please remove your persons. My office will keep you apprised of events."

"Three..."

Jennifer Cady, no fool, grabbed Sara's arm. She pulled her through the open door.

"Let's go, Sara."

She dragged the TV host out.

"Four." Richard slammed the door on their faces.

"You empty a room quite handily," Morris said.

"It's all in the delivery."

"*Merde,*" Jean-Louis said. "I should have known something was up when that woman told us to stay away from the set."

"They had everything well-orchestrated," Julien added.

"By the time things calmed down," Hays added, "no one knew what had happened to Mrs. Martinez. Only one person can verify she was rushing toward the Blue room."

"Start setting up interviews. Everyone present or near her when this mess started," Morris said. "Last person to see anything first."

Hays nodded and walked out at the same time Jeremy strode in with Herb Bryce at his heels.

"What's going on here?" The man, from the tone of his voice, was tetchy. "This muscle drags me upstairs without a word, repeating it's important police business. Explains shit."

"Mr. Bryce," Morris said in his calmest voice. "We need to see your photographs during the past hour."

Herb Bryce's eyes bounced from one man to the other, gauging mood, interpreting expressions. "What's going on? Does this have anything to do with Mrs. Martinez?"

"Your cooperation will be greatly appreciated."

"Yeah. That's code for screw me."

"Alternatively, we can give you a tour of our newly refurbished interrogation room and take this discussion there. I'd prefer otherwise, although I would be happy to accommodate you, if that is what you prefer."

"What's in it for me?"

"Exclusivity," Richard said before Morris could come up with an answer. "A real story, rather than the shit you've been publishing."

Bryce smiled.

"One caveat," Richard warned, in reaction to what he read in the man's eyes. "After your exclusive, you close your chapter on Mrs. Martinez. You don't bother her ever again."

Pause.

"Ever," with emphasis.

Bryce considered. "Alternatives?"

"None."

Richard stared at Bryce, silent now. Herb Bryce was savvy enough to interpret his glance accurately. Richard saw the calculations in Bryce's expression, the pros and cons of a future without seeing Gabriela through his viewfinder. Saw the decision.

"Fine. So, what's the scoop?"

Morris didn't look too happy, but brought Bryce up to speed about the probable kidnapping, some of the threats Gabriela had been receiving, summarizing events and leaving out names and certain crucial information.

"You've been her protection?" Bryce's voice said he didn't buy the bull dished out to him.

"Yes."

Bryce stared. Eyes lit in sudden comprehension.

"You were the one, the mystery protector four years ago."

Richard confirmed nothing.

"Shit, we thought you were a ghost invented by that close-mouthed Frog in order to protect Mrs. Martinez. Rumors were flying she'd killed the bastard in self-defense, while others claimed someone else had pulled the trigger." Bryce considered. "What a scoop."

"Off limits," Richard said.

"What?"

"No." Said more fiercely. "Not part of what's on the table."

"You can't really…"

"No. Or we're done here."

After a few seconds, Bryce shrugged. He had enough headlines to pad his portfolio nicely.

"I barely got here in time to capture her exit from the limo, but these are the freshest pics." With the ease of familiarity, Bryce's thumb rambled across the camera's back, pressed buttons here and there in rapid spurts, and waved the men over.

The men huddled around Bryce. Richard studied the first photo: Jeremy opening the limo door. Next: Jean-Louis and Julien bracketing Gabriela. Afterward, three consecutive photos of the trio captured walking to the station's entrance.

For the first time, Richard got a taste of the tedium of this man's professional life. A slew of photographs, with a second or two pause between each, showed a freeze frame of other paparazzi in the area, talking, smoking. Bored. Waiting for anything. More random faces. Photos of traffic, including foot, people entering and exiting the building.

"There's April," noted Jeremy.

Bryce inspected the photograph. "Stamped fifteen minutes after Mrs. Martinez showed up."

"We were in makeup at that time, *n'est-ce pas,* Jules?" Jean-Louis asked for confirmation. Julien nodded.

The next photograph was a close-up of April, smiling like a coquette at the camera. Bryce shook his head. "I'm surprised she's alone."

"Her boy toy was in my office," Richard said.

"He was?" Jeremy's face showed his bewilderment. "What for?"

"Berating me for my treatment of April."

"He had the balls to do that?" Jeremy smiled. "He usually pisses his pants whenever you are around."

"April set him up to it, to delay me." Richard clenched his fists. "The bitch."

Bryce nodded. "That boy better get a major set of cojones. Pussy-footing around that one won't get him anywhere."

Richard cocked an eyebrow.

Bryce shrugged. "Hey, I've been at this for a long time. I can assess within a minute, sometimes seconds. She's a ball buster if not kept in line. Like a rabid dog, when she gets hold of something she wants."

Bryce looked at Richard. "And she wants you."

"Don't give a shit what she wants," Richard told him.

Bryce didn't respond. He flipped more photographs. They were of the surrounding buildings.

"Boatload of nothing there, man," Jeremy commented. "Waste."

"This is a new digital. Memory card. Costs a shitload of money up front, but worth it on the money I save on film. Quality is also crisp. Detailed. In-your-face clarity. I develop what I want, discard or save the rest. These cameras will become standard in the industry in a couple of years."

The miscellaneous photos became a steady stream, but none showed Gabriela exiting or being abducted.

"Wait," Jeremy said. "Back up."

Bryce accommodated.

"Stop. Let me see that."

Jeremy squinted to focus.

"What?" Richard's voice held the tension he felt.

"I've seen this bloke before."

"What?" Morris pressed in to get a clearer view.

"I've seen him before." Jeremy looked at them. "But, damn, I'm drawing a blank. Give me a minute."

"Can we get this enlarged?" Morris asked.

"Sure," Bryce said.

"Hays," Morris turned to his man as he stepped into the room. "Get Mr. Bryce to a computer posthaste. Get him anything else he needs to have that photo enhanced and sent to our office and to this control room. We need to see who is in it."

Richard turned to the engineer. "Anything?"

"Got some possibles."

They all gathered around. The engineer pointed to the monitors. He'd cued everything on screen in sequential order. He pointed from left to right.

"Got studio A cam, the tail end of the corridor leading to the Blue room, the emergency exit hallway, and loading dock at street rear synched real time. Cued everything from slightly before the interview was over."

Appalled did not cover the emotions burning through Richard as he watched Gabriela's face show the pain, the shock, and the agony she felt at every attack. His vision glazed for a moment, his chest constricted, and anguish grated flesh. Richard's knuckles paled from the pressure exerted on the back of the engineer's chair.

"*Dieu*," Julien said, expressing out loud what everyone in the room was feeling.

"*Ma pauvre petite,*" Jean-Louis whispered.

Richard pressed his palms against his eyes until he thought he might push his eyeballs into his brain. He needed to concentrate. Needed to be strong and smart for her.

Morris squeezed his shoulder in solidarity.

His eyes focused on the monitors once more. Saw Gabriela tear off the mike, rush, and weave through the set. She disappeared at the bottom of the screen.

"Wait." Morris pointed to the first monitor. "Freeze it when Miss Cranfield comes into view. Slow motion frame by frame after."

They could all see April mouthing some words, lean toward Gabriela. Saw Hays moving in and address April. Gabriela seemed disturbed by the interchange. She spoke to Hays and did not wait for the man to steer April toward the studio exit. What the hell had April said to make Hays interfere and Gabriela look so spooked?

"Hold it." Morris looked at Richard and Jeremy. "Did you see that?"

The engineer replayed the last frame. A shadow detached from the foreground. Skirted Hays and April who appeared to be insulting Hays and resisting his guidance. Normal reaction. Richard would have avoided them as well. But the man, after a quick look at the bodyguard, did not lose focus of Gabriela. Moved casually behind her. Took what looked like a box out of his suit pocket. Disappeared, trailing her.

"Can we zoom in on the face?" Richard asked.

The engineer rotated knobs, sliding others for optimum stabilization. "Best I can do."

The image blurred a bit as it enlarged. It did not help that the particular section of the set was in shadow, masking the man's features to mush. Couldn't make out specifics, except the man was a big-framed Caucasian, with rough features.

"He looks similar to the *mec* the paparazzo showed us," Jean-Louis commented. "Doesn't he, Jules?"

"Same build," Julien agreed after a few seconds of scrutiny. "Similar profile, at least."

"Jeremy?" Richard asked.

"Maybe."

"Nothing?" Morris asked.

"Not yet."

Morris shifted, sat next to the engineer. "Can you play back once more, please?"

Richard watched Hays forcibly lead April out, the man following Gabriela. His eyes shifted to the monitor showing the corridor. A minute or two passed. Nothing.

"There we are," Jean-Louis said. He and Julien dashed on screen for a second or two then disappeared off screen.

Richard shifted focus to the other monitors.

"Shit." He leaned forward. Gabriela was held tightly by what looked to be the man who had followed her. Same build, size.

"Her feet are uncoordinated," Morris noted.

"What the hell did the guy do to her?" Jeremy asked.

Richard studied the image of the two until the man dragged her through the stairwell exit door.

"Zoom and loop it," he ordered.

After the third rewind, Richard pointed. "He's got something in his right hand. See? Looks similar to something he took out of his pocket before he followed her. Can you make it out?"

Jeremy and Morris couldn't identify it.

"There." Richard saw the moment of feeble struggle, the object brought forward, a slight jerk, no further resistance.

"Do you think..." Jeremy started, but was interrupted by Morris.

"Size is about right. The lack of muscle coordination. The jerk in opposition. It's a stun gun."

Gulping for air, Richard bent over the second row of instrument panels. He wanted to throw up. *My God, not again. Don't hurt her again.*

Rage exploded. He grabbed the nearest chair and threw it against the far wall, a guttural groan torn from the bowels of his soul.

"The son of a bitch, the son of a bitch."

He turned his head as Hays entered the room with Bryce. Gabriela's bane was fanning a set of printed photographs in the air.

"Found another one of the guy." He stopped, looked at Richard. "You look like shit."

If he'd been a dog, Jeremy would have snarled. "Piss off, Bryce."

"Jem," Morris warned, taking the prints from Bryce's hand. "Let's concentrate on these."

Richard controlled his features and his heart as he turned to study the photograph spread Morris had created on top of the console. His finger rubbed his chest in manic moves.

Bryce pointed to the middle print. "I found another one of the guy. Not much, just his big-ass back. This dude is a professional bruiser. I stake my career on it."

"Wait up," Jeremy said after taking a closer look. He pointed to another photograph where the man was in profile, looking up at the building's directory. "I remember this fucker. He was in our building yesterday."

"You're sure?" Morris asked.

"Stake my ass on it. He was in the lobby. Near the elevator banks, when I followed Mrs. Martinez." He looked at Richard and stammered in embarrassment. "After you know when."

"What was he doing?" Morris asked.

Jeremy tapped the photograph. "He was waiting by the lifts, staring toward the building entrance, in profile like this. I glanced at him briefly while I rushed after Mrs. Martinez. Couldn't help but notice. He looked apish, out of place in his suit. Big."

"Hays," Morris said. "Get me copies of security footage from Richard's building. Meet us at headquarters. We need to run FERET on him."

"Is that your version of Phil?" Bryce asked.

Everyone turned questioning eyes toward Bryce.

"You know...Phil...the groundhog?"

Morris was disgusted. "No. Acronym for the new Face Recognition Technology. We can create an algorithm based on the photographs and video, run it through Interpol, see if we can get a hit."

"Ferret him out, sort of," Bryce quipped.

Richard thrust Bryce into the nearest wall and pushed his forearm into his throat. Bryce looked like a flopping fish in his struggles to breathe.

"This is not fucking *Comedy Central*, you asshole."

Morris sandwiched himself between the men. Richard had no choice but to release Bryce.

"Touch me again, and I'll sue your ass," Bryce said, coughing to clear his voice.

"My office, now," Morris ordered, pushing Bryce out of the way and out the door. "We'll monitor better from there. Outsource better. Let's go."

"Boss?" Jeremy looked miserable.

"Give me a minute."

Jean-Louis grabbed Julien.

"We'll be at the hotel, if you need us." He, for one, wanted to grab the nearest bottle of absinthe and rendezvous with his *fée verte* in order to dull the pain he was experiencing.

"Call me…" Morris said, extending a card.

"*Tout de suite,* if she contacts us," Jean-Louis said.

Julien gave Richard a quick hug, catching him by surprise.

"You'll find her," he whispered. "I know you will."

God, he hoped so. Hoped she was still in possession of her phone. Hoped she would be able to reach him. Hoped, if she couldn't, they'd be able to track her position through the cell phone signal.

"Coming, boss?"

Richard nodded, but stopped before exiting. He looked at the monitor playing its endless loop and focused on what he could see of Gabriela.

"Hold on, sweetheart," Richard said under his breath. "I'll find you."

Chapter Twenty-Four

Gabriela felt ill, disoriented. Her skin hurt, her muscles and stomach cramped intermittently, and certain parts of her felt as if she had been burned from long exposure to that electric devil with which this man had blindsided her.

She couldn't see, either. Some rough form of canvas bag had been placed over her head before she was thrust into the car. The fabric filtered light, but blinded her to everything else. She felt the movement of the car, sensed the heat of her tormentor near her, and breathed in stale, hot breaths, created by her own microenvironment of tropical humidity inside the pliable helmet from hell.

Gabriela still couldn't believe April had shown up on set and threatened her. How could they have misread her intentions? Actually, she blamed Richard for not gauging the situation accurately and for comparing April to Silvie. April was poles apart from Silvie. Heinige's mistress had been passive, manipulated rather than manipulator, and a coward at heart. This woman…well, this woman wanted Richard to the point of obsession. Did not bode well to ignore that type of personality. Stalker syndrome came to mind.

Gabriela almost laughed. What was another psychotic person added to her life? Normal fare, lately. Some daily bread. She was tired of it.

Trying to move her arms into a more comfortable position, Gabriela shifted in her seat. The bastard next to her had also taped her hands behind her back before dumping her unceremoniously in the back seat of a black sedan. They were not tightly bound, just uncomfortable. She arched her back and tried rotating her shoulders for some respite.

"Not move," the same accented voice said, shoving her back.

"Don't touch me again." Her voice sounded strange in her mini, muted echo chamber.

The man chuckled. As nasty a chuckle as one could get. The tone conjured images of sadistic torturers, lying to their captives, promising a release from the pain.

"Hear that, Dimitri? Woman gives orders."

A real chuckle came from the front. This Dimitri was either the driver or another person in the passenger side. Gabriela wished she'd paid more attention. She vaguely remembered another man near the car, but nothing else.

The name, however, didn't bode well for her. Now she understood the accent—Slavic undertones to the English. Russian. And if these were Wickeham's goons, it might well mean Russian mafia members. Hadn't he used Mexican gang members back in the States? Gabriela wouldn't put it past him to use any member of the underworld to function as his shady sideline—coercion and intimidation.

"Won't give orders soon, right, Bogdan?"

"Depends on boss."

Open laughter. "Charitable, our boss."

Gabriela forced her mind to concentrate on the pressure on her thigh and not on the insinuation from that snippet of cheer. She shifted, presenting more of her back to this Bod-whatever his name was. Let him think she was afraid, cringing from his presence. She just wanted to keep the only lifeline to Richard safe. Only God knew why they had not frisked her before forcing her inside the car. Maybe they thought she didn't have anything important on her person. Her purse was still at the television station. So was her coat. She just wished she'd kept the cell phone Morris had issued switched on. Unfortunately, from habit, she had turned the thing off before the interview in order to avoid embarrassing rings.

Before they discovered she had it, she needed to hide the phone in a less conspicuous place. That was crucial now. Where to hide it, exactly, was the issue. Gabriela had no illusions. If she hid it inside her bra cup, the thing would show. Inside her panties, well, may as well give it to the goons for safekeeping. She had not worn pantyhose today because the skirt's hem was low enough to cover her exposed legs and upper boots. She had made do with knee-highs. If she hid the phone in her underwear, the thing would slither down after she took a few steps to a point where it would be obvious she had something hidden. Worse. It could trail down and plop on the floor.

Gravity always worked at inconvenient times.

If only they would free her hands, just enough for her to grab it and stuff it...where? The only other place she could think of was her boots. They were wide enough for her to jam the cell phone inside, next to her calf. The leather material was loose and wrinkled enough to make that hiding place not obvious, as well as give her room to walk without too much discomfort. All she needed was time to switch hiding places. Would she have time to turn it on and dial? Would they give her time, period?

She closed her eyes and tried not to think about suffocating from her own breathing.

City traffic noises gave way to highway hum. She couldn't gauge where she was, what direction they were going, or how much time had gone by. This blindness to whatever landscapes or markers she could have remembered messed her up and added to the feeling of disorientation. Time had no meaning, only her prolonged discomfort.

How long had they been on the road?

"What time is it?" she asked innocently. The answer would be crucial information Richard could use.

Richard, her mind screamed in desperation. *Richard. Please. If only you could hear me.*

God, she hoped she had ifs left in her life.

"Not your business," Bogdan replied. "Stay quiet."

The car slowed down. Two rights and one left, before the car came to a stop. The goon up front got out, leaving the car in neutral and the door open. Gabriela felt the cold invading the warm interior, recognized a few outside smells mingled with her now stale breath. Exhaust and something fishy. She tried to hear above the hum of the car, but only heard the motor, some groaning hinges, and a loud bird call.

The car dipped and the door shut. Dimitri was back. The car shifted and glided forward slowly. Stopped. Motor off. Car doors opened, including the one beside her. Rough hands grabbed her forearms and literally lifted her off the seat. Dumped her on what felt like concrete flooring. Cold invaded her body, raised gooseflesh on her skin. She heard Dimitri walking away, closing a door with a metallic sound to it.

Without apology or care, a huge hand grabbed her by the underarm and dragged her forward for quite a few feet. Upon occasion, Gabriela stumbled over debris, only to be brought up painfully as the goon lifted her over stuff she could not identify. The smell of engine oil and fish grew more pervasive. But overlapping those smells there was another, a somewhat metallic afterthought of scent. And there was the sound of water, muted by the walls and the space. Some of it had the reverb sound of a leaky faucet in a big, empty cave. Some of it had the rushing quality of water over rocks. Was it because it was raining or because they were actually near water?

The man guiding her forced her to stop. Another door opened. She was dragged through it, taken somewhere inside another smaller room because of the lesser echo to their footsteps. Several steps in, she was pushed down onto a hard surface.

"Stay."

She almost blurted she was not a dog, but bit her lip. Better know what she was dealing with first before antagonizing a detrimental unknown. Besides, the man was muscled and big. She would not fare well antagonizing him.

Gabriela waited. Footsteps faded. The door nearby closed. She waited some more. Nothing, not even muted voices filtered from outside into her space, just the intermittent drip of water drops.

Okay, now what? With difficulty, she forced herself to immobility until she thought she would scream from the tension. But she had to make sure no one was inside with her.

An eternity passed.

"Screw this."

With what she could use of her covered teeth and chin, she hiked her skirt over her knees, bit by bit and body shift after body shift. Her shoulders burned, but she disregarded the fire in her tendons and muscles. Gauging the skirt was high enough for her purposes Gabriela bent at the waist and placed her head between her knees. It took several attempts, but she finally pinched enough of the cloth to get a good grip on it. With slight jerks she began pulling off the cover on her head.

"Shit." She tore some of her hair, but the suffocating canvas helmet finally came off. She understood taking it off involved risks she didn't want to even consider, at least not yet.

She didn't care. She was free of that cloth cage.

She gulped.

She expanded her lungs with the cold air and the dust floating around her. She opened her eyes.

Gabriela was, indeed, in a small, squarish room with very high ceilings—too high for her to reach the small, rectangular, latticed windows a good fifteen feet above the wall behind her. The room had an old, abandoned warehouse feel to it, with dust all over the floor and speckled here and there with the broken and cracked glass panes fallen from above. Those panes still intact in the windows were practically opaque from dirt. Through the broken panes, a cold breeze fought it out with daylight for supremacy and right of way. A small dusting of cobwebs decorated the high steel beams here and there, and the only furniture was the bench on which she was sitting.

The door she'd come through was directly in front of her. She walked over to it. No handle to turn and the door handle hole had been cemented. She pushed her shoulder into the door. Slight give, but it stopped immediately. Probably bolted with some sort of latch on the other side.

Gabriela turned, and using the door as anchor, bent over and stretched as best she could with her hands behind her back. She wriggled and wiggled, bent, squatted, and tried everything she could think of to bring her hands forward, similar to what she had seen actors do in movies. But, either her arms were too short, or what was depicted as possible in the movies was bull unless you were double-jointed.

Gabriela began to sweat from the effort and, with that slight film of perspiration, the cold invaded. She needed to get her hands free, she needed to stay warm. Her blazer would keep some of the cold at bay, but not nearly enough for her body temperature not to suffer. Spring in England was downright cold and this place had no heat. Hypothermia would kick in. It would make her sluggish. And she needed to keep her wits about her. She needed her responses, needed to act quickly if the occasion called for it.

Gabriela began looking for something, anything she could use to tear or slice through the duct tape. She meticulously examined the walls, the steel girders, the floor. Her hopes blossomed at sight of the shattered glass panes on the floor, but those hopes deflated almost instantly. How on earth was she going to pick those up and free herself when her hands were behind her? Even if she picked them up with her mouth, she would not be able to transfer the glass to her hands. She could cut her lips with the sharp edges. Besides, she was not putting her lips near that floor unless absolutely necessary. If she knelt and sat on the floor, she would cut her fingers to a pulp before she could grab the glass properly, and then...how to cut? Where to cut? She could even slash her wrists without knowing and bleed out.

What the hell could she do? She plopped onto the bench once more. How the hell was she going to get out of this mess? She couldn't even reach the cell phone.

She was helpless. And if she was helpless, her chances of survival would be nil.

Gabriela tried to clear her head, but desperation clawed its way to the forefront of her thoughts. An image of her children burst in. *God, her babies.* They needed her. She needed them. She couldn't leave them orphans. She had to find a way out. She had to.

But just the thought of losing them, of never seeing their faces, of never touching, cuddling, or holding her children tore through her. Gabriela succumbed to the pain and the desperation. Her chin dropped and she wept bitterly. How could her life go so wrong? There was so much hurt lately, so much grief. Her only moments of brightness were her children, her work, and Richard. Last night had been a miracle, a lifetime of rapture compressed to a few hours of bliss. It seemed so far removed from the now. Was happiness so unattainable for her, so ephemeral? Was her fate just to experience it, to touch it briefly, before it vanished forever? Would she ever be whole again?

Robertico. Gustavito.

Luisito.

Richard.

Her sobs became a keening.

Richard. Save me. Please.

***

"You're driving me barmy with your pacing," Morris told Richard without looking away from the screen. The computer continued its global search for a face match. It flicked images so quickly Richard couldn't understand how Morris didn't get nauseous from watching without a pause.

Morris's techies had done their magic with mathematical algorithms a while back. They had scanned facial dimensions and had fed those into their mainframe. The computer had begun its hunt through the Interpol database of thug images. No results yet. It still searched.

Jeremy pressed his shoulder. "He's right, boss. Go walk off the frustration. I'll find you if we get anything."

Richard knew his anxiety level was a distraction to the men. His blood felt like lava boiling inside his veins. He felt out of control, desperate.

He needed to find his center.

"I'll be right back."

Morris and Jeremy barely nodded as he stepped out of the computer lab room, a man driven by demons. People gave him a wide berth in the hallways. He found the emergency stairwell and plopped on the cold stairs.

He bent over, head in hands, his upper body rocking, trying to breathe. Gabriela. God, he couldn't lose her. Not now. His fingers clenched. *Please, please,* he pleaded to the universe, *please don't take her away from me. Have pity. She is my love. My joy. My hope. Earth would be worth shit without this woman who completes me, who gave me the greatest gift a man could wish for, who loves me without reservation. I'll die without her.*

A guttural cry echoed around the stairwell and his body trembled with anguish. His heart burned and he could no longer endure the pain. Dry, choked sobs shook him.

For the first time in his adult life, Richard cried.

Time passed. A new calm descended. Determination and a concentrated focus replaced his despair. He stood and walked back. He was turning left on the corridor when Jeremy rushed out, looking right and left.

"Richard," he shouted. "We got a hit."

Less than an hour after identification, Morris and his team had mobilized and they were now speeding through London traffic, sirens blaring, heading to Wickeham's house to serve a warrant. Once Interpol had identified one Bogdan Ljubic as the man who had abducted Gabriela, Morris had worked at an impressive speed, digging up fake visas, work permits, criminal backgrounds, and tax records in record time. They'd discovered Mr. Ljubic was ex-military from the Yugoslav army, had tenuous ties to the KGB, had been linked, suspected but not proved, to several killings across Europe, and had been under Wickeham's employ for about two years.

"Wickeham's a British citizen. He's got rights."

Richard didn't give a damn about Wickeham's rights. Morris's police badge hindered his actions, but Richard didn't have that problem, and he didn't give a fuck about Wickeham's rights. The moment his goon had grabbed Gabriela, the man had sealed his fate.

"I recognize that look, Richard. I did warn you we needed to do everything according to the law, remember. No muck or we lose the case and he goes free."

"This is different," he said, staring out the window. *Shit, it was different.*

"I'm serious," Morris turned in his front seat to stare at Richard. "You say nothing, do nothing. I will handle things. We still have shit on Wickeham, except for a possible hiring of an irregular, and he'll claim ignorance, knowing the courts will slap him with a fine and a stern 'don't do this again' warning. We want his ass in jail."

"I'll be a good boy," Richard said, but didn't mean it. From Morris's expression before he turned around, he didn't believe him, either.

"I hope I won't have to arrest you, as well."

Richard kept his mouth shut. Morris was right in not trusting him. He didn't trust himself at this point. His heart still hurt, his stomach hadn't unclenched, and his brain felt like a cotton ball in a tight space with too much water. Still, a ruthless, calculating, cold focus drove him. He had felt like this before he'd met Gabriela. He would nurture and use this lack of emotion to his advantage. Richard understood allowing his rage and pain to consume him would not help her. However, he would take any opportunity to pulverize the man who had kidnapped her, the one who had used the stun gun on her. The one who'd hurt her.

He wanted him to feel pain.

Once this was over and she was safe back in his arms, that man and his boss would never hurt anyone again. He knew the type of bastards with which they were dealing. Even defeated and jailed, they would plan revenge and hire out to carry that revenge. It was the nature of this beast. And, like beasts, they would have to be put down permanently. He would take care of that.

Chapter Twenty-Five

Gabriela had to go to the bathroom. It was getting to the point of discomfort.

She was feeling more like her old self after wallowing in despair and self-pity until there were no more tears left, until her eyes felt puffy and her eyelids burned. Anger had returned. She began to scheme.

She needed to go.

With clipped strides she walked to the metal door and began banging it with her boot heel. Despite the fact they were in an abandoned area, Gabriela knew Wickeham wouldn't take the chance of leaving her unsupervised. Someone had to be out there. She lifted her leg again and gave the door two swift kicks. Repeated the action. Once she almost toppled backward, but skipped a step or two and started the pounding once more.

"Hey. Hey. I know you're out there." Three more bangs, more furious now. "Open the damn door. I need to go to the bathroom!"

She paced the room, annoyed. At least the activity was keeping her warm. She returned to the door and began the merciless pounding.

"Open." Bang. "The damn." Two more kicks. "Door." She gave the barrier one last frustrated kick.

"Your bastard of a boss won't like to see me in the condition I'll be in in a few minutes." She shifted to her other leg. Kicked hard. "I've got to go." What was it the British called their bathrooms? "I've got to go to the loo. Open the damn door!" Real desperation laced her last words.

She leaned against the door, gathering her breath and almost toppled to the floor when the door gave way for her.

"You are an annoying bitch." An arm prevented her kissing the floor, and a gun was pressed to her throat. "Shut the fuck up."

"What?" she scoffed. "Afraid the neighbors will hear?"

The man shoved her out the door. He was her height, slim, with a few rotted front teeth and the breath to complement the rot. Blond hair, crooked nose. Probably broken in a fight. Scar on his chin.

"Our boss warned us you were a cheeky bitch." He dragged her across an empty bay. Steel staircases rimmed the edges of the walls, giving access to the array of windows all around. Several chains hung from what looked like rolling pulleys. Depressions on the floor slanted to empty space below ground level. As she craned to look and capture every minute detail of where she was, the area reminded Gabriela of the huge bay of a car factory or a garage.

The man shoved her into what looked like a small office, glass window overlooking a work area. He opened a small door and held it open. The smell that came out was rancid with old urine, feces, and a metallic smell. She almost gagged.

"There's your loo."

"You've got to be kidding me."

The man shrugged, letting go of her arm. He jerked the gun several times in the direction of the toilet.

"This ain't a posh flat. You want to go, this is it."

Gabriela turned around. "Please untie me."

The man laughed.

"Listen," she almost blurted "You asshole," but decided to play the distressed maiden in order to appeal to his macho self. She breathed in deeply and lowered her eyes. Once she knew she was in control, she looked back at him, her eyes pleading for understanding.

"Please. I'm a woman. I don't point and pee. This place is gross, so gross I don't think a rat would go there to relieve itself. I need my hands. Please."

Gabriela waited. Not all her distress was faked. She hopped around a bit to accentuate the point.

"Turn around."

The welcome words came after a lifetime of waiting. She followed his order with alacrity. But he wasn't gentle. He pulled her arms farther back and ripped the tape off. When she was able to pull her hands forward, the burn and ache was so bad she thought she'd pass out from the pain.

Think of something else—about the fact she was free and this crippling pain meant her release. As the sensation of hot needles punctured her muscles with laser-like precision in a billion nerve endings, she was grateful she had full mobility, finally. For a few moments she was in some serious negotiations with the Almighty about what she'd do if He kept her untied, safe, and helped Richard find her. When the paralyzing pain subsided, she glanced inside the bathroom.

"You wouldn't have some tissues on you, would you?"

The man guffawed and pushed her inside.

The bathroom was so repulsive it took all her ingenuity to do her thing without soiling or touching anything. Not even breathing through her mouth helped keep away the noxious smell of the place. It didn't help there was no working light fixture and she had to keep the door ajar for light to filter through. It didn't help either she had to keep an eye on the man as well, in case he got any ideas.

She finished as quickly as she could, thinking if it were the last thing she'd do it would be to get even with the bastard who'd placed her in this position. With the tip of her boot she widened the gap of the open door, holding her skirt tight across her thighs, making sure she didn't brush against anything. She stepped quickly out of the room, shivering in disgust and relief.

The man grabbed her arm and dumped her back in her small prison. He slammed the door before she had time to turn around.

Gabriela waited.

The man was an idiot to leave her untied.

She took the phone out of her pocket.

But the man came back too quickly. If he had not banged the door with the chair he was dragging, Gabriela would have been discovered. Without turning it on, she dropped the phone inside her boot and faced her jailer.

He sat next to the door, gun in hand. He gestured to the bench. She didn't argue, not with a gun pointing her way. She sat.

She would need to find another opportunity.

Time crawled by. Gabriela began to nod. In between lack of sleep, electric zaps, and the cold, sleep tugged at her eyelids.

She stood.

"Sit down," the man ordered.

"I'm cold."

"Tough shit."

"I need my coat."

Her jailer shrugged and pointed his gun to the bench.

"Lend me yours," she told him.

The man laughed and snuggled into his leather jacket.

"Figures," she said and began to pace, circling the bench in staccato steps.

"Sit. You're making me dizzy."

"Tough shit," she said. "I need to keep warm."

"Don't get any ideas." He waved his gun, making his point.

"What? With a gun pointed at my face?"

"Cheeky bitch."

Gabriela kept pacing, slapping her sides and her arms in order to get circulation back and her body warm.

Didn't this man ever go to the bathroom? He had been sitting in the same position for what seemed hours, his beady eyes missing none of her movements. It seemed he was used to this type of work.

Gabriela didn't know how much time passed before he glanced at his watch, stood, and stretched. Taking his chair, he left the room and locked it behind him.

Gabriela couldn't believe her luck.

She took out the phone and was about to turn it on when she heard voices. They were approaching fast.

How much time did she have? Usually, these phones took their sweet time to turn on, and she needed to know, to be absolutely sure the thing was transmitting. She couldn't take the risk of their finding the cell phone. Better wait for the right opportunity, one that afforded her more time to check for the little bars. She might even need to go to different places within this room, probably close to the windows, to make that happen.

Gabriela lifted her skirt and rammed the cell phone in between her lower calf and the boot. She fixed her skirt, stood straight, and faced the door.

It opened. In the gathering gloom, she saw Wickeham cross the threshold, followed by her current jailer and the apish goon who had abducted her.

She would never have had the time to get the phone working before they'd entered.

She smiled.

That smile seemed to take Wickeham off-stride. Was he expecting her to be a hysterical mass of female blubbering? Probably. Hours earlier, she would have been exactly what he'd expected. Now she wasn't, something for which she was grateful.

"You'd better release me before the entire wrath of Scotland Yard and Richard descend on you."

"No one can link your disappearance to me," Wickeham said.

"Richard will."

"Frankly, I'm not interested in your ineffective bodyguards. However, I am interested in obtaining your signature on this contract of sale. Bogdan."

Wickeham took the briefcase from the apish-looking man's hand, lifted it, and rested it against the man's forearms. He opened it with a fastidiousness that was somehow repulsive to Gabriela. Out of its shallow depths, he took out a very official-looking packet and a pen. With the same fastidiousness, he closed the briefcase and laid the contract on top of it.

"I have taken care of all contingencies, especially a future claim of fraud."

"You mean extortion," she blurted.

"You are rather unpleasant for a female, Mrs. Martinez. If I did not admire your work so greatly, I would have taken less care."

"Really? Let's see, intimidating me over the phone, paying someone to attack me at home, threatening to kidnap my children, attacking my mechanic, sabotaging my car, and now zapping me by this ape in your employ. How euphemistic of you."

Wickeham ignored her, although she could see he wasn't pleased with her response. "The contract has the proper seals and, as soon as I have your signature, I will date it and begin ownership transfer."

He clicked the pen and extended it toward her as if everything was a fait accompli.

"No."

There was a moment of incomprehension that led to his lowering of the pen. He seemed to recoup and, once more, extended the pen toward her.

She shook her head to emphasize her next words. "No. I will not sign."

"As you wish." He replaced the contract and pen inside the briefcase. Reclosed it.

"Dimitri. Give me your gun."

As her jailer complied, Wickeham jerked his head to Bogdan, a silent signal the man interpreted without verbal cues. Meanwhile, Wickeham retreated to the doorway, suitcase in one hand, gun in the other. It was obvious he was not planning on soiling his hands with what was to come.

Here we go again, thought Gabriela, remembering her battered body from four years ago. At least Heinige had the gumption to do his own nasty work. Wickeham bestowed on others that privilege.

Dimitri and Bogdan began stalking her from opposite directions.

Show no fear. Show no fear, she kept on repeating to herself as she began to back away from both.

The macabre dance took on bizarre moves in the gathering twilight. Gabriela kept to the center of the room, pivoting and shuffling, trying to keep the same distance between herself and the men, at least as much as she could, without making her flank vulnerable. If one got behind her, or grabbed her, she would be at their mercy. She could see in the apish man's eyes he'd done this before and had enjoyed it. He might be bigger, but she was quicker. The other one, however, was nimble. She had a problem. If she could get to Wickeham, get past him somehow. But she remembered he was also strong. Had felt it when he'd grabbed her at the auction house publicity bash.

"Dimitri." Wickeham's tone said he was getting tired of her game.

Dimitri rushed her. She waited, as she had been taught in self-defense classes. He was almost upon her when she stepped quickly sideways and shoved him forward with as much force she could garner. It added to his momentum. He crashed against the brick wall. He fell into a stunned mess on the ground.

She had never been so glad she'd taken those defensive courses. She had never been so glad she'd kept practicing those moves with Spike. Gabriela turned to move away from Dimitri, but Bogdan grabbed her right wrist. He pulled her forward. She lifted her arm, knowing he would not see this as a threat. She ducked underneath his arm and twisted. As she came behind him, her body and arm forced Bogdan's own to twist. She gave a savage jerk upward, heard his groan of pain, and smiled. He released her, but whirled around, arm outstretched and already swinging like a bat trying to catch a baseball. She was ready, knew she couldn't allow that arm to connect or she'd be unconscious. She ducked. He saw her move, reversed the swing. She ducked again, but immediately jumped up, close to him, and she crashed her palm against his nose.

The man howled.

Damn, but that hurt.

She was panting and about to get away when she felt cold metal press against her spine.

Gabriela had forgotten Wickeham and his gun.

Damn.

"Enough of these games," Wickeham said. "Dimitri."

Dimitri, who had finally gotten his wits back, grabbed her, dragged her to the chair, and pinned her arms behind the chair's back. She arched to relieve the pressure.

Wickeham came over with the contract. "Sign."

"No." She spit in his face.

He slapped her.

Gabriela felt and tasted blood on her split lip.

"Sign."

"No."

Wickeham stepped back. Bogdan's face loomed before her. The smile cracked the areas where blood had solidified from her blow. *God, he was going to enjoy this.* Pity the poor woman who sustained this man's abuse.

"Sign." Wickeham repeated.

Gabriela looked at him. "No."

Bogdan hit her stomach. Enough to be felt, not enough yet to be life threatening. They were going to take their time, punching her and torturing her in areas where it wouldn't be evident.

"Sign."

"Go to hell."

Another blow, this time to her ribs. Gabriela's breath came in agonized gasps from the pain. Another blow to the stomach, this time harder. She looked into her tormentor's face. Just before the other blow hit, she said, "I'll get even."

The ring of a cell phone froze everyone for a moment.

Oh, God. Oh, God. That wasn't her phone going off, was it?

But Bogdan was taking his out of his jacket pocket. He glanced at the ID and answered.

Gabriela grabbed huge gulps of air. A spate of words came out of his mouth that sounded Russian but were not quite Russian. Her body was in pain. She breathed in slowly, her ribs protesting and burning. She held her breath and slowly released it.

Bogdan approached Wickeham after the short conversation. His body language screamed emergency. He opened his cell phone, took out the battery, and whispered something in his boss's ears. She heard police and search. Wickeham's face reflected shock and fury after the short briefing.

He grabbed her by the neck and pulled her face near his. Gabriela tried not to flinch.

"You will sign the fucking contract, now."

Gabriela looked him in the eye and whispered a soft "Screw you."

Wickeham stared at her. For the first time, Gabriela realized he was truly seeing her, gauging her as herself rather than as a stereotype he'd dealt with before. She knew he could only go so far with the torture. He needed her and needed her in somewhat good health to sign without the signature being questioned. He was running out of time. The auction was in three days and, today, daylight had started to fade in earnest now. And if her deductions were correct, Richard and Morris were on his tail and the information Bogdan had relayed did not bode well for him. He had been so certain before they could not link him to her kidnapping. Well, it seemed they had.

She smiled.

Wickeham turned and walked to the door.

"Bogdan, change her mind. Leave the face and her signature hand without bruising. I need those untouched. Use your gadget."

Gabriela's face set into lines of determination as she watched Bogdan approach. She'd endured labor pains. She could endure this.

She heard the door slam at the same moment she felt the first hit.

Chapter Twenty-Six

They were back in Morris's office. They'd found shit. No sign of Wickeham, of the goon, or of Gabriela.

A frightened housekeeper with a Slavic accent had let them inside the home after Morris had showed warrant and ID. Had run to the telephone and spoken to someone in hysterical tones, while they had searched the premises. They had scoured the place with no results.

Richard was fit to be tied. Jeremy was cussing a mile a minute under his breath. Morris was issuing orders like a frantic sergeant-at-arms. Bryce was pissed at not having a single photograph exclusive enough to print, had excused himself, and gone outside to get something to eat.

"Any leads on business properties, Williams?" Morris shouted from his doorway.

"Checked all of them, sir," a young policewoman answered back, not stopping work. "All clear."

"Roberts. Phone pings?"

"None. Telephone is either off or in a dead zone."

"Can you expand your search to possible Russian mafia holdings?" Richard asked.

"Vice might know." Morris picked up his phone and dialed. "Ian? Need a favor."

Richard listened in while he continued to pace the small office. He was worried they had found an empty house. Where on earth could they have taken her?

One of the tech officers knocked on the doorframe just as Morris hung up.

"We've checked the CCTV around the surgery near the suspect's house, sir, but we got nothing."

"What about surveillance on the ground?"

"A car accident blindsided our team before we could set things up. Traffic was paralyzed. By the time our secondary unit could get into position, the suspect was gone."

"Shit." It was time Richard called in some favors. "Jeremy, let's go."

Morris grabbed his arm and stopped his momentum. "What the hell are you doing?"

"I'm useless here. Better out there, calling in a few favors."

"Can't use that in court, Richard."

Richard kicked the chair Jeremy had recently vacated. It crashed against the wall. The office quieted.

"Leads, Morris," Richard said, his voice low and cold. "We need fucking leads. Right now we have shit. Some of my old contacts may know more than your people. I can work in tandem with your vice officers. Snitches can get the info into our hands faster. Someone may have heard something—a recent hire, a potential job." He stared at Morris. "I need to do something. Anything. You'd do the same if it were your wife."

Morris stared back. "Go. I'll figure the legalities later."

Richard was out the door before the last words echoed around the office. His phone was pressed to his ear before he stepped into the elevator.

"Maurice."

There was a short pause, then a brief *Merde*. "Tell me."

"The bastard has taken her." His words almost choked him. "I need to find her."

"What can I do to help?"

Richard debriefed Maurice with everything he knew.

"Ex-Yugoslav army, you said?"

"Yes. I know your database is more extensive."

"Less discriminatory," Maurice answered.

"My friend, I'm running out of time. Leads." Richard didn't have to tell his friend the time frame for finding Gabriela alive was shrinking. "I need leads."

"I'm on it. Wait for my call."

Richard paced the sidewalk, placing feelers throughout his old intelligence network as he waited for Maurice to ring back. But he had been out of the intelligence loop for three years, and he was not about to talk to Seldon. Richard would owe him, and he would be damned if he were pulled back into his bastard of an ex-boss's claws again.

Fuck.

His cell phone pinged.

"Talk to me."

"Remember Liebowitz?"

Richard remembered the Jewish-American agent they'd worked with on his last mission to Paris.

"Yeah."

"Contact him. He's on the ground and has heard rumors. Sent you his number. He's waiting for your call."

"Can't pay you enough, my friend."

"*Buf.* Just get her back safely."

***

It was three in the morning. Richard was closeted in a small conference room Morris had turned into central command. A whiteboard was filled with an array of writing, photographs, and questions marks: a visual of the crime, leads, and any information or questions about their investigation.

"Some of my contacts fizzled out," Richard told Morris. Maurice, however, had come through. "But one gave me the name of a lowlife with possibilities." Liebowitz had been a fountain of information on the guy.

After conveniently opening the door to this lowlife's apartment, Liebowitz had requested Richard keep him and Maurice in the loop. Richard knew they would prove helpful, especially since they could still work around the fringes of legalities.

"You can run these for fingerprints." He pushed an envelope with money inside it with his pen. "I tried not to get any of mine on the thing, but you never know."

Morris shook a latex glove out of his pocket. Once on, he inspected the money and the envelope.

"How did you get this?"

"Let's say I was invited into the premises."

"Shit, Richard…"

"There is no evidence of breaking and entering. No proof I was there."

"Who is this guy?"

"A lowlife called Dimitri Karzhov. Offers Laundromat service. Job in—job out, cash only. My source told me word on the street was someone important had an easy babysitting job. Others confirmed this Dimitri had accepted. His type of job."

Morris began jotting down the info on the board.

"This ties in with the rumors on the street," a man Morris had introduced as Detective Inspector Ian Millet from vice spoke. He opened a file and passed a mugshot to Morris. "From the description of your suspect, this boy doesn't really fit the description of your kidnapper."

Morris inspected the photo and shook his head. "Too scrawny. Blond, too." He passed the photograph to Richard, who then passed it along to Jeremy and Bryce.

"He's not our guy," Richard said, disgusted. "He's probably the Dimitri fellow." And after experiencing how Gabriela had taken out her attacker back at her house, she could have taken on this guy. He was probably just that, the babysitter.

"Most of what I got from my sources," Bryce opened his steno pad and flipped a few pages, offering some tidbits into his own investigation. "Was the runaround, with some generic bull about Russian mafia activities." He took out the folded, clipped pages there. "A real gloss-over job, protect-my-territory-and-sources reporter shit. However, one pointed the way to a few of his bylines about criminal activity. Made copies of the microfiche. Highlighted the places he mentioned." Bryce pushed those toward Morris.

"I have a list as well," Millet said, taking out another sheet of paper. "I've crossed out the two we've been able to clear as of now. But their holdings are spread out across the city and beyond. Our resources are tight. Even adding your men to the mix, it will take time to search everything."

"Word is probably spreading we are already on the scent of something," Morris said. "My fear is that when it reaches Wickeham, he might move her from where they have her stashed currently."

"He was warned already," Richard said, certainty in his voice. "The housekeeper, remember?"

"She made that hysterical call after we arrived," Jeremy added. "Spoke in Russian or some sort of dialect. Recognized a few *das* and *niets* in her ramble."

"I would be hysterical if my boss regularly beat the shit out of me," Richard said.

Complete silence descended in the room.

"How'd you figure that?" Bryce asked.

"The woman had evidence of a dissipating shiner. Minor puffiness and yellowish discoloration under her left eye. Some bruising on her wrists. God knows what other bruises she had hidden underneath the uniform. Her gait was slow, and she winced a few times. Her nose was also crooked. Probably broken way back. She cringed whenever we came near, but did not display the same reaction when your female officers approached. She's somebody's punching bag, and my bet is on this Bogdan."

"Wouldn't surprise me," Morris added. "She's probably an irregular, too." He turned to Ian. "Marriage for citizenship, maybe?"

"Flesh peddling, more like," Millet said. "Promises of utopia, for a fee. But once these women arrive, reality and hell begin. Currently there are more than one hundred open cases. More than our department can handle. The lucky ones get the equivalent of brutalized indentured service. The others…" He shrugged. "Are not so lucky."

"Saw that in my army stint in Southeast Asia, back in my time," Bryce said. "Nasty business."

"Did you get a trace?" Richard asked Morris, but knew the answer before he spoke.

"No. The call wasn't long enough. Anir tried but couldn't get a clear specific antenna bounce. No live signal from the phone the woman called yet, either."

"Are there any properties here listed in common within that antenna bounce area?" Richard tapped both the article copies and the property lists. He wanted to think of nothing but solutions now, of finding Gabriela. If he didn't, images of her battered face and body four years ago surfaced. She could be in that condition, or worse. And if he allowed those torturing images to invade his mind, he'd be out of control.

Millet studied the list. "These two are abandoned properties on the big bend toward the mouth of the Thames."

Morris looked at the list. "This one is near Fiddler's Reach in Grays," he said, pointing to an address he recognized. "Don't recognize the other." He patted another address. "This one is northeast of London, toward Walthamstow."

Millet circled more addresses in both lists, labeling them all with corresponding identical numbers. "These four appear in both lists as well."

Morris pressed a button on the telephone and asked for Hays. "We should concentrate on empty or abandoned properties first," he said.

"I would on active businesses," Millet said. "Usual MO. More camo in busy places. More hidey-holes to stash her in with no one knowing."

"Lot to cover," Richard said. "We'll be stretched thin. And we're running out of time."

Hays entered. Morris held the copies out to him. "I want everything you have on these properties, including surveillance and satellite."

"On it."

Richard signaled Jeremy with left hand slapping right wrist. It was their silent signal to get out of there, something Richard had learned from the French.

Jeremy raised his eyebrow, but stood to get the car.

"You going?" Morris asked suspiciously.

"I need to freshen up, get more comfortable," Richard answered as Jeremy disappeared. "Suit pants and shirt don't make for a good hunting ensemble. I also need a shower, some coffee."

"We have…"

"Please, Morris. I need real coffee."

Morris grinned.

"Be back in an hour, tops. Call me…"

"I'll ring you as soon as we know anything."

Before he reached the elevator, Richard grabbed pen and paper from an empty desk. Once inside, he jotted down the warehouse addresses he'd memorized. He nodded to the night officer on duty in the lobby, signed out, told him he'd be back, and left the building. He began pacing the sidewalk, waiting for Jeremy to arrive.

"You don't fool me," a familiar voice said behind him.

Richard turned to face Bryce.

"You're going after them."

Richard said nothing.

"Damn foolish to do it on your own, you know."

"I'm simply going home."

"No shit. And I'm Santa Claus." Bryce shook his head. "No, seriously, dude, your macho protective hormones are flashing like supernovas from your eyes." He stared at Richard, his cynical expression vanishing. "I'd do the same, you know."

"Would you?"

"The way you love this woman?" Bryce saw Richard's reaction. "Yes, I would."

Richard turned. Jeremy rolled the limousine next to him.

"Don't go alone," Bryce warned. "Let me tag along. Three are better odds."

Richard considered. "Meet me at my place in half an hour."

Bryce watched the limousine roll away. Stop at the light, two short streets away.

Now, where the hell had he left his rental?

The sudden explosion of metal ramming metal startled him.

What the fuck?

The police officers on duty outside by the barriers blocking the entrance to the Yard began shouting. Others ran inside the building, others talked into walkie-talkies as they ran toward the accident.

Bryce ran and prepped his camera. He began clicking, arm in the air. Saw the limo almost wrapped around a light pole, a huge SUV pinning it. The SUV driver jumped out. More tires screeched. Another black SUV stopped on the other side of the intersection, at a place of access to the people inside the limo.

Bryce kept clicking. One more block. He saw three goons step out, leaving their doors open. One jimmied the passenger door of the limo open with a metal rod while the two others reached in. They pulled Richard out. He looked unconscious. Within seconds, they had dragged and dumped him inside the SUV, scrambling behind Richard's unresponsive body like rats. Two seconds later, the SUV was gone, painting a rubber wheelie on the asphalt and leaving the acrid smell of burned tires in the air.

Bryce was panting by the time he came to the intersection. He couldn't believe what he'd just witnessed. He kept clicking and clicking until the

SUV was no longer in sight. He heard sirens approaching but didn't have much hope they'd catch the car.

With a stitch in his side, he rushed over to where Jeremy sat slumped and bleeding over the steering wheel, the deployed air bag now flat against his torso. He took more photographs. Someone shouted for a medic. Another verified Jeremy was not dead, just injured.

Bryce didn't wait for more. He rushed back to the Yard building. Morris and several other officers ran pell-mell toward him.

"What the fuck happened here?"

Bryce stopped and breathed in jerky spasms. "Snatch and grab. They got Richard. Got it all on camera."

"Shit."

Everyone understood the ramifications of what had happened. With Richard in Wickeham's hands, Gabriela had no chance. Wickeham now had an effective negotiating chip to persuade her to sell that manuscript.

Chapter Twenty-Seven

Time took on conflicting proportions for Gabriela. Minutes of torture seemed like hours. Acute pain took eons to decrease to a tolerable throbbing. The first hitting bouts had been followed by hushed, angry discussions outside her torture chamber. From that moment on, the electric zapper had become the torture instrument of choice.

The last session had been brutal. The bastard electrified already sensitized, bruised areas in her body, adding to the pain level with every contraction of her muscles. This Bogdan had his brutality pinned down to a scientific method. And after every session, Wickeham came in, arrogant in his certainty she would sign.

She hadn't.

That had pissed him off royally, the last time around.

Gabriela looked at her watch. Five a.m. They usually took one hour at most between their brutalizations of her. This time, however, more than an hour had gone by and there was no sign of activity on the other side. That probably did not bode well for her.

Dimitri just sat in his chair and stared, looking bored. Knew she was no threat to him now.

She tried to get up, but her entire body burned like hellfire. She gagged. She forced her legs to lift her body and, once upright, she wobbled. Took a few tentative steps to the corner. Braced herself with her right arm against the wall.

She vomited and regretted it the moment her stomach muscles went into convulsive spasms of pain.

"Gross."

She turned at Dimitri's words and saw him get up and leave the room. He was gagging. It was obvious he empathized with her heaving.

This was her second bout of retching. Her breath was rancid with the bile she couldn't rinse away. The light the bastards had brought in to see the details of their torture did not reach this corner. Gabriela hoped the darker spots of her upchuck were not evidence of blood.

She wobbled back to the bench. Sat down, feeling as if the Furies were ripping her flesh, and inched her hand to her boot. It was still there. She fumbled inside with her fingers, but the cell phone slipped out of easy reach, down toward her ankle. She bent at the waist but the pain paralyzed her. She lost her breath and couldn't move.

Time. She hoped Dimitri would give her enough time to inch the phone upward, take it out. She would go to the darkest corner of the room, hit the power button on the phone, and hope to God there was a cell tower near to capture her signal.

Gabriela moved her leg into a more comfortable position, where she could access her boot and phone without excessive duress to her body. Every action felt as if she were a snail, moving in millimeters rather than inches. She took an inordinate amount of precious seconds for rest, more than she would have liked.

The glaring light in the room exposed her actions, she knew, but she needed to take the chance. She needed to help Richard find her. If not, she was screwed.

Gabriela couldn't hold the position much longer before passing out. Sweat pooled and dripped from her forehead, both from the effort and from the pain in her stomach and ribs.

But she got the phone into position finally. She took it out and stood, clenching her teeth against the pain. She moved to her vomiting corner, and bent at the waist far enough for her forehead to rest on the cold wall. She pressed. Waited five seconds. Nothing. She wasn't sure if she had pressed the volume button or the power button. At this point in time, she pressed any button in the hope she'd get the damn thing working.

Another finger press, this time followed by a minute vibration. Could that be it? God she hoped so. She straightened and tried not to gag against the pain. Shifted her body and looked at the screen.

Nothing.

Damn.

Wait. She closed her eyes and looked again. Her eyes were not deceiving her. The thing was on.

Gabriela straightened carefully, slowly, and kept herself from crying. She had done it. She had done it.

She leaned forward again, hiding her actions, and disregarding as much of the pain as she could. She couldn't see the numbers too well because the keyboard was not lit and her body was blocking the little light there was in this corner of the room. She felt for the numbers. She made sure her thumb was at the edge of the phone and between the plastic screen and the barely protruding numbers. She moved it slowly. Stopped when she felt two edges. Slid it back. Pressed. Counted to five and prayed the speed dial worked.

A number one appeared on the screen. She almost cried when she saw it. Now for the dial button. She worked her fingers the opposite way. Pressed. The phone screen flickered and she saw the dialing message. Tears welled in her eyes. Gingerly, so as not to aggravate the pain, she lifted the phone to her ear.

"Hello?" she whispered. "Hello? Is anyone there?"

Only ringing answered. No one was picking up.

Outside her cell, she heard Dimitri curse at someone. He was very close.

Taking care she didn't turn the cell off, Gabriela placed the phone inside her skirt pocket. She'd done all she could. Now it was up to Richard to come save her.

***

Morris had a mess in his hands and he was truly worried. His supervisor was chewing his ass about this latest setback and incompetence, threatening demotion with every breath and every flaying.

At the moment, he was processing the area of the ramming. Bryce was with Hays back at the Yard, scanning through all his takes. Jeremy was arguing with the paramedic while he sat on the NHS ambulance, an ice pack held to his head. Morris's men were photographing, bagging, and fingerprinting everything. The lab was checking all footage from the CCTVs in the area.

"Detective Inspector."

The urgency of the tone caught his attention. A cell phone was ringing.

Morris practically ran to the man.

"When did this start ringing?"

"A moment ago, sir."

Morris connected. Listened. "Gabriela. Gabriela!"

He could barely hear anything.

"Shut up everyone. Shut the fuck up. I need to hear."

He listened. Muted ambient noise. A boot scrape and a cough. A hushed but very explicit curse. Female.

Gabriela.

Morris grabbed one of his technicians. "Tell Anir to start tracing Richard's cell and taping everything that comes through it as well." He pushed him forward and followed practically at the same run, all the while listening and hoping she would stay on the line.

***

More time passed. She was grateful for the reprieve but was suspicious as to its cause. She began to doze on and off. Once she practically fell off the bench.

She dozed again, but woke up when noises began to filter through the closed door. Her muscles tightened. She recognized the hum of a car's motor, the slamming of doors. Dimitri left his post. Then all hell seemed to break loose out there. Men shouting, heavy grunts, more shouting.

It sounded like a fight.

Could it be?

More cursing, more grunts. A lull. The clank of chains moving.

Quiet.

"Hey, hey." She screamed and crouched a bit. With her head down, she directed her next words in the direction of the phone. She hoped her voice was clear and loud enough.

"Dimitri. Bogdan. Wickeham. What the hell is going on out there?"

The naps had restored part of her energy. Her body still hurt like a bitch, but she could manage.

"Hey, you assholes." Gabriela had never in her life been this foulmouthed. But she also knew they expected it after the abuse she'd suffered. "Answer me, Wickeham, you sniveling, kidnapping coward. What the hell is going on out there?"

Please, Richard, she thought, *please be recording this. Please, let the microphones on the cell phone be powerful enough to capture my voice.* If the police were recording, she was supplying proof of her kidnapping, together with the names of her abductors. *Please, let the signal be strong.*

The bolt outside her door rattled. Bogdan stepped through the threshold first. Gabriela gaped. The man was bleeding from the mouth and from his right eyebrow. The eye underneath was puffy, almost closed.

Gabriela couldn't help it.

"Looks like a fist bumped into you," she said with an overabundance of sweetness.

The message in his eyes did not bode well for her future, but it lifted her spirits. Someone had tried to beat the crap out of him.

Unfortunately, Wickeham appeared next and he sported a satisfied smile. That did not bode well for her at all.

"Bogdan, take Mrs. Martinez to our guest."

Guest? What the hell was Wickeham talking about?

"Don't touch me," she told Bogdan, getting up and giving him a wide berth. Adrenaline flowed the moment he'd entered, numbing some of the pain.

Wickeham nodded to Bogdan once more and the man stopped. Bogdan pointed the gun at her as he stepped away, giving her space to walk through the doorway.

Gabriela looked around. There were three additional men in the area. They stood near another spotlight, standing guard around a man suspended in the air by the chains she had seen on her way to the bathroom. Said chains surrounded his wrists and kept his body a few inches above the floor. His body was swinging slightly in pendulum fashion, as if he'd been placed there recently. At the same time, his body twisted three hundred and sixty degrees full circle. He must be in excruciating pain. Chin down to his chest, it looked like the man was unconscious. Water had dripped and was still dripping on his body, his white shirt dark from a drenching.

Wickeham was watching her like she was tomorrow's meal to a famished man. What was he waiting for? Gabriela looked at the hanging man once more. Squinted as she approached. Something was familiar.

"Richard?" she asked, her tone incredulous.

Richard's battered face came up. "Hi, sweetheart."

Oh, God. Her heart was going to break. Incredulity gave way, however, to such viciousness, such fury, she shook with it. She had never felt anything similar.

"You son of a bitch," she said. "You son of a bitch!"

Gabriela lashed out at Wickeham with her fist, catching him by surprise. She nailed him twice, in the chin and on the nose, before Dimitri grabbed one arm and Bogdan the other. They pinned both at her back.

Wickeham spat blood on the floor, his own face a mask of incredulity mixed with anger.

"Attagirl," Richard said, smiling.

Gabriela knew Wickeham had never, in his sorry-ass life, ever envisioned a termagant such as she. He had expected a cowering female, had expected instant capitulation. Had never, it seemed, dealt with someone who pushed back as hard, even harder than he pushed.

"I've had enough of this bullshit," he told her, wiping the blood from his lip and nose with a handkerchief he'd taken out of his pocket. "Bring her over."

Dimitri and Bogdan dragged her close to Richard. They stared at each other with remembered pain, remembered injuries.

"Are you okay?" he asked, after a quick inspection. He didn't see too much bruising.

"Yeah. You?" His face showed signs of a recent battering. But from what she saw, he had given better than he'd gotten. All the men, including Dimitri, showed signs of Richard's fists coming into contact with their faces.

"We'll need to compare notes." He smiled.

She choked and held back her tears. God, they were both a mess.

"Since you've been so uncooperative," Wickeham began, "I brought a little persuasion to the bargaining table."

"I'm not signing."

"Mrs. Martinez, you truly take the fun out of negotiations. But, no matter. You'll rescind your decision." He walked around Richard. "You see, Bogdan so likes his little electric toy. He's been experimenting with it for a while, widening the electrode gaps for maximum results. The water will further enhance the effects." He stared at Richard. "I wonder how long he'll live?"

Gabriela could only stare. "You wouldn't dare."

He pivoted, the violence of the move almost upsetting his balance. He went to the chair with the open briefcase. He took the document out once more and shoved it under her nose. His hand was shaking.

"Sign."

He must have seen the denial reflected in her gaze because he turned around, his hand crushing the contract at the edge. "Alexei."

The man closest to Richard took out a small box. She heard the crackle before she screamed.

Richard's body jerked from the pain and the electricity bursting through every cell in his body. It was as if the atoms that made up his essence had gone nuclear, berserk in the explosion, transmitting a shock of energy so powerful he thought his heart would blow up. The chains holding him up burned his wrists. The water augmented every second of exposure. He convulsed over and over, until he thought he would black out.

Gabriela struggled like a madwoman against the restraining arms holding her back, uncaring of her injuries or the pain. *Oh, God. Oh, God. They were killing him.*

Richard slumped, panting and gasping for air. Alexei removed the stun gun.

She went beyond crazy, alternately crying, calling his name, and cursing at Wickeham.

"If you want me to stop, sign." Wickeham extended his pen and the contract.

"Gabriela," came Richard's hoarse whisper. "No."

"Stop wasting my time," Wickeham said viciously. "Sign the damn contract." He pointed to the line bearing her name. She read it for the first time. Looked at Richard. Turned to stare at Wickeham. Looked back at the signature line bearing her name.

"Don't fuck with me. I know what's going on in your calculating mind. Alexei."

The man stepped forward. Static crackled the air.

"No." She practically screamed it. She looked at Richard. "Wait."

"Gabriela, no."

"Release him, or I won't sign a thing."

Wickeham nodded to the men. One grabbed Richard by the ankles while another released the mechanism, lowering his body slowly until he lay on the floor. The men stepped a few feet away, guns aimed at Richard.

Gabriela struggled to get away, but the arms pinning her were merciless. She stopped struggling the moment she saw Richard move, curse, and gag. With infinite care, he stood, but immediately grabbed his knees for support and breathed harshly.

"I want your promise you will release us," she told Wickeham. "Unharmed. If not, I won't sign."

"I'm no fool. When the transaction is complete and I have the manuscript in my possession, then I will call Alexei and release you."

My ass. She knew, as soon as he got his greedy hands on the manuscript, he would skip town, and give the order to kill.

Wickeham extended the contract and the pen once more.

"Gabriela, sweetheart. No." Richard's chest hurt. His breaths came with more difficulty. Damn, but that had been brutal. "He's not letting us out of here alive."

Gabriela knew this, but she couldn't allow Richard to be tortured because of her work, however precious and important it was to the charity and the children who would benefit from the money. She would not have his death on her conscience.

She extended her hand and grabbed the pen.

Wickeham smiled with triumph. "Bogdan."

Bogdan stepped over to the chair, closed the briefcase, and held it for Wickeham as an impromptu desk. Wickeham placed the contract on top and motioned for Dimitri to bring her forward.

"Here and here, please."

Gabriela stared at her printed name again. Lifted the pen.

"Don't expect to fool me. I have a facsimile of your signature."

He showed her a copy of an old document. Where the hell had this man gotten hold of that? She'd have to have a very serious conversation with her lawyer.

"No, Gabriela."

The eyes she turned to him were brimming with love and with something else Richard couldn't quite make out.

"Trust me." No other words.

Gabriela signed her name on both pages and returned the pen to Wickeham.

The smile was triumphant. "Excellent. Bogdan, with me. Dimitri, Alexei, take them to the room."

They hobbled, in different degrees of pain, back to the same room she'd stayed in for so many hours. Watched the door close and heard the latch fall into place.

They gravitated to one another without words. Kissed as if the world had stopped and time from all eternities was theirs. She melted into his body. She didn't care if she was in pain or getting wet from his garments. She wanted to become one with him. He tightened his hold. She winced. He released her immediately, but kept his hands on her shoulders. He needed her near.

"What's the damage?"

Gabriela lifted her shirt. Hematomas and burned areas were visible. "Punches. Zapper. The man is easy with his fists and electricity."

Richard closed his eyes. His body hurt from the ramming and from his abused muscles. There was a spreading pain in his arms. He wanted to kill. To kill.

"Not as nasty as the zap you took." She began exploring his body. "Are you okay?"

"A fried circuit must feel the way I do." Richard cupped her face between his hands. He really wasn't feeling well. "Have I told you how much I love you?"

"Not nearly enough."

He kissed her softly.

Bangs reached them. To Richard, it sounded as if some ramming mechanism was being used. Screams of "Police" and "Stand Down" followed, shouted over and over again. The sound of loud pops filtered into their room.

Gunfire.

"Come. Now."

The urgency in his tone galvanized her.

Richard grabbed one corner of the bench and began dragging it. Gabriela understood and picked up the other end. Her sides burned and she wanted to scream from the pain, but Richard needed her help. With surprising efficiency, they placed the bench across the entryway. A bit lopsided, but it would work.

Richard rounded the obstacle and pulled her to the most protected corner of the room. On his way there, he kicked the lamp. Upon impact with the cement, the bulb cracked, plunging them into darkness. Only a sliver of light could be seen under the door. They would at least be invisible to anyone who entered and tried to use them as hostages. And the bench would trip them and slow them down.

More pops. More screams. Richard pulled her into his arms, making sure she was shielded.

The door rattled.

"I love you," he told her.

"Love you, too," she whispered.

She felt his muscles tense, felt him gather her more protectively into his embrace.

The door opened.

A bump.

"Bloody hell."

Outside light flooded the room. Richard turned to see Dimitri spread-eagled halfway on the bench and the floor.

"Don't move," he ordered and moved to neutralize this threat. Before Dimitri could get up, Richard dragged him onto the floor and straddled him. He was about to deliver an uppercut when Morris, wearing a bulletproof vest with POLICE printed in bold white letters in front, stepped into the room.

"Nice booby trap." He smiled, nodded to several officers to take over for Richard, and stepped over the bench. Two others followed. They pushed the obstacle out of the way.

Richard stood with effort as the officers handcuffed Dimitri and began leading him away.

"How did you find us?" Gabriela asked.

"Been connected since you first dialed."

"I hope to hell you got all that recorded, because I'm not going through this shit again. Ever."

"And then some," came Morris's cheerful voice.

"Gabriela needs a medic," Richard told Morris.

"So does Richard," she cut in.

"Already dispatched," Morris said. "Couple of minutes behind us."

Bryce entered, clicking away, flashbulb blinding them.

"Get that thing out of my face," Gabriela's tone was murderous. "What the hell are you doing here?"

"Actually, he's with us. He's cataloguing everything, injuries included, until our forensic team arrives."

"I made a deal with him," Richard told her.

"You what?"

"An exclusive for not following you ever again," Bryce said, not smiling.

"Where's Wickeham?" Gabriela asked. "Did you nab him?"

"Gone," Morris told her. "Placed surveillance on him for now. Phone taps as well. If he moves, or tries to escape, he'll be arrested before he opens the door to his house."

"That bastard will not leave without that manuscript." Richard couldn't get enough air out.

Gabriela frowned. Richard looked like shit, pale, and panting a bit. He seemed to be in pain. He began to rub his arm and he broke into a sweat, despite the cold.

"What's wrong?"

"Sorry, sweetheart, it's just that this bitch of a…"

Pain hit. Richard's features cramped. His heart did a tremendous Jello wiggle and skipped rope. He began to crumple slowly on top of Gabriela.

"Richard?" Gabriela grabbed him. "Richard."

She went down with him.

"No…no…no…no…no!"

She screamed like a banshee. Richard slumped on the ground beside her. His skin was chalk and it felt cold to the touch from the sweat.

"Where the fuck is that ambulance?" Morris shouted.

Gabriela grabbed the front of Richard's shirt and shook him.

"Richard. Richard. Damn it, look at me." She slapped him. "Damn you, Richard Harrison." Gabriela banged his chest. "Get up."

Someone tried to pry her from Richard's side.

"Get the hell away from me." Gabriela continued her panicked, staccato stroking of Richard's body.

"Richard." She shook and kissed him.

She closed her eyes. Sobs racked her body at his continued unresponsiveness.

"Don't leave me."

She cradled him, rocking him to her weeping.

"Don't."

Softer.

"Please."

This couldn't be happening.

"Oh, God. Oh, God."

Gabriela traced his face with a finger.

"I love you." Her voice held an abyss of pain. She touched his nose, caressed his lips. "Please, please, don't go. Don't leave me alone."

She looked around without seeing anyone. Didn't realize someone pressed fingers against Richard's carotid.

"Pulse there. Very weak," someone said.

She couldn't breathe, her chest tight.

"What am I going to do?" She mewled the words.

For a moment the world stopped. Only the pain in her heart and her keening were her reality. Then anger overwhelmed her and she shook him with enough force to rattle his teeth.

"Damn you. How could you do this to me? To our son? You are a goddamn selfish man. Just like Roberto."

She hit his chest.

"How dare you take the easy way out?"

She grabbed his shirt and almost pressed her face to his.

"Don't you dare die on me, Richard Harrison." Her voice was raw, angry, and desperate. She thumped his chest. "Don't you dare die on me, or, or, I swear, I'll sic Seldon on you for all eternity."

She felt the briefest pressure on her arm.

"Nag, nag," came the hoarse whisper. "Is this my future with you?"

Gabriela began rocking him in earnest, her sobs shaking them both while she held on to his hand as if she could push her life force into him via osmosis.

The world faded, time held no meaning. She fought every hand that tried to move her away from Richard. Her breathing synched to his shallow breathing. Her hands massaged his arms, trying keep his life's blood pumping.

When Bryce peeled her off Richard to give way to the paramedics, she became a wild woman. She lashed out and connected with his chin.

"Ow, Mrs. Martinez." He bear-hugged her from behind. "Let the paramedics look at him, stabilize him."

She stopped struggling, seeing a man and a woman step forward and begin to work on Richard with quick efficiency.

"He's fibrillating and his BP is erratic," she heard one say.

"What does that mean?" She asked one of the paramedics. "What does that mean?"

"Madam, please. We need to get him to hospital or he won't make it."

She froze. The paramedics bundled Richard, loaded him onto their gurney and the ambulance with impressive speed.

"What hospital?" Morris practically shouted.

"St. Matthews."

Morris rushed to her. "I know where that is." He dragged her to the police car and opened the door. She scrambled in, her weeping now hiccupy, Bryce next to her.

The car was rolling in less than five seconds.

"He'll make it, Mrs. Martinez." Morris looked at her ravaged face, her raw emotions ramming him. He reached over and squeezed her hand.

"He'll make it. You'll see. He'll make it."

She prayed to God he would. She didn't think she would be able to survive his loss.

By the time they reached the hospital, Gabriela was frantic. An orderly tried to stop her barging into the area where the doctors were working on Richard, but Morris flashed his police ID and whisked her through.

Standing in one corner of the cubicle, she watched nurses hook Richard to heart monitors, blood pressure cuffs, pulse clips, and an IV. Morris's

voice filtered through the curtains, directing the investigation from out
there. Bryce slid next to her, undetected by everyone but Gabriela.

"How is he?" he asked.

Gabriela seemed to surface from a deep abyss. "They stabilized him."
She listened to the now steady heartbeat beeping rhythmically to the visual
blips on the monitor. Moments ago that blip was everywhere and nowhere,
skipping beats every so often. She'd died a little with every silence.

"I'm glad," Bryce said.

"Where's Jeremy? I need to tell him."

"He's in another hospital, with a concussion."

"What?"

She hissed. She'd jerked at that bit of info and her muscles and ribs
burned in brief reminder of her own injuries. She was still riding the
adrenaline rollercoaster, but it was slowing down, ready to stop. When that
happened, she would be in worse pain.

Bryce recounted the snatch and grab, how Richard had ended up in
Wickeham's hands, Jeremy injured, and how Morris had finally tracked
them down.

The phone. She'd forgotten the phone.

She pulled it out. The screen reflected a schizophrenic array of
numbers, but the light was still on.

"And is it true? What Richard said?"

"About leaving you and your family alone from now on?"

Gabriela nodded.

"Yeah. I'm not a monster, you know. I'm only making a living. After
this," he pointed at Richard's prone figure. "I'll leave you alone."

Gabriela didn't comment. Only those on the receiving end of Bryce's
ilk really understood how much of a monster his type could be.

"I'll give you your exclusive," she dismissed him by turning to watch
Richard. He was so pale, looked so weak.

Morris walked in. "They will be admitting him shortly."

She passed him the phone.

Morris looked at it and, without comment, placed it inside his jacket
pocket.

"How's Jeremy?" Gabriela asked and shifted to a more comfortable
position. Her ribs were killing her.

"Cursing up a storm. Relieved. Wanting to come over." Morris began
leading her out the cubicle, but Gabriela resisted.

"I'm staying."

Morris sighed. "Your injuries need to be check out, and I need to
round up Wickeham before he takes that contract to Christie's."

"Let him. And what I need is a shower, some new clothes, and something with codeine." She looked at Morris, and even when wincing, she stood her ground.

"What do you mean let him?" Bryce said, perplexed at her nonchalance.

"Detective, I want to be there when you arrest him with the hand in the pot, so to speak." *I need to be there.*

Morris studied her face. He gestured for the doctor to come over, explained she needed triage as well but was refusing to leave Richard's side.

The doctor glanced at Gabriela and nodded to Morris. He gave his nurse orders to start with the preliminary vitals check-up.

"If the doctor gives the okay…"

"I'm fine," she countered. A blood pressure cuff was placed on her arm.

"*If* the doctor gives the okay," Morris insisted, "then, and only then, will I let you accompany me."

"I may be in pain, but I am ambulatory. Ow," she complained to the nurse, who was pumping away as if her arm's muscle and sinew were collapsible. "I have to be there when you arrest the bastard." *I can collapse afterward.*

Morris studied her stubborn expression and the hardness reflected in her eyes. "I'll notify Hollister to bring a change of clothes for you. Together with Hays, she'll be in charge of your protective detail."

"Why the protective custody, Detective?"

"Insurance. Until we have both Wickeham and Ljubic in custody. I'll pass by later to pick you up. We'll gain custody of Wickeham then. I'm sure Richard would want you to be present."

Yes, he would. Gabriela walked stiffly to the bed as soon as the nurse removed the cuff. She placed her index finger within the crook of Richard's hand, the only one without tubes. She caressed the inside curve of his palm.

Yes, Richard would be pleased. But he'd be more pissed, because he wouldn't be there to brain the bastard.

Chapter Twenty-Eight

Wickeham placed his final signature on the contract with a small flourish. He'd slept for about four hours after leaving the warehouse, had bathed as soon as he'd gotten out of bed, and had finished dressing to his fastidious code by lunchtime. He wasn't pleased, however. The bitch had forced him to put concealer on his chin and cracked lip to hide the bruising by her fist.

She would pay for that, as well as for the violation of his home by the CID, and for the fact he would need to disappear for a while. No matter. He would hide in style. Years ago, in expectation of such a possibility, he had bought a secondary home in Vietnam, where no extradition existed. Still, Mrs. Martinez would pay for displacing him and disrupting his business in the UK. The cost would be ownership of her manuscript and snuffing out her life.

Wickeham smiled. Soon, the manuscript would be legally his. By the time the idiots in CID realized what had transpired, he would be halfway to his destination. His lawyers could handle the rest.

In the meantime, he finished his lunch. He placed a call to the director's office at Christie's, made an appointment to finalize sale and commission within a half hour. The man had sounded a bit confused at Wickeham's request, but no matter. Everything was in order and on schedule. Just the way he liked things.

He waited until his housekeeper removed the lunch dishes. In a rare mood, he placed the finalized contract in his briefcase, stepped outside, and into his waiting car. He instructed Bogdan about the best possible route to avoid traffic snarls on the way to the auction house. He was now rather impatient to claim his booty, leave the country with it, and dispose of the two inconveniences his men were guarding.

Afterward, on his way to Vietnam, he could wallow in his good fortune.

Upon his arrival at the auction house, Wickeham was shown courteously to a plush office and was offered some refreshments, which he declined politely. He leaned back in a comfortable chair and waited.

"Your request has rather nonplussed me." The director held himself rigid, a look of disapproval on his face as he entered.

"Understandable. Understandable. But Mrs. Martinez sold the manuscript to me for the amount specified in the contract of sale, you understand, and I have the document here to prove it."

"Mrs. Martinez never made her desire to sell outside the auction known."

Wickeham took out the contract and placed it in the outstretched hand of the director.

"I understand, but she said a family crisis forced her hand and, since she knew of my prior interest in obtaining the piece, she contacted me."

"I simply can't stop an auction on such short notice or without her written approval. The cost to cancel this event two days before it is scheduled to run is impossible, not to mention the blow to our reputation."

Wickeham's lips curled in a polite smile, but his eyes held a hard glint in them.

"Mrs. Martinez could not delay the sale any further. That," Wickeham pointed at the contract, "is her written consent to pass ownership to me." He watched the director read the first page, then the next, and finally scrutinize the signatures.

"Everything is in order, I hope?" he asked, confident of the answer. His lawyers had created a foolproof document.

"I'm so sorry." The director looked at him. He tapped where Gabriela's signature was visible. "You have been duped. I cannot release the manuscript to you."

"What do you mean you can't release the manuscript to me?" Wickeham's smile was half-polite and half-tremulous. It took effort to rein in his incredulity and anger. "That is a binding contract of sale. Signatures properly witnessed."

"But that is the issue. Mrs. Martinez did not sign this."

"Is this a game, sir? Because I am not amused."

"This transaction is worthless," the director said more forcefully, shoving the contract across his desk toward Wickeham.

Wickeham's eyes narrowed. "Trying to defraud a client from his rightful product is a serious mistake on Christie's part. I will have my attorneys here within the hour."

"Your threats don't impress me. You, on the other hand, are trying to defraud this auction house, making outrageous claims, and presenting a forged signature. Your attempt to swindle this institution is prosecutable."

"Forged signature?" Wickeham stood. "Mrs. Martinez signed that document. I saw to it. It was properly witnessed." Wickeham was nearly shouting.

The director, his facial expression showing he'd had enough, buzzed his assistant.

"I will not be removed like some petty thief," Wickeham warned. "I am the rightful owner of the manuscript."

"Did you get that?" the director said into the speaker.

Wickeham would not be dismissed.

"Mrs. Martinez signed…"

"Actually, no, I didn't," Gabriela said from the doorway.

Wickeham gaped in shock.

Morris walked in with his ID raised high, a pleased smile on his face. Two other police officers followed.

"Arnold Wickeham, you are under arrest for larceny, kidnapping, battery, coercion, among others. You do not have to say anything, but it may harm your defense if you do not mention, when questioned, something which you later rely on in court. Anything you do say may be given in evidence."

"What do you mean you did not sign the contract?" Wickeham began to struggle against the constraining arms of the arresting officers. "I saw you. We all did."

Gabriela, who had walked inside very carefully so as not to jar her body too much, stood next to the auction house director and watched as Wickeham was led to the doorway.

"Wait, Morris. I want him to hear this."

With slow movements, and grateful she'd been pumped with pain pills, she reached for the contract. "May I?"

At the director's nod, she picked up the worthless piece of paper, flipped pages over until the signature showed, and turned it around for everyone to see.

"This," she pointed to her name, "is not my signature, Wickeham. Not my legal signature, that is."

Wickeham's face altered. Gabriela, despite the pain, felt inordinately pleased. Her only regret was that Richard was not here. He would have loved walloping this man who had caused such havoc in their lives. She regretted she could not punch Wickeham again, herself. It would hurt too much.

"When my husband opened his business and my career took off four years ago, we created different corporations for tax purposes. Mine was an LLC under my maiden name. Any legal transaction having to do with my career has to bear that signature, if not, it is null and void. The director here knows this."

She smiled at Wickeham. A very nasty, satisfied, almost disdainful curl to her lips.

"I gave you my autograph, Mr. Wickeham. It is what you demanded and what you deserved."

"You are lying." He struggled now in earnest against the restraints.

"Nope. You demanded a signature, and I wasn't willing to barter Richard's life for my work," she said. "He is worth more to me than a thousand of those manuscripts. But you, in your greed, gave me the out I needed. When I finally saw the contract and realized everything was under Gabriela Martinez, I knew you had screwed yourself."

She walked a few painful steps toward Wickeham, but stayed away from his reach, just in case.

"You are a nasty man. I'm glad you will be thrown in jail to rot."

"This is not over," he said as the police officers began to drag him out the door.

"Yes, it is," she answered and paused. "You should have kept asking for it nicely, you know. I might have considered selling."

Morris watched as Wickeham was escorted out of the office.

"Would you have?" he asked, his eyes curious.

"Nah. Not on your life." She breathed shallowly, the pain she felt finally reflected on her face and eyes. "Now, would you mind terribly taking me to the hospital before I pass out?"

***

The phone next to Richard's hospital bed rang. He rolled over, reached awkwardly for it, and answered. His tongue felt like cotton balls and his speech was slurred.

Damned drugs. He'd be out of it again soon. Maybe even for twenty-four hours this time around.

"You really can't stay out of hospital beds, *n'est-ce pas?*"

"Maurice."

"Is Gabriela back in the fold?"

"Yes. One of Morris's men said her ribs are bruised, not fractured."

"Vital organs?"

"Not compromised. Her torso and skin, however, are not in great shape. Some sections sport first-degree burns from the effects of the bastard's electric toy," Richard answered. "She should be back soon. Went with Morris to arrest the son of a bitch."

"Wanted to be there, eh?"

Richard grinned and wiped some sweat from his forehead.

"Wouldn't you?"

Maurice chuckled. "Just like before. Wanting to hear from the horse's mouth herself and brain the bastard."

Richard chuckled. "She already walloped him. Twice."

Maurice laughed with gusto. "A hell of a woman."

Yeah, she certainly is. My woman now.

"I've touched base with some gentlemen here on the Continent who are extremely interested and eager to get their hands on the ex-Yugoslav package. They had lost track for a while. Arrangements have already been made for retrieval from the UK and delivery into their good hands in about a day or so."

Richard's lip curled. Comeuppance. He hadn't felt this nasty satisfaction for a while.

"Any plans for the second *mec?*" Maurice asked.

Richard knew Maurice meant Wickeham. Heard the whoosh of breath as Maurice exhaled smoke from his lungs.

"British citizen. Rights and all that bullshit. Can't do anything about him, yet. Once I'm given a clean bill of health, I want to take Gabriela out of here, reunite her with her family. After I've done that, I'll deal with him."

"Why don't you let me take care of that small issue as well?"

"Maurice…"

"*Buf,*" Maurice said, humor lacing his tone. "We both know this man will never leave you alone." There was a pause. The next words held no inkling of humor. "Don't soil your hands with this *mec,* Richard. You are out of the business for good, and you shouldn't start a new life with his blood on your hands. Gabriela doesn't deserve that. Besides, it is not an inconvenience."

"No. It's not your responsibility."

"I owe Mrs. Martinez," Maurice said, disregarding Richard's objection. "Recuperate, *mon ami,* and make sure she arrives home safely. Take care of her. Be happy for once. Create more babies. I'll call when the tasks are finished."

Chapter Twenty-Nine

Two days later, Christie's bidding room was at full capacity. Austere in color and elegant in the articles displayed for auction, the big room was rectangular in shape and gargantuan in proportion. All local bidders sat facing a cherrywood lectern, next to which, on a raised dais, two employees monitored the auction from behind computer monitors. A big, closed-circuit television hung on the wall behind their heads. All bids were displayed there when auctions went live.

It was early evening. Gabriela stood next to Richard, Jeremy, her managers, and cousin at the back of the room. They had found a private corner beside the videographer recording tonight's session. In front of her, double-sided white doors proportionally separated the room so what decorated the right side was a mirror image of what stood on the left, sans lectern. At the sides of the room, both right and left, solid cherrywood balustrades spanned the entire length. It separated the representatives of anonymous or foreign bidders from those within the room.

"*Chérie,* why don't you sit down?" Jean-Louis said, impatience now lacing his voice. He still oscillated between joy, impatience, and angst, depending on how he thought she felt.

"He's in a better mood than two days ago," Richard whispered and chuckled.

Gabriela sighed. After learning she was in the hospital recuperating from her injuries, Jean-Louis had barged into the room like an avenging Valkyrie, with Julien and Father Ramirez in tow. He had broken down in tears the moment he'd seen her, and, before she knew it, had almost stripped her naked in front of everyone, Richard, Hollister, and Hays included, in order to catalog her injuries. If Julien and her cousin had not stopped him, amid her own complaints, it would have been an embarrassing moment. Richard's amused laughter had blended with the chaos of the moment.

"Last auction this evening is lot six," the auctioneer began.

"Actually, my ribs complain less if I stand, thank you," she told Jean-Louis.

"You should be in a hospital," Father Ramirez whispered. His eyes still reflected the horror over what she had experienced. He looked at Richard. "You, too."

"Trust me, *padre*. I've suffered much worse." Richard looked at his bodyguard. "What about yours, Jeremy?"

"Piddling little injuries, boss. Not hospital worthy."

"And I only have bruised ribs, guys. Meds have taken the edge off." *That, and the two days of rest I've had.* Ironic, too, that she was grateful to Wickeham. She knew she would have fared much worse if he hadn't needed her in somewhat good shape to sign his blasted contract. If not, the Yugoslav bruiser would not have pulled his punches. "I can manage this."

"Bruised ribs, first-degree burns, and hematomas worthy of a Picasso," Jean-Louis said, disgusted. "*Oui,* you can handle standing up."

"Never heard the Picasso analogy before," Jeremy said. "Not a bad one."

"*Salaud,*" Jean-Louis said.

"Jeremy, my man," Richard said, patting his bodyguard's shoulder. "You've just been called an asshole."

Gabriela smiled.

Jeremy grinned. "Been called that by many other assholes."

"Charity auction for the *Book of Hours* by renowned artist Gabriela Martinez is next," the auctioneer said to the room at large. The man spoke calmly, in a beautiful British baritone. "The item is currently showing to my right in the room and on the screens above."

Gabriela glanced around the room, which was abuzz with the hushed, excited voices of more than two hundred bidders as the auction's start was announced. Her joy in the moment would have been perfect if she hadn't spotted April. Flanked by her father and Edmund, she sat toward the middle of the room, her cold eyes fixed on Gabriela.

"What do we do about her?" she whispered to Richard, none too pleased at the woman's presence. April was not finished with her yet, she was almost certain. Her own gut feeling.

"Taken care of that with Hollister and Hays," Jeremy said. "Morris gave orders to remove her forcibly if she tries anything." Morris had also promised to be there with his wife for the auction.

"I doubt April will be that brazen, not after what happened," Richard said, his voice devoid of emotion. "But, if she is, she will never do it again."

Gabriela pulled down his arm. When he leaned over, she kissed him on the cheek. She had heard about the fiasco at the television station after her abduction. She'd also told them about April's words and her obsession with Richard.

"We'll handle her together," she said.

Richard smiled. "Love you."

She pulled him closer.

"Love you back," she mouthed, her words barely reaching him. In honor of her cousin's priestly sensitivities, Gabriela didn't want him to witness her words, at least, not until the divorce was finalized.

"Have you spoken to Spike yet?" Richard asked, scanning the room. "Is he back home?"

"No. He promised to call us as soon as he lands."

"There's Michael." Jeremy pointed.

Gabriela saw Morris enter the room inconspicuously. He scanned the area quickly. Upon spotting her entourage, he wove his way toward them.

"Am I late?" Morris asked, a bit breathless.

"Just about to start," Gabriela said.

"Was the Yugoslav finally extradited?" Jeremy asked.

Gabriela felt the alertness in Richard.

"Two Interpol officers served the extradition papers today," Morris said. "He's on his way to the continent to face trial."

Gabriela leaned into Richard. "What are you not telling me?"

For the first time in four years, Gabriela could not read the message behind Richard's expression. It had been the same in France, at the safe house.

"Nothing to tell," he said. "Where's your wife, Morris?" Richard asked.

"The twins are sick. Down with a fever since early morning. Sends her regards and regrets."

"Shh, shh," Julien said with enough emphasis to make some heads turn. "Talk later."

"Two hundred thousand to start," the man in the lectern announced. "Two hundred thousand."

The bidders in the room settled. The representatives lining the walls placed phones to their ears, their assistants alert and focused.

"Two hundred thousand this side of the room. Two hundred one."

And so it began. Five minutes later, she was in shock.

"Nine hundred thousand. Nine hundred thousand this telephone."

One bidder raised his finger, silently asking for more time to consult with his client on the phone.

"Just a second?" the auctioneer quipped. "Sure."

The room erupted with laughter.

A pause later, the man by the lectern resumed. Unlike some auctions in the States, the auctioneer seemed in no rush and didn't trip over unintelligible words said at lightning speed. The man was determined to sell, but he was not rushed. "Fair warning now. Nine hundred thousand on this phone against all the room."

A small, elliptical banner went up on the left. And the bidding resumed.

When it was all over, the final bid came from, of all places, Taiwan. Some rich industrialist had dished out a million six for the privilege of owning her work. Her managers were beyond ecstatic. Frank looked like he needed a good pinch from time to time, his face incredulous.

Morris was about to pat her back in congratulations but stopped. He smiled, grabbed her hand, and shook it.

"Amazing, Mrs. Martinez. Simply amazing."

The room began to empty. Her cousin grabbed her by the shoulders and squeezed. "Thank you, Gaby. Thank you."

"Nothing to thank." She gave him a soft kiss on the cheek. "Those children deserve it."

"They didn't deserve your pain," he said, choked up.

"It's over. We won."

When her cousin released her, Richard took her by the waist, pulled her in with infinite care, and kissed her. Her cheeks exploded from the heat, but she kissed him back. She couldn't help it. Everyone now knew she was divorcing Roberto. Finally she could relax, enjoy her success, her liberty, and her peace. The physical healing would take care of itself, with the help of a few more pain pills. Life would get back to normal with an added bonus…Richard.

"*Mon Dieu, chérie.*" Jean-Louis grabbed her face and kissed both cheeks. "You are extraordinary."

"Yes, I am." She grinned.

"*Extraordinaire,* yes. Also beautiful and smart," Julien added, imitating Jean-Louis with his kisses.

"Not to mention sly," Richard said.

"I am an improvement over the 1993 model," she quipped.

"Still can't believe you got the better of that cretin with something so simple," Morris said.

"Would have killed to see his face when she told him he only had her autograph." Richard couldn't help it. His smile was nasty.

"Didn't think telling Wickeham the contract was worth less than toilet paper was to my benefit."

"Ah, boss?" Jeremy's tone of voice warned them.

Gabriela turned. The auction room was practically empty now. However, Lord Cranfield, Edmund, and April were still there. They were approaching. Gabriela felt the same warning shiver as when Wickeham had approached her at the promotional party.

Something wicked this way comes…

"She wouldn't dare," Richard said, his voice taking on a threatening tonality with which Gabriela was very familiar.

Jeremy, Morris, Hollister, and Hays flanked her. Jean-Louis, Julien, and her cousin stood on the side, near enough to help, if needed. Richard stood silently beside her.

"Congratulations, Mrs. Martinez," Lord Cranfield extended his hand. Gabriela shook it. It was obvious the man was oblivious to his daughter's shenanigans.

"Wonderful event. Good cause. You should be pleased."

Gabriela eyed April. The woman was quiet, almost meek in her demeanor. Her eyes, though, told a different story, especially when Richard draped his arm around Gabriela's shoulders.

"Very," she answered. Her cell phone rang. Gabriela looked at the caller ID and smiled. "Will you excuse me for a moment, please? I have to take this call."

Richard nodded to Jeremy and Hollister, who kept an effective barrier around Gabriela as she stepped to the side. Hays stood near April, vigilant.

"Will you be attending the Clarke event tomorrow?" April asked Richard. She began to fidget when Richard looked at her in evident distaste. "Afraid not."

Lord Cranfield glanced from his daughter's face to Richard's harsh one. "You'll be making yourself scarce from now on?"

"Afraid so." It seemed Lord Cranfield had drawn a few conclusions of his own.

"Pity." Lord Cranfield shook hands all around and took his daughter out of the room. Edmund, who usually did not smile too often, never looked happier.

"Good riddance," Jean-Louis said.

Let's hope so, Richard thought.

"The kids are back home," Gabriela said, returning. "Spike is relieved, especially with Lupe taking over."

"A fitting ending to a wonderful evening," Richard said and hugged her.

They exited the room.

Outside the auction house, the air was cold and crisp. The sidewalk, as well as the street, was brightly lit from the building's floodlights. Gabriela breathed deeply. She loved the sights and sounds of this vibrant city surrounding her. She was about to ask Richard where they would go celebrate when she spotted April hovering a few paces away from the building's entrance. She stood sans Edmund, holding her ermine coat collar close to her face. She seemed to be waiting for something, one fingernail raking her bottom lip.

She was staring at them.

"What the hell is she still doing here?" she asked, a bit disturbed at having the woman so near. Hell. A whole lot disturbed.

"Ignore her," Richard said. "She's probably waiting for her boy toy to bring the car around."

Logical, but Gabriela didn't quite believe in April doing things logically. The woman looked rather smug, in contrast to her demeanor indoors.

"Are you a Mr. Harrison?"

The strange voice caught everyone by surprise. A man no one knew, with a cheap camera hanging around his neck, waited for Richard's answer.

Richard looked at the man suspiciously. "Who's asking?"

Taking Richard's question as affirmation, the man extended a plain manila envelope. "For you."

Morris took the envelope from the man's hands before Richard could. He examined it, turned it over. "No address or name."

"Wickeham, you think?" Gabriela asked.

"Possible, but doubtful." Richard accepted the envelope Morris extended. He glanced at her. "Didn't Bryce say he would send copies of what he would publish to us?"

While in the hospital, Gabriela had finally given Bryce the exclusive he'd wanted. She had never seen the man so happy.

"Yeah. But I never thought he'd do it this quickly."

Richard opened the envelope. Peeked inside. "Photographs."

"Let's see them." She leaned in. So did everyone else as Richard slipped the photographs out and flopped them on top of the envelope.

He froze.

Everyone else froze as well.

Visible to all, the photograph showed the naked bodies of a man and a woman in the middle of sexual intercourse, the woman on top, enjoying the ride.

Gabriela stared. The woman had her head thrown back in wild, pleasurable abandon while the man smiled, holding her as she rode him. Gabriela stared harder.

Her heart skipped a beat. Good Lord, that was Richard. Her stomach plunged and her blood pounded in her ears. The woman was definitely April. Her eyes shifted back to Richard's smiling face.

Gabriela frowned.

"Fuck," Richard said. "The fucking bitch."

Gabriela glanced up. April was watching, an intensity to her pose, an expectation to her expression.

Richard cursed, about to tear the photographs and the envelope, when Gabriela stayed his hand.

"Wait."

"Sweetheart, this is bullshit." His gaze was anguished.

"That woman is seriously fucked up," Jeremy said.

Morris was speechless. The others in the group, in different degrees of embarrassment, were looking everywhere else but Richard.

She took the photographs from Richard's grip.

"What the hell are you doing?" Richard tried to snatch back the photographs, but Gabriela wouldn't let him.

"Trust me," she said.

"Mrs. Martinez," Morris began, but she shushed him.

Gabriela examined the top photo. At first glance, it looked like Richard's face. But she was an artist. She knew body proportions, having studied human anatomy for years. She'd also bedded Richard. She knew every contour of his chest, his arms, and his luscious body.

She began to chuckle.

"Gaby." Her cousin was appalled at her reaction and embarrassed at what they were all seeing. "This is not funny."

"Jesus. It is." The chuckles turned to laughter.

"Mrs. Martinez?" Jeremy's voice sounded uncertain, as if he believed she had finally succumbed to the stress of the past few days.

"Gabriela, stop." Richard was not happy.

But she couldn't stop laughing, not until the pain in her ribs stopped the laughter.

"This is really hilarious. Ineffective, but hilarious." Gabriela glanced at April. The woman stood as if petrified. It was obvious she'd expected another reaction.

"This is not you," she told Richard and addressed April next. "Next time, pick someone less scrawny than Edmund." She began to laugh once more.

"Let me see that." Richard snatched the photograph from her hands. He stared. "Well, I'll be damned."

"Gaby, how do you..." After one look at her face, her cousin decided to remain in ignorance. "Never mind."

Jean-Louis and Julien no longer kept their distance. They crowded in, scrutinized the photograph for another moment, and shook their heads in agreement with her assessment. "*Oui.* That is not Monsieur Harrison."

Morris stared at the photograph. "I can have my lab analyze this. See if your face was superimposed on that one. If that is the case, I can prosecute."

"You can sue for libel as well, boss," Jeremy said, pleased.

"Want me to arrest her?" Morris said loud enough for April to hear. Everyone turned to face her. The woman looked as though she would faint.

Serves her right, Gabriela thought. *The pétasse.*

A car slid to a stop next to her. April opened the car door without waiting for Edmund to do the gentlemanly thing. She practically dived in.

"Want me to arrest her?" Morris watched the car speed away. "Peddling pornography with the intent to blackmail is a felony."

Richard shook his head in denial and placed the photographs inside the envelope. He handed everything to Morris.

"Why don't you hold on to these? If she tries anything, we'll talk about prosecution." He reached over and pulled Gabriela into his arms. "Come here."

Richard kissed her as if the world were ending.

"Thank you," he whispered.

"Whatever for?"

"Believing in me."

Gabriela smiled and kissed him back.

Chapter Thirty

"Let me talk to the doctors. I'll be right back."

Gabriela had uttered those words about twenty minutes ago, and Richard was still waiting for the doctors to leave and for her to show up. He stood and began to pace around the living room of Gabriela's mother-in-law's house. Jeremy and Spike shook their heads.

"What's keeping her?" he asked, not too pleased.

"Past meetings have taken longer," Spike told him. "Be patient."

They had arrived at the airport that afternoon. Only Spike knew they had returned. Earlier that morning, at two o'clock to be precise, Gabriela had received an urgent call from home, one that demanded her immediate return. He had not asked what the urgency was. Only knew that it had to do with Roberto. Richard had simply made the necessary arrangements for them to leave that morning, no more questions asked.

"I'm going back there."

Spike groaned, exasperated, but he got up. "I'll talk to Maureen. Be right back."

Spike walked to Roberto's room. The doctors stood speaking softly to one another. Maureen, the day-shift nurse, was taking care of her patient, but her eyes were overflowing with tears.

"What's going on?"

Maureen shook her head. Pointed to the backyard, where Gabriela was sitting at the edge of the property.

Spike turned and walked out of the room. He stopped at the edge of the hallway, but did not go into the living room. "You'd better get back here. It's Roberto."

Richard followed, Jeremy not far behind. *What the hell was going on?* "What about Roberto?"

"Be prepared."

Prepared? What the hell?

Richard heard the sound first, breathed in the antiseptic air mixed with another smell second. Spike stood next to an open doorway. He waved the men in.

What greeted Richard shocked him into immobility.

"Bollocks," Jeremy blurted behind him.

Richard stared at the body on the bed. He recognized the features, but nothing else. What faced him was not what Gabriela had intimated after her attack here at the house. The man Richard had known, and of whom he'd been jealous before leaving for London, was a pile of wasted flesh. The man who lay there was a dead man chained to earth by the instruments of man.

"He's been like this since the accident," Spike said. "He's brain dead. Has been since they brought him here. Mrs. Martinez has been dealing with this and everything else for months."

"Why didn't she tell me?" Richard whispered.

"She's told no one. Not a single soul, apart from the immediate family. She needed to keep Roberto's condition a secret in order to keep the company going. She needs to have the patent approved before she tells anyone."

Richard turned to face the doctors. "What the hell did you tell her?"

It was Maureen who answered.

"The therapy is not working, not anymore. Everything is shutting down slowly. They asked her to remove the tubes and take him off life support." She began to cry in earnest. "Poor Mrs. Martinez. Her poor babies, too."

"Where is she?"

Maureen pointed outside.

Richard spotted her, opened the door, and stepped out.

***

Roberto was dying. The doctors had given their final recommendations. It sounded logical, even humane. Then why did she feel as if they had just asked her to kill her husband?

Gabriela sat on the bench at the edge of her property, the one that offered a magnificent view of the western ocean and sky. The view had always invigorated her. Healed her. Now? Now it held no beauty, no healing. At this moment, she was numb, felt numb, and thought she would be carved and trapped in this frozen stasis of numbness forever.

It was the shock, she knew.

The doctors had been more brutal than normal during the meeting. It was pointless to continue current treatment, they had explained. They recommended removal of Roberto's feeding and breathing tubes to allow

Nature to take its course. The minerals and calories injected into Roberto's body maintained organs; the air blowing into his lungs brought oxygen to his blood; but the body kept deteriorating, cannibalizing its own muscle and sinew despite all efforts. The brain transmitted no electrical impulses. He was already dead.

She had listened politely and excused herself. Inside, she was suffocating. She'd told them she would come back with her decision.

Pull the plug. How could she do that?

Her eyes roamed across the horizon. She usually reveled in the by-play of gold and reds as they blended and highlighted the soft blues at the edge of the earth. Not today. Today, her eyes focused on the gray clouds hiding the sun. How could she do this to her children? How could she snuff out their father's life? How could she do that to the man who had been her friend, her husband, and her lover for so many years? How could she do this to Roberto who, despite his foibles, had always been a good man, a good provider, a good family man?

God. Oh, God. She should trademark her life as the perfect model for the tragic heroine. Her life's story would give Shakespeare a run for his money.

Her tired hands rubbed her face. She would not cry. She would not. She still had things to be grateful for. Her children were safe. She was safe. Richard was alive.

A soft breeze, heavy with the smell of the ocean, caressed her skin. She shivered and hugged her body. She felt as if she bore all the tragedies of the world on her shoulder. Her bruised ribs protested slightly. They, at least, were practically healed.

She wondered if her bruised soul ever would.

Gabriela began to weep.

Arms picked her up. She was placed on top of warmth. Hard muscles surrounded her, held her.

She looked up.

Richard.

"Why didn't you tell me? About his real condition?"

"What am I going to do?" she asked, a world of misery coloring her words. "He wanted to live so badly. Wanted his company to be successful. Wanted to see the children grow, get married. What am I going to tell them? How can I do this?" Tears brimmed and fell, creating meandering rivulets over her cheeks. "I don't know what to do."

"You will figure things out, sweetheart." He kissed her face, tasted her tears, and wanted to howl with pain. "You're strong. You've handled a situation most people would have been crushed under from the weight of the responsibility."

He kissed her again. "But more importantly, you're not alone in this. Not anymore," he said. "Whatever you decide, we'll tackle this together. Tell the children together. I love you. I've got your back."

Out of the darkness, something raw clawed out of her soul. He saw it. Felt it. Prepared for it.

An eerie wail ripped its way out of her body, floodgates opened, and Gabriela came apart.

She cried and cried and cried until she thought she would drown in her tears.

Richard yelled for Spike and Jeremy. They came running.

"Is she okay?" Jeremy asked, his voice full of concern.

"She will be. I'm taking her to the pool house. Don't tell anyone." He looked at Spike. "Get rid of the doctors as well. She'll talk to them tomorrow."

"You won't be disturbed," Spike said.

Richard lifted her, cradled her in his arms, and carried her to the pool house. Jeremy rushed ahead of him, opening doors for them to go through. He finally closed them in the privacy of a bedroom.

Richard locked the door and placed Gabriela on the bed. He lay next to her and held her. He held her through the endless crying, through four years of bottled ravaging pain bursting from her. He soothed her until she was spent, until there was no more pain, guilt, fear, and regret left.

Her body trembled and she tried to push away from him. "I've got to go. Take care of the children."

"Not tonight. Spike, Lupe, and Jeremy will take turns with them. Let someone else take over for a change. I'm taking care of you, tonight."

Her weeping renewed. He cradled her and reassured her throughout the long hours. When she finally quieted down, Richard veered her toward the bathroom. He turned on the shower and undressed her carefully.

Gabriela simply stood in the middle of the room, unable to move, lethargy invading every pore of her body, and glad someone had the energy to take care of her. She sat when she was asked, lifted a foot when ordered, raised an arm when prodded. She felt like a rag squeezed to the point of fraying.

Once naked, Richard stared at her body. She didn't need a mirror to know what his eyes saw. Her body was a fading map of yellow-green bruises, with some brownish scabs marking the spots where the brute had applied the stun gun for longer than necessary.

"Dear God."

He placed a forefinger to the scab on her side and began exploring every bruise and burn on her torso. Gabriela's skin twitched at his roving finger.

"I'm going to kill the bastard."

"It always looked worse than it felt," she whispered.

His eyes showed he knew the game she played.

"Really, Richard. Thanks to Wickeham, Bogdan pulled his punches on the first rounds. He gave orders to use the stun gun exclusively after. Not that that was any easier to bear."

Her eyes reflected a moment of deep pain renewed. "You fared worse." She began to weep.

Richard took off his clothes, draped her in his arms and rocked her. Slowly, he guided her to the shower and went in with her. He washed her hair with enormous care, rinsed it with long strokes, and soaped her, his touch as delicate as a baby's. He kissed her and kissed her, trying to erase her memories of pain with his mouth, with his hands, with the soap, and with the water. He toweled her dry with as much care, draped her in another dry one, and took her back to bed.

Gabriela slept the exhausted sleep of the devastated, with Richard next to her, cradling her body.

Richard's phone rang just before dawn.

"Did I interrupt anything?" Maurice asked and chuckled.

"Screw you, my friend."

"I don't think that is what's on your mind or on your bed." The chuckle got louder.

Richard got out of bed. He stepped outside the bedroom, but left the door ajar. "You've got news for me?"

"First package captured and broken apart. Will never see the light of day again."

"Hope the bastard suffered."

"Oh, he did, with more brutality than he dished out himself." A pause. "The other package was also dispatched."

"Details?"

"Better if you don't know. Only, rest assured, he won't threaten the future Mrs. Harrison ever again. Think of it as my wedding present."

"Thanks, Maurice."

"*De rien.* Enjoy yourself. You have four years of catch-up to do."

Richard hung up with Maurice's laughter echoing in his ears.

He returned to Gabriela. Yes. He had four years of catch-up to do. He woke her up with his kisses, divesting her of the towel. Entered her slowly. Skin to skin, heart to heart, he made love to her, showing her his need. She came apart in his arms in the knowledge that this was permanent, that this would be the beginning of something that would last.

Epilogue

Monterey Bay, June 1998

"Gabriela, sweetheart. Come on."

"Give me another minute," she yelled. She arranged the hydrangeas in the vase, shifting the stalks until she had a satisfying pattern.

"The kids are really excited, Roberto," she said. "You should see the place we're going to live in. The house is warm brick with a half-moon wrap-around deck in the back, a pool, and a view of the lake to die for. The house is on a landscaped acre, with another acre on each side. Tons of trees there." She dusted off the dirt gathering around the lettering on the plaque. "You would have loved it."

"Sweetheart," Richard said, approaching from behind. "If we don't leave now, we'll miss the plane. The kids are antsy. Besides," he bent down to where she was kneeling next to Roberto's grave. "I don't think Spike can babysit for one more minute."

Gabriela chuckled. She finished dusting the plaque, picked some weeds out of the grass, and extended her hand.

"I'll need the other one to lift you," Richard said.

"Very funny."

She was heavy with child, this wife of his. Richard had cajoled and begged until she'd caved in. This would be her last child, she had warned. Period. But Richard didn't care. He had wanted to experience what he'd missed with Luisito. Caress what grew within her. Revel in her changes, feel the life that was half his and hers.

Richard lifted her, turned her, and hugged her from behind. He loved touching the swell of her belly, taut with their child, shifting as their child moved. Loved to place his ear on her belly and listen.

"How's he doing today?"

"Would serve you right if it was a she."

He had not wanted to know the sex of the child. He wanted to be surprised. And as he never missed a doctor's appointment or a sonogram, she didn't know the sex either.

"Are you okay?" he asked, his breath caressing her ear.

Gabriela knew what he meant.

"Yes," she answered. "I grieved long before he died, Richard. I just needed to say the final goodbye."

"I'm glad."

He kissed her lips softly, took her hand, and maneuvered her through the graveyard to the waiting car and their future.

THE END

Acknowledgments

A novel is never created in a vacuum, and I would like to acknowledge those who have helped and advised me throughout the journey.

To my husband, Rolando, whose support and love never flags. Thank you, my love.

To Anita, from Mumm's the Word: Editing and Critique Services (www.anitamumm.com), for guiding me throughout the sequel. She made sure I stayed true to Gabriela and Richard with her wonderful suggestions.

To Toni Lee, for all her incredible proofreading. She did an absolutely magnificent job. I wouldn't have been able to publish a polished and professional novel otherwise.

Thanks go, as well, to my friend, Leo Cabanas. Thank you for being the most enthusiastic BETA reader ever.

To my sister, Victoria Saccenti, for always believing in my story (her own novel, *Destiny's Plan*, is coming out soon. I'm stoked!). Thank you, Sis, for always being there. Love ya.

To my wonderful, incredibly talented friend and assistant, Mari Christie (www.MariChristie.info). I would have gone completely bonkers without your help, your encouragement, and your patience (with me). Thank you, thank you, for taking care of everything I couldn't, for creating wonderful websites, blogs, and pages, for keeping me in line, and for keeping me organized.

Finally, to my late mother, Elena del Cueto. She never got to see the finished product, but I am sure she is smiling from heaven.

About the Author

Maria Elena Alonso-Sierra lives with her husband in the NC area and has been a professional dancer, singer, journalist, and literature teacher. She has a Masters in English literature, specializing in 12th century French romances. Throughout her life, she has lived in many countries, including France, where she set her first novel.

Connect at her website:
www.MariaElenaWrites.com

A Note from the Author...

Dear Readers,

Thank you all for allowing me to take you on the rollercoaster ride that has been Gabriela's and Richard's stories. As you have read their tales in *The Coin* and *The Book of Hours*, I hope you have laughed, cringed, and teared-up as much as I did while writing them. It has been one heck of a ride, but a wonderful one.

Now for the next story...Detective Nick Larson.

I would appreciate, as well, if you would help others enjoy this book, too.

Recommend it. Please help other readers find this book by recommending it to friends, readers' groups, social media, and discussion boards.

Review it. Please tell other readers why you liked this book by reviewing it at the following websites: Amazon, and/or Goodreads.

Join me at www.MariaElenaWrites.com to keep up with my latest releases and appearances. I would love for you to visit.

Once more, thank you for your support.
Maria Elena Alonso-Sierra

Don't miss the rest of Richard and Gabriela's story.
Make sure you pick up Book One:

THE COIN

For a preview, turn the page...

Prologue

France, May 1993

He was safe.

The man surveyed the clearing, inspecting the rearranged landscape for the last time. The mounds of rock and dirt surrounding him dropped unevenly, pock-marking the ground in no visible pattern. Nature had spread her hand, healing the upheaval she'd caused a year ago by covering the ground with short-cropped grass, dehydrated moss, bramble, lavender, thyme and the local version of oregano bushes. There was no evidence anywhere of his search, past or present, nor did the metal detector sound any signal of Nature regurgitating the remaining strongbox it had so callously devoured.

The man's hands curled around the plastic bar of the metal detector, tightening into a fist so fierce his forearms vibrated. Years of planning, of careful manipulation, of evidence gathering, of assuring no one could trace the puppeteer pulling the strings of mayhem, had been nullified without trace by the whim of a capricious mountain. Even when luck had remained stubbornly by his side, helping him recuperate many of his records and videotapes, he'd only gathered a pittance of the arsenal he'd had. If Nature had been a real woman standing before him, he thought, he would have relished killing her.

He skimmed the area once again, his eyes methodically covering more ground, his features darkened by the approaching twilight. His job here was almost over. After this final sweep, he could finally disappear and begin to plot again.

"Oh, danke Gott."

The strange voice caught him by surprise. He whirled around to face the intruder, his body rigid. A wiry young man, looking tired and terribly frustrated, now stood a few paces into the clearing. The man watched as the hiker shrugged off his bulky backpack, grabbed his knees for support, and gulped down several cool breaths of mountain air, grateful for the respite and his luck.

"Please forgive me," the hiker said, his French atrocious. "I've been roaming this godforsaken mountain for hours and can't seem to get back on the trail." His gaze turned hopeful. "Can you help me?"

The man nodded, but his eyes narrowed, intent on this intruder, this new threat to his carefully plotted safety net. He began to close in slowly.

The hiker visibly relaxed. "Thank God. I thought I'd be forced to camp out tonight."

The mouth and eyes that smiled back at the hiker chilled the surrounding air. The man loved fools such as this hiker, blind idiots who never suspected a normal façade could harbor the blackest of souls. Such naïveté always delighted him, made his hands itch with the anticipation of the kill. But for now, he gestured to his left, toward a dirt path barely visible through the trees.

As expected, the hiker turned, eager for directions. The man's smile widened. He lifted the metal detector.

The calculated blow to the head was swift, but not lethal. The hiker stumbled, caught off guard. The man waited patiently for his victim to recognize the danger, for the eyes to widen with dawning horror, and for the futile attempt to flee. Staggering, disoriented, the hiker backed away from what he now realized was a man gone mad. Smiling, the man lifted and struck again, this time on the upper arm. A whimper rose to a wail that bounced over the mountain. The man closed in once more, considering several options. With calculating precision, he aimed at the hiker's left thigh, reveled as he felt the femur collapse with a soft, moist crack. The hiker screamed, tumbling into a wriggling heap on the ground. The man swung again and struck his victim's abdomen. He watched the hiker painfully inch backward. Such foolishness, the man thought. Escape was impossible. No amount of begging, sobbing, or sniveling would stop him—had ever stopped him. The laughter he'd held back bubbled and spewed forth, noxious, tainting the surrounding air. He lifted the metal detector and struck again, and again, and again, calculating the most effective areas to hit, watching his victim with a chilling, benign emptiness. The macabre choreography increased the man's joy as each blow landed. By the time the man was satisfied, the hiker's agony had shifted from screams, to supplications, and finally to barely audible moans, twitches, and sobs.

The man paused, evaluating his handiwork. Bruises and hematomas discolored the exposed skin on the hiker's body. Perfection, he thought. Utter perfection. Later, under cover of darkness, he would take his burden and toss him down the ravine underneath the village of Gourdon. He chuckled. The stupid *gendarmes* would label the death a hiking accident. His only concern was that dead men didn't talk, or point accusing fingers at anyone.

His cold eyes swept over the hiker. Yes, he would do. He dropped the metal detector and stretched, ignoring the pathetic twitching and sobbing of the young man at his feet. He inhaled deeply, reveling in the pungent perfume of the pine trees mixed with that of human fear and excrement. Yes, everything was in order, he thought, pleased, as he knelt beside his victim. With strong arms, he captured the hiker's head in a chokehold. He caressed the hiker's face, grabbed his chin, and gave the head a vicious twist. The neck snapped like a soda cracker.

Oblivious now to the lifeless heap at his feet, the man examined the clearing in the rapidly fading light. He reached into his pocket and retrieved a ten franc 1945 French coin, no longer in circulation. His fingers lovingly caressed the etched image of Napoleon, and thought that his only regret was not finding the coins, his unique password. He'd keep this last one as his lucky charm, and start over again.

But that was for the future. For now, he was safe.

Chapter One

June 1993

Gabriela Martinez arrived at *Les Clos* ten minutes later than planned. She jerked open the heavy door of the restaurant—a 13th century monastery converted into a lucrative four-star gastronomic heaven ten years ago—and figured her day was developing into an exact replica of yesterday's chaos. Actually, for the sake of accuracy, today was the postscript resolving yesterday's mess of broken answering machines, canceled appointments, and ruined illustrations. The saving grace in her muddled schedule was the coin she'd found in the middle of *La Marbriére* yesterday. She smiled in recollection. She had been frustrated, lost somewhere in the middle of the mountain, not at all where she had wanted to go. The coin, half-buried in a magnificent clearing cocooned in gray cliffs, emerald forest and sheer ravines, would have remained undiscovered if the afternoon sunlight had not bounced off its surface, making it wink at her. She had been delighted with her discovery, amused that even though she was lost in the middle of nowhere, she continued finding money in the most unusual places. This latest find would raise her loot to about ten dollars, give or take a few French centimes.

She stepped into the blessedly cool interior of the restaurant and shook off the oppressive heat sticking to her. Well, there was nothing she could do now about her tardiness. It had been her idea, after all, to have the coin added to the collection already gracing her great-grandmother's bracelet. If it hadn't been for Michel, her jeweler, and his love of political debates, she would have arrived sooner and been prepared to face Albert today.

Gabriela sighed and rushed in the direction of the dining room, wondering how she would discuss unwelcome sexual overtures with a man who had been her mentor and friend for the past three years. She simply couldn't hurl accusations at Albert's face—not arrogant and powerful Albert. She wasn't even sure she wasn't misconstruing things herself. Her logic told her she was being a fool. After all, didn't Albert have Silvie by his side? With a mistress so absolutely ravishing, why would Albert have an interest in plain old Gabriela? It was stupid. And yet, there was that ineffable something that kept jabbing at her subconscious, making her now uncomfortable whenever Albert was around. And, if her suspicions proved true, she would then need a good dose of diplomacy to resolve things. If not, she risked losing an influential adviser and a friend.

She paused behind a tall floral arrangement, just short of the arched entrance into the spacious, elegant dining room. "Please, please, don't let him be here," she whispered, crossing her fingers. Her hazel eyes quickly scanned the lunch crowd. Hopefully he would be late, giving her the needed time to calm down and think through her approach. Albert's suggestion yesterday to meet for lunch had been providential, and the opportunity to meet with him in a neutral place had also been ideal. He was always mellower during a meal and, even if he reacted strongly to her subtle reproach, at least it would be less unpleasant in a restaurant full of people.

Albert's autocratic silver head came into view, towering above the rest of the diners. Damn. Jean-Louis, Albert's art gallery manager, was also at the table. Well, she thought ruefully, scrap the *tête-à-tête*. She would have to confront him without rehearsal or a plan. Her stomach suddenly heaved as if she had swallowed a rock. She knew that whatever she did, Albert's reaction to her candidness would be very unpleasant. The results could possibly be catastrophic…for her.

She strode casually toward the men, and Albert rose to courteously slide back her seat as she approached the table.

"*Bonjour, ma belle.*" Jean-Louis planted a feathery kiss on both her cheeks. Gabriela greeted him fondly, always a little sorry for womankind by the loss of such a handsome man.

In the lull after ordering their drinks, she glanced from one man to the other. Albert's eyes held a satisfied gleam in his usually impassive glance, while Jean-Louis's face could barely contain showing his excitement.

"You two seem to be in an especially good mood, gentlemen," she commented, closely studying Albert's smug face.

Albert squeezed her hand, lifted it to his lips, and planted what Gabriela thought was an overly fond kiss on it. His smile crinkled his eyes.

Gabriela's cheeks turned an embarrassed pink.

Jean-Louis leaned across the table, eyes wide, hands clasped in his usual manner. "Gabriela. You'll never, ever, guess."

"Kindly curb your womanly excitement," Albert stated calmly as he sipped his recently arrived Talisker. "Gabriela needs to hear an objective, unflowered account of events."

"What that really means," Jean-Louis said, "is that he wants to personally handle everything concerning you and your work, even the breaking of important news. Selfish beast." He winked.

Gabriela laughed, her dimples showing. "Okay. So..." She nodded playfully in Albert's direction.

"A little more respect, please. Especially for the man who achieved an exhibition at the Cercles Club in the Casino."

"As in Monte Carlo," Jean-Louis added.

Gabriela's entire body suddenly froze. "You're serious?" she whispered.

Albert smiled, his face acquiring a sensuous look. "Absolutely. Tomorrow, I'll close the deal over lunch. We've agreed to make it an informal affair, lasting, oh, four, five days. Enough to create an appetite for your works, but not enough to be tiresome. I want you there with me tomorrow when I meet the director of the club."

"Seeing you in person will definitely clinch it," Jean-Louis said, bobbing his head in approval.

Gabriela shook her head, trying to clear her thoughts. Jesus. Was this really happening to her? With this prestigious showing, her reputation in Europe would really skyrocket. She shook her head again, incredulous, cautiously excited. In nervous reflex, her hand went to twirl her great-grandmother's bracelet, but quickly aborted the movement. She'd left the bracelet at the jeweler's. She fidgeted awkwardly with the tablecloth instead.

Jean-Louis clapped his hands, amused. "Look at her, *mon Dieu*. Your face is so expressive, Gabriela." He turned to Albert. "I told you she'd be shocked."

Gabriela's cheeks reddened even further. "It's so incredible."

"But soooo exciting! Think of all the people who'll finally get to know your works. The attention. Fame. Glory." Jean-Louis wiggled a finger at her. "I'm envious."

"Enough of your blabbering," Albert interrupted. "We need to get down to business, Jean-Louis. Where's Julien? I specifically demanded he be here at noon."

Jean-Louis had worked for this dictatorial man for over ten years, and he recognized the underlying anger in his voice. Suspecting an imminent explosion, and always one to avoid them, Jean-Louis quickly scrambled to his feet. "I'll call the gallery. I'm sure he's only delayed in traffic."

Gabriela waited until he was out of earshot, then surprised herself by asking, "Why, Albert?"

"Why what?"

Gabriela held his questioning green stare. Calm down, she told herself. Be cool. Unemotional. Logical. Oh, God. How was she going to get through this? She went for the missing bracelet again, cursed her forgetfulness, and grabbed her wrist to keep her hand still.

"You've been going more than out of your way to promote my works lately. I just wondered—" She swallowed nervously. This was definitely not going the way she wanted. She gripped her wrist until her knuckles turned white. "Honestly, Albert," she blurted suddenly. "You're an important business man. Men in your position just don't spend so much of their precious time promoting an unknown artist's illustrations—mentor or no mentor. I would have expected you to hire a manager, not personally handle the tedious, day-to-day marketing." Her cheeks turned an even stronger hue of rose. "I just hope it's not...you know... Heck," she finished lamely.

Albert studied her blushing profile, amused at her obvious embarrassment. He knew why she'd been skittish these past two months, but also understood he had to allay her suspicions if his plan to make her his mistress was to succeed. After all, he had rushed things. It was a mistake, a rare one for him, but he could excuse his faux pas simply because of her illustration. He had not been prepared for the rush of emotion, or the impact Gabriela's powerfully ferocious drawing had had on him. He had lost control, plain and simple, and had instinctively reached for her, placing in that kiss all his appreciation, his pride, his possessiveness, and his lust for her.

Albert took a sip of his scotch, rolling it over his tongue before letting it slide down his throat like velvet. "Does this outburst have anything to do with my kiss?"

Gabriela thought her face would vaporize from the heat in her cheeks. Her hand was like a tourniquet on her wrist.

"*Ma belle,*" Albert smiled. "Don't be so prudish. It was the excitement of the moment. You have to agree that your St. George shocked me."

"It left you speechless," she admitted.

Albert chuckled. "A first for me, *n'est-ce pas?*"

"Definitely," she said, and took a sip from her drink. The cool liquid didn't alleviate the dryness in her throat. "It still doesn't clarify things."

"Then let's," Albert said, suddenly serious. "No one can do a better job of promoting your works than I. I have the good taste, the influence, the connections, and the advantage of knowing you personally. That gives me insight to choose the right places to exhibit, places where you will feel comfortable. Apart from that, your talent is extraordinary, my dear, but you are too timid to promote yourself."

Gabriela sniffed. "You sound like Roberto."

"But unlike your husband, I'm not glued to the computer screen, working non-stop on a pet project, oblivious to anything or anyone." Catching her expression, Albert changed the subject. "But we digress. You are a friend, Gabriela. You're unselfish and not mercenary. Who better than I to do this small service for you, who never abuses our professional partnership, nor our friendship?"

Made in the USA
Monee, IL
30 January 2020